A MARRIAGE OF INCONVENIENCE

Also in the Series

A Rooftop View
A Different View
Godmother's Footsteps
Lies & Consequences
Haste to the Wedding
Looking for Henry
Stormclouds
Things that Go Bump in the Night
Time to Say Goodbye
Full Circle
Winds of Change

Also by Jane Hatton
A Dream of Dragons

A
MARRIAGE
of
INCONVENIENCE

Jane Hatton

Copyright © Jane Hatton 2004
First published in 2004 by RaJe Publications
Garth Cottage, Little in Sight
Mawnan Smith, Falmouth, TR11 5EY

Reprinted 2020

Distributed by Lightning Source worldwide

British Library Cataloguing in Publication Data
A catalogue record for this book is available from the British Library

ISBN 978-1-8380372-0-8

Typeset by Amolibros, Milverton, Somerset
www.amolibros.com
This book production has been managed by Amolibros
Printed and bound by Lightning Source worldwide

About the author

Jane Hatton was a child during World War II, and grew up in the unpermissive fifties, when career options for women were largely confined to Secretary, Nurse, Teacher, Physiotherapist. She opted for the first, thinking the skills required would be useful in her preferred career as a writer, but has also worked in hotels, as a sailing instructor, in a craft workshop and as a cookery demonstrator – a remarkably unstructured career – while continuing to write whenever there was a spare moment: sometimes there were not many! She has had two children's books published in the mainstream (a while ago now), followed by three novels in the genre of "literary fiction", plus The One Too Awful to Mention – which  we don't mention – and has also independently published a long series about the Nankervis family and their friends and relations, all set in various areas of the West Country. Apart from writing, her interests include sailing, painting – including at one time scenery for the local pantomime – archaeology, photography and cooking. She lives in Cornwall, on her own these days, with a small black cat for company and a background of family and friends.

The lines of poetry that Oliver speaks on his wedding day come from Inisfail by C. Fox-Smith

PART ONE

SOWING the WIND

I

Tracy got off the bus with a child on each hand, lightheartedly ignoring the fact that most people would have considered those hands to be full.

Six-year-old Micky was screeching. There was no other word for it. He wanted to go home to watch Blue Peter, and although he had been repeatedly assured that Nanny had a television set in full working order, he refused to believe that it would have the same programmes as his own. There was a precedent for this (Grandad was a football fan), but even so, Tracy felt his behaviour to be unreasonable, and so did not give it the dignity of parental attention.

Candy, two years his junior, was more devious. Unlike her brother, she had learned early that although tantrums were treated with the contempt that they deserved, there was nothing like a good whinge for wearing an adult down. Therefore, although she had no particular end in view herself, she had come out in sympathy with her older sibling, maintaining a persistent, monotonous grizzle calculated to try the patience of a saint. Candy liked attention. She had no particular preference between admiration or sheer fury, so long as it was directed at herself. It was therefore sad for her that her mother's attention was directed entirely at the letter in her bag and its dynamite enclosure, successfully obliterating more familiar problems.

If it was a problem. Tracy, who lived firmly in what her husband, Tom, liked to call the Real World, believed that if her younger sister, Cheryl, and her boyfriend, Jonathan, chose to live together without getting married, that was nobody's affair but their own. Her father emphatically didn't agree. Their mother hovered uneasily between a sneaking feeling that Dad was right and a strong wish not to be branded as a pre-flood fossil. Thus, whenever anything that touched the subject came up, family life became an uneasy battleground where neither side was likely to be victorious. The only consolation was that the south coast town of Embridge was a long, long way from the Suffolk village of Whytham St. Giles.

But this time, Cheryl at least seemed to have made it into the national press, and although Jonathan wasn't obviously involved, there was no doubt in Tracy's mind that he was at the bottom of it. The photograph had the words "popular journalism" plastered all over it, even before Cheryl's cheerfully unrepentant letter of explanation that had accompanied it. Dad was going to love the idea of his youngest child displayed all over the tabloids in the arms of a complete stranger!

Somebody shouted out 'the shot needs a pretty girl', Cheryl had written, and Tracy could almost hear her giggle as she wrote it. *Jonathan just picked me up and threw me – it was a very good thing that he caught me, or I might have fallen into the sea! And after that they all took pictures, this is one of them! It was tremendous fun, you've never seen such an atmosphere – people waving and cheering, and a whole flotilla of boats and things churning along beside us – quite mad!*

Like Cheryl, reflected her sister, who appeared to think that atmosphere was visible. At home, at this moment, it could very likely be cut with a knife, so perhaps she had a point.

The thing that bothered Tracy, although not seriously, was the fact that, so far, there had been no repercussions on the home front, whereas Cheryl's letter had been written nearly a week after the event. Tracy herself didn't take a lot of notice of newspapers and considered the television news one of the most boring programmes on the box – but her father did. Both read newspapers and watched television news, and with almost the same dedication that he brought to football. So why had there been no reaction? It couldn't be shame. This was the nineties, for heaven's sake! And Cheryl, mercifully, had been fully clothed. There was yet something to be thankful for.

'I want to go *home!*' wailed Micky, hauling back on her arm as hard as he could.

'*I* want to go home!' echoed Candy, standing still in order to stamp her feet. A woman coming out of the village shop gave Tracy a sympathetic grin.

'Got yourself a full-time job there, Trace,' she said, in passing.

Tracy returned the grin wryly, and gave Micky's dragging arm a tug.

'Shut up Micky, you're too young for Blue Peter anyway!'

'Not!' he yelled, and echo answered, '*Not!*'

'It could be worse, Mrs. Peasgood, there could be three of them.'

'And when's that sister of yours going to settle down and start producing?' asked Mrs. Peasgood, artfully twisting the conversation to where she wished it to be. 'Saw her picture in the papers the other day. Well, when you're young's the time for having a good time, but what I say is, there have to be limits.'

'Oh, it was just a picture,' said Tracy airily.

'Starting up as one of them models, is she? She'd better be getting married. There's that nice young man she brings up here now and then, when's they going to tie the knot and make it right?'

Villages! thought Tracy. Mind your own business, you silly old bat!

She put her hand on the side gate beside the shop wall.

'I mustn't keep you, Mrs. Peasgood. Got to get these two indoors before they scream the place down.' The gate stuck, it always did. She gave it a shove. Micky and Candy, sensing something interesting going on, had gone quiet. Candy stuck her thumb in her mouth, eyes round as saucers, drinking everything in and no doubt, even if subconsciously, filing it for a suitable awkward moment.

'You can see your Dad's none too pleased about it,' said Mrs. Peasgood, with a satisfied nod. 'Flaunting herself all over the papers like she has, I'm glad she's no daughter of mine! You'd best get in and talk to your Mum.'

She sniffed, disappointed at not getting a rise out of Tracy, and stumped off down the street. Tracy sighed. She wondered if the picture in the papers had been the same as the print that Cheryl had sent to her. Even by Peasgood standards you could hardly call that one *flaunting*. She hustled the children along the narrow path to the back door, her head full of alarming possibilities, and with a terrible desire to laugh. Real storm-in-a-teacup stuff, this, but in a small community, mortifying for everyone. Thank goodness she and Tom didn't have to live here any more.

Marilyn Wainwright was at the sink, peeling potatoes, when the children burst through the door. Micky ran to her and clutched his arms around her legs.

'Nanny, Mum won't let me watch Blue Peter!'

Tracy sighed. Marilyn bent to disentangle herself.

'What's this, Trace, censorship?'

'I told him your telly still worked. He wouldn't believe me.'

'Naughty Mummy tells porky-pies!' cried Candy, and flung herself, too, on her grandmother, making her reel on her feet.

'That I'm sure she does not, miss!' Marilyn stooped and swung the child onto her hip, taking Micky's hand with her own spare one. Her eyes met Tracy's. 'You get on with those spuds, Trace, and I'll get these two settled. Dad's in the shop. You could slip through and say hullo first thing.'

Tracy tossed her bag onto the worktop and went through into the passage, pushing open the door that led into the rear of the shop. The familiar shop scent, compounded of fruit, flowers and bakery goods, with faint savoury undertones of cheese and bacon, reminded her of her own childhood, and later years spent working behind the counter before she married Tom. Cheryl had escaped that, lucky Cheryl, gone to secretarial college, then fled south to train in hotel management at a big seaside hotel. She was still there, chief receptionist and trainee manageress. And, apparently, photographer's model.

Bob Wainwright was slicing cheddar for a customer when his elder daughter came through the door at his back. He grunted, but in a friendly way. The customer, yet another of the gossipy village women, greeted her with a bright smile.

'Hullo Tracy, what you doing here then? And what's all this about your sister? Given up on her young man, has she?'

Tracy saw her father's neck go red, and made herself laugh lightly.

'Nothing like that, he just took her on the assignment with him – for the fun of it, you know – they went down to Falmouth for the weekend. And then the photographer wanted a girly shot, and she volunteered – or Jonathan volunteered her, more likely. Good picture of her, wasn't it?'

She heard Bob mutter *girly shot, is it, indeed?* but his neck was going back to a more normal pink, and the customer, like Mrs. Peasgood, looked disappointed.

Such a lot of fuss over one little picture! She kissed her father's ear.

'I'm out the back with Mum, Dad. Tom's working overtime, so we can stay on for tea, he's picking us up later.'

Bob gathered up the wedge of cheese onto some waxed paper.

'Just serve Miss Wallis will you, while I take for this at the till.'

Peel the spuds, serve Miss Wallis, no wonder Cheryl ran for it! Old Miss Wallis took simply ages to choose between smoked and unsmoked bacon, and then bought two rashers of unsmoked streaky. The potatoes were finished by the time Tracy escaped back into the house, and Marilyn was pouring boiling water into the teapot. On the kitchen table, a newspaper was folded back at the offending picture, ready for discussion. It wasn't the same one, Tracy noted, by this time without surprise. It was a lot worse. Cheryl had her arm firmly round the man's neck, and the expression on her face, frozen in time by the brief exposure, was one of utter delight. Her legs kicked in the air like a can-can dancer's. No wonder Dad's neck was red. She picked up the paper and studied it. Marilyn watched her.

Behind the entwined pair could be seen what were presumably bits of yacht, or catamaran, or whatever you called it, and a distant vista of boat-scattered sea and a lighthouse. The predictable caption, *Home is the Sailor, Home from the Sea – and Wouldn't You Come Home for a Welcome Like This?* headed a brief paragraph that Tracy didn't bother to read. Cheryl had put it all in her letter anyway. Heroic stuff, round-the-world yachtsman braving terrible dangers to raise funds for hospital back in his home town. Wonderful, up-to-the-minute new spinal injuries unit to be built with sponsorship money contributed by grateful townsfolk. Records smashed in all directions. Local boy makes good, blah blah blah. The lighthouse, Tracy noted in passing, was St. Anthony's at the mouth of the river Fal. She put down the paper and Marilyn passed her a mug of tea. Their eyes met as they sat down at the table.

'Dad raising a riot?' asked Tracy, sympathetically.

'A bit. Cheryl's always been his special pet, as you know. She could of warned us.'

'She didn't know,' said Tracy. 'She wrote to me. She thought it was just for the local rag, silly fun stuff. She didn't expect Jonathan to syndicate it, or whatever the word is. And perhaps he didn't – he *says* he didn't. There were other photographers there, too, not just the *Herald*.'

'It might of helped if *you* had warned us, then.'

'I only got the letter this morning. She hadn't heard from you. She wondered if she ought to throw her hat in the door, first.'

Marilyn primmed her lips together to hide a smile. 'Your Dad was fairly foaming at the mouth! Why *didn't* she warn us? Or at least ring to explain.'

'She was down in Cornwall for the weekend. She didn't see a paper until they got back home. And then there was no message from you, so she thought... well, that she'd better keep her head down for a bit. She wrote to ask me to explain and make her peace, and she'll ring Sunday, when Dad's not busy in the shop. You better see the letter.' She reached for her bag and took out the envelope. Marilyn pulled out the two closely-written sheets of Cheryl's explanation and the photograph, which Tracy had temporarily forgotten, fell onto the table. It lay there between the two of them, and they looked at it. Transgression in full colour.

The picture showed a slender young woman with long, curling, red-gold hair, apparently in mid-air. She wore close-fitting jeans and a tight, boat-necked T-shirt neither of which left much to the imagination, and her arms were flung up in the air, her legs flying, her midriff bare. She was laughing. Beyond her, a man stepped forward to catch her. Not much of him was visible behind Cheryl's levitating torso, but he was obviously young and handsome, dark, bearded and sunbrowned. He, too, was laughing, white teeth startling in the close-trimmed black beard. Tracy imagined trying to explain a picture like that over the phone to an irate father, and her sympathies, on the whole, were with Cheryl. She looked at her mother.

'Come to that, why didn't *you* phone *me*? That letter was the first I'd heard of it.'

'I didn't want to make too big a thing of it, I suppose.'

'It's hardly the crime of the century, is it?'

'It was a bit of a shock, even so, suddenly seeing our own daughter all over the tabloids.' Marilyn had unfolded the letter to read it, now she laid it down on top of the photo. 'It isn't just that. It's everything. Your Dad grieves over Cheryl.'

'Goodness! Why?'

Marilyn propped her elbows on the table and lifted her mug in her hands, but held it there, not drinking. 'You know why. Living with Jonathan without being married. It's not your Dad's way.'

'She doesn't live with him. She has a room in the hotel, she lives in that.'

'No,' said Marilyn. 'Her clothes live in that. Cheryl only sleeps there if your father or me goes down to see her. Don't try to kid me, Trace. I'm not a fool.'

'She doesn't want to hurt you... and it's her life, Mum.'

'I just wish she'd marry him, and be done with it. There's no reason why not. We all like Jonathan.'

Tracy was following a line of thought.

'She doesn't actually live with him, Mum. If she's on duty, or he's on an assignment, she sleeps in the hotel.'

'You're splitting hairs, Trace. Lives with or sleeps with, is there that much difference?'

Tracy thought that there was, but this wasn't the moment to argue about it. Micky burst through the door, wailing.

'Mum, Candy keeps playing with the thingummybob and I can't watch My Programme!'

Candy tumbled through behind him.

'Mummy, Micky pulled my's hair!'

Tracy scooped her up and sat her on her knee.

'You're a naughty girl, and you deserve everything you get. Now you stay here, and leave your poor brother in peace – off you go, Micky, or you'll miss it all.'

Micky dived purposefully out into the passage, and Candy wriggled and tried to get down.

'Want to go too.'

'Well, you aren't.' Tracy took a firm grip. Marilyn had picked up the letter again, and Candy's eye was suddenly caught by the photo, still lying on the table.

'That's Auntie Cheryl!'

'It certainly is.'

Candy lunged and grabbed her aunt's picture, holding it in both hands to peer at it.

'Auntie Cheryl's flying, Mummy. Nanny, look at Auntie Cheryl, flying!'

Marilyn raised her eyes from the page and gave a quick look, although she would sooner not.

'So she is, isn't that clever?'

'I 'spect the man threw her,' said Candy, studying the possibilities. It was an option, Tracy conceded, looking over her shoulder. Throwing her overboard, perhaps. But no. No such luck.

'Who's *him?*' Candy demanded, pointing.

Marilyn had come to the end of the letter. She laid it down.

'It sounds quite reasonable as Cheryl puts it,' she said.

'It *is* quite reasonable, Mum.'

Candy stabbed with an imperious finger.

'Him, him, him!' she insisted. 'Who's him?'

'Can I keep this and show it to your Dad? It might cool him down a bit.'

'I should hope so! It was only a bit of harmless fun, after all.'

'It's got the whole village talking. It's hard for Dad, in the shop all day.'

'He should learn to laugh about it. You can't blame poor Cheryl. Anyone would think she was starting on a rip-roaring affair, not just being a fill-in! She doesn't even know the man!'

'WHO'S HIM?' roared Candy, tired of being ignored. She poked the photo so hard that she bent it. Tracy removed it from her hand, not without difficulty.

'Careful pet, you'll tear it! He's nobody. Just a man.'

'He must be *somebody*,' objected Candy, with unimpeachable logic. 'He's throwing Auntie Cheryl into the sea. Mummy, why's he throwing – '

'He isn't throwing her,' interrupted Tracy, firmly. 'He's catching her. And a very good thing too, or she'd have fallen – splash!'

Candy pushed her thumb into her mouth and stared solemnly at the laughing dark face in the picture.

'Who threw her then?' she asked, indistinctly.

'Jonathan threw her. And before you ask *why*, he threw her for a joke.'

Candy removed the thumb.

'Why? Why for a joke?'

'Ask no questions, hear no lies!' said Marilyn, adding, with a rueful laugh, 'I always swore I'd never say that to a child.'

'Candy makes a business of breaking good resolutions for people,' said Tracy.

Candy returned to her original question with the persistence of a thrush murdering a snail.

'Who's him then?'

'Who's *he*,' Tracy corrected, automatically. 'His name is Oliver Nankervis, and he sailed a big boat all round the world. Does that answer your question?'

'Why?' demanded Candy. 'Why did he sail – mmph!'

Tracy placed a gentle hand over her small mouth and kissed her forehead.

'I should know better, after all this time,' she said.

'You should, too,' said Marilyn.

Later, much later, when she woke, as she often did, in the early hours of the morning, Marilyn reflected that even nine-day wonders ended sooner or later, and Cheryl's letter had at least managed to soothe her father's ruffled feathers. He had even laughed, reading her account of her day spent in a small boat with a crowd of journalists, Cheryl had a knack with words. The story ended with the climax of her unexpected flight through the air. The remainder of her letter dealt with her weekend in Cornwall with Jonathan, with particular attention paid to the scenery. The scenery had had a calming effect on Bob, too.

'A pity she didn't tell us all this before,' he had said, folding the sheets and putting them back into the envelope. 'She might have known it'd be easier for us to explain if we knew the explanation in the first place.'

Which was true, but you could hardly expect a giddy girl like their Cheryl to think of that. Her concern had been, quite simply, that they might have been upset by the pictures in the paper. Marilyn was fairly certain that she had never given village gossip a second thought. She had been away too long.

And if she married her journalist, she would be away for ever.

Marilyn turned over, facing the window, a pale square against the dark wall. There was a good moon outside, bright as day it would be in the garden. Children did leave home, it was the natural thing for them to do. There was Richard, married and living up north, and Michael in the army going all over the place ... but it was different with the youngest, and a girl at that. The darling of her father's heart ... so easy to hurt the people who loved you best.

Jonathan was a nice young man. They had been together for eighteen months now, and whatever Tracy said, they did live together. Bob knew it too, although he liked to pretend that he didn't. But Jonathan took care of her. He loved her. When they married, as eventually they would, of course, the whole family would be pleased as well as relieved. Jonathan fitted in.

Beside her, Bob snored gently, mind now at ease. Now that the drama was over, they could all relax, and Cheryl would ring on Sunday ... that was the day after tomorrow. Bob could never resist Cheryl, wind him round her little finger, she did.

Funny how it was different with daughters. Richard and Michael had both had live-in girlfriends, and if Bob had disapproved, he had never said so. Trusted the boys, but it was different with girls ... girls were more vulnerable, that was it. But it would be all right. Wedding in the village church, Bob smiling, Cheryl radiant in white... little Candy as a bridesmaid and Micky, bless him, would make a lovely page boy. Dippy old Auntie Maudie reading the tealeaves and munching wedding cake, just like when Trace and Tom got wed ... her eyelids were growing heavy, the fabric of the pillow was cool under her cheek. Marilyn smiled, planning, drifting into sleep.

Cheryl was safe with Jonathan, married or not. He worshipped the ground she walked on.

Three o'clock in the morning, and all's well ... Marilyn slept.

It was a very good thing for her peace of mind that she had no idea what Cheryl was doing at that precise moment.

II

She sat at the foot of the fire escape. It was half-past two in the morning, and the soft night wind blew cool on her hot skin, the cold iron of the newel post was hard against her forehead. Behind her, the sleeping bulk of the Queen's Hotel was silent, in darkness apart from the emergency light over the back door and a very dim glow behind the stairway windows. At her feet, a hastily packed holdall and a rolled sleeping bag bore witness to an impulse that she might live to regret. Acting on impulse had always been her besetting sin. She waited – for a stranger, if she was honest, or perhaps simply for the moment when she would pick up her luggage and return, stealthily as she had come, to her little room in the staff quarters.

He probably wouldn't come.

The light above the door glinted on her hair as she moved, striking a spark, red-gold, that shone a moment and fell into shadow. He wouldn't come, but she would wait a while longer just the same.

She was tired now. Memories of the day went through her head in a blur, tangled with emotion, confused. Pictures...

There was herself, was it only that morning? – on duty in reception, leading her humdrum life, juggling with reservations, being charming to the guests, advising on coach trips, beaches, shops. There was the cup of coffee on the shelf beneath the counter, that she hadn't had time to drink, growing a disgusting scum as it grew cold. There was Mrs. Fellowes-Harper, who must surely have been born complaining, stalking away towards the lift after trying to make a scene, and she had been so busy containing seething indignation, she remembered, that she hadn't even noticed him as he walked through the door. Unbelievable! He had stood by the desk, and when she had turned with her polite receptionist's smile to see what he wanted, he had smiled at her for one bewildering moment, and said, 'Hullo again. Remember me?'

In her mind, a thoroughly startled Cheryl took another look. Dark, clean-shaven. Thick, straight hair, well-cut but untidily ruffled by the wind, a sensitive mouth that flashed into an infectious grin, making deep dents in his cheeks that only just escaped being dimples. A blunt-ended nose a fraction too long from bridge to tip. An oval face with a wide brow, dark flying eyebrows over black-lashed eyes the colour of a stormy sea. Sun-faded jeans, white T-shirt, clean brown skin and an elegant grace, like a cat's, for all his six-foot height. She was almost certain that she had never seen him before, but a second later she could have drawn him from memory.

Tall, dark and handsome. A *cliché*.

Then she had recognised him, of course. Recollected the flash of sunlight on water, warmth on her skin, and Jonathan tossing her like a chattel to Oliver Nankervis, a legend come to life, who had just returned from sailing round the world, and laughing as he did it. She had laughed too. And Oliver. And everyone around them. The wildness of him, the care-for-nothing courage that had taken him so far and so fast, hung around him like a tangible aura. He had been drunk on success, dangerously charismatic. As he caught her in his arms, he had kissed her. It was like being struck by lightning. She had lost her head a little after that, but it hadn't mattered, it had none of it been real. Jonathan mattered, he was real.

Of course, Jonathan had never intended that she should become so integral a part of the homecoming celebrations laid on in Falmouth, but once included in that euphoric group of sponsors and friends, she had somehow remained there, on the catamaran called *Lawley's Girl*, and Jonathan's happy grin had become a steady scowl directed at her from the press boat. Unfair when it had been his doing, not hers – hadn't it? She wasn't a possession to be lent out and returned, and it had been fun, exciting, flattering ... but only a game, after all. Teasing Jonathan had been half the fun of it, and he had deserved that.

Better, though, she had decided, that her family shouldn't know the whole story, even though it had been meant, and taken, lightheartedly. She wouldn't see him again, after all, they didn't move in the same circles, far from it.

But she did see him again. And yes, she remembered him. Oh yes.

Cheryl's forehead slipped against the rail, and her head jerked forward, to bring her abruptly awake again. For a second, dazed with weariness, wine and the need to sleep, she stared at the deserted car park with blank eyes, uncertain of where she was, or why. Then it all came back to her with a shock that ran hotly through her, making her colour rise although there was nobody there to see.

What on earth did she think she was doing?

She was sitting on a cold metal fire escape in the middle of the night, waiting for a stranger – and it was all Jonathan's fault! Well, better be honest Cheryl. Where it isn't your own, or even Oliver's – but it was Jonathan who had thrown her into his arms, Jonathan who had been so unnecessarily jealous when he hadn't let her go, Jonathan who had blown everything up into something more important than it need have been, Jonathan, whose misfortune it was that Oliver Nankervis's home town wasn't Falmouth, but this south coast resort of Embridge, and that the excellent cause for which he had embarked on his adventure had been firmly rooted in this very town. All factors which had brought her to this point.

Back to this morning; Oliver leaning on her desk and smiling at her with the self-contained charm that was so much a part of him, knowing exactly what he wanted and meaning to get it. And what he wanted, amazingly, had been her company. Headily flattering once more – and one in the eye for Jonathan, who had made a silly quarrel out of nothing. The two lethal motivations for what had followed.

Oh God, what on earth had she been thinking about?

He wasn't here yet. She glanced at her watch and found that she had been on the fire escape for half an hour. It was beginning to feel very hard, and the cold of the iron struck through her jeans and made her shiver. She picked up her sleeping bag and placed it as a cushion, settling down to wait, wondering when – if – he would come. It was over an hour since they had left the reception.

Oliver's reception – or at least, given in his honour by the Mayor, the main sponsor and the Hospital. Not at the Queen's, which was not quite grand enough, but at the enormous wedding-cake Langland next door, which was very grand indeed. Jonathan, who was going, as before, on behalf of the *Embridge Herald*, had pretended that he couldn't get her a ticket, whether because he distrusted her or because he was teaching her a lesson wasn't quite clear, but in either case, it was a deception that had rebounded on his own head, since it left her free to accept a more exciting invitation. Jonathan had been astounded – and furious – when he saw her in the ballroom, the more so, she suspected, since he must have realised that he had only his own dog-in-the-mangerish attitude to blame. She tried to push away the memory. Perhaps she had earned his anger, or perhaps he was being unfair, but either way it made her uneasy. It had contained some element that she didn't quite recognise and it had led directly to this uncomfortable fire escape, and who knew what besides?

She had curtsied to minor royalty tonight, she had been formally presented to the Mayor – Jonathan's mother, unfortunately, her high-nosed stare directed at her son's familiar girlfriend in this new setting with injured surprise, and the mayoral chain of office rising and falling indignantly on her masterful bosom, for had she not made Cheryl welcome in the mayoral home and graciously bestowed her approval on the friendship? Utter disaster, the whole thing, in retrospect, and a mess that it wasn't going to be easy to clear up.

But what an evening! Wonderful food, lots of speeches (less wonderful), she had clapped until her hands tingled when the chief sponsor, head of a local engineering firm and owner of *Lawley's Girl*, had handed a handsome cheque to the Chairman of the Hospital Management Committee. And she had danced, as if her feet were winged, on a magical cloud that hadn't been only because of her Cinderella situation, and tasted a sweetness in her own unashamed pleasure that was something completely new. For this, she knew, her partner wasn't entirely blameless. He was something right outside her limited experience, and very heady wine indeed.

His father was a local solicitor of high standing and reputed wealth, his mother had been – presumably still was – a sculptress of international reputation, and beyond his name she knew nothing more about him. He had crashed into her life like a meteor and, like a meteor, left it in chaos.

Or ruins. Who could tell, at this stage?

Ten minutes over the hour now, and the car park was still deserted, the lines of parked cars metallic ghosts in the moonlight. She had been telling herself all along that he hadn't really meant it, so she had no real reason to feel so let down. After flying high, as she had been all evening, coming to earth was bound to be an anti-climax.

She should have had the resolution to say 'No'.

This unpalatable truth took her abruptly from fairy-tale to reality, and reminded her of Jonathan, glacially polite, inviting her to dance, as clear and painful in her mind as if it was happening all over again.

'I don't think –' she said, rather uncomfortable, but he simply took the drink she was holding from her hand and putting it on a table, swept her into the crowd of dancers. It was one of those smoochy numbers, wholly inappropriate. Holding her close, he danced her across the ballroom and out into the hotel foyer, and there he confronted her angrily.

'Now explain,' he demanded.

Cheryl looked into his hurt brown eyes and hot, cross face, and instead of the shame that she probably should have felt, was suddenly conscious that the heat in the ballroom had given her a thumping headache, and that her elegant evening sandals pinched her toes and had four-inch heels.

'Explain what?' she asked, coldly.

The conversation bounced thereafter like a tennis ball at Wimbledon.

'What are you doing here?'

'Why shouldn't I be here?'

'I would have brought you, if I'd known you wanted to come!'

'You *did* know.' She paused there, she recalled, and added with more truth than tact, 'You didn't want me to come, did you? You've sat glaring at me all evening, making a sideshow of both of us, just like you did in Falmouth!'

'Don't be silly!'

'You told me you couldn't get me an invitation, and now I've come anyway, you say you could!'

'I never said that.'

'You did.'

Here, Jonathan paused in his turn, dimly recognising that his just wrath was losing its edge in something perilously close to a playground squabble. He changed the direction of his attack.

'How come you're here with *him*, anyhow?' he demanded, in what was clearly meant to be a menacing tone of voice. Cheryl tossed her head carelessly, deliberately provocative, so that the overhead light struck flames from her hair. His mouth tightened, and the flames spread.

'Because he asked me, that's how,' she said. 'Which is more than you did.'

That had been neither wise nor kind, she knew it at once. She saw Jonathan's shocked expression, but although she was aware that she had caused it, she had no understanding of the sick twist that he had felt deep inside him, or of the helpless feeling he suddenly had that their time was running out like sand through an egg-timer, and nothing he could do would stop it. She only knew that he hit out at her, not with his hands but with words. Jonathan had always found words ready for his use.

'You're *my* girlfriend! You had no right!'

'Right?' Cheryl heard her own voice inside her head, and winced for him in spite of a surge of retrospective rage. 'You have no *rights* over me, Jonathan Holmes!'

'I was going to ask you to marry me – '

'What's *I was going to* supposed to mean?'

'You could have told me – warned me what you were up to – ' He was white to the lips.

She had, in fact, tried to ring him several times. She said so, sounding aggrieved.

'I tried. You never picked up. What was I supposed to do?'

'If you loved me as you said you did, you could have stayed at home!' It was a cry from the heart, and she heard it ringing down the vista of all the happy days they had spent, all the times she had lain in his arms, shared love-making, even passion, real at the time. *Meant*. She felt her own heart contract with pain, but it was on his behalf, not her own. He was the one who was hammering the nails into his own coffin.

'If,' she said, and the pain she felt made her voice sharp. Tears stung behind her eyes, because it was all so silly and pointless, and so very sudden. His nice face was all crumpled with pain like an unhappy child's. 'Don't, Jonathan,' she pleaded.

His voice was shaking with misery, and the awful nearness of complete breakdown.

'So where do you think it's all going to lead? He's mad – a complete nutter, without fear of God or man – or element! Programmed to self-destruct! A doomed man, Cheryl – is that what you want?'

There is no need to answer an obviously rhetorical question, and Cheryl simply stared at him with dumb resentment, giving him the opportunity to enlarge on this theme.

'What will you do, the day he breaks his damned neck, or drowns himself or whatever? Come and weep on good old Jonathan's shoulder? You know he'll make you unhappy, he'll make you sick with worry, he'll leave you and go off on some crazy adventure and hardly remember to write and tell you where he's gone. Is that what you want? Is it? *Is* it?'

Sitting on the fire escape in the cool night breeze, Cheryl could appreciate just how stupid it had all been. So many ties should have bound her to Jonathan, months and months, almost years, of mutual content, hopes, plans, dreams – all sweeping away in his fury like leaves on floodwater. In spite of her indignation at being berated in public, she kept her temper, and tried to defuse a situation that had blown into full-scale confrontation almost out of the empty air.

'Jonathan, it isn't like that at all – '

'Isn't *like* what?' he interrupted, bitterly. 'Don't you realise how you've humiliated me tonight, Cheryl? In front of my parents, in front of people I know, my God, how *could* you? All over tomorrow's papers – television news – when everyone in this town knows that you're *my* girl – you couldn't have made it more public if you'd yelled it on the rooftops!' He stopped. 'I loved you,' he began again, more temperately. 'I thought you loved me. I wish you joy of your new friend – and he of you – and goodnight.'

He had gone then, Jonathan whom she had almost loved, slamming out through the revolving glass doors into the spangled moonlit night, taking his hurt and anger with him...

and she had swallowed a lump in her throat for which there was no accounting, and turned away to see her evening's partner, the cause of all the trouble, standing in the ballroom doorway with a beautiful, dark-haired girl, and obviously engaged in a stimulating quarrel of his own.

Joanna Rendell – local landowner's daughter, very dark and intense, fond of dramatising everything – you know the kind.

Jonathan's voice echoed out of yet another memory, a whisper on the night wind that carried with it the chill of disappointment, telling her too clearly how stubbornly blind she was being. She wasn't beautiful, she had ginger hair, a snub nose and freckles, and witch's green eyes that only the charitable called blue. She could never afford to dress like Joanna Rendell either, not in a million years, she had no rich father to pay for it, she was a working girl. Something inside her, some lost bit of her soul that had, for an evening, had a dream, began to weep.

On a purely feminine level, if she was honest she had known it was all leading nowhere then, that she was throwing away everything for nothing. She had gone and shut herself in the cloakroom, which fortunately had been empty, and snivelled miserably into a tissue without even knowing for certain just what she was snivelling about. She might have stayed there for the rest of the evening had not Joanna Rendell come storming in with tears pouring down her face, too. No room ever built was large enough to hold both of them at that moment. Cheryl left on the instant, her own poise in shreds, the screwed-up tissue clutched in her hand, and walked straight into his arms, and it might have been intentional or it might have been coincidence, she was even now not quite clear about it.

'I was looking for you,' he said, and whether it was true or not, she had been oddly conscious that it should have been. His hands rested lightly on her shoulders, unpossessive and somehow reassuring. His eyes were stormy, filled with shadows.

'I was in the loo,' she said, on a shake that she had meant to leave behind there.

He looked at her more closely, taking in the brightness of her eyes and her flushed cheeks, and one or two other things which she had hoped he would overlook.

'You've been crying. Has someone been saying something?'

She shook her head.

'What then? The girls I take out don't cry.'

The girls he stopped taking out did. She had just seen one.

'Oh … just everything. Everything is *bloody!*' she said, and her voice didn't only shake, it cracked in the middle.

'Not everything… just people.' He lifted a hand and pulled her head against his shoulder, the touch of his fingers was like a burn on her skin even as she re-lived it. 'People are generally bloody, even when they don't need to be, or even mean to be – do this, do that, you ought to do the other – people never leave you alone.'

He sounded bitter, as if all the joy was gone out of him, and she felt that she ought to comfort him.

'They mean well – most of the time.'

Perhaps they were both a little drunk.

'I don't know why I ever came back here,' he said. 'I hate the place, I always did. I think I'll pack up and go.'

'What, right now?' She had only been half-teasing, the other half of her had been cold and still deep inside, where the weeping thing was, inexplicably lost, without reason.

'Why not right now? What is there to stay for?'

The jolt his words gave her went right down from her aching head to her pinched toes.

'To sea again?' She hadn't meant to speak that urgently. And now, here it came – that moment of crazy insanity that was going to end in humiliating disappointment here on these cold iron stairs.

'No – I don't know. High cliffs and open spaces and stars ...' He had paused then, and looked down at her, his face unreadable. 'Come with me.'

And an incandescent spark had seemed to flash between them, and she had said, 'Why not?' It had sounded casual, even offhand, but their eyes had met in understanding. At that moment she had known it was all right.

And now?

Well, now she was really in the mire. Falmouth would be hard enough to explain away, but tonight? As Jonathan had so rightly said, all over the newspapers, the television news. Dad would hit the roof, and nobody would ever forgive her. Even without knowing about this last piece of stupidity, she would be damned forever! And she had never meant any of it, it was so unfair, it had flown at her out of the sun, and knocked her flat.

Perhaps it wouldn't get further than the local papers. Oh please God, let it stop in Dorset. I'll never be impulsive again, I'll apologise to everyone, I'll even be nice to Mrs. Holmes if only it stays down south.

She was not only tired and uncomfortable, but cold. The cold had gone right through into her bones and taken the last dregs of excitement with it. She was being a fool, sitting here waiting for a man who had never really meant to come for her. Another of Cheryl's famous impulses, a joke spoken to comfort a girl who had been crying too obviously.

A casual date, that was what she was. A man didn't take a casual date away with him, and a sensible casual date didn't agree to go even if she was asked. Not with someone of whom she knew damn all. Unpleasant things happened to girls who did things like that, his own reputed craziness must have spilled over onto her.

The best thing to do now was to go to bed and forget all about it. In the morning she would be sober, and he would be gone ... alone.

Cheryl got to her feet and bent over to pick up her bag. Her hair, which was long and thick, fell forward and made a momentary curtain between herself and the world beyond, and when she stood up, flicking it back over her shoulders and pretending that it was bending down that had made her eyes water, it was as if light was swimming towards her through a sparkling mist, as delicate as her shattered daydream.

She blinked, and the diffused light resolved itself into headlights, dipped, coming towards her. The car, an open sports car whose dark colour was part of the night, slid to a halt beside her. Oliver Nankervis reached across and flicked the nearside door open for her.

'I never thought you'd really be here,' he said, and the light from the dashboard showed her that he was smiling. 'I nearly didn't come at all – get in, then, if you're coming, don't just stand there gawping! Just chuck your things in behind.'

The sound of her own heartbeat drummed in her ears. Cheryl picked up her things and flung them into the space behind the seats, and climbed in beside him. The car moved forward with a well-bred growl.

Behind lay the past, predictable and ordinary, family and friends, Jonathan who loved her, the job that she enjoyed and was good at. Ahead was only the open road, and a velvet night studded with stars.

III

Cheryl woke to the feel of wind in her face, the growl of a powerful engine, and a feeling of complete bewilderment. She sat for a moment trying to collect her thoughts, before opening her eyes and taking an experimental look at the world.

It was a dark world, slashed by bright headlamps that blazed a trail into the unknown, along which she whirled in an open car. Beside her, his hands lightly on the wheel, was a man she hardly knew, the wind of their swift passage through the night blowing his hair into wild disorder, his expression withdrawn, absorbed, unaware of her watching eyes.

In reality, she had known him for two days – well, half-days, really, if you discounted the interval between them, during which she had never expected to see him again. She felt a momentary jolt of shock. This had to be the craziest thing that she had ever even dreamed of doing.

'I must be out of my tree!' she said, wondering at herself. Oliver flashed her a swift glance.

'Hullo there. Awake at last?'

Cheryl yawned, and struggled to sit up in her seat.

'More or less, I think. Where are we?'

'Just coming up to Exeter. In a minute we shall spend about two minutes on the motorway, and then I thought we might stop for some petrol and a cup of coffee, if that suits you.'

Cheryl pinpointed Exeter on an imaginary map laid out in her mind. They were driving west into Devon and Cornwall. Next stop America. Well, why not?

'Fine,' she said, and relapsed into careful thought.

Bright lights and traffic roared up on their right, the M5, as promised. The car flew like a bird, winged, exciting, for a

25

brief moment of time part of this frantic westward migration of sound and light, and was away again, peeling off to the left, engine snarling like an angry tiger.

The all-night services were almost deserted at this early hour. They sat at a table and drank coffee, and Oliver looked at Cheryl and said, 'Are you sure about this?'

She didn't pretend to misunderstand him, but met his eyes honestly.

'I said I'd come, I've come. Won't that do – for now?'

'You were upset. And I don't think either of us was all that sober. I know what I'm doing, are you sure you do?'

Cheryl looked at him thoughtfully.

'What are you trying to say?'

'What do you want me to say?' returned Oliver, and grinned at her.

Cheryl tried to consider this question objectively, but found that it raised several others that she should have asked herself much earlier. She had made a commitment, however tacitly, by coming with him. Was she now prepared to honour it, with all that would imply?

'I think...' she began, and stopped.

'Yes?' he prompted her, when the pause had gone on too long. 'What do you think?'

'I don't know,' said Cheryl, surprised and rather horrified to find that this was true, when surely she should have been completely certain that she should get on a train back to Embridge – and Jonathan. 'I mean, I didn't think at all – I just came. It seemed the natural thing to do.'

'And now?'

She shook her head, not knowing what she ought to answer. He watched her in silence for a moment.

'I can take you home now, and nobody will be any the wiser,' he said, quietly.

'Do you want to?' countered Cheryl.

'No. But I will.'

Cheryl thought about home – or at least, about the Queen's Hotel and her job, which she could be throwing away. About Jonathan and his reproaches – justified, unfortunately. About his formidable mother who was already furious, and her own parents, who would be understandably grieved. About the events of the last twelve hours. It all seemed far less important than herself sitting here with Oliver.

'We've started this, let's finish it,' she said.

Whatever the link that bound them together, she knew that she couldn't cold-bloodedly break it. If she went back now, she might wish she had not for the rest of her life. She saw him relax and her heart leapt foolishly.

'Good,' said Oliver, with quiet satisfaction. 'Can you drive?'

'Well... yes,' said Cheryl, taken aback. 'But – '

'Good,' said Oliver, again, and yawned delicately. 'I'm shattered. You can drive the next bit.'

Cheryl's driving experience was limited to her driving lessons and the odd spin in Jonathan's rust-ridden old Ford Escort, and Oliver drove an elderly and idiosyncratic MGB. It was on the tip of her tongue to argue, but she bit back the impulse. This was an adventure, wasn't it? And the man with her had no understanding of fear, or even simple doubt. She had been told so, and she had in any case felt it for herself. She wouldn't start this new relationship, whatever it was going to turn out to be, by dithering.

'Fine' she agreed, casually, and knew by his smile that he had divined her thoughts.

The point of no return, she thought. The tingle up her spine could have been doubt – of him, or her own common sense. She ignored it.

They strolled together back to the car.

'Where are we going?' asked Cheryl.

'Does it matter? Just keep driving, we're bound to fetch up somewhere.'

Cheryl settled herself into the driving seat and studied the unfamiliar knobs and switches for a moment. Oliver, belting himself in beside her, spoke sleepily out of the darkness.

'I'm glad I look the same to you when you're sober.'

Cheryl spent the next few miles smiling over this comment, but indefinably uncomfortable, too. Oliver Nankervis knew his way around just a little too well, but she supposed it was only to be expected. She herself – well, up until a few hours ago she had assumed that she would move in finally with Jonathan quite soon, marry him one day, and that had seemed all right, but what could she assume about Oliver? What, for the matter of that, were his assumptions? Kiss and goodbye, here today, gone tomorrow – a brief rainbow and a vale of tears? She had no idea, and worse than that, she didn't think she cared either.

Later, maybe, later she would care.

As the car snarled its way along the dual carriageway from Exeter to the Cornish border, Cheryl gradually became aware that it wasn't black, or dark blue, as she had thought, but dark green. By the time they had crossed the border into Cornwall, the sky had turned from luminous grey to a pale, pink-tinged oyster pearl. Her knowledge of the geography of the Duchy was hazy, and the instruction to *just keep driving* unhelpful, but Oliver was sound asleep beside her and all the decisions her sole responsibility. She drove towards Bodmin Moor, with vague thoughts of Daphne du Maurier and *Jamaica Inn* in her mind, settling down now to the open road.

Oliver's confidence in her ability had given her confidence in herself, the unfamiliar and powerful car had soon ceased to bother her, she began to enjoy herself. It was going to be a beautiful day. Early morning mist lay in chunks and drifts and tufts all over the moor, filling the dips, catching on the trees and hedges, laying traps for unwary drivers. There was the heavy scent of gorse, and once two sheep trotted across in front of her. She braked and missed them, and beside her Oliver stirred and almost woke, but the rhythm of their resumed flight through the dawn lulled his instinct for danger and he went back to sleep.

He must, she realised, have brought sleeping with one eye open down to a fine art on his way around the world. It must be nerve-wracking to have to sleep, knowing that you were the only person there if things went wrong. It was a new and disturbing idea among many other new and disturbing ideas of this misty morning. Other people sailed round the world of course, but she had never given them more than a passing, admiring, thought. But Oliver was a flesh-and-blood person to her, not simply a name. All sorts of thoughts began to push into her head, giving her an unexpected and oddly touching awareness of his courage, and of the risks he must have run. He could so easily have never returned.

Considering this, although it would have made little difference to her at the time, chilled her over the next few miles, as the car swept on, breasted smooth hills along curling roads, sped across the open moorland. The only other living things to be seen were animals, there was almost no other traffic on this road at all so early, although there would no doubt be more later on. A deserted, dawn-bright world created especially for the two of them. Magic!

Later still, with Bodmin behind them, the question of where they were going arose again, more urgently. She didn't know Oliver well enough to guess what he had in mind, and she was getting hungry. It would be useful to stop, consult with him, look at a map if he had one, but she had an unreasonable feeling that if she did so she would lose Brownie points. She had been given a fast car and the whole of Devon and Cornwall to choose from, very well then, she would see what she could do.

A familiar name appeared on a signpost, Wadebridge. She took the turning instinctively, before she had remembered why it was familiar, but a few minutes later it came back to her. A summer holiday, years ago now. The family packed into the car, driving off to spend an August fortnight at ... yes, Tregothen Bay, that was it. Two weeks of complete enchantment, bleached in sunshine, and the first summer holiday that she could remember. A very small Cheryl playing on a golden beach with her older brothers and sister, great greeny-blue breakers crashing ashore in a tumble of surf, flowers thick on the clifftops, long walks on springy turf nibbled smooth by rabbits and burnt by the wind ... quaint little villages and towns, with narrow, twisty streets where it was nearly impossible to find a parking space, Padstow, Port Isaac, Tintagel. The names came back to her as easily as twice-times-two. The child Cheryl had dreamed of going back for years, and then pushed the memories to the back of her mind while she concentrated on the intricacies of growing up. The adult Cheryl – this new Cheryl full of such surprising anomalies – wondered if the ghost of the child might be an embarrassment to her now. The innocence of childhood is hardly the lasting kind.

A T-junction appeared ahead, Wadebridge to the right, Redruth and Truro to the left. Cheryl braked and stopped. She had a destination now, but how to get there? Seven years old takes no notice of routes.

'What's the matter?' asked Oliver drowsily.

'I'm thinking,' said Cheryl. 'Go back to sleep.'

She had it now. She waited for a milk tanker to trundle past and turned to the left. The right-hand turning off the major road, when it came, was an old friend, so perhaps seven years old wasn't so unobservant after all. Oliver glanced at the signpost, and then at his watch.

'You've made good time,' he said, and sounded surprised. 'It's only just after seven. That's a pity, I'm starving.'

'Me too,' admitted Cheryl, feeling this to be rather unromantic, given the circumstances. Last night's extravagant dinner seemed a year ago. 'I don't suppose there'll be anywhere open for hours yet. We're on the wrong road for a transport caff, or even a Little Chef.'

There was nothing to be done about that, she had no idea even of what they had with them. If food was included, Oliver didn't say so, and since they had left in the early hours of the morning, it had to be unlikely. They drove on and Oliver, apparently content to leave it in her hands, didn't even ask where they were going.

It was strange how familiar the twisting lanes appeared, she could follow the way faultlessly, St. Merryn along *here,* Constantine and Harlyn down *there*; the tiny lane leading off towards the cliffs was unmarked, but Cheryl turned down it without hesitation. Flowers and grasses brushed the car on either side, flicking Oliver in the face and splashing him with drops. He laughed and dashed them away as they breasted a rise, and there was the sea.

The familiar granite farmhouse still stood at the corner of the lane, and she remembered something else, and had laughed aloud before she could stop herself.

'What's the joke?' enquired Oliver, grinning at her, for the laugh had been infectious.

'Oh – just a silly thing! You see that field, there? When we were small, on holiday here, Tracy and me sat on the gate in the evening and talked to the pigs – the pigs aren't there now, but they were then – and I used to sing hymns to them ... one in particular, because it seemed to sum up the whole place. *Summer suns are glowing, over land and sea ...*' She hummed a bar or two of the tune. 'Do you know it?' Oliver shook his head. 'I don't know what the pigs thought about it,' said Cheryl.

'Is Tracy your sister?'

'My older sister,' said Cheryl. 'There's four of us. Richard, Tracy, Michael and me, in that order, very tidy. Trace is married now, and Richie. Mike's in the army. Engineers.'

A query hung in the air. Oliver ignored it. Cheryl wished suddenly that she hadn't mentioned her family. They would sit in judgement on her, and she had given them the right. Would anything, after this, ever be the same? She pushed the thought away.

The road curled round a bend, and an old inn, enjoying a new lease of life as an hotel, appeared on their right, white and clean in the early morning light, grey slate tiles, odd windows peeping out here and there. It was as if she had never been away.

'We stayed there,' she said, pointing. 'There's a caravan site down the road, but you couldn't see it from the windows. I should think it may have grown a bit by this time.'

Oliver was only half-listening. He said, 'Are you allowed to camp down here? Would you like to?'

'Do we have a tent?' asked Cheryl.

'In behind you. Yes.'

'I think they used to allow tents in the field at the far end – yes, I'm sure they did. Mind you, I'm going back a long time.'

'We'll go and see later on. When people are awake.'

The field overlooking the sea that was the car park was empty, the gate untended, the beach kiosk shuttered close. Cheryl parked the car and switched off the engine, and there was a sudden quiet, emphasised rather than flawed by the hushing of the sea around the rocks edging the bay below them, the song of a lark in the clear, pale sky, the whisper of the light breeze in the tamarisks over their heads. Oliver leaned across and gently kissed her lips.

'This is exactly the right place for the way I was feeling, clever girl,' he said. 'What shall we do, until it's late enough to hunt breakfast?'

Cheryl's eyelids felt like lead, and she was stiff and aching with driving and unslept sleep. Now that they had stopped, she realised how tired she was. Even that kiss, with all it had promised, took second place to sheer weariness. And sleeping would buy her time, but she didn't consciously think that.

'Can we find a quiet spot, and go back to sleep?'

Oliver was as bright-eyed and alert as if he had spent eight hours sleeping in a comfortable bed rather than less than three in a cramped bucket seat, but he could see the shadows of physical exhaustion under her eyes and agreed without argument, content to let events take their natural course. She was grateful to him.

'We'll try the beach,' he said easily. 'There's a rug in the back, under the tent, I'll dig it out.'

They left the car and walked slowly down to the sand. It was about half-tide, but in any case, she remembered, the sea never came right up the beach except at high-water springs, or in a storm. They found a sheltered indentation in the cliffs above the tideline, spread the rug and settled down. Cheryl shivered a little, it was still quite early in the year.

'Cold?' asked Oliver, beside her.

'A bit – it'll warm up soon.'

'Come here.' He reached out and scooped her towards him, putting his arm round her. 'Better?'

It felt strangely right to be so close to him, as if, she thought sleepily, she had been here many times before. The warmth generated by his body was comforting. How could she ever have thought they would never meet a second time?

'Mmm,' said Cheryl, and folded close, slept at once.

Consciousness began with hot sun on her skin, and the softness of wool against her cheek. There was the roar of surf somewhere close at hand and gulls mewing sadly overhead, and there were voices in the distance and a general feeling of a world that was wide awake and going about its business. She lay for a minute or two, eyes closed, remembering where she was and what she was doing there, and had already smiled before she had time to wonder if she ought to feel shame – or even alarm. She opened her eyes.

She wasn't lying beside Oliver so much as on him, and the softness against her sleeping face wasn't the rug, but his sweater. She could hear his heart beating under her ear, the slow, steady, even beat of total fitness. He had rolled onto his back as he slept, taking her with him in the circle of his right arm, and his other hand was right under her nose as she awoke. He had nice hands, she thought sleepily, long-fingered, elegant hands, not a bit what one might be forgiven for expecting in such a dedicated seaman. She recalled that his mother was some sort of artist. His wrist was encircled with a formidable-looking watch on a heavy strap, the dial ringed with a bevel engraved with numbers, but it didn't look quite like a stopwatch. She put up her own hand and turned it gently towards her, exploring the bevelled edge with her fingertips.

'It's an underwater watch, divers for the use of,' Oliver informed her, lazily, and she jumped.

'It's very grand. What are the numbers for?'

'Recording elapsed time. You can move it round to suit yourself. It's very important to know how long you've been down, if you get it wrong, nasty things happen to you.'

Cheryl remembered Jonathan saying that Oliver had been diving in the Mediterranean, if she had thought about it at all, she had imagined him finning about with a mask and snorkel. She now had a feeling that she had that wrong, that watch looked serious.

'You mean, you're one of those people who go down and explore sunken wrecks?'

'It has been known.'

'You're laughing at me!'

'Would I?'

Cheryl sat up, pushed a stray strand or two of hair out of her eyes, and looked at him sprawling on the rug, relaxed as a cat and nearly as untouchable.

'I don't know you very well yet, but yes, I think you would,' she said. 'And if that wonderful watch of yours is right, we've missed breakfast – and my stomach thinks my throat's been cut!'

It was nearly eleven o'clock. The beach was scattered now with family groups and windbreaks, and children digging sandcastles. Oliver sat up too and looked at the view thoughtfully.

'All self-respecting tourist-trap beaches have a taverna,' he stated.

They found it just up the road from the beach, nothing so exotic as a taverna; a simple British beach cafe established in somebody's garden and serving all-day snacks and soft drinks. They sat under a red sun umbrella to eat eggs on toast and drink coffee.

'Now what?' asked Cheryl, when they had reached the third-cup-of-coffee stage. Oliver, meditatively stirring sugar into his cup, looked up.

'It's Saturday, so I suppose we should round up some food for the weekend. After that, who knows?' He looked at her directly. 'What about your job? Hadn't you better let them know you're still alive? They might send out search parties.'

'I left a message on the desk to say I'd been suddenly called away on urgent family business,' said Cheryl doubtfully, for in the sane light of day the lie seemed shabby. 'I'll phone up later and explain.' Explain, how?

'We can still get you back before all hell breaks loose.'

'I've already told you,' said Cheryl. 'No. Why do you keep saying it? Do you wish you hadn't brought me?' The thought was a sharp disappointment. So much for doubt.

He looked at her, his brows drawn together in a slight frown.

'It seems a bit ... sweeping, somehow. You were right, it seemed natural at the time.' He paused. 'You hardly hesitated, and I didn't stop to think.'

The red umbrella had a white plastic fringe round it that flickered in the warm wind and made a twittering noise. The twitter filled a space of time that seemed endless.

'It's stupid,' said Cheryl, at last. 'I feel – I've felt all along – that I've known you for ever. Actually, I hardly know you at all. I thought I was in love – with Jonathan – you remember, he threw me at you? – and I was going to get engaged and married, and keep house and raise children, all the usual things. I don't ... well, sleep around like some girls I know, there was only ever him – but suddenly, there's you ... and that's how it is.'

It had been a difficult thing to say, and to a lot of people, she would never have said it. Oliver, for some reason, was different. They were on the same wavelength. He smiled at her bewilderment.

'Then we'd better settle up for breakfast and get ourselves some stores,' he said, matter-of-factly, and whatever it was she had been trying to tell him, he obviously understood. Like a foreigner understanding sign language, Cheryl thought, as they strolled hand in hand down the lane to the car park. The thought brought a new one in its wake.

'Nan-*kerv*is,' she said. 'It's a strange name. Where does it come from?'

'God knows,' said Oliver. 'I was born with it. Someone once told me it might be Cornish, but I never bothered to follow it up.'

'It sounds rather foreign.' She remembered the mention of a taverna. 'Greek, or something. Don't you think?'

'I've no idea. I can only tell you, I've never met anyone else with it.'

The beach kiosk was open when they got back to the car, and while Oliver had an argument with a car-park attendant who insisted that they were trying to cheat him, Cheryl went inside. She found it sketchily stocked with bare necessities, and as she chose the things that looked most useful for the coming weekend, she wondered if Oliver was a fussy eater, for she really knew nothing about him.

'You've left out butter,' said Oliver, joining her and running a swift eye over the contents of the basket. 'I refuse to eat that imitation healthy stuff. Don't go too wild, will you? I'm practically broke, unless we can find a hole in the wall. How about you?'

'I've got about sixteen pounds and a Visa card, which I don't think this place will take,' said Cheryl. They smiled at each other. It didn't matter.

They returned to the beach and spent the remainder of the day catching up on some of the things they needed to learn about each other, and preferences in food weren't mentioned.

'What do you do, when you're not sailing round the world?' asked Cheryl, as she lay on the rug and soaked up the spring sunshine.

'Not a lot,' he answered her. 'Why?'

'For a living, I mean. You must do something.'

He laughed.

'Oh, that ... I'm a professional skipper, I deliver yachts to places abroad for people who can't, or don't want to do it for themselves. I had a fling with a flotilla a couple of years back, and I've done a bit of professional diving out there in the Med, too. I do anything that looks as if it might be interesting, really.'

Cheryl remembered some of the things that Jonathan had said about him, and smiled.

'You're nothing but a beachcomber,' she said, and gave him a friendly push. 'An ornery, no-good bum! Are you going to bum around for ever?'

'I hope so!' said Oliver.

'It's hardly a career.'

'So what, if it gives me what I want?'

'Which is?'

'Excitement – variety – adventure. Enough money to live on and call my soul my own. Freedom.'

'One day,' said Cheryl, carefully, 'don't you think you might want to settle down? Have a proper home to come back to, children to carry on your peculiar name?'

He looked at her, and his lips twitched a little.

'Is that your ambition?'

Cheryl had never thought about it specifically, she had taken the idea of marriage and children for granted because that was the way she had been brought up. His simple question took her by surprise.

'I've no idea,' she said, the surprise showing in her voice.

'Good God! Why not?'

'I've just taken it as read, I suppose – about marriage and children. I love my job, but I don't see it for ever, I'm not a career woman in that sense. With no husband and no children, life could be a bit … well, empty, couldn't it?'

'Put like that, I suppose, yes, but why does marriage and children immediately mean settling down to you? Getting stuck in a rut, that could be pretty empty, too, don't you think? People keep on saying to me, *you'll have to give it all up one day, you know*, but I fail to see why. If I ever have a wife and children, I shall of course have to share some responsibility for them, but does it have to be behind a desk, in a so-called *respectable profession?* Not as I see it.'

'These days, wives help support children, if that's what they want. Lots do. They don't have to be a responsibility, who wants to, anyway?'

Oliver laughed, linking his hands together behind his head, closing his eyes against the bright sunlight. She knew a crazy instant when her heart turned right over and her breath caught uncomfortably in her throat, and pushed it away, afraid to study it objectively.

'Husbands and wives and children should work it out to suit themselves,' he said. 'It isn't any business of anyone else. My wife, should I ever have one, will do exactly what she wants, I hope, not as society expects her to – and so, for that matter, shall I.'

'It sounds perfect, but I suspect there's a catch.'

'Nobody has the right to somebody else's freedom and independence, married or not,' said Oliver, laying down the law. 'I've watched some of my friends – trying to muscle in on each other's privacy, trying to change each other all the time, refusing to let the wind blow between them. They won't allow any personal space at all, and so at the first bump in the road, they're so on edge that they take to the woods and lose everything – everything that they haven't lost already, that is. Then there's no end of an emotional mess to sort out, miserable kids, squabbles over property, lawyers rubbing their hands and licking their lips over the corpse of something that need never have died in the first place, if it had only been given room to breathe ... no, not for me. Nobody ever said it was easy to be free *and* married, and happy with it, but it has to be worth trying, surely, or marriage as an institution would have died out long since. And before you jump to conclusions, we are not talking sexual freedom here, that goes without saying. That never made any marriage work.'

Bitterness there. Cheryl filed the discovery for future reference, now was not the time.

'It all comes down to trust, then?' she said.

'It seems so, to me. People are people, individuals, not made to some master plan. You and I, for example, are not the prototypes for the human race. Marriage is supposed to be a good thing, and I can see that it could be ... one day, not right now.'

'It sounds funny, coming from someone like you,' observed Cheryl, studying him thoughtfully and trying to ignore that last remark. 'I would have thought that you'd be just the opposite – you look like the prototype lover, if anything, not solid husband material.'

He grinned at that, lightening an atmosphere that had become unexpectedly charged.

'People say that life is what you make it, but I think myself that you are what life makes you. I'm the child of a broken home myself, and I wouldn't wish it on a dog. And my mother has taken lovers enough, and I can't see that it's made her any happier. The happy people are those who feel secure.'

Another surprise.

'You pine for security?' asked Cheryl, startled; it seemed out of character.

'In human relationships – yes, I think so. Security, mind you, not prison and a ball and chain.'

'Isn't that an impossible ideal?'

'*Impossible* is a dirty word,' said Oliver. 'Feel like a swim? It's got to be warm enough now, even for you.'

He had succeeded – as perhaps, Cheryl decided, he had intended – in stopping the discussion in its tracks. She was disappointed, for it had surprised her that he should have such positive views on marriage and she would have liked to explore further, but the warning signs were clear enough. He had told her all that he wanted, maybe more than he had wanted, and if she wished to learn more she would have to wait and pick her moment for asking. She could accept that, there was time yet, and if she was wrong and there wasn't, it wouldn't matter anyway.

It was after five, and the beach was beginning to empty, when they finally gathered up the rug and their other possessions and walked back to the car. Cheryl wedged herself in under the box of stores, and Oliver drove up the field and onto the caravan site.

'What made you choose such an inconvenient car?' she asked, squashed.

'I didn't. It was a present – twenty-first birthday, from my father.' He pulled a face. 'It's what he liked at that age. Some people, I suppose, still do.'

'There's lots of enthusiasts about,' said Cheryl, including, she might have added, her own brother Mike.

'Not me,' said Oliver, but he still had it ... what? Seven, eight years later? Apathy, or consideration for his father's feelings? The first, she suspected, alas! She already had the suspicion that Oliver's father's feelings weren't a first priority with him. The reverse, though, couldn't be true, his father must have believed the gift would please him. Sad.

'If you could choose, what *would* you choose?' she asked, and Oliver laughed.

'Something practical. Rugged, spacious, plenty of pulling power. Disappointed?'

'You aren't really a car person, are you?'

'They're not a lot of use in the middle of the ocean.'

'True.'

They had arrived outside the site office, and Oliver climbed out, leaving Cheryl wedged under the box while he went inside to make inquiries. Tents, as Cheryl had remembered, were allowed in the top field, together with touring vans. They were allocated a space under the hedge on the seaward side and drove up through the lines of static vans to find it.

While Oliver put up a diminutive ridge tent, Cheryl investigated the contents of the boot, which seemed at first glance to be mainly composed of a wet suit, two cylinders of compressed air, and a miscellaneous collection of various valves, mask and flippers. Beneath all this, she found a minimal amount of basic cooking equipment, and a tiny camping stove. To one more used to the chaos that went with a large frame tent and a trailer full of gear, it was salutary. Oliver saw her expression and laughed outright, holding out his arms to her. She walked into them without thought, and held him close, her face tilted up to his.

'Well, my little sybarite?' he said, mocking her.

She didn't understand what he meant, but smiled at him anyway, yielding like butter melting in the sun.

'You're barking mad!' she told him.

For answer, Oliver kissed her again, his mouth searching hers with renewed promises of more to come, and if there was a breath of a whisper at the back of her mind, telling her that he wasn't the only one who was barking mad round here, Cheryl chose to close her ears to it. She returned the kiss with equal warmth, untempered by caution. Her heart began to thump unevenly and the kiss had kindled a glow that spread through her body like fire. Oliver looked down at her, his eyes glinting. He released her slowly, spinning out the moment, and held back the tent flap with a smile that made her heart lurch.

'After you, my lady.'

It was in keeping that Oliver should be as straightforward and lighthearted in his love-making as in everything else. He took her with laughter and used her with gentleness, touching within her a spring of awareness, both mental and physical, that she had never suspected could exist. Not tearing passion, not even sex simply for its own sake. Fun, and an endearing delight in the pleasure both given and received. No beginner, as she wasn't foolish enough to overlook. She had always enjoyed the physical side of love, but Jonathan was an also-ran, in spite of his often affirmed devotion. Cheryl supposed, for the last time, that she should have felt guilt at her betrayal not only of him, but of the standard she had set for herself, one man, one love – but that was the last doubt she allowed. Laughter was too close to the surface. It couldn't be taken seriously. Afterwards, she lay in Oliver's arms, his skin silky and warm against her own, letting contentment wash over her in honey-sweet waves, amazed at the richness of her newly extended experience.

But it hadn't been the first time he had made love since he left England so many months ago, of that she was certain. Hunger there was, yes, natural and under control – starvation, no. And she thought of Joanna Rendell's dark beauty and a shadow passed over the sun.

IV

Jonathan Holmes woke up on that Saturday morning no longer angry, but sick. Sick with himself, with Cheryl, and most of all, with Oliver Nankervis. Jonathan was a journalist, he prided himself on knowing how many beans made five. He knew that gossip had it that Oliver had taken to the great oceans to escape an entanglement with his stepsister's great friend, Joanna Rendell. He knew that Joanna Rendell had been waiting on the jetty at the Embridge Yacht Club when *Lawley's Girl* came quietly home on the evening flood tide. Nobody knew what had happened after that. A lot of wild surmises flew about, however. The reuniting had not appeared, to onlookers, to be a happy one. They had left, after the Commodore's welcoming cocktail party, in her car, but Oliver had looked tired and rather angry, and Joanna was on the verge of tears, he had that on excellent authority. Nobody had spotted them together since. If there was a story there, it was kept well hidden. Oliver's sister, Susan Casson, had a way of treating hard-working reporters as if they were cockroaches and gave nothing away. Joanna Rendell had similarly kept a carefree public face, until last night. Last night, and Cheryl.

Jonathan gritted his teeth. If Oliver's intention had been to upset Joanna, he must have succeeded beyond his wildest expectations, but why did he have to drag Cheryl into it? Cheryl wasn't his kind, she was a bystander – an innocent bystander. She deserved better than to be used as cannon fodder in a private war of the sexes.

She could have said *no!* She should have said it. Bloody opportunist, Oliver Nankervis! Flaunting his transient fame and all-too-evident charm, dazzling the poor girl – leading her on just to make some point or other, who did he think he was anyway?

44

Indignation felt good, but Jonathan found it impossible to sustain. Honesty is something that doesn't necessarily come easily to men of his profession, but unfortunately he had been strictly brought up, and sometimes found that it got in his way. It did so now. Oliver Nankervis would never even have noticed Cheryl if it hadn't been for himself.

Jonathan swore.

Belting his bathrobe with constricting fury, he went into the kitchen to make himself some coffee. His head was thumping and his mouth was dry, the pair of them had literally driven him to drink last night! He sat down, head in his hands, at the table. Nothing is more depressing than the conviction that you have made a fool of yourself, and Jonathan felt this in full measure.

Falmouth had been nothing – Oliver's fault, not Cheryl's – his own fault, for doing what he had, just to make a good picture. But how was he to know that the bastard would refuse to let her go? But even then, it had only been a bit of fun, hadn't it? Hardly love at first sight, like something in a tacky romantic novel. He had overreacted, and now look where it had got him.

He would be lucky if she ever spoke to him again.

The kettle boiled. He made a mug of strong black coffee and wandered miserably into his sitting room to drink it. Memories of her were everywhere – the book she had been reading, open face down on the coffee table, her sweater flung over the back of a chair, her photograph on the mantelpiece. Her scent on the pillow as he lay awake last night ...

'Damn, damn, damn, damn!' said Jonathan, and flung himself down into an armchair.

His mind went back over their quarrel. He had said, he recalled uncomfortably, some very hard things, jumped to some unforgivable conclusions.

There was only one possible way out.

He would have to apologise.

The thought immediately made him feel more hopeful – not better, precisely, but more hopeful. Couples fought all the time, after all, and it didn't always lead to the divorce court, or to a murderous assault with the bread knife.

He would like to take a bread knife to Oliver Nankervis. Now that *would* make a good headline. *HEROIC ROUND-THE-WORLD YACHTSMAN KNIFED BY JEALOUS LOVER! Blunt bread knife shown in evidence!* Real Sunday tabloid stuff, that. He contemplated the picture with pleasure. *Blood everywhere! Ginger-haired girlfriend weeps ...*

Whose girlfriend? And why would she weep?

'Oh shit!' said Jonathan. 'I've really buggered things now.'

Setting his mug aside, he went back into the bathroom and peered at himself in the mirror. White face, eyes like a dissipated racoon. Apart from that, his own unexciting, pleasant countenance stared back at him. Curly, light brown hair, dark brown eyes, stubbled square chin. The face of an ordinary man who played rugby and drank real ale, and loved a hotel receptionist. No charisma, though. Pity about that, but it had never seemed to bother her before.

The phone rang in the sitting room, but he didn't rush to answer it. A moment later, the answerphone kicked in.

'Jonathan?' said his mother's voice. 'Jonathan, are you there?'

'Ask a silly question,' remarked Jonathan, to his reflection, and reached for his can of shaving foam.

'Ring me at once when you get back, please. I shall be at home all morning.'

Click. Whirr. Goodbye, Mother.

A razor would make a nice mess, too. He hefted it in his hand. He had never suspected himself of such bloodthirsty inclinations.

If you are going to apologise at all, it's advisable to do it thoroughly. Jonathan, a romantic at heart after all, bought flowers and chocolates, rang the *Herald* on his mobile to tell a few untruths about what he was doing, and drove to the Queen's Hotel to get it over.

And Cheryl wasn't there.

Jeanette, the receptionist on duty, knew Jonathan well, but fortunately hadn't yet heard about last night's fiasco at the Langland. She greeted him with explanations, not ghoulish sympathy, he was relieved to find.

'She left a note on the desk last night,' she said. 'She had a phone call – she had to go home at once. Some family thing, urgent, she didn't say what.'

Jonathan stared at her. A newsman first and a disappointed lover afterwards, his mind immediately leapt to the day's headlines. *Shooting in Northern Ireland. Three killed.* Soldiers. Mike, Cheryl's brother, was stationed in Northern Ireland. Not Mike, oh please, not Mike! Cheryl would be devastated, she adored him.

'Is anything the matter?' asked Jeanette, looking at him curiously. She liked Jonathan, envied Cheryl. She would have envied her even more if she had known about Oliver Nankervis, at that very moment cuddling her workmate on a sunlit beach.

'No – it's OK. I'll give her a ring at home. Does she say what time she left?'

Jeanette shook her head.

'No, but it must have been very early. Nobody was on the desk.'

Jonathan frowned.

'Didn't the night porter see her?'

Jeanette shrugged.

'Not even when she wrote the note?'

'He went upstairs, he said – oh, about two o'clock, maybe later. Someone had a dripping tap keeping them awake. She must have left it then.'

'Damn! Nobody saw her go, then?'

'You can get out by the back way without setting off the alarm, if you know how. She knows how.' She giggled. Everyone knew why Cheryl knew how, Jonathan better than anyone. His returning grin was mechanical, his mind working fast.

'Well, thank you. I'll give her home a ring, ask her to call me when she gets there – if she's not there already. No problem.'

'Sounds good to me.' Jeanette was already losing interest. Jonathan went slowly back to his car.

Marilyn was surprised to receive his call.

'Cheryl? No, she isn't here.'

'But you're expecting her. She said ...'

'Not that I know of.' Marilyn shook her head, although he could not, of course, see her.

'I thought there might have been bad news of Mike,' said Jonathan, hesitantly, but Marilyn was quite definite about that.

'Mike's on leave. He's staying with Richie and Louise. Are you sure you got the message right?'

Jonathan was no longer sure of anything, but at least that news was a relief, of sorts.

'Would Tracy know where she'd gone?'

Marilyn considered. Tracy hadn't said anything yesterday, but something might have blown up since, out of a clear sky. She made a guess, and came close to the truth.

'What's the matter, Jonathan? Have you two had a fight?'

'No, of course not.' He sounded unconvincing, Marilyn thought, remembering the details of yesterday's discussion with Tracy. She decided that it would be best to stay out of it.

48

'That's all right, then.' She paused. 'She's going to ring home tomorrow. Do you want me to tell her you asked for her?'

'I expect I'll have seen her by then,' said Jonathan. 'I'm sorry I bothered you, it must be some misunderstanding.'

He rang off, then cursed because he had forgotten to ask for Tracy's number. By the time he had got it from Directory Enquiries, her line was engaged. Marilyn had lost no time.

That was that, then. Jonathan sat staring through his windscreen with eyes that saw nothing. After a while, an unthinkable thought came into his head.

She wouldn't ... would she?

He drove down to the marina.

Lawley's Girl, back now in her own berth, was immaculately tidy, locked and deserted. The stresses and strains of her recent voyage showed in worn ropes and bleached woodwork, and one or two bumps and bends, but she had come through well, all things considered. Her wealthy owner, who also owned a big engineering works on the outskirts of the town, should have no complaints. He had been the main sponsor, and what he had paid out in hard cash must have been more than recompensed by all the publicity. He had known that, of course, when he came up with the original idea. Jerry Nankervis, Oliver's father, was a member of the same Yacht Club. Old School Tie stuff. Jonathan pulled a face. Oliver, a known wild card and an experienced yachtsman, had been the obvious choice for the voyage on many counts, not least that it had removed him, for a while, from his family's orbit. Oliver wasn't the family favourite.

Jonathan knew a lot about Oliver, more, probably, than Oliver would have wanted him to know. Back at the *Herald*, there was a large file, full of interesting information, garnered over the years and brought together when he set out on his epic voyage. Oliver Nankervis was Bad News – or had been, up until the time he became merely News.

And Oliver Nankervis, like Cheryl, wasn't here.

Jonathan aimed an angry kick at the sleeping catamaran and stalked back up to the marina office. Yes, they believed that Mr. Nankervis was still living aboard, and no, he hadn't been aboard last night. He had told the night watchman that he would be back late, but his car had not been in the car park this morning. No, they didn't know where he had gone. Jonathan was left with the distinct impression that they wouldn't have told him even if they could, so perhaps they *did* know. Had he come back at all? Useless to ask. Sir Charles Lawley, and if it came to that, Oliver himself at this moment, were VIPs. Jonathan was just a stray journalist, asking tiresome questions.

He found himself sitting in his car again, wondering where to go next. He tried Tracy's number, but this time there was no reply.

The unco-operative Mrs. Casson would make short work of any questions that she considered impertinent. In any case, it was fairly clear from the files that Oliver would be unlikely to make a *confidante* of her. There remained Joanna Rendell.

Spoilt, beautiful bitch. But at least, spoilt, beautiful bitch spending the morning at home. A maid showed him in – a *maid*, would you believe! His mother had a daily woman, but a *maid?* Of course, her father was another one of that Yacht Club set. Jonathan, a committed socialist, sneered, while at the same time, a ribald little voice in his head that refused to be silenced, observed that a good sneer was cleansing for the soul.

It soon became obvious that a maid who let stray journalists into the drawing room wasn't exactly flavour of the month, and might soon find herself down at the Job Centre.

'What are you doing here – barging your way in like this?' Joanna could sneer too.

'I'm trying to find Oliver Nankervis,' said Jonathan, falling back on what was, after all, true.

'I don't know why you should be looking for him here!'

'I just thought you might know where he was. It's reasonable enough, isn't it? You go out together.'

'Do we? Perhaps you should tell him that!'

She spoke in angry exclamation marks. Jonathan didn't blame her. Under normal circumstances he might have tried to provoke her into a greater indiscretion, but somehow, today he hadn't the heart for it. He couldn't make copy out of Cheryl, and Cheryl had to be at the bottom of this. His heart felt leaden. Joanna, with belated caution, spoke carefully.

'Of course, we did go out at one time, but that was months ago. I'm afraid I can't help you. Now, if you don't mind, I'll ring for Carol to show you out.' She reached for the bell. On impulse, Jonathan reached out and stopped her.

'I think we're at cross-purposes here. I'm not after a story. I'm looking for a girl.'

'Oh, a girl *and* Oliver?' But she dropped her hand.

There was a pause. Then Jonathan said, soberly,

'I hope not. But it could be.'

'A girl with freckles, and squiggly ginger hair?'

Jonathan gave a silent nod. A look almost of sympathy passed between them.

'She was with him last night,' said Joanna, as if she was spitting out cherry stones.

'I know. I was there.'

Her lip curled. He thought that she was about to make some derogatory remark about paparazzi, and added, 'My mother is the Mayor. I was in her party.'

'But looking for scandal too, no doubt!'

'Scandal is not my line. There are gossip columnists for that.'

'I suppose you all scavenge for each other!' said Joanna, scornfully, which was true enough to be uncomfortable.

Jonathan had been about to tell her that Cheryl was his girlfriend, but decided against it.

Joanna walked across to a sideboard with drinks set out. She reached for a glass.

'Have a drink?'

Having the Mayor for his mother had been an advantage before, but he hadn't expected it to help here. Mayors were small fry for the Rendell family, definitively County. Jonathan accepted, wondering what was coming next, and she handed him a hefty measure.

'He's not here you know – not in Embridge. He's gone. Oliver.' She sounded desolate.

'What do you mean – gone?'

'Gone. Scrammed. Wented. How do you want me to mean it?'

'Gone, where?'

'Who knows? Who cares?' She tossed off her drink and poured another. 'He got in his car, and just drove away. Goodbye, Oliver!' The second drink followed the first.

'Alone?' asked Jonathan, hesitantly.

'Alone!' Joanna made an extravagant gesture. 'Of course, alone, what d'you take him for? *Alone* is all Oliver wants, all Oliver has ever wanted. You're a bloody journalist, don't you even know that much?' She began to cry. Jonathan wondered how much she had drunk before he got here, and decided that it was time to go. The passion with which she had spoken had convinced him that she believed in what she said, there was no help here. He thanked her for the drink and left, without benefit of Carol, and with a strong sense of relief.

Poor little rich girl, with everything but what she wanted.

Alone had been a comforting word. She believed it, but did he?

He wanted to, thought Jonathan, as he drove away. Nobody could imagine how much.

But even so, he didn't.

When, by evening, she had neither returned nor telephoned, then he accepted the truth. She had left him, and she might come back, true, when Oliver Nankervis had had enough of her, but nothing would ever be the same. The lonely flat, his solitary bed, the whole great world, rang with emptiness.

Only himself to blame, only himself. It was like a refrain, humming through his head like a dismal song, it even seemed to have music. Jonathan got angry, thought *Damn her, anyway!* and took himself down to his local and got thoroughly and gloriously drunk. It seemed the only sensible thing left to do. He did not ring his mother.

Back in Suffolk, Cheryl's family weren't unduly worried at first.

'They'd obviously had a row,' said Marilyn. 'Stupid girl! I expect it was over those photos again.'

Tracy objected to this. 'It didn't sound in her letter as if they were rowing. Well, not seriously. And that was all a week ago.'

Marilyn looked mildly worried.

'She wouldn't go off with someone else, after all that living together, would she?'

'I wouldn't think so. Gracious, Mum, they're practically joined at the hip! Anyway, she would've said – to me, if not to you, if there was someone else.'

'Your Dad would be real upset if she did. He likes Jonathan, in spite of all, and believe me, that's a miracle. There's not many'd be good enough for his special girl.'

Tracy, who had always been secretly relieved not to hold the position of Dad's special girl, in spite of a certain amount of sibling rivalry, sighed.

'He sets that much store by her, she's bound to trip up sometime, isn't she? No Mum, they may have had a bit of a fight, goodness, don't we all? She might be teaching him a lesson, he can be a bit of an MCP, just like Dad. Or it might just be a silly misunderstanding, he never actually saw the note, did he?'

'He didn't say he had.'

'There you are then.'

'I just think he was troubled when she wasn't here. Too much troubled.'

'Well, she's ringing tomorrow, and you can ask her about it.'

But Sunday passed, and there was no call from Cheryl.

V

The days in Cornwall became magical. Both Oliver and Cheryl were virtually penniless, and what money they had was spent on food, but they swam and surfed and sunbathed, and in the intervals made joyous and lighthearted love with each other, and if Cheryl ever felt a pang about that unmade phone call home, she managed to push it to the back of her mind. How could she have spoken to them, that dear but distant family? What could she have said that would explain? Nothing. So it was best left undone.

Her skin turned from winter-pale to a pretty shade of tourist pink, and developed even more freckles, and Oliver tanned, if that were possible, a shade of deeper olive brown.

'You look like an Arab,' Cheryl told him. 'Didn't you hear those people over there, asking each other how she, that's me, could go out with a coloured man, that's you? Are you sure that name of yours isn't Middle Eastern?'

Oliver gave a smothered laugh and took her by the shoulders, rolling her over on the warm sand with a strength that she had already found to be irresistible. He looked lightly built, but he was as hard as nails and as tough as whipcord. She already loved him passionately, from his tousled dark head to his heels, but she wouldn't admit it. Every inch of his body was beautiful.

'I always fancied myself as a sheikh,' he said, now. 'Perhaps it's hereditary. Do you fancy coming into my tent?'

'You've been too long at sea,' Cheryl said, thinking it was true, and hooked her arms around his neck, pulling his head down to hers. 'You know what sailors are!'

She had thought that she had him by the neck, but now found herself pinned down on the sand. They were both laughing.

'Oh, stop!' she cried, breathlessly. 'You're squashing me, and people are staring!'

He let her go and sat up, smiling at her with so much unshadowed pleasure that her breath stopped altogether. She lay on the sand and smiled back at him.

Just talking to him opened up a whole new world. Oliver might be broke personally, but he moved in circles where money talked, and loudly. He had been brought up against a background as different from her own as it could be. Her own parents kept the local Spar shop in a small Suffolk village, Oliver's ...

'How did you come to sail round the world, anyway?' she asked him, another time. 'Have you always done a lot of sailing?'

They were sitting in a froth of sea pinks at the top of a perilous cliff, with the seabirds perching on the ledges and outcrops below them. Oliver idly picked up a stone and threw it down towards the surf line, sending the birds wheeling and calling around their heads. His face had taken on a shut look, but he answered her easily enough.

'When I was very small, my father had a yacht, so I suppose you could say I was born to it. The yacht went soon after he married my stepmother. Dear Dot dislikes the water for children, but I'd got the bug by then, and I was always sneaking off to the harbour. I grew up with boats and sailing ...' He let the sentence tail off as if he had been going to add something else, and tossed another stone. The gulls, that had begun to settle, flew screeching into the air a second time. Cheryl hesitated, made acutely aware by his actions as much as his tone that she might be picking her way blindfold through a minefield. For all his sweet familiarity, she was still ignorant about his private life.

'Did you have a boat of your own?' she asked. It seemed an innocent enough question.

'No,' said Oliver. For a second she thought that the brief negative was all that he was going to give her, but its brevity must have sounded as snubbing to himself as it did to her, and after a short pause he turned and smiled at her. 'Mama wouldn't let me,' he said.

'Why ever not?' asked Cheryl, for privileged families that could afford yachts, she naturally assumed, could easily afford dinghies. Oliver's smile took on a rather derisive twist.

'She didn't like me,' he said, and then, seeing her expression, added, 'My stepmother, we're talking about. And I suppose she had her reasons.'

'Which were?' prompted Cheryl.

'I didn't like her, was one of them,' Oliver told her. Perhaps it was enough.

The gulls were beginning to glide back to their perches on the cliff, tentative, ready to fly again, fidgeting uneasily.

'Don't throw another one – please!' said Cheryl.

Oliver dropped the stone he was holding, and a silence fell between them. He sat contemplating the sea, coolly at ease with his arms folded round his updrawn knees, and Cheryl sat beside him trying to make something of the sparse information she had been given. Her own childhood had been short on luxuries, but in spite of the fact that her parents had to work long hours in the shop, it had still been full of love and fun and happiness. She herself, and her brothers and sister, had nothing to grumble about. Oliver's father, she already knew, was very wealthy and a prominent man in Embridge, but for the first time since she had met him, she wondered why Oliver chose to live such a footloose, wandering life. After a little while she asked again, tentatively, 'So how *did* you come to sail round the world?'

Oliver's reply fleshed out the cynical conclusions already drawn by Jonathan, but of course, he didn't know that and neither did Cheryl.

'We-ell,' he sounded a little self-conscious. 'When the hospital first launched the appeal for the new specialist unit, one of my father's cronies decided to launch a sponsorship scheme to help pay for it – he had a particular interest in spinal injuries, his favourite uncle fell out of an aeroplane in the Battle of Britain – don't laugh, horrible child, it wasn't in the least bit funny!'

'I'm sorry, it was the way you said it.' Cheryl hurriedly straightened her face. 'Of course it wasn't funny, particularly for Uncle. Go on.'

'He owns this big cat – Sir Charles does. Someone made the suggestion that it would be fun to sail it round the world, but that wasn't enough for old Lawley, he likes schemes with punch to them. He wanted something that would be more spectacular, that would catch the public interest so that he could pull as many people as possible in on it, make a big splash. He settled on going round the world single-handed, and he'd personally double the take if the trip set a record. You know all this already, why am I telling you again?'

'That might have made *you* make a big splash,' observed Cheryl. 'A fatal one. All that pressure, it can't have helped.'

'It didn't hinder,' said Oliver. There was a pause, not entirely comfortable.

'He's the man who owns that big engineering works at the back of the town, isn't he?' asked Cheryl, to break it. She did already know, but it had for some reason become necessary to say something. Oliver had that brooding look again. 'How did he fix on you? Because he knew your father, I suppose.'

To her relief, Oliver smiled, returning in an instant to his more familiar buoyant self.

'Not at all,' he said. 'It was my own brilliant reputation!'

'Stop teasing me,' said Cheryl. 'How was it?'

Oliver laughed outright, then relented and told her.

'*Lawley's Girl* was built at the Taverners' Shipyard, out at Emberton. I've done some sea trials for them from time to time

– she was one of them, actually – and made the odd delivery, so when they were asked to nominate somebody, they naturally suggested me as the right brand of lunatic. That's all there was to it, really – whatever anyone says.'

Cheryl missed the point of this – which was, of course, that he refused to owe anything to his father, as she realised only much later. She thought only that he was being too modest. She knew already the fever that had gripped the whole town when it was a local boy who had set off on the long haul round the world. Sponsorship had been a boom industry for months, they had taken hundreds of names on the reception desk at the Queen's alone, the pledges had run into tens of thousands. And interest had not flagged; when *Lawley's Girl* had lost radio contact for nearly two weeks, after a heavy storm in the Southern Ocean, the town had been in mourning. She would never forget the great wave of joy that had swept the place when a reconnaissance plane had reported seeing the brave little ship, still sailing on – and still more, she remembered the surge of civic pride and rejoicing that followed the realisation that the world record was going to be minced to shreds. She had been caught up in it all herself, and she hadn't even known him then. Oliver was a national hero, but it was in his home town that his reputation stood ten feet tall. She didn't think he could have been selected as casually as he made out. The new Spinal Injuries Unit, when built, would probably bear his name for evermore. Unless, her more cynical self added quickly, it was Sir Charles Lawley's name.

Oliver had had enough of the subject. He leapt to his feet and hauled her up after him.

'Come on,' he said briskly. 'I'm sick of doing nothing. Race you back to the beach!'

On the Thursday morning, they walked along the cliffs to the neighbouring village of Steps-of-Peace to buy unsliced bread and suntan oil at the shop there, and made the pleasing discovery that there was a fair setting up in a field just beyond the houses.

'I'm in favour of fairs,' said Oliver, with satisfaction. 'They're noisy and crowded and vulgar, and I like them.'

Cheryl sat on the wall outside the village store, quietly basting her glowing arms with *Ambre Solaire*. She looked at him indulgently.

'You're just a big kid!' she told him.

'So, what's wrong with that?' He perched himself beside her, cradling the crusty loaf in his arms, and looking at him, she felt quite giddy. 'What about you?'

She laughed.

'I thought I was grown-up until I met you. Now, I'm not so sure.'

'Sunk to the level of swings and roundabouts yet?'

She closed the top on the bottle and linked a friendly arm through his.

'I easily could. How long is it here for?'

'Three days, they say in the shop.' He spoke with a satisfied air that made her smile again.

'Let's go every night!'

'Now that really would be childish!' said Oliver, grinning appreciatively. He stood up and lifted her off the wall. 'If we start walking back now, there's time for me to buy you a drink at the pub before lunch.'

They went to the fair that evening, and strolled with the seething crowds among the sideshows and roundabouts. The bright coloured lights under the velvet night sky, the raucous music, the noisy, cheerful bustle of the fairground crowds, gave Cheryl a strange sense of unreality, as if her feet were an inch or two above the ground. *Cheryl in Wonderland*, and any minute now a white rabbit would dash by, calling to her that time was a-fleeting. The man beside her, with his arm so possessively round her shoulders, was still a stranger. She must keep telling herself that. If she forgot, she was liable to be hurt, for all that they were sharing paradise.

Contentedly eating hot dogs that leaked onions at every bite, they toured the fairground like a couple of kids let out of school. Cheryl couldn't decide if it was the lonely days at sea that made Oliver view this unsophisticated night out with such childish delight, or if it was something born in him. He was into everything with the shameless glee of a nine-year-old, she hadn't had so much fun in years. Jonathan, she was certain, would never be so undignified as to ride with her on a spotted roundabout horse, or career around in a dodgem whooping like a Red Indian. Jonathan's idea of a night on the tiles was far more predictable, tending to centre around a beer at the pub with his mates. It was true that they had had some good times, but nothing to touch riding on the Ferris Wheel with Oliver.

Perhaps it would be wiser not to compare Jonathan with Oliver.

She tumbled off the Ferris Wheel in Oliver's wake, feeling slightly sick and smelling of fried onions, clutching a large pink panther that he had won for her on the rifle range, and beginning to have serious doubts as to her ability to stay the course. She lacked his tireless energy, and she would have liked to sit down, except that there was nowhere obvious to sit, apart from the Ferris Wheel itself and the roundabouts and swings. She must have wilted a little, for he slid his arm around her waist and gave her a hug.

'Tired? What time is it? Do you want to go back?'

'Of course not!' Cheryl denied. 'But don't you ever stop to get your breath? It's like going out with a whirlwind!'

'Sorry,' said Oliver, but with no sign of real repentance. 'Have a rest, then.' He stopped dead, and the crowd divided and eddied round them, jostling, pushing and carelessly jolly. Cheryl began to giggle, but it appeared that there was a purpose here.

'There,' he said. 'I knew I'd seen it somewhere – you can cross the gypsy's palm with silver, and sit down at the same time, Madame Zsa-Zsa is sure to have a chair. Do you believe in fortune-telling?'

'I've never really given it a thought,' said Cheryl, pushing through the crowd behind him. 'I've a great-aunt who reads teacups, but all she ever told me was that my life would take a surprising turn. Oh – and that my Fate would be tall, dark and handsome, with sapphire blue eyes, but she said that to please me, because she thinks it's every young girl's dream.'

'And is it yours?' asked tall, dark, handsome and almost blue-eyed Oliver, laughing down at her, so that she blushed suddenly scarlet as she realised how what she had said might have sounded to him.

'I don't care what he's like, so long as he's fun to be with,' she said hurriedly, and of course, Oliver qualified there, too. But they had reached Madame Zsa-Zsa's wigwam-like seat of custom, and fortunately for Cheryl, the subject had to be dropped.

It was quiet inside the tent, the heavy curtain over the entrance fell to behind them, muffling the cheerful fairground music, shutting out the noisy crowds, and leaving in their place a stifling semi-silence. The gypsy sat at a round table covered to the ground with a heavy black velvet cloth, in the centre of the table was a round glass ball about the size of a baby's fist and a pack of Tarot cards, neatly stacked. A lamp, hanging high in the pitch of the roof, gave out a dim light that reflected off the rings and earrings and bracelets which she wore in profusion, glinting from among the folds of a black shawl that enveloped her head and shoulders. From her face, in that uncertain light, it was impossible to tell how old she might be. Cheryl had an odd feeling, just for a moment, that time had stopped and none of the three of them had any age, or face, or meaning – and then it had passed, and she was simply Cheryl Wainwright, standing beside Oliver Nankervis in a stuffy tent, looking at an impossibly theatrical gypsy and trying unsuccessfully not to start giggling again.

Dark eyes viewed them across the table, calmly and without offence, slender, beringed hands reached out for their money.

'I don't give both readings together,' said Madame Zsa-Zsa. 'One at a time is my rule.'

Cheryl wanted Oliver to stay with her. She felt obscurely that he might disappear and she herself wake up if she took her eyes from him in all that shifting, seething mass of humanity outside.

'Supposing we want to stay together?'

The calm, dark eyes surveyed her, and flicked across to survey Oliver.

'He'll still be there, never fret. His fate is twisted with yours for today, and for many days. You'll not lose him unless you want.'

Oliver laughed as if the idea pleased him, and said, 'I'll wait around outside.'

'Oliver –' began Cheryl, but he had already gone.

'Sit down, maid.' The unfamiliar west-country idiom started her off giggling again, but it was more from nerves than amusement this time. The giggle, nervously suppressed, escaped as a snort and she felt her colour rising. A hand gestured to an upright kitchen chair set on the fortune-teller's right and a jewel flashed in the uncertain light, flashed and was dimmed in the folds of the shawl. It was probably glass, but could as easily have been a diamond. Cheryl sat, seeing no help for it, the stuffed panther sitting on her knee like a bizarre toddler. She thought that it was just like Oliver to land her with this pointless mumbo-jumbo, and that they could laugh over it together afterwards.

'Give me your left hand.'

Cheryl held it out. The gypsy took it in both her own, she held it for a moment or two and Cheryl waited. The gypsy's hands were cool and impersonal, but she thought uncomfortably that they read her like a book, and dismissed the thought as silly. Everyone knew that hands couldn't read. But she had lost all desire to giggle.

'I see,' said Madame Zsa-Zsa, and sounded surprised. 'You have powers of your own, did you know that?'

'I have?' asked Cheryl, equally surprised. 'No, I'm sure you're wrong. I'm as down-to-earth as – as steak and kidney pie.' It was the first ordinary thing that came into her head, and struck her in her present hyped-up state as hilariously funny, but Madame Zsa-Zsa didn't smile.

'That's what you think, but the power is here just the same. It's in your head and in your hands, and its extent will astonish you one day.' She paused. 'You should have guidance for it. I can give you the name of a man who will help you.'

Cheryl was silent, keeping her doubts to herself. The gypsy held her hand a moment longer.

'You don't believe me. Listen. You're the youngest of a large family, I think four children, or maybe five. I see you against a background of marshland and seabirds crying, huge skies, and I can feel the land stretching away, away on either side, flat and open, so that the wind is always blowing. You don't live there now, you've come a long way and you work among people, but not in a dedicated capacity. Your father keeps a shop. Am I right?'

Cheryl answered, honestly surprised, 'I've got two brothers and one sister, and my mother had another child that died, and I was born and grew up on the east coast. It's just as you describe it, the wind and the birds and everything. I've left home now, and I work in catering.'

Her hand was dropped, but gently, onto the velvet cloth.

'You'll believe the rest in time, and then you must seek the help you will need. Will you have the cards, or the crystal?'

Dippy Auntie Maudie had a set of Tarot cards, and Cheryl, in spite of her avowed scepticism about tealeaves, for some reason hated them, she would never have them cast for her. She had always had a senseless fear of the Tower Struck by Lightning, that is supposed to foretell destruction, imprisonment, or death, and all the bitterness that goes with them, almost as if it had some special significance for herself. She knew that if she let this stage-gypsy read the cards for her, the Tower would turn up, as clearly as if she could see it lying on the table in front of her, and however little she believed in such things, she didn't want to see it there.

'I'll have the crystal,' she said firmly.

The dark eyes regarded her impersonally.

'Your choices are written in either, and in both. You can't pick and choose about that.' She took the crystal and held it for a moment. 'Take it, maid – cover it between your hands and try to think of nothing.'

The crystal was cold and hard, and fitted snugly in the curve of her two palms. Cheryl held it, and felt the glass warming between her hands, and tried to think of nothing, but this, as anyone knows, is nearly impossible. Into the void came all sorts of things and people; her job, Jonathan and the life that she had planned around him, her amazing meeting with Oliver and all the things she had done since, the crumbling tower of the Tarot, the flat Suffolk marshes that were her home, a kaleidoscope mixture of tangled vision and emotion that seemed to go on for ever, so that it gave her a jump when Madame Zsa-Zsa said, 'Now give it to me.'

The crystal dropped from palm to palm, thin brown fingers curled around it.

'You stand at the parting of the ways,' said Madame Zsa-Zsa in a slow sing-song that nevertheless gave Cheryl no inclination to laugh. 'Behind you lies your life up until this moment, and everything you have done, good, bad or foolish. Ahead of you lies a choice. The known, the unknown. One way lies contentment and happiness, security, love, children, all the familiar things you ever wished for. The other way ... oh yes, the heights and depths, the shining stars, the thing you fear so much and that, one day, you must confront. The test of your courage, the fulfilment of yourself, and the powers that you deny, that can bring you safely home.'

'And which should I take?' asked Cheryl, and was surprised to hear her voice unsteady.

'That's for you to decide when the time comes. But it will come – and sooner than you think.'

'It's a deliberate choice, then?'

'Of course. Our fates aren't written in our hands, or even in the stars, but in ourselves. One choice, another and another, all different paths leading to the final goal – and that, we choose for ourselves.' She hesitated. 'You're one of the lucky ones, maid. Your road runs east and west, and both lead home. It is only the road itself that may be stony.'

'But I *shall* come safely home?'

'If that's how you choose. There are other paths, too, as you go. If we could all choose wisely, maid, which of us would ever weep?'

'And is Oliver – is the man who was with me for me to choose?'

'A man that you've only just met?'

She didn't know why she had asked that about Oliver. Not only did she hardly know him, but apart from these few stolen days, she wasn't even a part of his world, or likely to be. And then she had a sudden picture of life as a series of junctions and forks in a winding road, to the left, to the right, to east or west, and herself picking her way through them – to what end? *The final goal – and that, we choose for ourselves.* She had chosen, and more or less deliberately, to go with Oliver.

'If he is, and if that's the way I choose – is that the way that what you called *the thing I fear* lies?'

66

Madame Zsa-Zsa did not answer directly.

'Even the cards are affected by those around them. Perhaps destruction will be in your choice, but that, I can't tell you. You'll choose for yourself, and travel your chosen road.'

Cheryl spoke on impulse. 'Would you read the cards for me?'

'It's extra. One or the other, that's the rule – both costs extra.'

'All right.'

Under the gypsy's guidance, she cut the cards, shuffled, cut again, and watched as the gypsy dealt them face downwards on the velvet cloth. One by one, Madame Zsa-Zsa turned them up.

'Never let a stranger deal or turn your cards, maid, particularly one with the gift. Now, see, these represent your past. The star, that is the powers that you despise, but will find in yourself; they come through the blood. These three in conjunction are security and a happy home, opposition overcome, a new beginning. These are the present, the man for whom you left your happy home, he's yet to play a big part in your life. See, he's a fair man, and you've hurt him deeply, he has no defences.' She paused, shuffling the upturned cards together, and Cheryl had time to reflect that Jonathan was fair, in spite of his brown eyes, and once she had met him she had gone far away from her home to work in Embridge to be near him, against her parents' wishes, finding a whole new career in the process, and there was no way that this woman could have known it.

The thin brown hands hovered over the last line, began to turn up the cards one by one.

'And these are your future. The dark stranger who is to influence your life for good or ill, as you allow, the children that you may, or may not have, the – ' She stopped abruptly, and laid the card in her hand face-down on the table. 'No,

I told you, I don't do both. I can't do both for anyone. You must be content with the crystal and trust to yourself, I can tell you nothing more.'

Cheryl thanked her and left the tent totally disinclined to laugh, and certain in her own mind that the card left face-down was the Tower Struck by Lightning, and that whatever it portended, Madame Zsa-Zsa hadn't wanted to tell her. She found Oliver waiting close by.

'Hi,' he greeted her. 'What did she say, anything interesting?'

'Not a lot. A lot of stuff about choices.'

'What, no tall dark strangers and voyages across the sea?'

'Oh, you were there, as if you didn't know – and I'm standing at a crossroads. Are you going to have a turn?'

'Me?'

'Why not you? You made me.'

'You're the one who wanted to sit down.'

'I'll wait for you,' promised Cheryl.

Oliver, it now appeared, was game for anything, even fortune-telling, if it would amuse her.

'All right,' he said. 'But don't expect me to believe in it.'

He was gone for twenty minutes. Cheryl wandered about watching the crowds, fended off a couple of unwanted advances, and bought herself an ice-cream, wondering if Madame Zsa-Zsa would have anything to tell him about hotel receptionists with ginger hair. He rejoined her eventually, as unperturbed as he had left her.

'What a load of bullshit!' he commented, irreverently.

Cheryl fell into step beside him, licking her ice.

'Why, what did she say to you?'

'She told me that I took too much out of the Bank of Life, and the time would come when I had to pay it back.'

'Well,' said Cheryl, carefully licking. 'She could be right. Did you have the crystal, or the cards?'

'She didn't offer me any cards. She made me hold this glass ball and think of nothing, but all I could do for her was to think of flying fish.'

'Flying fish?'

'Nobody can think of absolutely nothing. Except possibly the odd yogi.'

'Is that *all* she said? You were long enough.'

'She told me that I was dangerously wilful, very self-centred, and wouldn't grow up until I learned to recognise fear, not very complimentary really. And she warned me against putting all my eggs in one basket. I got the feeling that I'm about to drop the lot and end up with omelette.'

'No veiled hints about choices? No predictions for the future?'

'Only the usual thing – *beware the Ides of March* and all that stuff.' He spoke lightly, but Cheryl thought his voice sounded odd. She peered at him in the shifting light from the Ferris Wheel.

'Beware the Ides of March?'

'Oh, she didn't mention them by name. But she said that I was spiritually a long way from my goal, that I was travelling a hard road of my own making, and that I must always beware of acting without thinking because one day it would bring me down.' He hesitated. 'She said that I was a celebrity for now, but the thing that's going to make me really famous is something I haven't yet done, have never imagined doing, and it will arise from something that I'll wish I hadn't done. And then she said ...'

'What?' prompted Cheryl, when he didn't immediately continue.

'She said that I'll die without issue, but my name will live after me, and I don't believe a word of it. But I wish,' he ended suddenly, and with unexpected violence, 'that she hadn't mentioned dying. I don't want to die, I want to live – and I don't want to look that far ahead.'

'It doesn't sound as if it's imminent,' Cheryl comforted him. 'You've got a lot of ground to cover yet, my lad, some of it flat on your face. Self-improvement and fame take time!' She was pleased to see that he was smiling again and with real amusement, and added, curiously, 'Would it worry you, to think you'd die without issue? Do you want children?'

'I've no feelings one way or the other. One day – some time – children would be fun, I think. Now? Certainly not, there's too much to be doing!' And he grinned at her, so that any lingering gloom dissolved in laughter.

She hadn't thought that the gypsy's words had made any deep impression on her, for nothing specific had been said, and of course fortune-telling was arrant nonsense, everyone knew that. But that night, when Oliver had long been asleep, she found that her thoughts were going round and round in circles, keeping her awake. She lay in the darkness with Oliver close against her, listening to his quiet breathing and thinking – and trying not to think.

The trouble with crystal-gazing was that you could twist it any way you liked. It was logical to believe that contentment and security and all the familiar things should go with Jonathan, and the heights and depths and the shining stars with Oliver, but that alone didn't make it so. Jonathan had ambitions, she knew, that if achieved would take him to disaster areas, into war zones, trouble of all kinds. It was only the past that she could legitimately judge by. Taken in that context, the thing she feared, whatever that was, disaster in whatever form, well, that could apply equally well to either of them, for you could die without issue as a centenarian if that was the way it went. But more probably, it would apply to Oliver, he had that undomesticated, feral aura that invited trouble like honey invites bees. Her mind made pictures, and in each of them, because Jonathan had put the idea into her head, the crumbling dark tower spelt death – death on the sea, under the sea, death by drowning, fire, accident – Oliver's death, early in life, childless, leaving her alone, for Jonathan to comfort, to bring her safely home?

Would it be worth it to go with Oliver, knowing or fearing that the dark tower lay so close ahead? Did it, in fact? Was it connected with that unpremeditated action he would wish he had never taken, and forewarned, would he take it? And would she even be offered the chance to be around when he did so?

Oliver wasn't the kind who listened to warnings.

She lay in the dark, sleepless and plagued with ridiculous fantasies, and beside her Oliver slept a sound, untroubled sleep, his head pillowed against her shoulder and his breath stirring the nerves along her arm into tingling awareness of his nearness.

It was an endless night.

VI

The next morning, Oliver awoke restless and fidgety. 'Time we were moving on,' he said.

Cheryl looked at him in surprise.

'Where to, particularly?'

'I haven't thought. Any ideas?'

Cheryl was content where they were, and tired after a sleepless night. She was conscious of a strong wish to stay here, where they had been so deliriously, ridiculously happy, and not to tempt fate by leaving. Only, she supposed, it was impossible to mark time for ever.

'No. None,' she said, and heard her own voice, flat.

Oliver studied her carefully for a moment or two.

'You look tired. Do I snore, or something?'

'Not often,' said Cheryl, smiling in spite of herself.

'No regrets? No second thoughts?'

'No. None. None at all.'

'All right,' said Oliver, mildly. 'There's no need to sing a song about it. What was I saying? You've made me forget.'

'About moving on,' said Cheryl.

'Oh yes. That. There's a lot of Cornwall that we haven't even looked at yet. Shall we go and see what it's like, or have you had enough adventure?'

Cheryl gave up, accepting that she had elected to throw in her lot with a chronic wanderer.

'We haven't seen Land's End yet,' she offered, and he grinned, making fun of her.

'I saw it only about ten days ago, remember?'

'So you did.' She managed to grin back, but it was unexpectedly difficult. 'But you didn't set foot on it.'

'Nor I did.'

The weather was showing signs of breaking up today, the endless sunshine of the past week dissolving into flying clouds and spattering showers as they drove westward, so that they had to put up the hood of the car. They ran into Trelewan around teatime, on the wings of a short sharp shower, with Oliver at the wheel and Cheryl yawning beside him, and pulled up outside the post office to ask after a suitable campsite. The post office was small and cluttered and the postmistress busy serving, she broke off what she was saying to smile at Cheryl and Oliver, and tell them she wouldn't be above a minute. Cheryl passed the time looking along the shelves but the selection of goods here was even more basic than in the beach kiosk at Tregothen Bay. She was just wondering whether the general store she had noticed opposite might be more helpful, when the long-winded transaction at the counter came to an end, and the customer turned to leave, nodding to Oliver as she passed him and saying that it was a shame about the weather. The postmistress turned to serve them, but broke off at once to exclaim,

'There look, she's done it again!' She picked up a purse from the counter and called shrilly,

'Mrs. Nankervis, Mrs. Nankervis! You've forgot your purse again!' She turned back to Cheryl as the woman came bustling back to claim it. 'I'm sorry, my lover, what can I do for you?'

Cheryl had temporarily forgotten why they were there. She looked after the retreating back of the absent-minded woman, and remarked,

'Nankervis. That's an unusual name.'

'I told you it wasn't Greek,' said Oliver, and the postmistress looked scandalised.

'Indeed it is not, it's a good Cornish name! There's many Nankervises in these parts, the churchyard is full of them, you've but to look.'

But Cheryl was looking at Oliver.

'You're Cornish after all,' she accused him. 'Did you really not know?'

The postmistress looked at him too, critically.

'You're a Nankervis, are you? Yes, I can see it now I come to look at you.'

'Really?' asked Oliver, startled. 'I'm always told I take after my mother.'

'It's the eyes of you. And all the Nankervises are wonderful handsome men.'

Oliver coloured a little at that, and the postmistress began an exploration of his possible genealogy, which rambled discursively by way of the Jacksons of Church Farm and Old William Nankervis down at Vellanzoe, and finally settled on Simon Nankervis, who ran away to London in the early nineteen hundreds at the age of fifteen, and was never seen or heard from again.

'They thought he must be gone in the first war,' she said pensively. 'Many a young one was lost in those years. But perhaps he wasn't. If so, they'll be glad to know. Old William was his brother, you know. It's always been a grief to him.'

Oliver looked wary, and Cheryl said, regretfully, 'He's from Dorset, not London.'

'Nankervises do get about some,' said the postmistress, admiringly. 'There's one has even gone around the world, you know, tho' not one of our own, all alone on a little boat.'

'No, really?' asked Oliver, managing to look suitably impressed.

Not many of them, Cheryl thought, would have travelled as far as he had. It would have been fun had he unwittingly come home. She brought the conversation round to campsites.

Five minutes later, armed with the information that *Jeff Jackson up to Church Farm has a campsite out the back road,* they returned to the car, and Oliver grinned at Cheryl as he opened the offside door.

'Would you be very surprised if I told you that the founder of my father's boring old-established firm of solicitors was my grandfather, Simon Nankervis?' he asked.

'No, was he? Why didn't you say?'

'I thought we might be there for the rest of the day, and anyway, I already have too many relations,' said Oliver, adding, as he folded himself in under the steering wheel once more. 'In any case, we sailed close enough to the wind with the eyes of me – they run in the family, you know, you can see them in the Founder's portrait over my father's desk at his office. Deb has them, too.'

Deb, Cheryl supposed, must be his sister, or perhaps a cousin, for she had only ever heard him credited with one sister, Susan Casson. She didn't ask, having learned already that Oliver fended off questions if they became too personal – from lack of interest, she rather thought, not secretiveness, or emotional involvement. But grandfather Simon was a subject of his own choosing.

'And you didn't know – that he came from Cornwall, I mean?'

'I believe it's part of family lore, but to be honest, I've never been that interested. I don't remember him anyway, I was only a baby when he died.'

The tone of his voice ruled a neat line under the discussion. It wasn't an intentional snub, just Oliver's way. Simply not a family man, Cheryl told herself, and without consciously doing so, she saw it as a romantic attribute rather than a warning. She was in deeper water already than she would let herself believe, and it wouldn't be long before she began to feel the cross currents, pushing her off her feet, trying to sweep her away.

There was plenty of room at the Church Farm campsite, for it was still early in the year, and Cheryl and Oliver were allocated a site adjacent to a large frame tent occupied by half a dozen or so of their own contemporaries. It took only about ten minutes for Cheryl to discover that the imposing underwater watch on Oliver's wrist, taken in conjunction with the air tanks filling the boot of the car, was the same in essence as a Masonic handshake. Ten minutes again after the discovery was made, they were all drinking tea together outside the larger tent.

Their new, and for Cheryl at least, unwanted friends were all members of a branch of the National Sub-Aqua Club from the Manchester area. They had already been in Trelewan for a week, diving on a wreck with the local diving club.

'Not a wildly exciting one,' said the leader of the party, whose name was Mike. 'She's a trawler that got herself torpedoed off the Wolf in 1944 and sank trying to creep home to Falmouth. But she's interesting – there's a surprising amount of her left, and some simply colossal fish! There's a conger down there that must be first cousin to the Loch Ness Monster, we give him a wide berth, I can tell you!'

'You must dive with us one day,' offered someone else.' Nobody will mind – we're trying to do a proper underwater survey, just for the experience, and the more of us there are, the more diving time we can put in while the weather's good.'

The weather didn't look particularly good to Cheryl, it had developed into a blustery wind and gathering grey clouds, but she caught the gleam in Oliver's eye and was amazed at her own sudden angry disappointment. Mike and the rest were enthusiastically endorsing the invitation, and she took a firm hold on herself. She had no rights in Oliver, and to try to assert any could only lead to disaster, if he wanted to risk his life diving on a sunken ship in company with a hundred-foot conger eel, she must let him, and the effort to recognise it was as conclusively exhausting as trying to raise the same ship single-handed. When he turned to her and asked her if she would mind, she said, 'No, of course not,' quite naturally, but had a horrid sensation of having stopped barely in time on the edge of a crevasse of unknown depth. Shaken, as much by her own reaction as anything, she picked up her mug and drank.

It occurred to her that it might become more than one day, and the realisation that she didn't want to share him, or to have other people encroaching on their precious time together, brought her up all-standing. She had met Oliver properly – for you could hardly count that first time in Falmouth – just a week ago today, and their association was all in the present, no past, no foreseeable future, so why then this overwhelming surge of possessiveness?

Her heart answered her at last. Because of days spent in the shining sun, of nights when she had lain in his arms in the warm darkness, the glamour and excitement of him and a totally irrational feeling that she had in his company of having come home. Because she was infatuated with him, swept with hero-worship, intoxicated – and if it went further than that, her head stepped in and denied it. Only a week, and it couldn't go on much longer. She had her job to think about, if it wasn't already lost, and her family, who would never understand. They would go home – or she would have to, and quite soon if she was to contain the damage to her life – and that would be that. She looked on the prospect with unhappy eyes, and the way that things were between them, in the midst of all the laughter and talk Oliver sensed it, and put his arm round her, drawing her close to him, unconsciously staking a claim in front of all those friendly eyes.

That night, when they were alone in the tent, Oliver said, 'You know something, Chel? The more time I spend with you, the more surprising you are.'

'I am?' asked Cheryl, doubtfully. She loved the way he had of calling her *Chel*, but she was a little ashamed of herself today. 'In what way?'

'Oh – because of your courage, and the way you understand things – and now I find that you don't cling and you aren't possessive – am I dreaming you, or something?'

Cheryl knew that she hadn't deserved any of that and felt guilty. She took refuge in absolute truth.

'I've got no right to stop you doing anything you want.'

'It's generous of you to say so, but even if it were true, you didn't even hesitate. You smiled, and let me go. Chel ...'

'What?' asked Cheryl.

'I like the way you come with me as smoothly as a bird, and not just tagging along for the ride, but is that the way you like it?'

'I'm willing to give it a try,' said Cheryl, through lips gone suddenly dry. He rolled over and propped himself on an elbow to look at her in the dimness inside the tent. His free hand traced the line of her eyebrows with a delicate touch.

'You are unbelievably wonderful, and I'm a lucky man.'

There was something about the way that he said it that reminded Cheryl suddenly of Joanna Rendell, who had reputedly made scenes when he left her to go round the world, and lost him thereby. But that had been a bigger thing than a day's diving, and she wasn't sure what she would have done herself. Her thoughts twisted themselves into a speechless little prayer.

Oh God, don't let me ever make a scene.

If she had behaved generously, she was to have her reward. By showing Oliver that she could let him go, she had drawn him closer, and by stepping outside their enchanted private circle she had also stepped, for the first time, into the position of his recognised girlfriend, bracketed with him, accepted – Chel and Oliver, bubble and squeak, strawberries and cream. It began a new phase in their relationship, which was already galloping full speed ahead.

At first, she didn't recognise it. Oliver took his day's diving and to begin with, Cheryl felt rather out of things. Although there were other girl friends and even wives in the group, they were all used to diving and divers where she was not, and she felt as if Oliver had gone away from her into enemy territory. Clad in his wet suit, with his breathing equipment flung casually over his shoulder, he had become crisp and competent and different, one of a fraternity of which she wasn't even an honorary member. It was only when the leader of the team, a local man, asked to know his name and how much diving he had done, and where, that she began to see things in a different light.

Oliver tried to dodge the issue by simply saying 'Oliver,' but Jack Soames, responsible for the safety of each member of his team, wasn't having that.

'Oliver what?' he demanded, his pencil poised over his clipboard.

'Nankervis,' said Oliver, as if it didn't matter, but his public and triumphant return home was too recent, his name in the world outside Trelewan too unusual, his port of entry after his voyage too near. There followed a moment of disbelief when all of them stared, followed by a sudden outcry as they all realised what he had just said. Jack began to change his rota without further argument, his only comment being,

'Oh God, you're a pro, then.'

Cheryl had known him for a well-known professional yachtsman, but she hadn't fully realised that his name was also familiar in diving circles. She was still digesting this new fact about him when the divers – eight of them – left the cove aboard their inflatable dinghy, and the backwash of the sensation he had made rebounded on herself. The three or four girls left with her on the beach looked at her with new eyes, seeing in her a reflection of Oliver's glory. Jack's wife, Maggie, who had so far said little to her, now gave her a friendly grin.

'Who's a lucky girl, then?'

She was an attractive, if rather spreading young woman with brown hair done up in a knot on top of her head, and a taste for ethnic prints and jangly neck chains and beads. She had a baby on one hip and a toddler at her skirts. On closer acquaintance, she turned out to be one of those comparatively rare people who look exactly what they are, in her case she taught art in a local comprehensive school, but she had no idea herself that she was typecast. She was entirely natural and Cheryl returned the grin, liking her for her friendliness even though she suspected it was on Oliver's account rather than her own. It came as no surprise, later, to discover that she and Jack lived a vegetarian existence in an isolated cottage with a well for a water supply and no electricity. They kept chickens and goats in the back garden, and their little girl called them by their Christian names. It all seemed both idyllic and alien.

Cheryl found the hours apart from Oliver less unbearable than she had feared, she was encouraged to talk about him as much as she liked, and the envy of her companions was pleasant. She swam with them and shared their lunchtime picnic, basking on the sheltered beach. She was kept too occupied to wonder or worry over what Oliver might be doing, knowing that he was only diving for fun and unable to appreciate any risks involved. Even so, by the time that he came ashore, exhilarated on a soaring high, she was so glad to see him that their mutual excitement met and mingled like the meeting of two waves in a tide rip. It was a sweet and heady moment that outstripped reason, made all the sweeter by the first hours that they had spent apart.

'You two have got it badly, haven't you?' commented Maggie, a little jealously, as they made their way in a group up the slipway and back to the car park, and Cheryl, to whom the remark had been made, simply smiled and said nothing in reply.

VII

Cheryl had found the suggestion that she might have psychic powers more funny than anything, and she hadn't mentioned it to Oliver. Vellanzoe, therefore, came as something of a shock.

They had been down to Sennen Cove, just the two of them, surfing, for the day's diving had not so far been repeated, apart from Oliver having taken Cheryl snorkelling round the same cove from which the divers had embarked. It had been her first experience of the intricately beautiful world beneath the surface of the sea, and had left her breathless with wonder, and with the first faint and inadequate glimmer of understanding as to what made him tick. The diving party in the tent alongside theirs had urged him to go with them again, but he had his own defences that repulsed too much intimacy, and beyond the odd drink in the village pub, their friendship remained casual. This suited Cheryl perfectly. She was too bewitched to see it as another straw in the wind.

On this particular evening they had spent most of the day on the beach, eaten a fish and chip supper on a green clifftop overlooking the wide breadth of Whitesand Bay, and were drifting home in the car with the hood down, pleasantly weary and relaxed with sunshine and fresh air. The lane they were on was narrow and twisty, running through farmland and moorland in uneven patches, bordered with wild flowers and practically deserted. Cheryl could feel Oliver's inner contentment radiating off him like warmth from a glowing fire, and wondered what he was thinking, and if he, like herself, ever speculated as to what might happen tomorrow. The day really couldn't be far ahead now when this interlude – she was always aware that it was no more than that – would be over. She tried to shut the thought out of her mind, but it kept coming back. They had no future beyond this holiday romance that she could see.

Jonathan, the past.

Oliver, the present.

Nothing, nobody, the future.

Don't think about it.

Flat fields lay on either side of them, scattered with occasional houses and lit with the slanting light from the low sun. Oliver's roots ran back to this quiet place, the moors and the patchwork fields, the ruined tin mines with their tall chimneys, the sandy coves and granite cliffs, and the fringes of the broad Atlantic. His ancestors must have worked these fields, seen this same view, been born here, lived and died. Oliver was at least partly Cornish, even if he had never valued it. She wondered if he felt the pull of it, whether it touched any inherited memory, and if it was those distant ancestral Cornishmen that had bequeathed him his love of the sea.

A screen of blackthorn and hazel on their right momentarily hid the fields on that side, and a farm track opened up to their left. Cut into the granite stones of the wall was the name HIGHER VELLANZOE, and Cheryl said, 'Oh, look! That's the place that the woman in the post office talked about – William Nankervis, remember? Your great uncle.'

Oliver braked – they were not going particularly fast, but he slowed to a crawl and looked around him with interest.

'So this is Nankervis country. A long way from the middle east, wouldn't you say?'

'Oh, shut up about the middle east, fool!' said Cheryl. 'Stop a minute.'

Oliver pulled into the side of the road and obediently stopped, switching off the engine. The silence of the spring evening poured in around them.

They were parked close under a Cornish hedge adrift with wild flowers that cut off their immediate view. On the other side of the road, the blackthorn screen curved round to reveal another narrow lane approaching the one they were on, twisting off out of sight within the copse, and opposite the turning a building threw its stark silhouette against the evening sky. It was unlit in the gathering dusk and in what light remained it was possible to see that the land immediately surrounding it was thick with bushes and young, self-sown trees, and the tiles were slipping from its roof. It was biggish, set side-on to the road, and with a chimney rearing up at each end. There was no doubt that it had been empty for many years.

Cheryl might laugh at psychic experiences and would have unhesitatingly claimed that she had never had such a thing in her life, but just for a moment, as she sat there with Oliver's shoulder touching hers, she clearly heard the sound of tears in the soft night wind, and the keening of a soul called too soon and unfulfilled. A terrible cold feeling crawled on her skin, for a brief instant she knew a heartache beyond easing. She both heard and felt these things, but before she had to believe in them, Oliver spoke and his voice broke the spell. The whispering among the hazels and sloes was only a breeze, and it was only its evening coolness that touched her arms with goose-pimples.

'What a weird place,' he said. 'Fancy an exploration, Chel?'

He was opening his door as he spoke, so that Cheryl had little choice. Shaken, for what she had felt had been very real for that brief moment, she climbed out onto the verge and stood beside him under the lee of the hedge.

As they walked towards the house it was possible to see it more clearly. There was a double gable on the end, and a deep gulley running back between the pitch of the two roofs. The nearer slope, facing them as they approached, was moss-grown and sagging with slipping slates leaving occasional gaps where they had slipped too far, but the slope beyond the gulley was torn from end to end by a great ragged, gaping hole, that allowed a glimpse of sagging rafters and broken beams within.

A lean-to built against the end wall beside the road had a young tree growing right through its roof, and the small space between the house and its garden wall was filled to overflowing with roses, once maybe tamed and cultivated, but long since reverted to the wild and climbing everywhere. The runners dripped in long swathes over the wall and caught at their hair as they went past.

Beyond the building, the garden wall, if there had ever been one, had disappeared, carted away maybe, stone by stone, to mend another wall somewhere else, leaving this part of the garden open to the road. It was nothing more than a narrow, scrubby field now, with a tangle of brambles at its further end half-masking two small outbuildings, doorless and roofless and well settled into decay.

At the front, a huge privet, that must originally have been planted for ornament, had grown and spread itself across the place where the front door might be expected to be; the roses had again rioted joyously over everything. Closer to the ground, the brambles and stinging nettles were slowly taking over so that the whole of the lower front was a mass of seemingly impenetrable vegetation. Above this, the upper windows, square and sightless, made dark patches against the granite walls.

'We can't get in,' said Cheryl, with relief, but Oliver was already pushing his way through the brambles.

'It's not that bad.' His voice came to her from the depths of the undergrowth. 'It's quite clear under this bush, and the door is off its hinges. Come and see.'

Cheryl picked her way after him reluctantly, and stood beside him under the privet. Immediately beside the door was a window, glassless now, and its frame rotting in the wall. He looked through it.

'What a mess! The place looks as if it's been hit with a thunderbolt! Coming in?'

'If you like,' said Cheryl doubtfully. 'Is it safe, do you think?'

'Probably not, but we can be careful.' He stepped past her, pushing aside the rotten door on its broken hinges and picking his way carefully over the threshold. They went under the lintel and stood inside the house.

Here, it was clear that there had at one time been not one cottage but two, standing side by side. The second front door was there, hidden from the outside under the privet, but the centre dividing wall had crumbled and lay on the ground in a welter of rotting laths and fallen beams, and the floor of the upper rooms lay with it. The front section of the cottages was open to the sky, they could see it, and the tops of the surrounding trees, through the gaping hole in the roof.

'Poor little houses,' said Cheryl, and her voice echoed back queerly from the broken walls. There was the crack of breaking wood as Oliver worked his way across the room to the doorway on the far side, and anxiety leapt at her like a pouncing beast. 'Oh, do be careful! It can't be safe!'

'It's all right,' said Oliver, from the doorway. 'The ceiling is still up in here, whatever did all that must have missed this side. Have a look.'

The floor was a muddle of rubbish and broken planks. Cheryl picked her way carefully round a rusty bath, pathetic in a heap of rubble and a tangle of twisted piping, and followed him, peering over his shoulder into a dark room – dark, because the surrounding bushes had completely covered its one small window. It was just possible to see a dirty stone floor littered with broken plaster from the ceiling, and damp-stained walls with once-flowered wallpaper hanging off in discoloured strips.

Oliver had moved away to the left, and Cheryl stood in the doorway and looked in, thinking that she didn't like it much, before she turned to follow him. As she turned, the blood left her heart in a painful wave, and every nerve on her skin sprang into screaming life. Oliver had gone.

She stood there, rooted to the spot, and in that chaotic instant the shutters in her mind flew wide and let in a sudden tide of shock and regret, overwhelming agony, utter, horrified disbelief and grief, that broke about her like a storm. She felt herself trapped, weighted down, and there was a pain in her head that pressed unbearably so that she felt her brain must burst, rivulets of agony pouring through her body. Her ears rang with cries – surely not her own? – *Help, help me, don't go, oh please, don't go and leave me* – that seemed to tear right through her. Her breath came only with difficulty. Her own voice, shrill and distorted, cut across the nightmare like a knife.

'Oliver!'

He reappeared swiftly from another opening beyond, and she stumbled towards him through the mess on the floor and fell into his arms, quite forgetting to be brave and unclinging, trailing shreds of pain along with her.

'I thought you'd fallen!' she said, and her voice jerked painfully. Oliver held her tightly, his own voice was warm with amusement.

'Silly woman! Fallen, where?'

The terrible pain, the crying voice, had gone away.

'I don't know – a well, a cellar – even a mineshaft, out here. You went so suddenly!'

She was clutching at him, she suddenly realised, and deliberately relaxed her grip. She was ashamed to find herself trembling.

'Oh Oliver, I'm so sorry! I don't know what got into me.'

He laughed, but she thought that he sounded strained himself as he said, 'Let's go outside again. There's nothing more to see even if we could get upstairs, which we can't. Anyway, everything's rotten. You were probably right about it not being safe.'

He went ahead of her, choosing their path in the fading light, reaching back to take her hand and guide her, and she followed him with relief. Out in the overgrown garden it was cool and sane and ordinary. The air was heavy with the scent of roses and bats flew in the dusk, squeaking, very tiny and faint as they passed. Oliver put his arm round her and drew her back towards the car.

'What a place!' he said. 'I wonder what happened to it? It must have been derelict for years.'

Cheryl shivered a little, she couldn't help it.

'There's been some dreadful tragedy there,' she said. She paused, because that had almost said itself, and she hadn't realised that it was even in her head. She wouldn't have blamed Oliver if he had laughed at her again, but he didn't. He gave her a curious look in the fast-fading light, and said, 'Let's go and find a stiff drink, shall we?'

It was stupid of her, she knew, but as they drove away and left the derelict house to its loneliness, she could have sworn that she heard again a bodiless voice crying on the wind, *Come back, don't go* – She shivered again, and was glad to see the lights of Trelewan.

The bar of the Cornish Arms was brightly lit and cosy, and all the usual crowd were there, including Jack Soames, although not Maggie. Maggie would be doing her fruitful earth-mother bit, looking after her sleeping children, as deeply involved in the part she played as ever. Cheryl and Oliver were greeted with shouts of welcome and demands as to where they had been.

'You're always getting lost, you two,' said one of the girls, laughing. 'Anyone would think you were on your honeymoon!'

Oliver grinned at her, unoffended and not in the least embarrassed.

'We're just naturally anti-social.'

Cheryl, who had found the comment a little embarrassing, said quietly, 'We've been on the beach all day – and speak for yourself, Oliver Nankervis!'

He had, of course. The idea, which had been trying to get her attention for some time, brought her up short. She would have liked to explore it, carefully and preferably on her own, but Oliver was speaking again, enlarging on what she had said.

'We stopped on the way back to explore a ruined house. A place a couple of miles down the road, with a great hole in the roof. Rather spooky.'

'Vellanzoe Cottages?' asked Jack, looking up with interest touched with derisive amusement. 'That's supposed to be haunted. Did you see any spooks?'

'No,' said Oliver. 'Do people?'

'They say they do,' said Jack, who had the total scepticism of the aggressively down-to-earth.

'Who haunts it?' asked Cheryl, curiously. She felt better in the friendly, ordinary atmosphere of the bar. What she had felt at the ruined cottages didn't amount to her own, admittedly stereotyped, idea of a ghost, it was more like a nightmare. Well, it would be – it hadn't been real, after all. Things like that were not. She was unaware that her chin had taken on a defiant tilt until she saw Oliver looking at her with quiet thoughtfulness. She lowered her eyes and the chin together and wouldn't look back at him.

'You might well ask,' said Jack, grinning ferociously. 'Somebody flew a light aeroplane into the roof – in a fog, so the story goes – around thirty years ago – fortunately there was nobody there at the time. He's supposed to hang about there, crying for help and shouting out that he doesn't want to die – but he did, trapped up there, before anyone could get him down. Those that have heard it say the cries are terrible, but as with all ghost stories, you never meet anyone who has heard it themselves, just friends of friends of the people who say they have.' He laughed, inviting them to share his amusement that people could believe such rubbish.

Crying for help ... Cheryl felt as if she had a block of ice in the pit of her stomach. She didn't believe in ghosts – she thought that no sensible person possibly could – so –?

The pub was suddenly neither so friendly nor so comforting.

'What's the matter?' asked Oliver, quietly, in her ear. 'You didn't hear anything there, did you?'

Cheryl heard herself give a nervous laugh.

'What would you say if I said yes?'

Oliver looked faintly scandalised.

'But you didn't – did you?'

He wanted her to deny it, she thought, and wouldn't believe her if she told him anything else. Oliver had to be as practical as Jack, even if he had more imagination, otherwise he would never have got himself safely round the world. You couldn't believe in hobgoblins and stay sane under those circumstances.

'Of course I didn't,' she said firmly.

'Then why have you suddenly turned green?'

'I'm tired, that's all. It's been a long day.' She managed a smile.

'We'll go soon,' said Oliver, but he gave her a strange look before changing the subject.

But she was quiet for the rest of the evening, remembering the gypsy at the fair, who had in fact told her very little that she didn't already know... but had somehow known it herself, which was impossible to explain. She and Oliver had laughed over the veiled predictions, which could be interpreted however they liked, as she had already tested for herself. In any case, life couldn't be lived by the crystal or the Tarot. She had liked the idea of an element of choice though. It meant that nothing was immutably written – and even to think this way argued that she half-believed in it all. Which she did not.

As for such powers in herself, well, what a laugh! Come through the blood, ha ha! – from Auntie Maudie and her teacups, no doubt, even funnier!

... and the voice in the gathering dusk had cried *help* ...

'One more, and then we're going home,' said Oliver, briskly, watching her, and for one panicky moment she thought that he meant that literally, but of course, he meant it only figuratively. The tent, for now, was home, so far as he was concerned. She wondered suddenly if he even knew what the word *home* really meant, but that was a question to which she was unlikely ever to learn the answer.

'Oh come, it's early yet,' objected Jack, but Oliver shook his head, gathering glasses for the refills.

'The child has had too much sun,' he said firmly, and Cheryl realised, with sudden and consoling warmth, that he was protecting her. She wondered, with tenderness, if he had any ideas as to what from.

They passed Vellanzoe the next day, in full sunlight, headed again for Sennen. It looked quite different in the bright sunshine, lonely and pathetic, but not at all disturbing. The rose bushes reached after them over the broken wall, and bees buzzed among the nettles and brambles. Coming from this direction, you couldn't see the tearing hole where the little plane had gone through, but Cheryl thought of the man who had died there, trapped and bleeding and crying for help that never came, and her own blood chilled a little in her veins. A horrid way to die, in agony and alone, and knowing what must be coming.

'What's the matter?' asked Oliver, casting her a swift glance. 'You can't be cold!'

He sounded incredulous, as well he might since it was another beautiful day.

'Oh ... a goose walked over my grave. I was thinking about what Jack said last night. How awful to die slowly like that, knowing you were going with your life unlived and everything left undone. Why couldn't he have gone out with a bang, and not known anything? It was such a cruel way to go.'

'Perhaps it wasn't like that at all,' said Oliver. 'It's only a story, after all. Thirty years is time for quite a lot of embroidery. And if it was true, there's no point in tearing yourself to bits over it. What can you do about it, anyway?'

'Well ... nothing, I suppose.'

'Well, then.'

The sad little houses were behind them, the Vellanzoe fields were coming to an end, giving place to an estate of modern bungalows, the bustle of the A30.

Dusk, a ruined house, the awareness of personal grief to come, too much imagination, not sleeping properly, not knowing what was going to happen next, any or all or these could have caused the phenomenon. She had not truly heard the screams of a dying man, nor shared his agony.

There was no such thing as a haunted house. Fortune-telling and psychic powers were one big joke.

So there!

VIII

On the tenth night, the fine weather finally broke in a storm. They had driven back to the campsite that evening under a steel-grey sky and in a sticky stillness that Oliver said meant some nasty weather in the offing, and he was right. Cheryl woke suddenly at two in the morning to find that the elements – wind, rain and thunder – were roaring around them in a terrible battle that outraged the night.

Beside her, Oliver slept on. Elemental excesses were commonplace fare to him and his subconscious, accepting that he was safe on land, let him rest. He lay relaxed on his side with his right arm flung across her and his head against her shoulder, breathing quietly, miles away from her in spirit but in body so close that she could feel his breath on her skin.

She lay for a while and listened to the wind roaring in the hedge behind them, watching it plucking at the tent so close above her head, making it billow and plunge like the sail of a ship riding out a gale. Flashes of lightning illuminated the whole interior with terrifying frequency, the thunder seemed almost continuous. In Cheryl's imagination, the surf crashed into the quiet coves where they had swum and lazed and sunbathed, and made her shiver under the warm rug. It would swirl cruelly round the rocks where they had watched the sand eels dance, that new undersea world that she had discovered would be a very different place tonight.

Inevitably, there came the moment when she wondered how many storms, even worse than this one, Oliver had ridden out alone with his boat on the wild seas, and if he had ever wondered if this was the end and given way to despair and fear. Perhaps his natural fearlessness hadn't allowed it. She thought that the gypsy at the fairground had been right when she had implied that his total lack of fear had made him immature.

He was sophisticated, experienced, courageous and charming, but he also had that self-centred streak that was childish in its intensity, an irresponsibility towards anybody or anything, including his own life – or herself, for that matter – that more rightly belonged to extreme youth. He was twenty-seven years old, with the basic outlook of a teenager, and what, if anything, would ever change him was something that Cheryl couldn't visualise. Maybe, of course, nothing ever would.

But was it important anyway – to her, that was? Men like Oliver were for dreamy days spent in the sun, not for ever and ever, not for the dull days of ordinary life. The cream on life's instant coffee, the lone currant in the dreary bun of everyday living. These were not given to everyone. She had been lucky.

Or desperately unlucky ...

The thing that she had tried to shut out for days now suddenly hit Cheryl with blinding force out of the blue. To live without Oliver, as she would soon have to, would be the hardest thing that she had ever had to do.

The admission brought a wave of desolation that stuck, choking, in her throat and stayed there as physical pain, and it went on for far too long. It was quite dreadful. Her defences had tumbled at last and left her exposed, all pretence or laughter gone, to an unacceptable truth.

She had let herself fall in love with Oliver. Of all the stupid things to do!

Stupid, but probably inevitable.

Oh God, how had she let him make such a fool of her? And she would cry miserable tears, and he would go on, free as the air, to the next adventure.

Leaving her with less, even, than she had before she knew him, nothing but thrown-away chances and a comparison that she could never avoid making.

He had never offered her anything else. She knew that all along. She had only herself to thank.

A heavier gust of wind than the others roared down the campsite, and the tent flapped and struggled like a wild thing, tugging at its ropes, longing to be free to fly with the gale and be gone. Cheryl, who a moment before had been lying on her back, staring inconsolably down the black tunnel of her coming loneliness, was whisked straight back to here and now by a swift and genuine fear that it was going to succeed. She sat up with a jerk, and cried, 'Oliver!'

The urgency of her cry woke him at once, where the storm had failed. He rolled onto his back and opened his eyes, instantly fully conscious, his reflexes in perfect working order.

'What is it?'

Cheryl turned to him, and a passing flash of lightning lit her face, showing him her immediate fear and a lingering echo of misery.

'The storm – we're going to blow away!'

Oliver pulled her down, and put his arms around her.

'No we're not. The tent might try, but it isn't going to succeed.'

The tone of his voice said as clearly as words that a tent put up by the great Oliver Nankerkis wouldn't dare. As always with him, Cheryl felt impending crisis dissolving into merriment.

'Are you quite sure of that?'

'With both of us plonked down on a fitted groundsheet? I should like to see it! What's the matter?'

'Nothing,' said Cheryl. She couldn't share such private thoughts. He would be embarrassed and it would spoil everything. She said instead, 'It's cold.'

Oliver laughed, and pulled the rug up to cover her shoulders.

'You're a proper little towny,' he told her. 'It's only a bit of wind, for God's sake!'

Cuddled in his arms, she listened to the wind and the rain beating against the flysheet, and the thunder rolling around like monstrous pandemonic marbles for a while without trying to talk above the noise. She had accepted Oliver's assurance that the tent wasn't going to blow away without further question, and even began to enjoy herself. She realised, now that she had stopped panicking, that the hedge was breaking the force of the storm, and there was something particularly cosy about being shut in this little capsule of shelter in the midst of such an enormous disturbance. Her thoughts of a few minutes ago seemed silly and inappropriate. Oliver stood for laughter, not tears, surely. After a while she became aware that he was laughing now, shaking against her with some private joke.

'What's funny?' she asked drowsily, for in spite of herself, sleep was creeping up over her in a stealthy tide. The future, after all, was just that. She couldn't be robbed of here and now, unless she consciously chose to forget it was hers to keep always.

'You,' said Oliver.

'Me?'

'Going off to sleep, and now you've got me at it.'

'At what?'

'Wondering if the tent is going to blow down. Do you really want to go to sleep?'

Cheryl yawned and snuggled closer.

'I've been awake for hours, quaking. It's your turn.' After a while, when he didn't answer her, she said, 'I suppose you're used to storms – at sea, I mean. What is it like all alone in the middle of the ocean in a raging hurricane, like this one?'

'You thank God for seasick pills and the radio,' said Oliver, flippantly.

'Are you never serious about anything?'

'Sometimes, about some things. Try this, shall we go back to Embridge, and get married?'

'What?' asked Cheryl, when she had recovered her breath.

'Well, we can't do it here. Even for a register office you need a residential qualification. I don't think they'd count a tent. Anyway, if we go back we can probably do it more quickly.'

Cheryl very much wanted to say something, but when she opened her mouth, no sound came out. Finally, she managed a squeak.

'But –' She sounded like one of the bats at Vellanzoe, she thought, and cleared her throat to try again. This time the words came out as if someone else was saying them. 'But you haven't known me a fortnight.'

Her heart was trying to batter its way through her ribs, making breathing a conscious and uncomfortable effort. The thunder grumbled about overhead and crackled in the distance, as Oliver appeared to consider what she had just said. At last he spoke out of the concealing darkness, and he, too, sounded unlike himself.

'It seems to me there's no choice. We go together – it feels, from way back.'

She couldn't answer him. If she spoke, she was afraid this moment would shatter like a glass bubble, leaving nothing but sharp splinters.

A terrific flash of lightning, brighter than all the rest, lit up the inside of the tent, momentarily showing her his face, serious, etched with black shadows, watchful. He said, 'All right, it's unreasonable. When we first met, I thought that I already knew you. This past week, everything about you has been dear and familiar, as much a part of me as my own body. I thought you felt the same.'

Speech came back in an unexpected rush.

'But it's so soon,' pleaded Cheryl, panicking. She felt as if she was being rushed along on a huge wave, and couldn't see through the surf to a safe shore. She wanted to go with the wave, but her courage faltered so that she instinctively struggled. In the uncertain twilight, she thought she saw a glimmer of amusement in his eyes.

'How does it go? *There's so many things to do, and so little time to do them,*' he said. 'Let's not waste any of it.'

So little time, with a lifetime ahead of them? Cheryl had a momentary picture of that lifetime, packed with incident and excitement, and then, although she didn't consciously think of the man who had crashed to his destruction in the creeping mist thirty years before, to cry in the lonely darkness for the help that never came, he was there in her mind. She had imagined him as young and daring, just like Oliver. Nobody could know what would happen tomorrow, and Oliver invited trouble – perhaps that unknown pilot had done the same, and left someone behind to live with regret for a lost opportunity all her life. The confession leapt out of her almost of its own accord.

'I love you,' she said, and every lover who had spoken them before her sang in the words.

'We'll go back tomorrow,' said Oliver. He didn't, she noticed, use the word *home* this time.

She hadn't actually said that she would marry him, Cheryl thought, much later, as she lay in his arms and listened to the storm growling away over the sea, but she would, and he knew it.

The wind rattled the flysheet and the thunder rolled again, fading now.

- *it will come – and sooner than you expect –*

The echo seemed to come out of the roaring wind.

… the shining stars and the thing you fear so much, the test of your courage and the fulfilment of yourself, and the powers that you deny that can bring you safely home …

… I must always beware of acting without thinking …

Was he acting without thinking now? Was it she who was going to bring him down?

... I'll die without issue, but my name will live after me ...

She wanted children. She did. But everybody died some time and nobody had said that it would be young. And there were the choices, and the twists, and the path that ran from east to west with both ways leading home... something like that. She could marry Oliver and travel with him in safety along his stony road. Nobody, surely, believed in Happy Ever After anyway.

Nothing was ever this easy, of course she knew that. *Oh Oliver, Oliver, I'm not sure I'm brave enough for this. I love you with all my heart and soul, and I know ... I know ...*

But what she knew escaped her and fled away on the wings of the dying storm, so that she lay all night close in the arms of the man she loved and would marry, and grieved in her heart for something that, although she couldn't identify it, she knew that she would lose thereby.

They packed up and turned for home the following morning, on a dull and windy day with spurts of rain whipping in the wind and scudding clouds whisking across a pale blue sky. Down in the coves the surf roared and tumbled, the flowers threshed wildly in a confetti of torn petals on cliffs flattened by the gale, and the new grass in the fields swelled and curtsied like a green and silver sea.

Cheryl had forgotten most of her misgivings of the night before, dismissing spooky things to the shadowy realms in which she considered they belonged. She had slept, in the end, with her head in the hollow of Oliver's shoulder and his arms close about her, and she had woken with no misgivings waiting to taunt her, to recall with a shock of surprise that she was going to marry him. She sat up under the tumbled rug and stared at him, wide-eyed.

'Did I dream that?'

Oliver looked up at her, one arm crooked behind his head and his eyes so full of love that her heart gave an uncomfortable lurch.

'Dream what?' he teased her.

'I said I'd marry you,' said Cheryl, dazedly, and Oliver grinned at her.

'Well actually, you didn't, but I take it as read.' He reached out to her. 'Come here.'

Cheryl flopped back into the curve of his free arm and laid her cheek against him. Some of last night's misgivings were not so easily dismissed as the spooky things. Possibly, in some ways, they *were* the spooky things, translated into ordinary terms.

'Oh Oliver, how can I love you so much? What will everyone say?'

'Do you care what they say?'

'A bit, I think. Don't you?'

'Not a lot. Why do you?'

She thought about it.

'Because ... well, because it will upset people, I suppose. My family, I mean – Mum and Dad.' She hesitated. 'I don't mean that they'll dislike you, how could they? But they've got it fixed in their heads that I'm going to marry Jonathan, although I've never said so. They think it's the right thing for me to do, and this will be ... well, rather a surprise, I suppose.' She didn't say the word *shock,* but that didn't stop her from thinking it. Oliver looked at her, quizzically.

'I'm reasonably honest, I earn myself a living, and I have all my arms and legs and faculties. What has this Jonathan got, that I haven't?'

'Familiarity,' said Cheryl, and sighed, because it was impossible to explain to Oliver that there was a general, as well as a more specific familiarity involved here. 'They'll say that I've lost my head over you.'

'And have you?'

She looked back at him, and couldn't help smiling. She knew that her parents would immediately recognise, and instantly distrust, the fact that he was a very attractive man, but she didn't think that she had in the strictest sense lost her head. She was sure she knew exactly what she was doing, with all its risks and possibilities, even without Madame Zsa-Zsa to stir the pot with her soothsaying nonsense.

'Of course,' she said, and kissed him. The kiss began as a swift caress to tease him, but began to run out of control because Oliver was stronger than she was, and not at all interested in their conversation. She fought him off to say, 'No, Oliver! Be serious a minute! My Mum is going to stand out for a church wedding, and my Dad is going to say, *wait and be certain.*'

'And aren't you?'

'I'm quite certain, but they won't believe me.'

He looked at her, seriously now.

'Are you going to make me serve seven years in the wilderness, like Jacob? Is it Jacob I'm thinking of?'

'No. At least, it might have been Jacob, but no to the rest.'

'We could be married in a couple of weeks, if it all goes right.'

'It's so quick – '

'But you'll do it?'

'That's what you meant – last night, when you said, let's go back and get married?'

'It is.'

'Oh, goodness!' said Cheryl, and felt a sudden sinking sensation in her stomach.

'Your parents would probably prefer it to your going on like this. If they're anything like mine, that is – be respectable, even if it kills you!'

That wasn't quite fair to her own parents, but even so, probably not too far from the truth.

'All right, all right,' said Cheryl. 'I'd marry you next week, I promise. I must be barking mad but I'll do it, but we must be practical too.'

'Why must we?'

'Because ...' It was strangely difficult to explain what she meant while he was looking at her with that particular expression on his face. She said, 'People will expect it.'

'I wouldn't bet on that – of me, anyway. My family will all rush to tell you that I've never been practical in any way that matters since the day I was born.'

'And mine will expect you to be,' said Cheryl. 'No –' as he opened his mouth to speak. 'Be quiet a minute, and listen. It isn't true, what I just know you're about to say, that it isn't anyone's business but ours. At least, it is true, but it isn't.' She paused to frown, and Oliver blinked in surprise.

'I hope you know what you're trying to say, because sure as hell, I don't,' he said.

'Yes you do – you're just being awkward.' Cheryl rolled over onto her front and propped her chin on her hands, so that she was looking down on him. 'My family aren't like yours. I don't have a wicked stepmother, or any of the awful problems you seem to have.' A giggle bubbled up and refused to be suppressed. 'Do you have ugly sisters, too?'

'Not ugly ones, no,' said Oliver, but absently. 'Go on. You were saying?'

The giggle had gone suddenly. Cheryl said,

'I love you with all my heart and soul, and I'd marry you today if I could, but I don't want to upset other people by doing it.' She saw his brows twitch together in a frown, and added, quickly, 'Not if it can be helped. You make it all sound simple, and it isn't.'

'Why isn't it?'

Cheryl took a deep breath and told him.

'Because I have probably lost my job, and you haven't even got one. We have nowhere to live. That's just for starters.'

'OK. You can get another job, I'll find one, and we'll find a room or a flat somewhere.'

'It sounds easy when you put it like that!'

'I don't see why it should be difficult.'

She looked at him seriously.

'What would you do? Go back to delivering yachts?'

'Hardly – unless you want to get rid of me already.'

She was relieved, but knew that she dared not say so. She knew what he was all along, after all.

'I don't want you to give anything up – not for me.'

'Don't you think that might be being over-generous?'

'No. You'd do it, but you'd never forgive me, in your heart. I'd be the prison, and the ball and chain – we can find a better way.'

'My God,' said Oliver, staring at her. 'What are you saying?'

'That I love you just as you are – free. If I tied you down, I would have made you ... less.'

He removed the hand from under his head and used it to stroke her hair, very gently, curling the ends round his fingers.

'I can't do all the taking, and leave you to do all the giving. That's not fair.'

'I want you to – if you do anything else, I can't marry you. I don't want to be a ball and chain.'

'I wish I'd never made that silly remark!' said Oliver, with unexpected violence.

'But you did, and I know you meant it. Let me give you what you need – let me do that much. Please.'

'You're twisting it round to make me feel better,' he accused her.

'I love you.'

'You're binding me with a heavy burden, you know that?'

'Then accept it, along with the rest. That would make it fair.'

Oliver let out a long breath. He looked up into her face very seriously.

'You're asking too much of us. We can't do it. Nobody could.'

'When we talked about it, on the beach that day, you said it meant working at it. We won't fail – I promise you.'

'You can't promise me. Whoever even knows?'

'I love you too much to fail you.'

'And I love you,' said Oliver, rather unevenly.

'You told me your wife would do what she wanted, and I want to do what you want.'

'I must have been out of my mind!'

'Uh-uh.' She let her elbows collapse and put her mouth against his, ending the argument, her boats all burning on the far side of the watershed that lay behind her.

IX

Things began to turn sour as soon as Cheryl arrived back at the Queen's. The moment she walked through the door she knew that, to put it at its lowest, the shit was about to hit the fan. She was greeted with a daunting pile of messages – ring Jonathan, ring Mrs. Holmes, Mrs. Nankervis called in to speak to you, your mother phoned, and phoned, and phoned ... She looked at the pile of post-it notes in horror, and then at the duty receptionist, who was not sympathetic Jeanette but a smart young opportunist with an eye on Cheryl's job. Her heart sank like a stone.

'There's going to be a row,' she said, and the duty receptionist, who wouldn't have offered comfort even had there been any, simply said, 'Old MacDonald wants to see you the moment you get back.'

Cheryl said a word that made the duty receptionist blink, and then sniff.

'It's easy to see *you've* been keeping bad company,' she observed.

If she had already been sacked, Cheryl reflected, there wasn't a great deal of point in trying to keep the peace. She allowed her lip to curl suggestively.

'Better than no company at all,' she suggested.

This gave her a brief, cheap satisfaction, but altered nothing, of course. There was a row. It reverberated from all directions, and caught Cheryl and Oliver equally, both separately and together.

'How could you, Oliver!' cried his sister Susan. 'It's just so typical of you, it isn't true! There was Sir Henry Pearson, pulling strings for you, and coming all the way down here to see you personally, although he's always so busy, and where were you?

Off heaven knows where, with some tacky bit of crumpet out of a shop! Couldn't you even hang on for five minutes?'

'Don't be so bloody vulgar!' said Oliver. 'I didn't invite your comments, and I didn't ask for the great Sir Henry's patronage either, and you can both go and jump off the pier!'

'Joanna blames herself –'

'She *what*?' roared Oliver, interrupting without ceremony. 'What in hell's name has it got to do with her?'

'Don't swear at me, Oliver.'

'Why the fuck not? At least swearing is honest and straightforward, unlike your bitchy innuendoes –'

'You're utterly selfish!' accused Susan, not inaccurately and with indignation. 'You never consider anyone but your wonderful self! You might have some consideration for the family sometimes, instead of leaving us to clean up the backlash of your scruffy little *affaires*! Poor Daddy had that dreadful Mrs. Holmes nagging at him all last week –'

The sheer injustice of this drove Oliver to interrupt yet again.

'And I should like to know what it had to do with either of them, or you if it comes to that!'

'Her dreary son is going into a decline.'

'More fool him!'

Oliver had lived in a permanent state of war with his family for years, and incidents like this slid off him like water from a duck's back. Cheryl, who cared more about the opinions of other people, fared less happily.

Ronald MacDonald, the manager of the Queen's, was naturally known as Old MacDonald among his staff, although he was not, in fact, particularly old. Fortunately for Cheryl, he was a shrewd businessman who lived in the present and could see all round a problem, and he had already worked out that if Oliver Nankervis and Cheryl were to become what is known in modern parlance as an item, he would hardly come up smelling of roses if he threw her out. The town loved Oliver, his flight from publicity, apparently in company with the girl he had only met on his arrival home, had caught the public's romantic imagination. The *Herald*, over-ruling the Mayor's cuckolded son and even the formidable Mayor herself, had run the story as a fairy-tale romance for all they were worth, for the Mayor only bought one paper, the townspeople bought thousands. The *Herald* knew very well that it could bring political disaster to the Mayor any time it chose, and did exactly as it liked according to the mood of the moment, which right now was that Oliver Nankervis could do no wrong. Therefore it followed as the night the day that, for the moment, Cheryl could do no wrong either. There was also, of course, the consideration that Cheryl was extremely good at her job, while her obvious replacement was an ambitious little schemer. Old MacDonald believed in keeping life smooth for himself.

All of which made things difficult for him, but he handled the situation, he flattered himself, with his usual personnel skills. He called Cheryl to his office and didn't offer her a chair. With her standing in front of him like a rebellious little girl, he gave her to understand that he would overlook her behaviour this time, since the other girls had covered for her and she had had some holiday owing. Blessing Jeanette, whom she assumed had done most of the covering, and not realising that her deputy too had been flaunting her efficiency under the manager's eye, Cheryl nevertheless knew that she wouldn't get off this lightly, and nor was she wrong.

'But I wish it clearly understood,' continued Old MacDonald in a voice that could have chilled an iceberg, 'that if it should happen again, no matter how influential your friends, you will be out of a job. And moreover, should one breath of scandal touch the good name of this hotel over the incident, you may pack your bags and leave the next day. Do you understand?'

Cheryl was astonished that she wasn't packing her bags today, but resentful that her private affairs should be referred to as "scandal". She apologised, since that was obviously expected of her, with rebellion in her heart, knowing that there was no point in making matters worse, and thanked Old MacDonald with as much gratitude as she could summon, which wasn't as much as it should have been. She then had to listen to a lecture on modern morals – or the lack of them – that made her turn scarlet to the tips of her ears. Being thus made aware that her private life had been inadvertently conducted under a public spotlight made her want to crawl into a corner and die of shame, and a growing realisation that she was only being forgiven because Oliver was who he was made her cringe. She would have liked to be able to give in her notice then and there and storm out, but it wouldn't help, as she had just sense enough to see. The fact that she had kept her job was a point on the side of herself and Oliver. It did not, however, console her for the rest.

The duty receptionist sneered at her as she returned to the foyer, which was a mistake, as an already furious and seriously upset redhead who hates your guts is the wrong person to annoy.

'What's the matter with you, Mavis – gut ache?' demanded Cheryl, taking the war straight into the enemy's camp. 'Well, good! – and get that sloppy coffee cup off the counter!'

Her subordinate, whose name was Maeve – *my grandmother was Irish you know, her people kept racehorses on their estate in County Kerry* – looked affronted. She was still gobbling with indignation when Cheryl's hand sliced across the counter top and sent the offending cup and saucer bouncing into her lap. The dregs spilled over Maeve's immaculate blouse and skirt. Drinking coffee behind the reception desk was contravening reception etiquette, although everyone did so – circumspectly. The fact that Maeve felt secure enough to do so openly was simply the last straw.

'Now look what you've done!' Maeve howled.

Cheryl peered over the counter top, and smiled, not nicely.

'Oh dear, what a mess. You had better not let Old MacDonald see you on duty like that, he won't be at all pleased.'

Maeve mopped indignantly at her stained white blouse with a tissue. For such a little slop, it had covered a wide area. Cheryl gave her a deliberately irritating smile, and headed towards the service door at the back of the hall, just as the manager, to her great pleasure, came out of the office behind reception. Feeling better, she pushed through the door and went up to her room.

A shower and a change of clothes should have made her feel better, but didn't. Some kind person, and no prizes for guessing who, had left the previous week's *Herald* on her chest of drawers, folded open at a page of gossipy speculation as to where Oliver had taken his lady, under the predictable heading **YOU *SHALL* GO to the BALL, CINDERELLA!** Everyone, she realised with a sinking heart, had deduced what they had done, even though nobody had found them. She should have thought about that before she left, but the truth was that she had not – she had barely stopped to think at all, and in any case, this was something that she would probably not have thought about even if she *had* thought. Realising that she was confusing even herself, Cheryl mentally boiled this down to the simple statement, *if I had gone away with Jonathan, it wouldn't have made the newspapers*. No doubt, if Maeve had taken any of her mother's calls, as from her handwriting on the post-it notes she obviously had, nobody in Suffolk had been spared the knowledge that she had run off with a stranger, either. Jonathan, also no doubt, would have filled them in on the details. Things couldn't possibly be worse, she thought, which only proved that she had yet to meet Oliver's family.

It was too early to ring home. There was no point in trying to speak to her parents until after the shop was shut. She ripped the page out of the newspaper, stuffed it into the pocket of her jeans, and went out to find Oliver in the marina.

Oliver, too, had seen the newspapers. He, too, had realised that he had been guilty of not thinking, and was furious with himself for having made Cheryl's name a byword, even if, as seemed the case, it was in the nicest possible way, and the excuse that neither of them was used to being in the public eye was no excuse at all. They sat side by side in the main cabin of *Lawley's Girl*, where nobody was likely to see them, and tried very hard not to contrast their happy time in Cornwall, with Jack and Maggie and Mike & Co., where nobody criticised them, with their present situation where it seemed as if everybody did.

'It's no business of anyone but us,' Cheryl told Oliver, miserably. 'Why won't people leave us alone?'

'That's my line,' he reminded her, a little grimly.

'They're making us look cheap. I never meant to be cheap Oliver, I didn't!'

'You weren't,' said Oliver. Cheryl said, 'I didn't want to make a scandal. I didn't know you could any more – not like that.'

'You can't,' said Oliver. 'Come on sweetheart, lighten up – we're getting married a fortnight tomorrow, and then they'll all have to shut up.'

Cheryl caught her breath.

'So soon! Oh Oliver –'

He put his arms round her and pulled her head down against his shoulder.

'Is it too soon?'

'I'd marry you tomorrow, you know I would –' She bit her lip, humiliation still too close for comfort. 'You're the only person who can understand why ... and I love you so much.'

'People don't matter,' Oliver assured her – mistakenly, she thought. She sighed.

'Your stepmother came to the Queen's.' she said. Oliver pulled abruptly away from her.

'Aagh!' he said, crossing his fingers in the age-old sign against evil. Possibly he was trying to make her smile, she decided, but he wasn't smiling himself.

'Is she that bad?'

'I don't think you'll like her.' He was undoubtedly serious now. She wished that she hadn't mentioned his stepmother.

'What do you think she may have wanted?'

'Nothing that you need take any notice of,' said Oliver, brusquely. 'To hell with the lot of them, Chel.' But as he pulled her roughly back against him, she heard real anger underlying the words.

They were silent for a while, enjoying the simple pleasure of being so close together, and into the silence there came the sound of footsteps approaching along the slatted wooden jetty. The footsteps didn't go past. They stopped alongside *Lawley's Girl*.

'Hullo. Is anyone aboard?'

Cheryl lifted her head from Oliver's chest, where it had been resting, and looked at him with a question in her eyes. He placed a finger on her lips and shook his head, speechlessly. They sat still.

The footsteps moved again, and the voice said, tentatively,

'Ahoy there. Anyone at home.'

The boat rocked as someone stepped aboard. Cheryl pushed Oliver's hand away and mouthed the single word,

'Who?'

'Press,' he mouthed back. Someone banged on the fore hatch.

'Anyone home?'

If he walked aft, he would find the main companion hatch and the saloon doors open. Cheryl held her breath. Oliver's fingers, gently stroking the back of her neck as if she was a frightened cat, sent tingles down her spine. She suddenly wanted to giggle, and buried her face again, smothering it.

But whoever it was obviously was unfamiliar with boats. There was a lurch as he jumped ashore again, and then the sound of retreating footsteps. Cheryl got to her feet and peered through the window. She caught a glimpse of him, a tall man in jeans, swinging a large camera case, and drew a slow breath.

'I think you were right. How did you know?'

'Witchcraft,' said Oliver, and then laughed. 'I recognised his voice, no mystery. I know him. He's a mate, but not this time.'

'Oh.'

'Chel, do you mind very much?'

'It won't go on for ever. Nine days, they say, don't they?'

Oliver grimaced.

'Eight to go, then. Chel, I'm *sorry.* I've really loused this up, haven't I? You do believe I never meant to?'

'*Beware of acting without thinking,*' said Cheryl. Oliver caught her hands and pulled her back into his arms.

'Omelette all the way,' he said.

If the news was out that they were home, they decided, they must not now spend the night together. Cheryl was past caring, but Oliver was adamant on the subject.

'They're already talking about us,' she objected. 'It can't be worse, surely.'

'They don't *know* anything,' said Oliver, firmly. 'For all they know, we went to a temperance hotel and slept in separate rooms, the rest is simply surmise. Let's not add fuel to the fire. It's only a couple of weeks.'

Cheryl thought that the time would last for ever, but she saw that he was serious. He walked her back to the Queen's quite early, and when they arrived, she was forced to admit that he was right. A harsh flash of light in the dark car park lit their arrival, a man ran out from among the cars waving a pencil.

'Oliver! Give us a story, be a mate! I've been looking for you all evening.'

Oliver paused, lifting an eyebrow.

'Is that the action of a mate?'

'Is this the lady friend?' The flash came again, making Cheryl jump, and the photographer strolled across to join them.

'Get lost, Andy,' said Oliver. The pencil pointed to Cheryl.

'How about you, my darling, will you speak to a poor bloody journalist? Where've you been hiding yourselves?'

Cheryl smiled.

'That's for us to know, and you to wonder,' she said. 'Excuse me, won't you – I'm on shift in a minute.' The first excuse she thought of, and a lie.

'Give us a kiss then!' cried the photographer, camera at the ready.

'Certainly not! You're a perfect stranger!' She squeezed Oliver's hand, swiftly. 'Goodnight Oliver. See you tomorrow.'

'That's not –' But Cheryl had vanished through the back door of the hotel, and Oliver was walking away. They leapt after him, clamouring.

Hounds baying at a fox, thought Cheryl, climbing the backstairs to her room. Be careful the fox doesn't bite you, doggies! Oddly shaken, for there had been nothing at all frightening in the encounter, she sat down on her bed. It wouldn't last, of course, something else would happen and the hounds would race off after some other unfortunate quarry. Nevertheless, it was horrible now.

The post-it notes were still stuck to her mirror, where she had left them. She pulled them apart and looked at them. Jonathan and his mother, definitely not, she had nothing to say to Mrs. Holmes and too much that would have to be said to her son. Mrs. Nankervis could call again if it was that urgent, Cheryl wasn't going looking for her. Her own family ...

'Oh, shit,' said Cheryl, inelegantly, to her reflection.

It had all seemed so simple down in Cornwall. She had even sent a postcard, showing Tregothen Bay, announcing cheerfully that she was taking a break in old haunts with a friend. At the time it had seemed only fair to stop them worrying, now she thought that she must have worried them all the more. But she had never thought that there would be this much fuss. She had never stopped to think that Oliver was News.

I should have rung before, she thought. I should have rung the very first evening. I've made a mess of things, as well as Oliver, and now what do I do?

Be careful, she answered herself. How you handle this is going to be very important. Get it wrong, and Oliver is going to be on the next boat to the Mediterranean, and there's no guarantee that you'll be with him. Hopefully, he would regret that for the rest of his life, you certainly would. So think.

But the only counsel she found in her thinking was that they must somehow limit the damage. They must keep their cool, they must be reasonable but firm. They must stand shoulder to shoulder, even if it did feel more as if they were standing back to back with a gun each to fight everyone off. And they must speak out honestly, and stand by what they said.

Which meant that, first of all, she must find a place where she could make a private phone call.

In the past, that had meant Jonathan's flat, or his mobile; working as she did behind a bank of phones she had never bothered with a mobile of her own. For perhaps the first time, she regretted the economy. There was a pay phone downstairs, but she could hardly use that, too public, too awkward altogether. So where?

Finally, she got to her feet and went back downstairs, and out through the service door into the foyer. Maeve, thank goodness, had gone off duty, it was Jeanette who manned the desk tonight. Hopefully, this was a good omen.

'Cheryl!' cried Jeanette. 'You're back! Did you have a wonderful time?'

'Wonderful, but the bill's come in – live now, pay later, you know? Is Old MacDonald in the office?'

Jeanette gave her a sympathetic look.

'So long as it was worth it. Yes.'

'Oh, it was worth it,' said Cheryl. They exchanged a smile. She opened the flap in the counter top and knocked on the office door and opened it.

'Good luck,' said Jeanette.

Cheryl closed the door behind her, and Old MacDonald looked up.

'Oh, it's you again. What do you want, you're not on duty until tomorrow, are you?'

Since she was wearing her own casual jeans and shirt, the answer to this must have been obvious even had he not drawn up the rota himself. She stood, hands folded, feet neatly together, reciting to herself – keep calm, be reasonable.

'I wondered if I might use the phone in here – later, of course, if you're busy now. I need to phone home.'

'Ah.' He looked at her meditatively. 'Private call, I see.'

'Very private,' said Cheryl, thanking anyone who was listening for an intelligent boss. Old MacDonald gathered the papers on his desk together and set them aside.

'I'm just on my way to check the restaurant anyway. You can do it now, if that's what you want.'

'Thank you.'

When he had gone, Cheryl sat behind his desk with her hand on the telephone and her mind completely blank. What could she say, what in heaven's name could she *possibly* say, when she was going to hurt and upset them so much?

Pay up, or shut up. She picked up the phone.

'Give me an outside line, Jeannie.'

'Done.'

She heard the click, and punched in the familiar number.

If it hadn't been for Oliver being so well known, Cheryl might have got away with her postcard.

Hey, look where I am! Came down on the spur with a friend, having a wonderful time, it's hardly changed at all. Sun shining, everything fine, will ring when I get the chance, love you. Cheryl xxxx.

'I expect Jonathan just got up her nose,' said Tracy, when she was shown it. 'He gets up mine sometimes, and I don't have to live with him.'

'It seems a bit drastic to just run away. And she doesn't say who she's with.' Marilyn sounded worried.

'"A. Friend",' mused Tracy, holding the postcard to admire the coloured view. 'Sounds a familiar name – but Mum, Cheryl and Jonathan are like *that!* She must have loads of girlfriends we don't even know about.'

Candy came rushing into the kitchen, clutching a curious scarlet and green erection made out of Micky's Lego.

'Look Mummy, a jarff!'

'A what?' Tracy looked startled. Marilyn took the curiosity from her granddaughter's hand and held it up.

'Oh yes, dear, what a lovely giraffe! Did you make it?'

'I never was good at languages,' said Tracy. She gave back the postcard. 'Don't worry Mum, you know what it's like. She

115

probably just needed to get away. And now I must get down to the school, or I'll be late for Micky.'

Marilyn would have liked to talk more, but between the jarff and the time, she saw that there would be no opportunity. Tracy's lack of concern soothed her own, she drove home feeling much happier, although the customers she served that afternoon found her a little absent-minded.

Bob had stayed in all Sunday for Cheryl's call. The postcard was hardly the same. She was a naughty, thoughtless girl, but Marilyn supposed she had just grabbed an opportunity and you couldn't blame her, really. She had loved Cornwall as a child, bless her.

Half a pound of streaky bacon, four ounces of mild cheddar... oh, sorry, *six* ounces of mild cheddar.

She had probably sent Jonathan a postcard too. Or rung him. Poor boy, he would be very hurt, he was really absurdly sensitive for a man of his profession.

Cooking chocolate? Third shelf down, over there.

Such a fuss over nothing, too! All of them – Bob, Jonathan, everyone, making too much of a photograph, when from all accounts it was Jonathan's idea anyway.

... but a very good-looking young man, that Oliver ... what *was* his name?

Yes, the cabbages come from a local farm, fresh from the field this morning.

'Look out, Marrie,' said Bob. 'The lady over there has been waiting to be served for ten minutes now.'

Spring visitors, enjoying their holidays. Was Cheryl, too, enjoying hers?

Marilyn hoped so. Then she made herself concentrate, and got through the rest of the day until closing time without even thinking of Cheryl once.

Jonathan telephoned the following morning, early.

'Have you heard anything from Cheryl?' The anxiety in his voice was obvious.

'Haven't you?' asked Marilyn, cautiously.

'Not a word. Nobody knows where she is. They're all guessing she's run away with Oliver Nankervis.'

Nankervis. That was it, no wonder she hadn't been able to remember.

'Cheryl wouldn't do a thing like that.' Marilyn realised as soon as she spoke that she wouldn't have convinced even Candy.

'Oh yes, she would!' Jonathan sounded bitter. 'She was all over him like a rash at that dance! Marilyn – I'm sorry – I must find her. I must find her before she does something even more stupid – look, if you know where she is, you must tell me. I'll fetch her back. I'll say she was with me – anything. You must tell me.'

'Jonathan –'

'You don't know him,' said Jonathan, urgently. 'She'll get hurt. He's not her kind, and anyway, he doesn't care a toss for anyone, and he'd charm a hanging judge! Believe me.'

'She sent us a postcard,' said Marilyn, troubled.

'You must tell me! Believe me, the whole town's talking. It's got to be stopped before it all gets out of hand.'

She told him.

'You didn't!' cried Tracy, when she heard about this. 'Mum, whatever were you thinking of?'

'If she's gone off with this man, it's best Jonathan fetches her back before your Dad knows. This way we can perhaps see he never does know.'

'You think Dad won't hear, if the whole of Embridge knows about it?'

'Jonathan says he can hush it all up.'

'Jonathan's got to find her first!'

But Jonathan didn't find her. By the time he reached Tregothen Bay, Cheryl and Oliver were down at Trelewan, leaving no trail to be followed. All he succeeded in doing was proving for himself that they had been together, and he hadn't really believed anything different.

He loved her, did Jonathan. He told nobody where she had been, he confirmed for nobody whom she was with. He nursed the knowledge in his aching heart and pretended, even to his editor, that he knew as little as everyone else, and he didn't ring her home again. So that Bob and Marilyn, far away in Suffolk, knew nothing for certain until the evening that Cheryl rang to tell them what she had done.

'You've done what?' demanded her father.

'I've met someone. Not Jonathan. The right person for me, Dad. You'll like him, promise.'

At this point, of course, Bob Wainwright was still in the dark. He had no idea that Cheryl had already thrown caution to the winds, and he accepted her statement at face value.

'It seems very sudden.'

'Aren't these things always? It was just like a – a thunderclap, Dad. Bang, there he was.'

'Sounds more like the genie of the lamp,' Bob growled. 'Well, I don't know what to say, girl, and that's the truth. You'd better speak to your mother.'

He handed the telephone to Marilyn.

'Says she's met some man, and fallen in love. I thought she was in love with Jonathan, but poor, bloody fathers are obviously the last to know! Find out what's going on, will you, and talk some sense into her? No daughter of mine lives with a man all that time and then doesn't marry him without good reason, and that's final!'

'Oh Bob!' said Marilyn, and put the phone to her ear.

'I heard that,' said Cheryl. 'It's no good, Mum. Jonathan is yesterday's news, and I'm so sorry, but I couldn't help it. It just happened.'

'I suppose it's this round-the-world man. Cheryl love, are you sure you haven't just been swept away?'

'Of course I'm sure,' lied Cheryl, for that was exactly what she had been. 'Mum you'll really like him when you meet him. He's special.'

'You'd better come up for the weekend, the two of you, let us look him over. But I warn you, Cheryl, your Dad isn't in a mood to be won over easy. This is a real shock you've handed us.'

'Jonathan –'

'We're all very fond of Jonathan.'

It was hopeless, thought Cheryl, they had already made up their minds. How much did they know, up there on the east coast? Who had told them what? She said, feeling her way with caution,

'Mum, about last week …'

'Least said about that, the better,' said Marilyn, firmly. Bob was sitting in his chair with the paper, listening to everything she said through the open door. Best protect Cheryl for as long as she could. 'And as for Jonathan, well, it's early days yet. You've not known this Oliver a fortnight.'

'I feel as if I've known him always.'

'That's as may be. You bring him here, like I told you, and we'll see.'

Cheryl drew a breath. This was the wrong moment, but when would there ever be a right moment? Oliver had to break the news to his own family, she couldn't in all fairness expect him to face her own as well, but she did think that perhaps she had the harder part. Her family certainly packed less venom than Oliver's appeared to do, but that somehow made it worse instead of better. She let the breath out on a long sigh.

'There isn't time for that, Mum,' she said. 'We're getting married a fortnight tomorrow. You will come, won't you?'

'*What?*' cried Marilyn.

Later, when Cheryl had rung off after their short and unsatisfactory talk, Marilyn had a little weep over it. She felt as if a wedge had been driven between herself and her youngest child that had begun to force them apart. It was terribly hard to explain things to Bob. He went very quiet, and picked up his paper again.

'We must go to Embridge. We must go tomorrow,' she said.

'We can't.'

'We must. We must stop her. Trace will look after the shop.'

Bob lowered the paper.

'Marrie, I said, we can't.'

'And I said, we must. If we don't, she'll marry this Oliver person, Bob. She'll make a dreadful mistake, and we won't have lifted a finger to stop her.'

Bob was so angry, both with Oliver and with his darling Cheryl, that he could hardly think straight.

'If I see him I'll kill him with my bare hands, so help me!'

'No you won't.' She recalled the picture of the lithe young athlete and thought that he would be lucky to be given the chance, but wisely didn't say so. 'I'll ring Trace. Tell her what's happened.'

Bob grunted, and turned a page. As she went out into the hall again, he said,

'Ask her if she can do a couple of days – not this next weekend, I don't trust myself. Make it the one after and maybe I won't kill him. You're right, this has got to be sorted out.'

Marilyn's instinct was to rush straight down to Embridge, but maybe Bob was right, and it was better to let the dust settle. He wouldn't shift, anyway, and perhaps Cheryl would come down to earth in the interval, it might even give her a fright if they didn't rush. If they pushed her now, she'd only get stubborn. But there was so little time, if what Cheryl had told them was true, and Bob wasting it. She bit her lip, undecided, and picked up the phone.

'Trace? You're not going to believe this!'

X

It was paradoxical that the announcement of their impending marriage called down a fresh storm that threatened to eclipse everything that had gone before, but it wasn't only in Suffolk that the clouds were gathering. Things were fairly black down in Dorset, too.

'Oh, Oliver!' exclaimed his stepmother. 'How could you? Her father runs a shop, and her name is Cheryl!'

'What on earth has that got to do with anything?' asked Oliver.

'It might as well be Marlene, or Sharon!'

Oliver simply looked blank, having long ago decided never to give his stepmother the satisfaction of getting a rise out of him, but his father was more successful.

'Is the young woman to support you, I wonder?' he speculated, with heavy sarcasm. 'Or are you planning to be off to the Mediterranean again, while she supports herself at home? Since you've thrown away every opportunity that has been offered you since you came home, I think you should consider very carefully exactly where you stand.'

'I shall find a job, of course,' said Oliver.

'And what makes you so sure that you're different from the other three million or so unemployed in this country?'

'I said, I shall find a job.'

Father and son eyed each other across a chasm of misunderstanding, and Jerry Nankervis thought, as he had thought so often before, how far away from him this son of his had grown, and wished that he understood how it had happened.

'There's still an opening for you in the firm, if you want it,' he said, but Oliver thanked him and refused, which had also happened many times before.

'I shall never understand you,' said Jerry Nankervis, with truth. 'I just hope that this unfortunate young woman succeeds in making you settle down. You're too old to behave like an irresponsible boy, and marriage is a grave responsibility.'

'You should know,' said Oliver, with bitterness, and was immediately sorry, not because he realised that he had hurt his father, but because he knew he had hurt himself. He didn't see the need to apologise, therefore, and the interview ended on a familiarly sour note.

But Oliver had always been at odds with his parents. Cheryl, on the other hand, had enjoyed a normal, happy family life, so that the distress of her own parents was much harder for her. They came down from Suffolk a few days before the wedding was due to take place, determined to stop it if they could and full of concern for her welfare. The intervening ten days had been spent by Marilyn in trying to calm Bob down so that he wouldn't, as the saying goes, turn a drama into a crisis and make Cheryl do something that she might live to regret. She might as well have spared herself the effort, for as soon as their presence in Embridge was known, they found a great many people to tell them things that Cheryl didn't know, and that made her father very angry. She was at an immediate disadvantage and of course, Marilyn thought in despair, Bob had to push things to the limit. Men! You couldn't do a thing with them!

Marilyn tried to keep things calm. It was like sticking her finger into a leaking dyke.

'Poor Jonathan!' she said, persuasively. 'He loves you so much, too.'

'Jonathan's a nice lad,' said her father, but a lot more belligerently. 'You've given him a raw deal, my girl, and this Oliver Nankervis had better be as special as you say.' Marilyn kicked his ankle, and he scowled at her. Cheryl was the darling of his heart and it wasn't for Marrie to take her part.

'He is,' Cheryl assured him, but in the event, when they met him over a drink that same evening, they didn't like him. All the things that Cheryl loved in him, his looks and charm and style, his courage and sense of fun, were held up as faults and mourned over. Jonathan had done his work well.

'Oh Cheryl, how could you!' exclaimed her mother, when he had gone, leaving them alone in the foyer of the Queen's. 'When Jonathan is so nice, and so much more suitable. You're being very silly!'

'Oliver isn't unsuitable!' protested Cheryl defensively, and her father gave her a strange look.

'If that's all you know about him, that's it! The marriage is off.'

A mixture of indignation and sheer fright betrayed Cheryl into answering back.

'You can't stop me!'

'If that's his influence speaking, then I certainly will,' Bob told her. 'There's never been divorce in our family, but you're in a fair way to be the first!'

'Why?' demanded Cheryl, out of her depth and fighting hard. 'What's he done? What have you got against him?'

Her father took a breath to tell her, but Marilyn placed a restraining hand on his arm.

'Come on, both of you. Let's sit down and talk this over reasonably.'

They went into the lounge. Maeve, who was on the evening shift, gave Cheryl a derisive look, which further ruffled her already disarranged feathers. Her heart was thumping as they found an empty corner.

They sat at either side of a low coffee table, with Cheryl's mother sitting between them like the referee, which was appropriate.

'Now then, my girl,' said Bob, which wasn't a propitious start. Marilyn interrupted him.

'Hush Bob, that'll get you nowhere. Cheryl –' She turned to her daughter. 'Now, come along, let's be grown-up about this, shall we? Do you know anything at all about this man you're so set on marrying, or are you just carried away by a beautiful face?'

The adjective surprised Cheryl, and so caught her off guard.

'I know everything I need to,' she protested. Her father raised his eyes to the ceiling.

'Give me strength! What's that supposed to mean?'

'It means, I know nothing to his discredit,' declared Cheryl, getting angry. 'Everybody likes him!'

'You approve then, I take it, of hell's angels, and drugs, and running away from home?' said her father. Cheryl stared at him.

'What?'

'Listen here –' he began, belligerently, but once again, Marilyn stepped in.

'Bob – I'll tell her.'

'No, Marilyn, I will.' He looked grim. 'Now then, girl – this wonderful Oliver of yours has been in trouble up to his neck all his life. He's a record as long as your arm of skiving off school, breaking the law on motor-bikes, getting into bad company. He's only kept out of serious trouble because of who – and what – his father is. Don't tell me you hadn't even bothered to find out!'

'Who told you?' asked Cheryl, because it was the only thing that she could think of.

'Jonathan's mother,' said her own.

'Oh, and you don't think she might have an axe to grind?'

'She's lived in this town all her life,' Bob reminded her, grimly. 'Why should she tell lies? *Her* personal integrity isn't in any doubt, and I hope you aren't going to imply that it is.'

Cheryl had stumbled into a nightmare. She felt cornered.

'But not drugs –' she protested.

'He was in trouble at university for smoking cannabis,' said her mother. 'No –' as Cheryl began to speak. 'Don't bother to tell me that cannabis doesn't matter. It does.' She saw Cheryl's expression, and her own softened. 'I'm sorry, Cheryl. I know how you must feel, but it's not just Jonathan's mother, it's no secret. His own stepmother confirms it.'

Cheryl had yet to meet any of Oliver's family, it seemed to be an object with him to keep them apart; neither had they sought her out, although they must have known perfectly well where to find her. The omission had given the past ten days a gunpowder quality that had made her jumpy, perhaps that had been the intention. It was no real surprise to find that her parents were ahead of her, but was she being paranoid to suspect collusion? She said nothing, and her expression turned sullen.

'They want this marriage no more than we do,' said her father, gruffly, not looking at her face. He couldn't bear to see her distress. 'They're not our sort of folks, Cheryl. They don't want you, don't go pushing yourself in.'

'I'm not,' said Cheryl, in a strangled voice. 'It's nothing to do with them.'

'And nothing to do with us either, are you saying?'

'You know I'm not.' She felt as if she was smothering. Oliver, it appeared, carried a high price – and was all this true? The thought that it must be, or nobody would have dared to slander him so, shook her. Her loyalty wavered, and stiffened again. Her lips felt wooden. 'I'm going to marry him,' she said, and her father gave a derisive snort.

'It's good to see we brought you up to respect our advice!'

'Bob –'

Cheryl was already ashamed of that momentary wavering.

'We love each other,' she said. Her father snorted again, enraged.

126

'After less than a month? Not so long since, you were in love with young Jonathan! Well, who lives will learn – but remember what they say, marry in haste and repent at leisure!'

'Why should we repent? We know what we're doing. We're quite certain.'

It was the sort of futile argument in which neither side is open to conviction.

'Oh, are you?' asked Marilyn, with a shrewd look that Cheryl found intensely annoying. 'If you ask me, you aren't *certain* at all, or why the rush? All else apart, are you sure you're not afraid that if you wait, he'll be off halfway round the world, and forgetting all about you?'

'He wouldn't!' exclaimed Cheryl, indignantly.

'Don't be too sure. That young man was born to trouble as the sparks fly upward, and there's nothing to say in what I've heard so far that he has any sense of responsibility either!'

'To what? To who? It's his life.'

'To you,' suggested her mother. 'And it'll be your life too, when you're married to him. What are you going to live on, the pair of you, may I ask? Your salary?'

'And where do you propose to live?' asked Bob, glowering. 'I don't know what money there is in sailing round the world, but it seems to me that all he has is the credit for it, and a boat to live on for now that isn't even his own.'

'There's perks,' said Cheryl, but Oliver would have nothing to do with advertising sponsorship, or endorsements, or consultancies, or anything that looked remotely like the ball and chain he derided so much.

'He's not for you, Cheryl,' pleaded Miriam, almost with tears in her eyes.

'He's thoroughly unstable, and you'll not cure him of it,' said Bob, more robustly. 'Well, marry him if you must – we can't stop you, as you kindly reminded us – but don't come crying home when things go wrong, as they will, make no mistake. Just you remember, he who sows the wind, reaps the whirlwind! And make sure that young man of yours carries adequate life insurance, if you'll take my advice just for once!'

Cheryl felt miserable. She couldn't explain to them that Oliver was part of her, her natural pair, they had set their faces against understanding even if they were capable of it. They were, instead, not going to forgive him for not being Jonathan, and steady, or for his beauty, or for being different and a notch or two up the social scale. They were going to allow him no credit at all. Marilyn saw the pain in her face, and put an arm round her shoulders.

'Come on Cheryl, be sensible. Wait a while, and get married in a decent, Christian way, after a proper engagement – what have you to lose? Nothing! And everything to gain. If he really loves you, he won't go away, and you'll have time to get to know him properly. We wouldn't stand against you if you did that, not either of us.'

Cheryl looked from her mother's anxious face to her father, and saw him nodding in agreement.

'That sounds reasonable to me,' he said.

Nothing to lose ... except something that she couldn't put a name to, and which she knew Oliver prized in her almost above everything else. His own brand of courage, perhaps, that was so sure of itself that it need never count the cost, and if that was it, she had only herself to blame.

'There's no point,' she pleaded in her turn. 'We want to marry now. It's all arranged. We're both of age, why shouldn't we?'

More than anything else, Bob Wainwright couldn't forgive Oliver for taking his daughter away and living as her lover, making her the talk of the town. Children didn't tell you everything, but whatever she might have got up to with Jonathan, she had never rubbed their noses in it. Times changed, unfortunately, and you couldn't keep your daughters in a time warp, but Jonathan had been discreet and respectful, a thoroughly decent lad from Cheryl's own world, with a steady job and good prospects. This Oliver, who had flaunted her all over the newspapers, was, in spite of his antecedents and his fame, in the eyes of a hard-working shopkeeper nothing more than the beach bum that Cheryl had called him in fun.

'I suppose we should be thankful he's marrying you at all,' he said, grudgingly.

'Cecily Holmes tells me poor Jonathan is quite ill,' said Marilyn, firing her final shot. 'Doesn't eat, can't sleep, she had to send him to the doctor he's got so down. How can you do it to him?'

Jonathan was the one person who hadn't so far reproached her, but this was a reproach in itself.

'What do you expect me to do?' asked Cheryl, miserably. 'I can't marry him just because I pity him. Anyway, he never asked me. I'm sorry – that's all I can say.'

There was a silence.

'But you'll come to the wedding,' said Cheryl.

'We'll have to think about that.'

Whatever she had allowed her parents to think, Cheryl knew that she couldn't overlook what she had now learned. Her faith in Oliver might be absolute – she hoped that it was – but there were some things that would be better out in the open. She could gauge their importance, she thought, by his reactions. She owed that much to herself, if not to her mother and father, and she didn't think he would hold it against her. He would realise as well as she did that you couldn't take anyone or anything for granted, not when well-meaning people were nagging you on every hand. The smallest doubt could in time poison their relationship beyond saving.

The difficulty was, how to approach the subject. She was so sure in her own mind that Oliver was exactly what he seemed that it was almost an insult to imply that she thought anything else. Fortunately, in spite of outside influences, when they were alone together they were still empathetically close, and Oliver short-circuited her dilemma for her.

'What's gone wrong?' he enquired.

He had picked her up from work, and they were now in the MGB, bound for his parents' house, where she was at last to meet his family, and where her parents, as well as his, were assembling to *talk this thing through sensibly* – his father's phrase, and faintly ominous. Because there had been no opportunity to talk to him privately since her own parents had launched their attack, and because this occasion seemed dangerously unsuitable for such a talk, Cheryl had been sitting very quietly. Thus directly addressed, she looked down at her hands, twisted together in her lap.

'It's going to be a pretty awful evening.'

Oliver shot her a swift glance.

'We don't have to go,' he offered.

She knew very well that it was only on her account that he had ever agreed to what he considered an unwarrantable invasion of privacy. She had only to say the word and he would turn the car round now.

'Yes we do,' she said. 'I think we do. If they're all making the effort to meet us halfway, we ought to try to do the same ... I think we ought.' She had said it all before. She wasn't even sure that he listened in any way that mattered, but at least he didn't openly oppose her, after his first furious reaction.

He didn't answer her directly.

'It's very important to you, isn't it – to meet everyone halfway?'

'No – at least, yes. I hate rows.'

'You don't, do you, admit their right to make one?' asked Oliver, with an edge to his voice that she had heard once or twice since their return to Embridge. She sighed.

'It's not that simple. Nothing ever is, have you noticed?'

There was a short pause, then Oliver braked and pulled into the side of the road. He switched off the engine and turned to face her.

'All right, what is it? Someone has put the cat among the pigeons, haven't they?'

Cheryl met his eyes. It wasn't the moment she would have chosen, but it probably should be out in the open before they met the united opposition waiting for them ahead.

'Yes,' she admitted. 'Mum and Dad have heard things that –'

'What sort of things?' interrupted Oliver, defensively, she thought, and her heart sank a little.

'About raising hell and running away and taking drugs.'

'I see,' he said. There was a silence. 'And do you believe it?' he asked, eventually. Cheryl looked down at her hands again.

'Yes. It has to be true, doesn't it, or people wouldn't say it?'

Oliver said nothing, and after a minute she said, still without looking at him, 'Yes, I do believe it. But I don't believe that it makes any difference. It must all be a long way in the past. And I know you.'

'Thank God for that, at least,' said Oliver. He hesitated. 'Before we go any further, I'd like to know who told your parents.'

'Mrs. Holmes – that's Jonathan's mother – and your stepmother.'

'Bloody hell!' said Oliver.

Cheryl raised her head to look at him again. He was angry, she saw, and although she had seen him angry before, she had never seen him this incandescent. But it was not, thank goodness, ever with her, and it wasn't with her now, either.

'Kids who raise hell and get into drugs, all those sorts of things, either do it because they're dragged up anyhow, or because they're very unhappy, or else because they're too easily led. I don't believe that you were dragged up anyhow, and you certainly aren't easily led.'

They looked at each other in mutual distress, the days that had passed since their return like a wall between them.

'It all sounded so easy when we talked about it in Cornwall.' Cheryl leaned her head back against the headrest and sighed wearily. 'What's made it all go wrong?'

'People. I told you once before, they always do.'

'Why can't they let us alone?' said Cheryl, on an unexpected wail, and Oliver broke off what he had been about to reply and looked at her more carefully. It was getting dusk now, and the light from a nearby illuminated fascia cast weird rainbows across their faces, making sharp shadows that hid them from each other.

'We should have come back and got married, and told them all afterwards,' said Oliver. Cheryl, who was beginning to wish they had done just that, looked up at him miserably in the uncertain, coloured light.

'I'm so afraid that by the time they've finished with us, there won't be any magic left.'

He reached out and let his hand rest lightly on hers, staking a claim yet leaving her free to run if she wished, a summing up of his whole attitude to life – and to marriage, too.

'Do you feel any signs of its slipping away?'

'Not when we're alone. I love you as much as ever I did.'

'Then don't be afraid.' He drew her towards him and kissed her, very gently. 'It's not for much longer. Another four days, and there'll be nothing left to say.'

'What are we going to do?' she asked, and Oliver answered blithely, on an unexpected mood swing, that it would all be fine.

'Ignore them,' he told her, starting the car again and pulling out into the traffic. 'You kept your job, I've got one this afternoon – we only need a place to live and we've met all our own requirements, and who cares *that* about theirs?' He made a swift and crude gesture before changing gear, and made her smile, but the strain of the last few days had extinguished the giggle that had previously come so readily. Something that she had thought once before came into her head, that Oliver and his kind were for the days when the sun shone. She looked at his profile in the gathering dusk, and love for him made a painful twist in her stomach. She gave her courage a cautious poke, and to her relief found it sitting defiantly firm.

And then they had swung off the main road into a maze of quiet, tree-lined avenues. She was aware of ever larger, expensive-looking houses set back in gardens to be measured in acres, of a growing impression of space and affluence. They drove perhaps a mile, and then Oliver swung the car left between tall gateposts, and up a drive lined with flowering shrubs. A long, low, large and lovely house lay before them.

'Here we are,' said Oliver. 'Waterloo. Theirs, I mean, not ours.'

Cheryl, silenced, climbed out of the car and followed him up the curving front steps.

XI

This was the first time that Cheryl had been to Oliver's parents' home, and the first time that she had met them. His stepmother had never repeated her visit to the Queen's: once the truth was out she had contented herself, Cheryl had already realised, with stirring trouble behind the scenes. Even without Oliver's attitude towards her, which spoke clearly enough of his opinion, she was fairly certain that she was going to dislike the woman, and nor was she disappointed.

Her first impression was that the house was elegant, but not at all homely. The atmosphere in the tastefully understated drawing room – which at home would have been the lounge – was like falling into the freezer, no feeling of welcome at all. Her parents were already there, Marilyn on the very edge of a deep armchair, acutely uncomfortable with a drink clutched in her hand, and Bob standing uneasily in the bay window, looking as if he was wondering if his boots were clean. Cheryl felt irritated with them, they could try harder, she thought, to look less like country bumpkins. Then a moment later she was angry, because Oliver's stepmother and his smartly-dressed sister – he had two of them, she had now discovered, this one was Susan – seemed to her to be deliberately making the guests feel ill-at-ease, with their cut-glass decanters and their gracious background, and not least their beautifully modulated voices and worldly social poise.

She looked swiftly at Oliver to see if he had noticed what she had noticed, to see if he fitted in – she wasn't sure. He was still familiar, however. Not ill-at-ease, certainly, but as alien in his particular way as her own father against this rich, ultra-civilised background. Her mouth had gone dry, she licked her lips in nervous relief.

The news that Oliver had found himself a job, which should have been welcome to everyone, at first had the opposite effect.

He broke it to the assembled critics over the uncomfortable drink that began an evening to which nobody had been looking forward.

'How typical of you!' exclaimed Susan, in disgust. 'You fall on your feet like a cat, Oliver – I just hope it's a good one, and something sensible for once.'

'Who with, Oliver?' asked his father.

'Bill Rowlands,' said Oliver, and into the succeeding hush, Susan cried, 'Oliver, you can't!'

'Why not?' asked Oliver, genuinely astonished.

Susan looked nonplussed, but only for a second. She recovered quickly.

'Well, I hope the money's good,' she said. 'It'll need to be, with all the risk involved, if you really intend to marry *her.*' She jerked her head disdainfully towards Cheryl.

'There's no more risk to it than there is in crossing the street,' said Oliver, obviously irritated, and Bob broke in, with more haste than grace, before a full-scale sibling row could develop.

'Who's Bill Rowlands? What's his trade?'

Bill Rowlands, as Cheryl had already been told, headed up a diving company that specialised in salvage.

'Treasure hunters!' said Susan, scornfully. 'Isn't that just like you?'

'Look,' said Oliver, 'what do you want? Blood? You all said, get yourself a job and a decent living wage – all right, I've got them. Now that's wrong, too. Am I ever going to be able to do the right thing again? Because if not, tell me now and that way none of us need be disappointed!'

'She doesn't want to be worrying about you at the bottom of the sea all day!'

'Why should *Cheryl* worry at all? And I shan't be there all day. It isn't possible.'

'It's dangerous,' Susan insisted.

'Rubbish!'

Bob Wainwright had become interested, and forgot to be uneasy. He spoke to Oliver, for the first time, as if he could come to like him.

'You mean, you're going to dive on sunken wrecks? Spanish galleons and things?'

Oliver laughed. He had a natural, friendly charm when he took the trouble to use it. He was taking the trouble now. Cheryl saw Marilyn look at him, and then look away again quickly, her face troubled.

'First find your galleon! It's usually a lot less romantic than that – recovering scrap metal, removing obstructions, underwater repairs, that kind of thing. But there's always the chance.'

'Suppose you did find a treasure ship?' asked Bob, curiously. 'Is that Treasure Trove?'

'You'd think it ought to be, but generally, it's not. Just salvage.'

'How disappointing,' said Cheryl, relieved to see her father showing a sympathetic interest. 'So you aren't going to make your fortune?'

'Unlikely. It might keep the wolf from the door – if we found one.'

'Are there any around here to be found?' asked Marilyn, unwillingly fascinated, and Jerry Nankervis added, urbanely,

'Wasn't Rowlands looking for the *Hesperides*?'

'Isn't everyone?' countered Oliver, with a flash of amusement.

'What was the *Hesperides*?' asked Marilyn, now visibly succumbing to the male Nankervis charm, quite as strong, Cheryl noticed, in the father as in the son. She was surprised. She hadn't expected this from what Oliver had told her.

'She was an East Indiaman that went down after ramming the Bornhope Rocks, just outside the harbour here, back in 1810,' said Oliver, smiling at Marilyn in a way that seemed to disconcert her once again. 'Among other cargo, she's reputed to have been carrying over eighty-thousand pounds worth of coin, and the personal fortune in jewels and gold bullion of a highly important Company official, *en route* for Southampton and home. Legend says that his reputation was not untainted with piracy, or even slavery, but that's legend for you. What isn't legend is that the ship went down in a heavy storm, supposedly quite close inshore. There's probably not a lot of her left – but salvage methods at the time weren't up to the depth, or the currents and conditions, and it's fun to think she might still be down there – and all that treasure with her, of course.'

'How romantic,' said Marilyn, sitting back in her chair at last, but Susan spoiled it.

'And how typical of Oliver!' she said. 'Only he could call a hypothetical treasure ship a source of income!'

Oliver looked at her coldly.

'You said a living wage, not a get-rich-quick scheme,' he reminded her. 'It wasn't me that brought up the *Hesperides*.'

The brief period of truce was over, and there followed a difficult evening that achieved nothing that satisfied any of the critics.

'You can't live on a boat,' said Oliver's stepmother, firmly. 'Cheryl wouldn't like it.'

'I wouldn't mind,' said Cheryl, but it turned out to be the wrong thing, for her mother and Susan pounced on her from either side.

'You very soon would when it blew, and got cold,' said Susan, and 'How can you possibly tell, when you know nothing about it?' said Marilyn. Cheryl went pink, and Oliver said, 'She's not mine, anyway. We'll find somewhere.'

'You're getting married in only a few days,' objected his stepmother. 'It doesn't leave much time. Have you even looked?'

Cheryl and Oliver exchanged glances. Neither of them had, there had been too much on their minds.

'*The Lord will provide!*' cried Susan, and threw up her hands.

'There isn't even time to arrange a proper reception,' said Marilyn, fretfully, which at least seemed to indicate that she was coming round to the idea, if rather belatedly. 'And what about a honeymoon? It really is such a scramble!'

Susan looked at her as if she found this preoccupation with convention too bourgeois for words.

'They've had that,' she said scornfully, and her husband, an inoffensive-looking man, called, confusingly for the Wainwrights, Tom, and who had sat most of the evening in embarrassed silence in the background, gave her a poisonous look.

'Well, yes, that's enough said about that, Susan,' said Jerry, repressively, and it was Susan's turn to change colour.

'You really should have somewhere to live,' said Marilyn, hurriedly, rather pink herself. 'It's no good just hoping for the best.' If she had hoped for a breathing space while such a place was found, she was to be disappointed.

'We'll find somewhere tomorrow,' said Oliver, and it was typical of his luck that they did.

The landlord called it a flat, Cheryl's mother, when she saw it, called it a bed-sit. It consisted of one large, virtually unfurnished room on the top floor of a tall Victorian house that fronted the less exclusive end of the waterside. The ground floor was a tacky gift shop and tobacconist, the next two floors were divided into flats, and the attic was to be Cheryl's future home. One end had been partitioned off into a minute kitchen, and the shower-room was at the top of the stairs, outside the door, in what had once been a broom cupboard. The ceiling sloped until it nearly met the floor, and the two dormer windows, which overlooked the harbour and the commercial dock, were so low down that it was necessary to kneel to see out of them. There was a scrappy rug and some limp but clean curtains included in the deal.

'I suppose it'll do for now,' said Marilyn, uneasily aware that she was losing the fight. Oliver was out of her league and she knew it. 'You've really set your heart on having him, haven't you?' she added, and Cheryl agreed that yes, she had, and didn't meet her eyes.

'His parents don't like you.'

'They don't seem to like him much, either,' said Cheryl.

'How can you say that?' asked her mother, in surprise. 'His father thinks the world of him!'

Cheryl had noticed nothing of the kind. She had felt Oliver's father disapproved of both of them on general principles, and his stepmother she had disliked on sight. A stout, well-corseted woman with lacquered hair and a sugary kindness that Cheryl instantly suspected, she had a way of seeming to be on your side, and suddenly swinging round to reveal the sting in the tail. She thought her guess that Oliver had been an unhappy child, very probably from a dysfunctional family, had probably been right, although she hadn't pursued the subject at the time, using her lack of curiosity as reassurance that she still believed in him. He really didn't care any more, of that she was certain, so that in any case there was nothing to be gained from discussing it. Marilyn looked at her doubtfully.

'His family could make life very uncomfortable for you, Cheryl. You have thought about that?'

'They won't be given the chance,' Cheryl told her, for that much was already abundantly clear. 'Oliver won't have anything to do with them if he can help it.'

'It seems very unnatural,' said Marilyn uneasily. 'You won't like being shut out.'

But all Cheryl wanted was Oliver. She was deaf and blind to anything else. Her mother went on looking unhappy, thinking of their own closely united family, reluctantly accepting that there was nothing she could sensibly do but smother her misgivings as best she could. Thanks to Bob's intransigence, they had left it too late – probably it had always been too late. She was beginning to realise that the marriage would alter the balance, not only of Oliver's family but even more of their own, and her heart was heavy.

A noisy disturbance on the stairs announced the arrival of Oliver, and brought the discussion – if so one-sided an argument could be dignified by the name – to an end. He came into the room behind a big cardboard box, that appeared to Marilyn's critical eye to contain nothing useful, only a lot of miscellaneous hi-fi equipment. Any remarks about a bed to sleep on, she thought resignedly, would only be greeted by another of Oliver's conjuring tricks. She gave in.

'Well, if your heart is set on it, and I see that it is, we had better decide what you're going to wear on Tuesday,' she said briskly. Cheryl looked at her blankly.

'I thought, that blue summery thing we got in Ispwich last year,' she said. 'I think it's clean,' She hadn't, to be truthful, given the matter any particular thought, there was too much else that was more important on her mind. Her mother made a tutting noise of exasperation.

'No really, Cheryl, it's too bad of you!' she exclaimed. 'This may be the most scrambled wedding of the century, but no daughter of mine gets married to a celebrity – *any* celebrity – in last year's cotton dress, that may or may not be clean! We'll go back to the hotel and look into your wardrobe right now!'

'We were going to go out for a drink,' began Cheryl, but giving in had given her mother a new lease of life.

'I've put up with a lot from you these past weeks, one way and another,' she said, firmly. 'This time – for the last time –

you can do what I say! You can go out for a drink any other night of your life, but for now we've only got a couple of days to turn this muddle into something like a proper occasion. Do you want Oliver's family to think you come from a tribe of savages?'

Cheryl glanced swiftly at Oliver, who was head down in the box, unpacking a pair of speakers. He straightened up with them in his arms, mischief written all over him, and grinned at her.

'That sounds like an ultimatum you dare not refuse,' he said. 'At least make sure it's clean! Consider my feelings, if you turned up to marry me all grubby.'

'That's the first sensible thing I've heard you say yet,' said Marilyn. 'Say goodnight, Cheryl, you can tidy up in here tomorrow.'

Oliver put down his speakers, took Cheryl in his arms, and kissed her soundly.

'Don't worry, I'll see to it.'

Marilyn turned away and went briskly to the door, but her friendly intention to leave them alone for a moment was thwarted by the fact that the landing was blocked by two tough young men carrying a shabby, but serviceable, studio couch, so that any romance dissolved into straight farce and conjuring tricks, and the party divided on laughter.

Back at the Queen's, Cheryl's mother began to show the first signs of wedding fever, like a slow thaw after chilling snow.

'And who's coming to this wedding, I should like to know?' she asked, opening the wardrobe and starting to fling things out onto the bed. 'There's no time for proper invitations.'

So long as Oliver was there, Cheryl didn't care. They hadn't planned on a family gathering, she rather thought that Oliver had hoped for just the registrar, a couple of witnesses, and themselves. Some hopes! He had not then made the acquaintance of her mother.

'It'll be rather a matter of who turns up,' she said. 'I shouldn't think it'll be more than half a dozen of us – I can't see the Nankervises turning out, can you?' She picked up the blue dress from the heap and shook it out. 'This one, I thought.'

Marilyn gave it one look, and threw up her hands in despair.

'Cheryl, whatever are you thinking of? There's nothing here that's suitable for a wedding, not even in a registry office! There's only one thing for it, we shall have to go out after breakfast tomorrow, and shop!'

'Mum – tomorrow's Sunday.'

Marilyn made a tutting noise.

'All right, Monday then, don't be so *smug!*Oh my goodness, that's cutting it terribly fine! The wedding is on Tuesday, and what time is it to be, anyway? Oh Cheryl ...' She visibly took a hold on herself. 'Well, there's no point in hanging all this back in the wardrobe. Get it packed into your suitcase, I'm going to phone Tracy right away. If she gets a move on, we might at least have some of the family here. I'll see you downstairs – I must have a word with that nice Mr. MacDonald, perhaps we can do something –'

She was gone, leaving the unfinished sentence hanging in the air behind her. Cheryl sat down on the debris.

Her first impulse was to laugh, but it left her very quickly. Her parents and Oliver's, she was very well aware, were surrendering to *force majeure*, not to personalities. The Nankervises despised her, her parents distrusted Oliver. The only thing he had ever done right, in their eyes, was to offer her marriage after running away with her, and even that was debatable.

In a very short time now, she would be married to Oliver.

She tried to imagine what it would be like, and failed utterly. Her impending wedding seemed quite unreal, she didn't know who would be there – apart from themselves – or what they were likely to say, or do, although she wouldn't put it past Oliver's stepmother to leap up and forbid the banns, or whatever you did in a register office. She knew only that she stood on the shore of a wide and shining sea, full of hidden shoals and reefs and currents, and that she was going to trust her safety thereon to a man that in all honesty she hardly knew. It wasn't too late to back out, even now. Certainly nobody would blame her.

Nobody, that is, except Oliver himself.

For some reason, not clear to herself, he had singled her out from all the girls that he must have known in his twenty-seven adventurous years of life as the one with the qualities he looked for in a partner. She realised now, for the first time, exactly what that would mean, not just with her heart which had known it all along, but with her head. She could look forward to no steady nine-to-five routine, no secure home life, no permanent peace of mind. The days together would be precious, the inevitable times apart, long and lonely.

It was silly, even so, to sit here and tell herself that it wasn't too late to turn back. It had been too late for that the first time that she met him.

Cheryl pulled herself together. She had things to do if she didn't want to waste her off-duty time tomorrow packing, and Monday was obviously going to be spent shopping, like it or not. She had no time to spend on useless speculation. She fetched her suitcase and a large holdall and threw them onto the bed, and had just opened the first drawer when there was a knock at the door. She opened it, and there was Jonathan.

She was shocked to see how white and strained he looked, and how unhappy.

'Oh!' she said, and then a little belatedly, 'Come in.'

He came in, but walking stiffly as if he was reluctant to do so.

'Sit down – I was just about to start packing up.'

He turned to face her, rigid with pain.

'They say you're going to marry him – Nankervis – next week.'

'On Tuesday,' said Cheryl. 'Yes, I am.' Jonathan looked at her miserably.

'I know I shouldn't have come here. I wanted to ask you ... if I ask you a question, will you give me a truthful answer?'

Cheryl met his eyes, not without difficulty.

'I owe you that much. What is it you want to know?'

'If I had asked you to marry me – before you met him – and we had been engaged, would it have made any difference?'

The question was so abrupt, and came with so little warning, that Cheryl felt as if she had been physically slapped. But she had said that she would answer him truthfully, and she knew that he would recognise a lie.

'No,' she said. 'No, I don't think so ... no.'

'You said that you loved me,' Jonathan reminded her.

She hadn't known a thing about love until she met Oliver, she knew that.

'Oh, do sit down!' she said, irritated with him in order to avoid pitying him. 'It isn't the end of the world, you know.'

Jonathan sat down on the edge of the bed without speaking, and Cheryl picked up an armful of underclothes and dropped them into her open suitcase. She could feel his eyes fixed on her ringless left hand. She had no engagement ring, she wasn't even certain that Oliver could afford one, and didn't care anyway. She would happily plight her troth with a brass curtain ring if it came to it. She went on packing. After a prolonged silence that made her acutely uncomfortable, Jonathan drew a long, difficult breath.

'Cheryl ...'

'Mmm?' replied Cheryl, going on her knees to grope under the bed. Jonathan watched her morosely until she came out again.

'You might listen,' he said.

'I am listening,' said Cheryl, and wished that she didn't have to. She hadn't been very kind to him, she knew that. She thought that he looked very ill, and didn't want her heart to start bleeding so close to her wedding day. She dropped her rescued sandals into the case anyhow and sat down beside him. 'Look, here I am, listening. What did you want to say?'

'It's not easy,' said Jonathan. 'Look Cheryl ... I know you can't help it, not if you really love him and not me, and I've not come here to make a scene, I promise you, but I just wanted to say ...' He broke off and looked at his hands, spreading the fingers and inspecting them with care.

'Go on,' prompted Cheryl, encouragingly. Jonathan went on examining his hands.

'You know what he is,' he said. 'You must do, by this time – everybody knows, and I know they've told you. He's restless and unsettled, always reaching after the stars – feral, gone back to the wild. He'll go on, pushing himself further and further, doing crazy things because he's like that, and even if you think you will, you won't stop him for long.' He looked up and met her eyes. 'I love you, Cheryl. I see that you don't love me any more, and I know that I've said all this before, and been angry with you and upset you, but I wanted to tell you, just once more. I love you this much, that the day that he leaves you – and it will come, if he doesn't kill himself first, make no mistake about that – then I shall be here if you need me ... and if you don't want me then, so be it. I shall accept that.'

That *any more* was, quite unintentionally, the biggest censure that he or anyone else had given her.

'Don't be such a daft bunny,' said Cheryl, but even to herself the words lacked conviction, as if his echo of her own, surely empty, fears had stamped them with the seal of probability, ill-wishing her happiness out of his own despair. Jonathan reached out and touched her, quite gently, on the shoulder.

'I'm sorry, I didn't mean to stir everything up again,' he said. 'I wanted you to know – oh hell, what does it matter anyway?' He got to his feet. 'Come and have a last drink with me for old time's sake, how about it?'

Cheryl went down to the bar with him, not knowing how to refuse. Her parents were there, her father sinking his sorrows in a pint of bitter and her mother sipping a genteel sweet sherry and looking pensive. They were surprised, even startled, to see Cheryl with Jonathan, rather as if the sight was all that they needed to crown an intolerable few days, and she thought she detected, too, a gleam of hope in their eyes. But Jonathan only stayed for twenty minutes, talking politely but without animation, and left abruptly when he had finished his pint.

Marilyn looked at Cheryl.

'You are quite, quite sure, aren't you?'

'Yes,' said Cheryl.

Her father looked at her thoughtfully.

'Nobody would blame you if you decided you couldn't go through with it, you know. It isn't even as if it's at all official.'

'I do want to go through with it,' said Cheryl.

Her mother took her hand.

'Listen Cheryl – there's been so much opposition to you both, we want to say we're sorry for our share in it. We wouldn't like you to feel that you had to marry Oliver on Tuesday to prove a point – any point. If you want to go ahead, then we wouldn't dream of making your marriage the cause of bad feeling between us, but please – please – don't be too stubborn to admit that you're making a mistake if you've begun to change your mind.'

Cheryl had known that her parents distrusted Oliver, but she hadn't realised how much until this moment. She looked at her father, and saw the same sentiments reflected in his face. It wasn't just because she had gone away with him, it went much deeper. An instinct to protect, she thought, was part of it – but against what? The same inherent disaster that Jonathan had so gloomily foretold? She couldn't believe in it – and if she had any clairvoyance in her at all, from dippy Auntie Maudie or anywhere else, she hoped that it was working for her now.

'I love him,' she said, and thought that it sounded overworked and unconvincing.

XII

Although she would never have admitted it, Cheryl had been rather shocked by Oliver's home background, so very much grander than her own. She had also been left with a nagging impression that somewhere along the line she had missed something, and that what she had missed was important. The jig-saw puzzle had a piece missing, but unlike other puzzles, she had no idea of what shape the piece could be, or which colour, or even of what size. It had slid, she told herself, down the side of the great armchair of life, and if it was never seen again ...

A real jig-saw puzzle would then be consigned to the bin, or the jumble sale.

Not an option.

She was on the early shift that Sunday, and it always began quietly, as people came down in twos and threes for their breakfast rather later than usual, only pausing to pick up their Sunday papers at the desk as they went past. It gave her more time to think than she really needed. It was not, she told herself, that she was getting cold feet. It was just that she was beginning to wonder if, after all, it might have been better to take a bit more time. She didn't, whatever she claimed, really know a lot about Oliver.

That was other people talking, not her own heart. She *knew* it was the right thing that she was doing. But – there was a *but*.

Back where she began. X, the unknown quantity.

There wasn't a lot of time left to solve the problem. Tomorrow she would have no time at all, her mother would see to that. The day after that, it would all become academic anyway. That just left today, when from the time she finished her shift she wouldn't be working again until Thursday.

Matrimonial leave, thank you Mr. MacDonald. Honeymoon time.

They've had that!

To call Susan Casson a cow was an insult to the bovine creation; surprising, since she was, on the face of it, an attractive woman. There was another sister too – presumably the *Deb* that Oliver had mentioned in Cornwall, known among her other relatives as *Deborah*. The one who also had those beautiful Nankervis eyes. Susan didn't. Susan had brown eyes.

Odd, that; her mother's were pale blue – a rather chilly and unwelcoming blue, at that. Wasn't brown the dominant gene?

Seeking after a clue, Cheryl thought for a moment there that she had one by the tail, but it slid away. She was missing the obvious, she knew it.

So much for clairvoyance. She yawned, smothering it with her hand. Perhaps she should take to studying tea leaves, Auntie Maudie seemed to find them very informative. Had Oliver, she wondered, any oddities like that in his family tree? What *did* live up there in those immaculately pruned and espaliered branches?

Twenty thousand Cornishmen, all wanting to know the reason *why?*

She could relate to that.

'Good morning, Cheryl!' called Marilyn, walking past on her way to the dining room. 'Working hard, I see!'

'I didn't sleep very well,' said Cheryl, excusing herself. Old MacDonald gave her parents special staff rates, they revelled in the luxury of the Queen's, or at least, her mother did. She wasn't so sure about her father, but he went along with it. She wondered what they would make of the Langland if they ever went inside. Now that really *was* living it up!

Marilyn now gave her a strange look.

'No,' said Cheryl, before she could speak. 'I'm not having second thoughts. Morning, Dad.' She leaned over the desk to kiss her father good morning. 'What are you two planning to do today?'

'We thought that we might take a drive along the coast,' said Marilyn. 'Do you want to come?'

'Well ...' said Cheryl. Her father gave her an old fashioned look. Cheryl met his eyes, and decided to be honest.

'I'd love to come, Dad, but I think that Oliver and I need some quality time together, just to be quiet. It's been a – a trying week.'

'You can say that again!' said Bob, but he did not sound unsympathetic. 'When do you go off shift?'

'Half past ten.'

'We'll see you after breakfast, then.'

They moved on in the direction of the restaurant, and Cheryl looked at her watch. One more hour. She was meeting Oliver at the flat after that, for they had a nest to build. Would he be good at bringing twigs, she wondered, and then, if he was a bird, what sort of bird would he be?

Not an eagle, far too haughty. Something in the seabird line. An albatross, or perhaps a greedy herring gull, soaring white against the blue, wide sky? Certainly not! Greed was not a failing of Oliver's – except, possibly, for life.

Cheryl didn't know much about seabirds, but suddenly she found the right one.

A storm petrel!

They lived on the ocean, she found herself thinking, and reputedly never came to land, except presumably to incubate their eggs, she wasn't sure. But she knew that they were wild, wild, wild, and rode the storms on the open sea, and whatever else you could do, you couldn't tame them with a scatter of cake crumbs, even if it was wedding cake.

She was still thinking about this, when Oliver pushed his way through the swing doors, and stormy was exactly what he looked.

She hadn't expected to see him until later, and immediately jumped to the conclusion that something had gone disastrously wrong.

'Oliver! What are you doing here? I thought you were meeting me at the flat.'

'Change of plan,' said Oliver. He leaned over the counter and kissed her. 'Good morning, darling Chel, not that it is a good one.'

'What's happened?' asked Cheryl, alarmed.

'Nothing. We just have to take a trip to Surrey, if you can bear it. If you can't, of course, we needn't.'

Cheryl looked at him carefully. She had never seen him in quite this mood, edgy, harassed, and searching for reasons not to do something. None of that was Oliver, not as she knew him.

'Perhaps you had better explain,' she suggested.

'My father tells me I should take you to see Helen,' said Oliver. There was a pause.

'Helen?' said Cheryl, cautiously. The less Helens he had in his life, the better, she thought. She was sure she had never heard the woman mentioned before.

Oliver had himself in hand now. He had begun to retreat, as she had once seen him do down in Cornwall, into a cool withdrawal, as if ashamed of his melodramatic behaviour.

'Helen is my mother,' he said.

'Oh,' said Cheryl. There didn't seem to be much else to say. She was conscious of being considerably startled, for she hadn't realised that Oliver's mother was still in his life. She had assumed, without actually being told, that she had drifted away during his childhood. She realised now that this was almost certainly what she had missed, and that she should undoubtedly tread very carefully.

'Do you want to see her?' she asked, curiously.

'Not particularly, but he's right. We probably should.'

'Then if we should, perhaps we ought to.' She was still feeling her way. To her relief, at this elliptical remark Oliver's face broke into laughter.

'A typical Chel comment, if ever I heard one,' he said.

Cheryl was oddly relieved.

'Get it over with,' said Oliver, dismissively. 'In that case, I'll pick you up here when you come off shift. See you.' He paused, on his way back to the door. 'We need never go again, if you can bear it this once. Unfortunately, my father is probably right.'

He was gone, and Cheryl was left with a whole new set of problems to pass the time.

They had never discussed his mother. Up until now, she hadn't fully realised it. He had said a certain amount about his stepmother, none of it complimentary, and spoken of *my father* – never *Dad* – but his mother had been barely mentioned in passing. Searching deep in her memory for something that Jonathan had told her, a while ago now, she came up with the information that she was a sculptress, or something – some kind of artist, anyway. Well known, famous, even. And yes, Helen ... Helen Macken. Pronounced in the Scottish way. How could she have overlooked her all this time? You lost the plot there, Cheryl, she told herself sternly, and then immediately excused herself. He meant me to.

Which was true.

Such a lot of loose ends. Joanna Rendell was one, as she tried not to remember. Jonathan was probably another. And now Helen Macken. *People*, making trouble, as in the gospel according to Oliver Nankervis. Cheryl sighed. Such a muddle, and yet she was so sure.

Perhaps it was the result of all the stress, but for a moment Cheryl thought that she literally *saw* the fork in the road. Shocked, she squeezed her eyes shut hard, and then opened them again. In front of her, all around her, was the quiet, almost deserted foyer, just as it should have been. Her heart gave one great bump, and then began to race.

Oh no! She was having none of that nonsense!

Before you knew, it, she'd have Micky and Candy calling her *dotty old Auntie Cheryl*, or something equally unflattering.

I need some breakfast, Cheryl told herself, it's too much caffeine and not enough carbohydrates, or something. Low blood sugar. Anything. Not spooks.

Her heart beat more steadily now. Also, the shock seemed to have done her good. She realised that she felt calmer, all at once, than she had done all week.

Time to do something constructive, she was wasting time sitting here dreaming. The monitor screen of her computer had long ceased to show client accounts and dissolved into piranha fish in psychedelic colours, all merrily dining on each other, which would be a dead giveaway if Old MacDonald came along. With a sigh, for she really didn't feel like work, Cheryl reached for the mouse.

The holiday season wasn't really under way as yet, and the roads, even heading towards London, were reasonably clear on this Sunday morning. Cheryl and Oliver dawdled along in the MGB, enjoying the sunshine with the roof down, and stopping now and then to admire a particularly fine view. Cheryl became aware that Oliver was deliberately putting off the time of their arrival but decided not to ask questions, she would find the answers soon enough. His attitude towards the unknown Helen was subtly different from that towards the rest of his family, less take-it-or-leave-it, in some way cruder. Almost – although it must be her imagination, surely – as if he disliked her more than he did his sweetly venomous stepmother.

Helen Macken lived in a barn, Oliver had told her, but when they finally did arrive, Cheryl saw that this was a misleading statement. Certainly, it had once been a barn, and one end of it still bore some of the hallmarks of one, but the rest had been converted and extended into a charming home, and the original field in which it had stood was a well-established garden, and beautiful. Cheryl was aware even before the car stopped that this was a very different kind of place from the opulent, rather sterile mansion in Embridge. Whoever lived here had different values.

Oliver looked around the deserted driveway with satisfaction.

'At least it looks as if she's alone,' he said, and Cheryl suddenly recalled that he had once mentioned his mother to her – the only time he *had* mentioned her, surely? – as having taken lovers, in the very firm and unmistakeable plural, and having found no happiness therein. Considering the circumstances under which the remark had been made, he was hardly in a position to criticise.

The front door of the house opened as they approached it, and a woman came out. She was smiling.

'Oliver! What a lovely surprise, I wasn't expecting you!' she cried.

Cheryl thought that she was going to hold out her arms to her son, but she stopped the gesture before it had fairly begun, and Oliver, not noticing, said, 'Hullo Helen. I brought Chel to see you.'

Helen Macken smiled at Cheryl.

'Cheryl! I've been longing to meet you.' This time she did hold out her hands, and Cheryl took them. For the first time, in Oliver's family she felt welcomed.

'Come in – this calls for a drink, at least –' She swept them indoors, into a drawing room with wide french windows set open to display a breathtaking view of fields and hanging woods. It occurred to Cheryl that she was nervous, but surely that was silly.

'What will you drink? Sherry, Cheryl darling? Or would you prefer something a bit more robust?'

Cheryl agreed to sherry, although she didn't like it much, for she had already learned that the women of Oliver's family seemed to expect other women to drink it and she was still picking her way with great care among them, as the unwanted stranger in an alien land. While it was poured for her, she covertly studied Oliver's mother. She wasn't as much like him as Cheryl had expected, but he had her hands, long-fingered and elegant, with almond-shaped nails, and the flying eyebrows over his storm-coloured Nankervis eyes had certainly come from her. What she had bequeathed him more than anything, though, was her beauty. For Helen Macken was very beautiful.

Not more than medium height, very slender, with clear, pale skin and dark hair, she also had dark blue eyes, delicate bones, and a wide and generous mouth. Add to these graces a small, well-shaped head on a long neck and the figure of a girl half her age (for surely she had to be fifty, or near it) and you had a very attractive woman indeed. Her hair was thick and straight, like her son's, but in her case long, and piled into a loose knot on the top of her head that made her look almost top-heavy. She looked fragile, but being Oliver's mother, this was probably deceptive. It was easy to see how, when combined with the solid, good-looking sturdiness of Jerry Nankervis, Oliver had turned out the way that he had.

Even the clothes of this unexpected person were as different as they could possibly be. No studied, expensive elegance here. Helen Macken wore a long, flowing cotton skirt in smudgy colours of yellow and green, like sunlight through trees, and a yellow cotton top with short sleeves. She looked, if you discounted the threads of silver in her dark hair, about eighteen. Seventies hippie, with added style. Dorothy Nankervis would have – probably often did have, thought Cheryl, with some satisfaction – an attack of the vapours, if she saw her. Oliver's unexpected mother, she concluded, was an individualist just like Oliver, and exactly the person that she chose to be. But still nervous. Why?

And what on earth could have got into Oliver's father to swap this lovely woman for his solid, homely, bossy Dorothy? People were very strange!

'If I'd known that you were coming, I'd have cooked something,' Helen was saying, adding, with a grin absurdly reminiscent of Oliver, 'Isn't there a song about that? Oliver, there's some beer in the fridge if you like to get it – you will stay to lunch, won't you? Only a salad, I'm afraid, but there's some good cheese, and I've got eggs.'

Oliver had gone in search of beer, his visits obviously sufficiently frequent for him to know his way around, which was interesting. Helen poured herself a gin and tonic and sat down where she could see Cheryl, and smiled at her, saying with devastating frankness,

'I should have known not to believe a word that I was told. You're not a bit like they all described you, you know – you're delightful!'

It was difficult to know what to say to a remark like that, but Cheryl returned the smile.

'I've got a lot to live down,' she said.

'Oh, rubbish!' exclaimed Helen. 'If people have no imagination, why should you have to suffer for it? I will admit,' she went on, 'that when I heard Oliver had run off with you in that helter-skelter way I was a bit cross with him – but I can see straight away it's making him happy, and heavens! he's old enough to know what he's doing at his age, or if he isn't, then he isn't ever going to be. Are *you* happy?'

'Very,' said Cheryl, as Oliver returned, followed by two border terriers barking excitedly and racing round in circles. The conversation became more general, Helen had questions about the round-the-world voyage and talking about this, and looking at photographs that Oliver had brought, probably to fill in awkward conversational gaps, made an uncontroversial subject that lasted not only through the drinks, but through the preparation and eating of lunch as well. Cheryl decided that Helen wasn't her idea of anybody's mother, she was more like a contemporary, lighthearted and fun. More and more, she felt that she was moving in the dark, trying not to knock into things. Oliver treated his mother as if she was a slight acquaintance, more politely than he did his father or stepmother, but she drew no conclusions from this. She just found it rather sad.

After they had followed lunch with coffee, Helen asked Cheryl if she would like to come out to her studio.

'I must work. I have a trade exhibition in town next month, but I don't mind people talking to me when it's just routine stuff, in fact I rather like it. Oliver can come or not, as he chooses.'

Oliver chose not to. He vanished over the fields with the terriers, and Helen watched him leave with a sigh.

'I often wonder what we should have done differently with Oliver,' she said pensively, as she and Cheryl strolled side-by-side down a path awash with sweet-scented pink roses, just coming into bloom. 'It was so dreadful at the time ...' She let her voice tail off, and opened a door in the side of the house. 'Come in, and mind the mess.'

The studio was large, light and airy, with benches around the walls on which stood tall shapes shrouded in damp cloths, unfired pieces, and finished items in about equal quantities. There was very white clay everywhere, both dried and in wet smears, plastic bags of it stacked in a corner, and an enormous kiln with a red light shining beside its closed door. Because of the kiln, the room was very warm, and Helen left the door propped wide. Every window was open, the soft early-summer air, heavy with the scent of the roses, blew through the big room. Light poured in through an enormous skylight in the roof. Cheryl was enthralled, she had never seen anywhere quite like it before.

Helen pulled out a chair that had lost its back, and dusted it perfunctorily with a green overall before she put it on.

'Sit down,' she invited, and seated herself without further ceremony on a tall stool at one of the benches, pulling one of the shrouded shapes towards her on a board.

'May I have a look round first? It's all fascinating.'

'Help yourself.'

Helen worked in porcelain, figures mostly, some of people but mainly of animals, strange, almost heraldic representations of wild beasts, twined and scattered with delicate flowers and leaves. It was finely detailed, delicate work, very beautiful, but studying it, Cheryl didn't find it comfortable. She didn't think that she could live in absolute harmony with some of Helen's beasts, there was something bewitched about them, twisted slightly out of true, and her vines and flowers had a touch of the surreal that was rather disquieting. She fired, but often didn't glaze, or only partly glazed, her work, and she never made two pieces the same. She explained this, almost absent-mindedly, to Cheryl as she unwrapped an elongated giraffe with a neck entwined by a strangulating vine, and picked up a modelling tool to begin work.

'When Oliver was a little boy, I always hoped that he might have inherited something from me,' she said. 'He didn't, though. I don't think I ever met anyone so determinedly uncreative as he is.'

'That's strange,' said Cheryl, feeling that she was expected to say something. 'Perhaps he was badly taught – he has very artistic hands, after all. Like yours.'

Helen laughed.

'That thing about artistic hands is very largely a myth,' she said. 'One of the greatest painters I've ever known had square, rather blunt hands, more like an artisan. When it comes down to it, it's what you see that counts, and Oliver is like his father in that respect, whatever he bothers to look at is boringly practical. The rest just goes over his head.'

Cheryl remembered Oliver finning around a Cornish cove with her, lovingly pointing out anemones and fronds of floating weed and glittering, flashing shoals of tiny fish, but Helen seemed disposed to be confiding and she didn't interrupt. She perched herself on the still-dusty backless chair and prepared to listen and learn.

Helen was talking almost, it seemed, to herself, with more than half her attention on what she was doing.

'When he was very small, while I was still married to his father, he used to play in my studio while I worked, messing about with bits of clay like other children do with plasticine.' She paused, intent on some tiny detail, and Cheryl had time to reflect that that answered one question, at least. She had often speculated, privately, as to whether Oliver's parents had actually been married. The answer it now appeared was yes, they had.

Helen laid down her spatula and picked up another, finer tool, a tiny, nib-shaped loop of wire on a stick, tapping it against the palm of her hand and frowning, either at what she had just done, or what she was about to say, it was unclear which.

'I used to watch him, but he had no real feel for clay. He messed around with coloured crayons, like all children do, and I thought once or twice that there was something there ... but perhaps it was simply wishful thinking. Anyway, his father said I neglected him and sent him off to a kindergarten to play with other children in a sandpit, and that was that. They tried to teach him to draw spongiform trees and pin men, and he downed tools. He just wasn't interested. I sympathised, actually. But that was it. End of story.'

'He must have been very young,' said Cheryl. 'Does artistic talent show that early?'

'Not like music does – musical talent shows earlier in a child than anything else in the world – but yes, you can often see some promise. Oliver was a sensitive little boy, he appreciated beauty, but he grew out of it, unfortunately, and I often wonder how much I was to blame.' She let the sentence die, and resumed her work.

There was no way, thought Cheryl, that Oliver could ever really have talked to his mother if she believed that. Not only Oliver's awareness of the beauty of the undersea world, but his sensitive empathy with ships and great oceans, and the way that she had sometimes heard him speak of the lonely days and nights he had spent at sea with *Lawley's Girl*, all these contradicted her.

Helen had gone off onto a new tack, her brow furrowed in concentration as she scooped delicate slivers of clay from a tiny hoof.

'How do you get on with his family?' she asked.

'Oh ...' said Cheryl. That was a loaded question if ever she heard one. 'We don't see that much of them.'

'Which is to say, badly. Well, I'm not surprised.'

'His father is always kind when we meet,' ventured Cheryl, surprised to realise that this was true. Kind, and a bit apologetic. But unyielding anyway. Hopeless.

'Oh, he would be. About as imaginative as a mud puddle, but kind – very kind – you wouldn't think, would you, that he was such fun when I married him?' She added, apparently still concentrating, although her tool was held motionless, 'What about her? The Dreaded Dot?'

'Mrs. Nankervis?' Cheryl hesitated, and Helen looked up with a wry look.

'Don't mind me, I can't stand her. She ruined my son and turned him into an outlaw. I believe she set him against me, telling lies, although I can never prove it. You can say what you like.'

Cheryl felt her feet on shifting sand, and replied with caution. 'Actually, she's not my sort of person.'

'How terribly diplomatic! What you mean is, she disapproves of you and doesn't care who knows it. There's nothing like a self-confessed Good Christian Woman for dreary intolerance! Hymns and praying every Sunday, the odour of good works around her like incense, and a mind as closed and narrow as a coffin! If I'd known a woman like that would have had the rearing of Oliver, I'd have killed her first!' She broke off, looking embarrassed. 'I'm sorry.'

Cheryl said nothing, and after a moment, Helen said, 'Chel –' She had fallen almost at once into Oliver's name for her. Nobody else had done so, so far. 'Chel – you won't take it amiss, will you, if I tell you – don't make an enemy of her. It's not a good idea.' Her face had taken on a shut look, as if she looked on something inward and primitive and dark. Then she gave herself a shake and added briskly. 'How about Susan? She making a blight of herself, as usual?'

'We don't have a lot in common,' said Cheryl, cautiously. She was wary of Susan for a potential troublemaker, but didn't feel she knew her well enough to offer an informed opinion. To her surprise, Helen said, 'Poor Susan,' and sounded as if she really meant it.

Cheryl was surprised.

'Why poor? She seems to me very well able to look after herself.'

'Oh ... because whatever you think about her, she's had some rotten breaks. She's so under her mother's thumb, poor darling, and Deb is just as untamed as Oliver, bless her. If you're shut into yourself like Susan, being bossy and aggressive is your only defence, of course. She was jealous of Oliver right from the start, and it says everything you need to know about that woman that she said – to her own child, mark you – *Oliver is your brother now, we don't have favourites in this house*, so that the poor kid thought Oliver was her mother's favourite just like he was everyone else's. That's what heavenly impartiality does for you! And Oliver didn't even want her to like him, which only made it worse.'

Cheryl felt as she might if she had picked up a book from which the centre pages were missing. She did a little mental arithmetic to try to bridge the gap. Susan was perhaps two years younger than Oliver, but Oliver had been old enough to be sent to school while his mother was still living in the family home. Deborah, on the other hand, from the little she had heard of her, was only about nineteen or twenty. Therefore, since nobody could imagine Dorothy Nankervis in the role of a little bit on the side, it followed that Susan couldn't be Oliver's true sister, not even his half-sister. His stepsister, merely. It clarified one or two points that had been puzzling her.

'She was married before – Oliver's stepmother?'

'Oh yes, didn't you know? Respectably widowed, of course, not unrespectably divorced like harum-scarum me. I always thought he died to get away from her.' Helen sounded waspish. 'Jerry – Oliver's father – and she were old friends. He used to grumble with her about me, about all the rows we used to have, and the way his son was growing up a heathen under my influence, and later on, about the way I kept house – or didn't keep it. Most of it actually began with her and went full circle; she's one of those old-fashioned domestic women they don't make any more, and she thought, and I think made him think too, that I should give up work to polish the furniture, and see that Oliver went to Sunday school, which he didn't in the least want to do. There was never any suggestion that *he* should help too, when he got home. She used to say –' Helen's pale skin suddenly flushed with remembered anger. 'She used to say, *Helen darling, it's only a little hobby for you, not like a real job*, oh, so sweetly! And I had already had two exhibitions up in London, and I was getting enquiries and commissions from all over the world! It wasn't even as if we couldn't afford to have someone to come in and do the cleaning for us, I made almost as much as he did in a good year.'

There was more to this story, obviously, than she was being told, but a definite picture was emerging. Who had married first? Cheryl wondered. Dorothy or Helen? There were some dark threads in the weave, and several people, she instinctively felt, had suffered. And Dorothy had come out the winner, hadn't she? In the end. Or hadn't she?

Helen said, quietly, 'It was certainly she who sold him the idea that letting Oliver run wild about my studio instead of playing with him, and walking to the shops every day, was neglecting him, he would never have thought that for himself, the child was so obviously happy. He was a sunny little soul... you wouldn't think it to look at him now, would you? *She* did that! He was much, much happier than her miserable little over-protected brat, with never a minute to itself! But anyway, we had row after row – over everything, but mainly over Oliver – and then, in the end, I found out something ... and it was all suddenly beyond redemption. It seems silly now.' She gave herself a shake, and ended briskly. 'So I left, and Oliver has never forgiven me for leaving him too. I'm not sure that I've ever forgiven myself, either.'

'So why did you?' asked Cheryl.

'It seemed the only thing to do at the time – to Jerry, anyway, and he had the big guns, he's a solicitor.' Helen put down her modelling tool and rested her chin on her hands, her elbows on the table, staring out of the open window beside her. 'We'd been quarrelling for years by that time – all Jerry's patience and understanding, that I once so loved in him, seemed to have seeped away – and most of the rows were about Oliver, and he wasn't stupid, he knew what was going on. I'd completely gone to pieces between the two of them – Jerry and Dot – I could do nothing but cry when I was alone, I couldn't work or do anything sensible. I felt as if my head was stuffed full of cotton wool all the time. I was frustrated and hurt and angry, and I had been made to feel such a fool, Chel, you have no idea! Then, when the Big Bang finally came, she was the one who said it would be easier for me without a child to look after. I had no home to give him, she said, and it would be better for Oliver to have stability after all the upheaval, and a little sister to play with. Jerry agreed, of course, and I hadn't a leg to stand on, I'd seen to that myself.' She shrugged her shoulders. 'Everyone told me I'd done the right thing, but – oh, *I missed him so*, and I very soon knew they were wrong. He spent his whole childhood ensuring that his home was as unstable as possible, so it couldn't have been right, could it? And he'd run away three times before he was sixteen, and found something even more dangerous to do to upset everyone.' She paused, frowning. 'I took something from Oliver – not the obvious thing, some anchor point. I don't know exactly what it was, there are too many options. I don't think he knows either, but without it he's adrift. You know him – you love him – but even you can't deny that he's achieved precisely nothing, in real terms, all his adult life. He works hard, but sticks with nothing. He isn't satisfied, not even now, and he's always searching for something that he never finds.'

'Sailing round the world isn't nothing. And he's got himself a steady job now,' ventured Cheryl, offering a crumb of comfort, but Helen only laughed at her.

'Chel darling, we've seen it all before,' she said. 'He's never lacked a job, that I will say, but steady? Believe me, this time next year he'll be doing something quite different, and God alone knows what it will be. He's growing older every year, and his life is just drifting away.' She turned to look directly at Cheryl. 'Marriage, and children – what on earth will he make of them?'

'It's all new territory,' offered Cheryl.

'Uncharted, too! What will you do, Chel, when a year from now, he turns round and tells you he's going to sail the Pacific in a bathtub, or something?'

'Make sure he has the tap end?' said Cheryl, instantly, but Helen didn't smile.

'It's all you can do, I suppose, and at least that way you'll hang onto him for now, but what about if there are babies? What will you do then? Oliver might stay – for a little while – but he'll have to change out of all recognition before he does it willingly, or for long.'

Cheryl had thought about this sometimes, usually in the dead hours before dawn, and found no answers that satisfied her. She brought out the best that she had managed so far.

'Then he'll have to go on his own, and I'll wait for him to come back,' she said. 'Other women do.'

'And will you like it?'

Cheryl hesitated, but answered honestly, since honesty seemed to be what Helen expected from her. 'No. But I shall have to lump it.'

'You won't be tempted to make a scene and try to stop him?'

'Tempted – yes. I hope I shall manage not to.'

'Dot and Susan think that you're giving in to him too much, encouraging him to be even more self-centred than he already is, do you know that?'

'Not exactly, but I know they don't like me. But at the moment, what suits him suits me – if he's an adventurer, I think I must be a bit of an adventuress.'

Helen swung round on her stool and faced her. This left the window at her back, and made her expression difficult to see.

'Would you like to know why? Why they don't like you?'

There had been so many possible, even probable reasons that Cheryl had never felt it worth raking over the ashes to be specific, but at this she felt curiosity.

'Why, then?'

'Apart from the obvious one, that they consider themselves better than everyone else, which you mustn't take any notice of – it's to do with Joanna. You know about Joanna, I take it?'

Cheryl felt suddenly sick.

'She was going out with him when he went off round the world.'

'She considered herself virtually engaged to him, my darling. It would have been an unmitigated disaster, but she's a very attractive girl and they enjoyed similar things – sailing and driving fast cars – not that Oliver's bothered that much about cars, but she is – they knocked around together for a while. But she was terribly possessive, and when he started this sailing-round-the-world thing, she made scene after scene, until in the end I think he went just to get away from it all. Then she was sorry, of course, but when he came home, instead of letting her fall on his neck and say so, he went off with you and only came back to announce he was going to marry you. Joanna is a friend of Susan's, and whatever you may say about her – and you may – Susan is loyal to her friends. She accused Oliver of getting married on the rebound, and he didn't like it, but that isn't the point. What is the point, and what you shouldn't overlook, is that scenes or no scenes, Oliver went. And he'd do it again, in the same circumstances. He loves you, but he won't give you his freedom, and if I know Oliver at all, he's told you so.'

The prison, and the ball and chain ...

'Yes,' said Cheryl. 'He has.'

'Then you're very brave to marry him just the same, because he meant it.' Helen looked down at her hands. 'Oliver has a grudge against life. I don't think he realises it himself. I've told you he was a little demon as a child, and I'm sure dear Dot hasn't missed the chance to tell you that he was a perfect menace as a teenager, at least until his interest in sailing resurfaced. That gave him a legitimate outlet for his energy, of course. Did you know, she tried to keep him away from boats?'

'I had some idea, yes. Things Oliver said ... was it deliberate?'

'She said she was afraid he'd drown Susan, playing about by the water – some chance! He wouldn't have her near him! No, she did it out of spite, because she knew he loved them. What was I saying?'

'About Oliver – being a menace, and interested in sailing.'

'Oh yes. He's spent all his time since then, either on or under water, pushing himself to the limit and putting years on us all. He doesn't do it from any particular sense of commitment, he does it simply for the hell of it, as he's done everything, all his life. To spite us – to spite life – and the fact that he's one of the most charismatic people I know, for all he's my own son, doesn't alter a thing. His way of life frightens me silly.'

'He always seems to come back safely,' Cheryl tried to comfort her. Helen looked at her as if she thought that remark was stupid – as, on reflection, perhaps it was.

'I should like more than anything to see Oliver fulfilled and at peace with himself,' she said. 'Perhaps you'll find the secret, I do hope so. He's taken challenge as a substitute for ambition, and he's never cared enough for anyone to be afraid. But he cares for you. You've understood for yourself that you'll hold him best by letting him go, but it isn't enough. It isn't fair to you, and it doesn't help him.' She paused. 'Have you met Deb?'

'Not yet.'

'You will. She'll be at the wedding.'

'I doubt it. I doubt if any of them will. They'll boycott the whole show.'

'Don't bet on it, you know. Jerry will make them. And Deb, I have to tell you, will want to be there. There, have I surprised you?'

'Yes,' admitted Cheryl.

'You'll like her. Yes you will, don't look at me like that. I promise you. I don't know how she managed it, but she somehow managed to bypass Dot's stodginess, and she certainly bypassed her virtue. She's Oliver's sister, in every way but having me for her mother. I wish, very much, that she was mine. Deb builds bridges.'

A silence fell. Helen picked up her spatula again after a moment or two, and resumed her work, and when she next spoke it was to ask about Cheryl's brothers and sisters, and any intimate revelations about her son seemed to be over. Cheryl was left with a distinct impression of somone desperate to absolve her own guilt and trying for, but missing, understanding. Two things at least were clear enough, she had been right to sense that Oliver didn't like his lively, lovely mother, for whatever reason, and his family affairs were far more tangled than she had begun to guess.

'Will you be there on Tuesday?' Cheryl asked, when the sound of the dogs barking announced Oliver's return. Helen laughed, not in amusement.

'No, my darling, I will not. But I shall be with you in spirit, and wishing you well.'

'I wish you would. I'd like you to be there.'

'Thank you. But no. It wouldn't do.' Helen leaned across and kissed her, feather-light, on the cheek. 'There's a thing you must know about the Nankervis men. You don't stop loving them.'

Before Cheryl could find her voice, the dogs charged in through the door, Oliver strolling in close behind them, and the moment was lost for ever. Of all the things she had learned during that informative afternoon, that was the one, tossed into the pot at the last moment, almost casually, that Cheryl never forgot. She thought it was the saddest thing she had ever heard.

'What did you think of my mother?' asked Oliver, as they drove home.

'I liked her. She's good fun. And she loves you.'

'She had a funny way of showing it. When it came to the push, she didn't hesitate to ditch me for her own interests.'

That was unfair, Cheryl thought, but didn't say so. He didn't sound unduly disturbed by it, and it had been a long time ago. She wondered if he knew that nearly everyone around them expected him to do exactly the same to herself one day, and if he really would.

'One good thing, though,' said Oliver, carelessly. 'She doesn't bother me much.' And thinking of the stripped and hungry woman that they had left behind them, it was the first time that Cheryl had been angry with him.

XIII

'So, how did you like Oliver's mother?' asked Marilyn.

'She's OK. Good fun. She showed me her studio,' Cheryl replied cautiously. She felt she was being stalked, set up to be pounced upon. She had often felt it lately, it seemed to her. She was beginning to be very tired of it.

Marilyn opened her mouth to say something, thought better of it, and picked up her teaspoon. Around them, the department store coffee shop bustled with activity and buzzed with talk. There would never be a more private moment, not before tomorrow, that was certain, and there would certainly never be a good moment, not if she waited a lifetime, for what she needed to say. Like Cheryl, she was weary of the fighting, but she knew that if she didn't pursue the battle until the very last ditch, and after that something went terribly wrong, she would blame herself for ever.

'Cecily Holmes says that she's a very odd woman.' This was buying time, Marilyn realised, and therefore cowardly. She despised herself.

Cheryl looked derisive.

'She would! She's not a *conventional* woman, but odd? No. I didn't think so.'

Marilyn sighed.

'Yes love, but the things you think at the moment are very much governed by what Oliver thinks, be honest.'

'Oh Mum!' exclaimed Cheryl. 'Do give me credit for being able to think for myself! Anyway, I'm certainly not going by what Oliver thinks this time, he doesn't get on with her. I liked her.'

'Cheryl ...'

'Mum, unless you're planning to do a Yuri Geller, I should put that teaspoon down. You're not doing it any good.'

Marilyn dropped the teaspoon hurriedly back into the saucer.

'It's my life,' said Cheryl, quietly.

'I know.' Marilyn looked at her daughter, and a lump came into her throat. 'Cheryl, you've not known him a month. Please.'

Cheryl said, 'We've come out to buy my wedding dress. It was your idea.'

'I know, *I know*!'

'You'd better just say it. Get it over with,' suggested Cheryl. 'It's a background thing, isn't it? You're still worrying about his la-di-da family. Please don't.'

'No, it's not just that,' said Marilyn. Now or never. 'It's Oliver, too. Your Dad and me, we'd do anything for you, Cheryl. Anything we could do. But you must get it through your head that one thing we're never going to do is feel easy with Oliver. You say it doesn't matter about you not fitting into his family, because he has nothing to do with them if he can help it. We find that sad. And I just want to remind you that you're different. You *do* have something to do with your family, and we hope you plan to go on having it.'

'What are you saying?' asked Cheryl, her throat suddenly tight. 'That Oliver won't be welcome in Whytham?'

'Of course not! Don't be so silly. I'm just trying to make you see that things won't be the same. When you and your husband come visiting, it won't be like Trace and Tom and the kids piling in. It can't be. There's nothing in common, don't you see?'

'There's me in common,' said Cheryl.

'Yes.' Marilyn picked up the spoon again, stirring her tea without looking at Cheryl.

'You mean,' said Cheryl, speaking carefully, 'that I'll change. Don't you?'

Marilyn looked at her sadly.

'You already have. In just this few weeks, you've grown away. Don't you feel it yourself?'

'Everyone changes when they get married. Tracy did. It's called growing up, but you never made this fuss about her marrying Tom. She's changed still more since she had the children, but she's still Tracy, isn't she? And I'll still be Cheryl.'

'No, you won't,' said Marilyn. 'You'll be *Chel.* And she'll be someone who belongs somewhere else.'

'Not to the Nankervises!' cried Cheryl, revolted.

'Oh no. And not to us, either. She'll be someone very slightly ashamed of where she comes from.'

Cheryl stared at her in horror.

'Mum! How can you possibly think that!'

'Because it's already happened. I was watching you, that night at their house. You thought your Dad and me was behaving like country bumpkins. And perhaps we were. But that's what we *are*, to them.'

'I would *never* look at you through their eyes!'

'You did,' said Marilyn.

Cheryl went scarlet, and tears started to her own eyes.

'I just wanted you to stand up to them a bit. They were being horrible!'

'No, Cheryl. They were just making a point, and so are we. Trying to, anyway.'

Cheryl wiped a finger under her eyelashes and felt the tear run hot over her skin. She was angry, but clearheaded, feeling this continuing, even if gentle, opposition shoring up her own determination. Was she just being stubborn? She did hope not, because an awful lot – her whole life – rested on this.

'You're putting a very high price tag on Oliver,' she said. Marilyn shook her head.

'No love. It was always there.'

'Bugger!' said Cheryl, with deep feeling.

'If it's any comfort to you,' said Marilyn, reluctantly, 'it was there for anyone. Not just you. Your Dad and me, we just want to be sure that you'd read the ticket.'

'Oh *Mum!*' Cheryl hesitated. 'Not everyone, surely. Joanna Rendell – Susan's friend – she wouldn't be frozen out by his family. She's one of them.'

Marilyn gave her a faint smile.

'You still haven't seen it, have you, Cheryl?'

There was a silence. Cheryl stared defiantly across the table and Marilyn met her eyes sadly. It went through Cheryl's mind, absurdly she knew, to confide to her mother her conviction that Oliver had spent the night of his return home with Joanna, and come to her only the day after. She couldn't know this for certain, of course, she never would *know* it. Had they quarrelled, had he really walked into the Queen's that morning just to spite Joanna? Helen didn't think so. Helen thought that Joanna had been history long before then. Scenes. Never make scenes. To cover an impulse that she knew would be a terrible mistake, she said instead, 'Seen what?'

Marilyn said, 'Oliver isn't a family person. It's him that puts up the real barriers. I can't believe you haven't noticed.'

An outlaw. Was that what Helen had meant? Cheryl swallowed, and was about to reply, when Marilyn went on, 'He won't be interfered with. And when you marry him, that will go for you, too. He'll draw you in and shut the door, and it'll only be opened on sufferance.'

'You make him sound like a recluse! He's got lots of friends.'

'Oh yes. You'll always have lots of friends around, though close friends, I wouldn't bet on. It's we relations you may find you miss.'

Cheryl said quietly, 'I can't help it, Mum. If you insist on making it a choice between Oliver and you, then it's Oliver.

But I wish you wouldn't.' She hesitated. 'But you did mean it, when we come, we'll be welcome?'

'Of course you will!' said Marilyn. 'Both of you. You're our child, whatever happens, aren't you? Dad's girl, particularly, he won't change. It's just ...'

'Just what?'

'I don't think you'll come very often,' said Marilyn, simply. 'Drink your coffee, it's getting cold. Then we'd better go and choose this dress, if your heart's set. What about little Candy for a bridesmaid?'

'Mum, the wedding is tomorrow. Anyway, Oliver –'

'It's *your* day, Cheryl. That's traditional. Yours and maybe mine, for he's got you for the rest of your life, or that's the idea. If you want a bridesmaid, you have one, just this once do what *you* want.'

'And Micky too, rampaging around as a page boy? It's a tempting idea, but I think not, thank you!'

'Well, perhaps you're right. There's not a lot of time.' She sighed. She did it quietly, but Cheryl heard it just the same.

'Mum, isn't there just one thing that makes you feel better? Just one plus among all the minuses?'

But Marilyn wouldn't answer her directly.

'I'd sooner have seen you marrying Jonathan, and that's a fact,' was all she would say.

This conversation might have boded ill for the rest of the day, but having said her say and allowed Cheryl hers, Marilyn made herself accept that there was nothing more she could say, or do, that would alter things and she set out to be generous. Cheryl, relieved that the third degree was now over and that she seemed to have made her point, was happy to meet her mother halfway. Both of them, perhaps, realised that they had passed some point of no return, both of them felt a small, premonitory chill of loss.

That fork in the bloody road, thought Cheryl, trying on dresses, and the wind of change whistling round the corners like a tornado! Oh Auntie Maudie, you're going to have a lot to answer for, I never expected *this* when I was eleven years old, and you told me my life would take a surprising turn!

'Is Auntie Maudie coming to the wedding?' she asked Marilyn, twirling to display a cream silk dress and jacket.

'God forbid!' said Marilyn. 'She must be about ninety! Anyway, we don't want her rushing in crying *Woe, woe and thrice woe!* like some old soothsayer, we've troubles enough without that!'

'*Mum!*'

'Oh, I didn't mean your Oliver, I've had my say on that subject. I just hope, Cheryl Nankervis-to-be, that when your daughter gets married, she at least lets you know how many's coming to the wedding!'

'What do you think?' asked Cheryl, spreading her hands to display her finery. Marilyn looked at her. The dress was low-necked, narrow waisted and wide-skirted, the jacket a tiny bolero, the rich fabric was shot with gold. It wasn't Marilyn's idea of a wedding dress, which surely ought to be white and long and frothy, with a veil and flowers, but even so a lump came into her throat. Cheryl looked lovely. Her skin was pale brown from the Cornish sun, her hair like red gold, shining on her shoulders. The cream and gold fabric suited her a treat. Marilyn held out her arms, gathering her daughter to her.

'You look like a princess!' she said. They hugged each other, differences forgotten.

'Perhaps Madam would care to try this hat?' said the salesperson.

They arrived back at the Queen's, tired but satisfied and loaded with boxes and bags, to find that Tracy and Tom and the children had just arrived. It hit Cheryl then.

'Oh God!' she cried, hugging her sister. 'I'm getting married tomorrow! Oh Trace, I can't believe it!'

Tracy hugged her back. Candy tugged at her skirt.

'Auntie Cheryl, I've got my party frock.'

'Have you, sweetheart?' Cheryl released Tracy and bent to pick up her niece. 'I bet that looks smart!'

'She wanted to be a bridesmaid,' said Tracy.

'I don't,' said Micky, glowering.

Cheryl kissed Candy.

'That's a good thing, because you'd look pretty funny in a party frock! Sorry, Candy love, I'm not having bridesmaids, but your dress will look lovely anyway, I just know it!'

'I want flowers!' said Candy, aiming a swipe at her aunt's nose. Cheryl reared away.

'Oi, I don't want a black eye for my wedding! Be careful, you big bully! Aunt battering is a criminal offence!'

'What's a kimmel fence?' demanded Candy.

'It's what you keep jarffs behind,' said Tracy, firmly. 'Put her down, Cher, you'll do your back in and end up crawling to the altar on your hands and knees!'

'No altar,' said Cheryl. 'Registry office. Remember?'

'*I* wouldn't get married in a noffice,' said Micky, scornfully.

'Face like yours, you'll be lucky to be married at all!' said Tom. He gave Cheryl a hug. 'Congratulations, Cher. You can see your nephew is really happy for you!'

Cheryl returned the hug. The warm family tide flowed round her in a babble of talk, comforting as coming home after a long absence. Although this was all about her marriage to Oliver, that suddenly seemed unreal. I belong here, she found herself thinking. Is Mum right, does he belong nowhere? Does he like it like that? I never felt anything like this with Jonathan.

Stop! I've made up my mind. If it's worth doing at all, it's got to be worth the cost.

'Mike had to go back to Belfast, and Richie can't get the day off at such short notice, but Louise is driving down early tomorrow,' Tracy was saying. 'There's a stack of presents in the car – fetch them in, Tom, and give them to Cheryl. Micky, you go and help him – and you Candy, and don't drop anything. Give her Auntie Maudie's parcel to carry, Tom, it's squashy.'

'Presents?' said Cheryl, blankly, as her family obediently ran to do Tracy's bidding.

'You know. Those things people give you when you get married. Antimacassars and things.'

'*Antimacassars?*'

'I wouldn't put it past Auntie Maudie,' said Tracy, darkly. 'She crochets them. Now then, where's your lovely Oliver? I'm dying to meet him!'

Cheryl, for some reason, hadn't imagined anyone giving them presents, the whole idea of their marriage had met with such a storm of protest, and anyway, they had planned it to be quiet and private. But Tom was coming through the door now carrying a large square box, with the children staggering behind with their arms full of coloured parcels. Tracy hurried to meet them.

'Watch it, Tom, don't drop that – Cher, what should we do with this? It's a cake. I made it and Mrs. Peasgood's niece iced it for you, it's all over little flowery things and I've been terrified all the way down that – what's the matter?'

Cheryl burst into tears.

Marilyn and Tracy lunged forward together, but it was Bob who got there first. Sweeping his daughter into his arms, he rocked her as if she was a child again.

'Don't cry, my lovely, there, don't cry.' And then, 'I'm sorry, love. It's all right. Please don't cry.'

Cheryl, her face buried in his shoulder, said something inaudible that ended in a howl. Guests passing through the foyer turned their heads to stare. Jeanette, watching sympathetically from behind the reception desk, offered to send for tea and mentioned that the bar was open. Candy dropped her armful of parcels on the carpet and ran to fling her little arms round her aunt's legs. The whole group teetered dangerously.

'It was the cake,' sobbed Cheryl, when she had regained control of her voice. 'I never expected a cake, or anything! Oh!'

'Here, don't start again, or I shall wish I never made it.' Tracy handed her a tissue. Cheryl blew her nose, still in the shelter of her father's arms.

'I'm so sorry, I don't know what came over me. Oh, I do love you all!' Tears welled up again. Marilyn said briskly, 'That's enough, you'll have Candy coming out in sympathy in a minute, and you know what that will mean!'

Cheryl looked at Candy. Candy's eyes were screwed tight, her mouth opening ready to wail. Her heart ached with emotion, not just for the little girl but for them all. Her family. She did love them, it was simply that she loved Oliver more, and that she couldn't help. She fell on her knees and hugged Candy tightly. Nothing, nobody, would ever come between them! Her tears mingled with the child's, helplessly, and Oliver pushed through the swing doors to be faced with this perfect family cameo.

'Waaaaa!' bawled Candy, and Cheryl snivelled helplessly. Marilyn looked a little watery too. Oliver's eyes met Bob's in mutual, and totally masculine, horror.

'Time for a beer,' said Bob, firmly.

Later in the evening, another scene, rather less amusing took place in the foyer.

Oliver had joined the family for dinner, once the children had been put to bed. Cheryl had wondered, after her mother's

178

little talk that morning, if this was a good idea, but Oliver had behaved beautifully, and then taken Tom out with him to have a drink with some friends, as yet unknown to Cheryl, to celebrate his last night of unwedded bliss. He and Cheryl were only able to snatch a few quick moments together, while Tom went upstairs to squash Candy, who was refusing to go to sleep in a strange room. Tracy had refused to go.

'I've been up three times already. You're getting a whole evening off, so you can go up and do your worst now.' She smiled at Cheryl and Oliver, and drifted tactfully towards the door of the lounge, through which Bob and Marilyn had already gone. 'See you tomorrow, Oliver. Don't let anyone put you on a train to Edinburgh.'

''night,' said Oliver. He drew Cheryl through the swing doors and out onto the step. The soft May evening closed round them. Isolated among the people strolling along the seafront, he took her in his arms, and just held her there, comfortably. Cheryl rested her cheek against his chest.

'I'm sorry,' she said. 'It's all running away with us, isn't it? You didn't want a fuss.'

'Don't worry about it,' said Oliver. 'It's only a day. I can stand it, me! I've seen the icebergs in the Southern Ocean in the middle of a storm, your family doesn't faze me. Not even young Candy.'

Cheryl giggled, just a ghost of her old self.

'You were marvellous. I couldn't believe it, she ate out of your hand.'

'Ah, but then you don't give me credit for being an uncle of some years experience.'

She raised her head.

'*Are* you?'

'One nephew, one niece. Annabel and Sebastian, poor little buggers. They'll be yours, too, this time tomorrow.'

'The things I don't know about you,' said Cheryl, snuggling close. His arms tightened round her, she felt his breathing quicken.

'You aren't having any regrets? It's still all right?'

My family don't like you, yours don't like me, they hate each other. She knew what he was thinking without him putting it into words. Against the background of the family meal they had just sat through, it had a whole new meaning. He knew now, at least in part, where he couldn't have known before, just what he was asking her to give up. She didn't expect to see a great deal of Annabel and Sebastian Casson.

'I love you best. You're enough,' said Cheryl.

He kissed her at last, gently, on the lips.

'Then I'll see you at the register office at eleven. Goodnight, Chel my darling. Sleep well.'

Tom came through the swing doors, and hesitated when he saw them.

'Goodnight, Tiger,' said Cheryl.

'Tiger?' Oliver sounded startled.

'The sort you get by the tail.'

All three of them laughed. Cheryl went back indoors, strangely comforted.

She went through to the lounge to join her parents and Tracy over a cup of coffee, where they were shortly joined by Candy, trailing a depressed-looking stuffed duck called Sage'n'onion, and complaining that she couldn't sleep because Micky was making silly nòises. Tracy gathered her up without argument onto her knee.

'He snores,' she said, resignedly. 'It's his adenoids. I think he'll end up having to have them out.'

Having got her own way as usual, Candy's eyelids drooped heavily. None of them was feeling talkative, the events of the past dramatic week had left all of them drained. It had been a struggle, Marilyn reflected as she sipped her coffee, in which there could be no winners. But at least Bob and his beloved Cheryl were back on good terms with each other, and Oliver, whatever he might have been thinking, was far too well brought up to let anybody know what it was. In fact, dinner had been quite a pleasant meal. She supposed that was what people meant when they talked about *breeding*. Not something that the Wainwrights had ever had much of, although they knew their manners, of course. Not that there had been any suggestion of condescension on Oliver's part, but Marilyn knew that he had fitted in with Cheryl's family far more easily than she and Bob, or even Cheryl, had with his, and that, in some way, it had been calculated. She frowned, unable to work it out to her satisfaction, but relieved that he was at least prepared to go that far for Cheryl. Bob had picked up a magazine and was idly turning the pages, the two girls talked quietly over the head of the sleepy child. Marilyn realised that she would be glad when tomorrow was safely over. She had never before been so uncertain of what was going to happen at a wedding. Tracy's had never been like this!

Out in reception, Maeve had taken over the shift from Jeanette, and was finding it unexpectedly interesting. She had seen Oliver and Tom leave, and not ten minutes later, three people, a man and two women, had come in to have a drink in the bar. The couple, Maeve didn't know, but she knew the other girl. Dark, dramatically beautiful, and already slightly tipsy, Joanna Rendell was a well-known figure in the town. Maeve found herself thinking, wistfully, that it would be pleasant to bring her and Cheryl face to face, she looked ripe for making a scene already, after a drink or two more her performance could be spectacular. What a shame that she had just missed Oliver, that would have been really something.

Unfortunately, she couldn't think up a pretext to bring her face to face with Cheryl. Maeve felt spiteful towards her immediate superior. From being the one most likely to find herself signing on at the Job Centre, she had announced her engagement and suddenly become flavour of the month, and in some strange way, in doing so she seemed to have sent Maeve's own star into decline. There was also Oliver himself. Maeve envied Cheryl, as well as feeling spiteful about her. She didn't deserve such spectacular good fortune in Maeve's view.

It was quiet tonight, nothing much seemed to be happening. Of course, Monday was always a dead night, people were recovering from the weekend. Maeve covered a yawn and glanced at her watch. Nearly ten o'clock. A while to go yet. She yawned again.

A girl pushed through the swing doors. Maeve looked at her with boredom, she had never seen her before. A scruffy blonde in tight jeans and a skinny sweater, with a big leather bag slung over her shoulder. She came over to the desk.

'I'm looking for Cheryl Wainwright. That's not you, is it?'

She had bright eyes that missed nothing. Another journalist, thought Maeve, with a stab of unholy glee, there had been a few already. Oh, what a wonderful evening this was turning out to be!

She knew exactly where Cheryl was. She could have directed the journalist to the lounge, or gone to fetch Cheryl herself. She chose to do neither.

'No, but she's in the hotel.' She smiled. 'I'll page her for you. One moment.'

'Thank you.' The blonde girl wandered away to peer into the showcases at the jewellery and scarves and china displayed there. Maeve, with a flicker of pious content, picked up the pager. Oh Cheryl, you are going to have such a surprise! I hope.

'Cheryl, there's a visitor in reception for you. Cheryl to reception, please.'

It would be heard all over the ground floor. It would be heard in the bar. Maeve smiled more widely, she couldn't help herself.

'She should be here soon.'

The journalist merely nodded her thanks. Oh girl, get your notebook ready! Maeve silently crowed.

In the bar, Joanna Rendell, already worked up into a state that was making her companions uncomfortable, was steadily drowning her sorrows. The couple had tried to dissuade her from going to the Queen's after their dinner treat "to cheer you up, darling," next door at the Langland, but without success.

'*She's* there,' had said Joanna. 'I want to see her – just see her, that's all.'

'No you don't, Jo,' said Caroline, her friend.

'I won't make a scene, I promise I won't. I just want to remind myself what she's like.' Joanna's eyes filled with tears. 'She's going to marry him tomorrow. I want to see what she's got that I haven't. You understand, don't you George?'

Caroline's husband made a sound that could have been taken to mean anything, but probably indicated nothing more than embarrassment.

'It's not a good idea,' said Caroline. 'Leave it, Jo. Please.'

'She stole him from me,' said Joanna.

Caroline was of the opinion that the truth was more along the lines of, Joanna drove Oliver away, or even that she had never been in with a chance, but she knew that it would be another bad idea to say so. In any case, of the three of them, Joanna was by far the strongest character and so, to the Queen's they went. Here, things went from bad to worse, as both Caroline and George had known they would. Wherever else Cheryl was – and what did she look like, anyway? Joanna couldn't quite remember – it wasn't in the bar, and they could hardly wander all over the hotel hunting for her. There was only one thing to be done, said Joanna, in heartbroken tones. Keep drinking. That way, perhaps she could forget.

George was sympathetic, because after all, Joanna was a lovely girl, poor cow, and that bastard Nankervis had treated her like shit! Caroline, more pragmatic, would have found a sympathiser in Jonathan Holmes, who also had disliked the dramatics. This was turning out to be one really ghastly evening!

Caroline toyed with the idea of slipping off to the ladies, finding this Cheryl, and warning her to keep her head down, but it seemed a bit extreme. The girl was probably out with Oliver anyway. She watched with resignation as George bought yet another round of gin and tonic for her hapless friend, and made an abortive attempt to get them all off the premises.

'Just one more, Jo, then it's time to go,' she said. 'You've had enough, and it really isn't going to help. You know that.'

Joanna wiped a hand across her eyes. Oh God, Caroline thought, with sinking heart, she's gone past the stage of worrying about her mascara. She's pissed as a newt, and no, this is *really* not a good idea. George came back with the drinks. She muttered into his ear,

'No more, George, please, make this the last. She's had enough.'

'Don't be so heartless, Caro! Can't you see the poor girl's in black despair? That shit Nankervis –'

'Oh George, grow up! The poor girl's legless, more like!'

They were about to plunge into a quarrel, when the paging system burst into life.

'Cheryl, there's a visitor in reception for you. Cheryl to reception, please.'

Caroline made a grab, but Joanna was too quick for her. She leapt to her feet, glass in hand.

'*That's her!*'

'George! Grab her!' cried Caroline, but George, staring bemusedly, was too slow. Joanna whisked past him and headed for the door into the hotel foyer.

Cheryl had been a little slower to react. It wasn't until Tracy said,

'That's you, Cheryl. Aren't you going to go?' that she moved at all.

'I'm not expecting any visitor,' said Cheryl. She got reluctantly to her feet. 'If it's another prying pressman, I'll set Candy on him! Back in a minute.'

She walked out into the foyer. At first, all she saw was Maeve, smiling, and Joanna Rendell apparently wrestling with two people at the entrance to the bar, and her immediate reaction was, *Oh no! Not tonight, of all nights!* Then Joanna saw her, wrenched herself free, and strode across the carpet like an avenging fury.

'*That's* for you!' she cried, and threw the contents of her glass into Cheryl's face.

It was a wonderful gesture, even Cheryl later had to admit that. At the time she didn't see the funny side.

'What was that in aid of?' she asked, indignantly. The gin stung her eyes, she rubbed at them fruitlessly, it only made things worse.

Maeve watched in high glee. When it reached punch-up point, which might not be long, she would send for Old MacDonald. Great stuff!

Caroline had Joanna in an armlock learned at her gym, but Joanna went to the same gym and squirmed free. George dabbed at her arm with his hand.

'Come on, old girl, you can't make a scene here.'

'Watch me!' cried Joanna. 'Just watch me!' She swung back her arm, hand flat. Cheryl, still half-blinded, flung out her hands to ward her off. The blonde gave the sorry scene a swift, critical look, allowed her bag to slip from her shoulder to the floor, and stepped forward.

'Get lost, Joanna!' she said.

Everything froze. Caroline said, 'Oh!'

'Nobody'll thank you,' the girl went on. 'Oliver certainly won't. Why don't you just go home and stick your head in a bucket?'

Joanna, as Cheryl had done earlier, standing on almost the same spot, burst into tears. The journalist, handing Cheryl a tissue, went on, 'If she turns up at the register office with a black eye, and it's all over the papers that you hit her – as it would be – how would you feel then? Get a life, for God's sake! Go away! Take her away, Caro, why don't you?'

The fight had gone out of Joanna. She let Caroline and George lead her to the main door, still hysterically sobbing. The girl now turned her attention to Cheryl.

'Go and bathe your eyes, or they'll be bright red tomorrow. I'll wait here.' Without waiting to see what Cheryl would do, she then turned to Maeve. For a moment, she didn't speak. Maeve returned her look, at first defiantly, then with less courage. There was something about the girl – she could only be in her early twenties at most – that was not quite as expected. Was she not a journalist at all? It was an oddly disquieting thought.

So far, the scene had gone without an audience, which Maeve had at first considered disappointing. Now, meeting that unnerving stare, she was changing her mind. First impressions had let her down, she saw. The light brown hair, streaked blonde, had been styled and coloured by an expert, the jeans were designer jeans. Dark grey-blue eyes fringed with black lashes surely reminded her of someone ...

'My name is Deborah Nankervis,' said the girl, and allowed the announcement to sink in. 'And you can wipe that silly smile off your face. Did you know Joanna was here, and in that state?'

Maeve blustered. 'It's no business of mine what people coming in from outside do in the bar. It's the barman's responsibility, dealing with drunks.'

'I asked you if you knew,' Maeve didn't answer. 'I think you did. Who did you think I was, the press?' Further silence answered her clearly enough. 'You are utterly despicable!'

She turned without saying anything more, and went to pick up her bag. Cheryl came out of the cloakroom, rather pink around the eyes but able to see clearly again. They met in the middle of the floor. Deborah Nankervis held out her hand.

'Hi, I'm Debbie. Helen said you were beleaguered, so I came to say hullo. Hullo!'

'Oh – hullo,' said Cheryl, taken aback. She took the offered hand and then found herself being hugged with real warmth.

'Get you!' said Debbie. 'You look like the condemned prisoner, not a bride on the eve of her wedding!' She held Cheryl away from her, and looked at her critically. 'Gin is a bugger when you get it in your eye, but I think it'll be all right. Perhaps it was heavy on the tonic, good thing if so. Where can we go to talk?'

'My family are in the lounge.' Cheryl felt at a loss. No Nankervis she had yet met or imagined had behaved like this. Except possibly Oliver, in a way. She looked like Oliver – slightly squarer in the jaw, blonde, different eyebrows, but no mistaking the relationship even so. His half-sister, of course, not his stepsister, like "poor Susan". Daughter of Oliver's father and the Dreaded Dot.

'Good. Let's go and join them.' Debbie slipped her arm through Cheryl's and turned towards the door of the lounge. Maeve watched them go with mixed feelings. She didn't think that Deborah Nankervis would report her to the management, but she wasn't sure, which was exactly how Debbie had meant her to feel.

The Wainwrights looked up as Cheryl and her companion came over to them. Even Candy, always afraid of missing something, forced an eye open and then closed it again.

'This is Oliver's sister, Debbie,' said Cheryl. Everyone shook hands and Bob drew another chair into the circle so that they could all sit down. For a moment, conversation foundered.

'Do you live in Embridge?' asked Marilyn, politely. Debbie shook her head decisively.

'No fear! Would you? I've just driven down from London for the wedding. Someone had to be there to cheer on our side of the family.' She paused, wondering if that had been the right thing to say, and was relieved to see Tracy suppress a smile. 'Sorry, me and my mouth. We're always getting each other into trouble.'

'You're going to cheer?' asked Bob, folding his newspaper now that better entertainment seemed to be offering.

'Loudly. Anything Oliver wants has to be OK by me. Oh, it's all right, I know they all made a fuss. Take no notice. Really. He won't.'

Candy opened her eyes, properly this time, and sat up to stare at this vivacious stranger.

'Who're you?' she demanded.

'Candy! That's rude,' said Tracy. Candy wriggled off her lap and went to stand in front of Debbie, dangling the unfortunate Sage'n'onion by his beak. Debbie looked down at her.

'I'm Debbie. I'm your almost-aunt, or I shall be tomorrow.'

'My aunties is Auntie Cheryl and Auntie Louise.' Candy scowled.

'That's right, and Auntie Cheryl is going to marry my brother, which will make him your uncle.'

'No she's not. Auntie Cheryl is going to marry Oliver.'

'That's right. He's my brother.'

'He *can't* be your brother!' said Candy, firmly.

'Oh? Why not?'

Candy thought about this for a moment. Perhaps deciding that she was on a sticky wicket here, she changed the direction of her accusations.

'My uncles is *Mummy*'s brothers.'

Debbie picked her up and sat her on her knee. To everyone's surprise, not to say relief, Candy accepted this without protest.

'I want to be a bridesmaid,' she announced.

'Really? That sounds like a nice thing to be.'

'Candy ...' began Tracy.

'Auntie Cheryl says NO!' cried Candy, loudly. Debbie made a tutting noise. The Wainwrights sat entranced.

'Rotten old Auntie Cheryl. Why's she saying that?'

'She says she doesn't WANT ANY!'

'All right, I'm not deaf! I call that mingy – I want to be a bridesmaid too, what d'you think she'll say to that?'

'She'll say –' began Candy, and drew a deep breath. Debbie placed a gentle hand over her mouth.

'OK, OK, no need to tell the whole world! Perhaps we should ask her nicely, and see what she says then.'

'I've got a frock.'

'Really? That's lucky! What colour is your frock?'

'It's PINK!'

Cheryl saw the whole thing galloping out of hand. She watched helplessly. Marilyn was laughing openly, and Bob smothering his laughter with a cough. Tracy had her head in her hands. Debbie shook her head.

'I don't think pink is quite my colour, but I'll have a look in my wardrobe, or perhaps someone else's wardrobe would be a better idea. We'll be the finest bridesmaids in town, you bet on it!'

Candy looked at her as if she didn't quite believe her.

'With flowers?' she asked, belligerently.

'Of course with flowers. Auntie Cheryl will have flowers, we must have flowers too. And a wreath on your head, don't you think?'

Candy nodded vigorously. Cheryl said, apologetically,

'Actually, I wasn't going to carry flowers. It wasn't going to be that sort of a do.'

Debbie settled back in her chair with Candy in her arms. She looked at Cheryl, and then, more searchingly, at Marilyn and Bob. She drew a breath.

'Oh-oh. They *have* spoilt everything for you, haven't they?' She paused, hesitantly. 'Look here, there isn't time to be diplomatic. Will you all forgive me if I'm horribly honest? I really won't mean to be speaking out of turn.'

There was a pause. Nobody was laughing any more, and Debbie looked at them all anxiously. Finally, Bob said,

'All right then, have your say.' He had liked Debbie instinctively, and his voice was heavy with disappointment. Just another Nankervis, then. Debbie drew a breath. She looked uncomfortable.

'I'm in the hot seat here, I know, but we couldn't think of any other way...' She turned to Cheryl. 'Dad sent you to see Helen, right?'

Cheryl was surprised.

'I suppose so ... yes. Or he made Oliver take me, which comes to the same thing.'

'You must understand,' said Debbie, carefully, 'that Dad is in a difficult position. He doesn't think you quite realise ... I mean, you've got to live in this town when it's all over. It's no good expecting Oliver to do anything, he's not bothered about other people and he doesn't see why anyone else should be ...' Her voice tailed off into an awkward silence.

'I think you had better come straight out with it, whatever it is,' said Bob.

'It's just so *embarrassing*.' Debbie bent her head over Candy, hiding her face. When she looked up, she was flushed a delicate pink. 'Oh *bugger!* It's a good thing they never meant me for the diplomatic service, isn't it? Dad was afraid that you were allowing them to trample all over you. Mum and Susan. They do that when they want their own way, there must be juggernaut blood in them somewhere. In me, too, I wouldn't wonder, only I'm more careful where I put my feet.'

'Except when you put them in your mouth?' suggested Bob. Debbie looked uncomfortable.

'Get back to Helen,' said Marilyn, quickly.

'Oh yes.' Debbie looked relieved. 'Dad thought perhaps Helen could help you. He thought ... well, never mind that. Helen liked you, Cheryl. She liked you a lot. When you'd gone, she rang Dad and told him he must straighten things up so people couldn't ... well, she meant Joanna, and that set, really, and haven't you fallen foul of the Mayor, too?'

'Just a bit,' said Cheryl.

'He wants to make sure that there's no nasty gossip. That there's no cause anywhere for anyone to say that Oliver is ashamed of you. Because he isn't. And nor is Dad, actually. And they will, if they can. They'll tell everyone it was a hole-and-corner marriage.' She hid her face again, cuddling Candy to her. Her voice came muffled. 'It's a bloody awful thing to have to say.'

'Hence bridesmaids and flowers?' asked Marilyn. Debbie nodded, without looking up. Bob said, slowly,

'If you are Cheryl's bridesmaid, that puts the Nankervis seal of approval on the whole business, is that it?'

Debbie nodded again. She looked up, and this time she wasn't just pink, but scarlet.

Marilyn said, 'So everything must be small, but perfect tomorrow, so that nobody can criticise?'

'There'll be reporters,' said Debbie. 'Dad wondered if you realised – you know, it'll be a bit public in places. It's bound to be. The dust hasn't settled yet. So it's got to stay The Great Romance. Mills & Boon stuff. For everyone's sake. Oliver can be a bit of an oaf, sometimes – he just doesn't see things like other people!'

The thought that the Nankervises – *any* of the Nankervises – should go to such trouble to protect her amazed Cheryl. Partly, she realised, they were protecting themselves, but even so it was unexpected. Helen must really have liked her, she thought, and was glad. About Jerry and his daughter Debbie she was more circumspect, in their case it was certainly Oliver that they were mainly protecting. Even so, it was pleasant to meet a relative of Oliver's that she could actually like.

'We've done our best,' said Marilyn, a little sadly. 'Trace brought a cake.'

'It's only sponge,' said Tracy.

'Good, I hate fruit cake,' said Debbie. 'Anyway, you must have a bit of attitude – it's not *only* sponge, it's sponge, hooray! That's the line. And there should be music and flowers, and as many of the proper fixings as you can get done in the time. There's going to be a reception, isn't there?'

'Mr. MacDonald is arranging something in one of the conference rooms,' said Cheryl.

'Good for Mr. MacDonald, whoever he is!'

'Only we don't know how many for,' said Marilyn, suddenly realising that she had an ally – of sorts – in the enemy's camp. 'There's no getting any sense out of Oliver, and your mother ...'

'Just sniffs, and says *I really don't know?*' asked Debbie, with deadly accuracy. 'Look, they wanted him to marry Joanna. County set, money, all that rubbish. He didn't. Want to, I mean, and who can blame him? Take no notice of them, when it comes to the crunch they'll bite the bullet.'

'That's what Helen said, but will they?' asked Cheryl.

'Dad will, and Mum will do what he does. You mustn't mind about Susan, it won't be about you.'

'You mean, she won't come to the wedding?' said Marilyn.

'Who knows? Probably not even Susan, at this minute.' She hesitated, looked as if she was about to speak and then changed her mind. She continued smoothly, 'Oliver has a good many friends, and some of them must know he's getting married. They'll be there. Bill Rowlands, and the Ravenscourts, and Bob ...'

'Flowers,' said Marilyn, helplessly. 'There's no time. I never thought.'

'Leave them to me, if you like. I was born in this town, I've got contacts, me!'

She sounded just like Oliver.

'The music will have to be taped.'

'Musak? If we have to, I suppose, but I know some people at the Music School. Will you leave that with me too? I'm not trying to interfere,' she added, hurriedly.

'You're very kind. We appreciate it. If there had been more time ...'

'Look, you don't need to explain to me. I know Oliver, I've known him all my life. He's a law unto himself and he doesn't understand about weddings and things. He can't have been any help at all, don't even bother to tell me!'

'He seems to think that all you need is a date, a time and a registrar,' said Marilyn. 'So very *barren* of him.'

Debbie spoke unexpectedly soberly. 'Cheryl should marry Oliver with all the trumpets and flowers and razzmatazz that you can manage. You love him, Cheryl, tell the world! He needs you to do that. Truly.'

Cheryl didn't think that Oliver needed anything of the kind, but she suddenly realised that she did. She had been put in her place enough by the Nankervises, or what they considered to be her place.

'That's everything, really,' said Debbie. 'You didn't mind, did you? Me saying ... I mean, it seems awful. Really.'

'A dirty job, but somebody's got to do it,' said Tracy.

'I prefer to consider it more as cutting the Gordian knot,' said Debbie. She looked down. 'This child is asleep.'

'I'll carry her upstairs,' said Tracy, standing up. Debbie got to her feet, carefully cradling the sleeping Candy.

'Let me. She'll wake, else. Show me where to go.'

They left the lounge together. Marilyn looked helplessly at Cheryl.

'Now I *really* don't know what's going to happen tomorrow!'

But Cheryl was feeling better than she had done since she and Oliver came back from Cornwall.

'Leave it to Debbie. I have a feeling she'll start at dawn and have it all sewn up before eleven!'

'And you've got bridesmaids, it seems, whether you want them or not. How do you feel about that?'

'Great!' Cheryl stretched her arms wide. Her eyes still stung, but her heart was suddenly light as a bird in flight. Debbie had the same gift that Oliver had, of turning the world upside-down in an instant. She hadn't realised how much it had hurt her, being so completely rejected by Oliver's family, until Debbie had unexpectedly hugged her out there in the foyer. *Deb builds bridges*, Helen had said. Her wedding day, which had, up until now, been lurking in the background as a formality that would have to be got through somehow, suddenly looked joyful.

'And all you wanted was to sneak off together, with a just a couple of witnesses, didn't you? *Didn't you?*'

'Dream on!' said Cheryl.

She had expected her parents to share her own relief, but to her surprise, they both looked unhappy.

'You did like Debbie?' she asked, suddenly doubtful.

'She's a very beautiful girl,' said Bob.

'You'd never take her for anything but his sister,' said Marilyn. This sounded so much like damning with faint praise that a small cloud drifted across Cheryl's sun.

'But –' she began.

'All that business with Candy was very clever,' said Marilyn. 'What it boils down to is, they didn't trust us not to let them down. They sent that girl here deliberately to make sure we did things right.'

'Oh no, I'm sure they didn't!' Cheryl was horrified.

'Looked like it to me,' said Bob. 'Her and her music and flowers and that – as if your mother didn't know what was proper.'

'Maybe they're not wrong, at that,' said Marilyn. 'I wouldn't never have thought about the newspapers, nor people gossiping. We don't live that sort of life where we come from. And those people she mentioned – Ravenscourt, was it? – they've got a place near us, they're titled folk. You know that, Cheryl, if you ever stopped to think.'

'I don't suppose it's the same family,' objected Cheryl.

'I don't know how to entertain folks like that,' said Marilyn, ignoring her. 'We better let her have her way. I'm out of my depth with these grand people you're marrying into.'

'Mum –'

But Marilyn refused to discuss it, and Bob didn't help when he said, 'Leave it, lass, your mother's upset, can't you see?'

What Cheryl saw was that Jerry Nankervis, Helen Macken and Debbie could turn cartwheels if they felt like it, but would never be credited with doing so out of a genuine wish to be friendly and helpful. The damage was already done, the cultural gulf too wide.

'If it's anything to do with Oliver, you just won't have it, will you?' she said, before she had thought. Bob reached for his newspaper.

'We'll pretend you never said that, Cheryl,' he said.

Marilyn had tears in her eyes. Cheryl knew that she ought to have felt sorry, but she simply felt angry. Anger, as well as the effects of gin when applied externally, made her eyes smart warningly. One more minute and there would be a terrible scene, and she suddenly found that, just like Oliver, she couldn't bear the thought of it. They had no right to behave like this, any of them! It was her wedding, hers and Oliver's. Just for a second she even thought wistfully of finding Oliver and running away again, but before this was more than a passing idea, Debbie and Tracy came back into the lounge. Tracy fell into her chair in an attitude of complete exhaustion.

'I now declare this lounge a Candy Free Zone!' she intoned, and closed her eyes. 'She's fast asleep at last, and snoring louder than Micky. Oh bliss!'

'And I must go,' said Debbie. 'I haven't been home yet, they'll wonder where I've got to. I'll see you all tomorrow.'

Marilyn and Bob rose politely to say goodnight, shook hands, murmured all the right things. Debbie stooped to kiss Cheryl.

'Flag nailed to the masthead, remember,' she said. 'Some of us are on your side. Most of us. I'm sorry about the bridesmaids, but you do see, don't you?'

'Yes of course. I'm really grateful.'

Debbie, like her brother, was far from stupid. She must have sensed an atmosphere, for she hesitated. Cheryl willed her to say nothing.

'Until tomorrow then.' Debbie walked to the door, turned and waved, and disappeared from view.

'Nice girl,' said Tracy, in a way that invited comment. Nobody said anything. When the pause became awkward, Marilyn broke it, saying brightly,

'Well, let's all have an early night, shall we? Tomorrow will be quite a day!'

'She said that you –' began Tracy, caught Cheryl's eye and said, 'Oh. Oh, all right then. I'm tired anyway.'

Cheryl walked with her to the stairs.

'She told you about Joanna Rendell, didn't she? Don't tell Mum. I think it would be the final straw.'

'Will you tell Oliver?' asked Tracy. 'Perhaps he ought to know.'

'Perhaps he ought, but he isn't going to. Goodnight Trace.'

'Cheer up, this time tomorrow it'll all be history,' said Tracy, and started up the stairs.

Cheryl turned and made her way, for the last time, towards the service door, the back stairs, and her little room in the staff quarters. Maeve, still on duty for another half hour, pretended to be terribly busy.

'Sleep well with your conscience, Mavis,' said Cheryl.

It was a cheap gibe, she knew it was, but it did make her feel better.

XIV

It wasn't surprising, after such an evening, that Cheryl should sleep badly. Although she fell asleep the minute her head hit the pillow, she awoke after only a few hours, the events of last night teeming in her head, and knowing that she had no hope of dropping off again.

This is just what I don't need, she thought crossly. Bother them, and all their fussing, why couldn't they all leave us alone?

Because *you* didn't want them to, she answered herself. *You*, not Oliver, dragged your family into this, and you must have known they'd want to do things right. They love you, and just because of that, they're going to conflict with Oliver for ever and ever, amen. And part of you is going to want them to, because if they stop you'll have lost them.

At least we didn't fall out over it.

Because he knows damn well that they'll go back to Suffolk after the wedding and leave us in peace. Which is what he wants, Mum's quite right.

Damn what I want.

What *do* I want?

She sat up and hugged her arms around her knees. You couldn't alter people, they would be as they chose to be, and were responsible only for themselves. Her mother and father would think as they chose, they would never shift unless they chose. The same went for Jerry Nankervis and the Dreaded Dot. They would have no influence, ever, on Oliver, and whether or not they influenced herself was up to her. Helen was an outsider anyway, the Dreaded Dot had seen to that somehow. *She made my son an outlaw.* Be careful of the Dreaded Dot. Oh yes.

Did Oliver really need her to make a public display of her love? Had Debbie been trying to say that he was *un*loved? Surely not!

Cheryl rubbed her eyes, they were still sore from the gin. Joanna Rendell and Susan, would they really try and spoil things for her by malicious gossip? Could they, even?

And strangest thought of all, what was Oliver's life really like? Who were his friends, what did they do together?

Tom probably knew more about that than she did by this time.

Tomorrow – no, today now – she was going to marry him. It would be her life too.

What the hell did she think she was doing?

The moonlit square of the window slowly brightened into dawn. Cheryl could see the pale shape of her wedding dress hanging against the wardrobe. Just a simple dress and jacket, Tracy had worn white lace and a veil and carried a huge bouquet.

Debbie would bring flowers.

Debbie probably always would.

Oliver's family were wealthy. What did that make Oliver? She had never asked, never cared. He was just himself. How impractical of her! She was fairly certain, though, that she wasn't marrying a private income, or they would surely have been able to find a bigger flat.

Perhaps those who said she was rushing into this had a point.

Cheryl got out of bed and pattered barefoot to the window. Her room was at the back of the hotel, overlooking the car park and the town. Over the rooftops to the east, the sky was blushing gold and ivory, fading into palest blue. A few tiny clouds puffed across it like a child's drawing. Her wedding day.

Quite suddenly and unexpectedly, her heart lifted. Only a few short hours, and then, for better or worse, it would be over and their new life would start. The family – her family – would go home, his family would have nothing more to say. Happy ever after begins here!

She was about to fling the window wide to let in the morning, when a movement caught her eye. Someone was sitting on the wall behind the rows of parked cars. Just sitting, not doing anything, in an attitude of slumped misery. It was still shadowy down there, but she thought that it was Jonathan, and her heart sank again.

Oh no! Oh no, Jonathan, not today! I won't have it!

The lovely dawn was calling to her to go out. With Jonathan sitting there like Romeo, there was no way she was going out by the back way, what was the matter with him, anyway? Couldn't he take "no" for an answer? Driving himself into a breakdown on her account was unfair!

He had never asked her to marry him, never so much as mentioned marriage, until Oliver appeared on the scene. Cheryl hardened her heart.

She dressed quickly in jeans and a sweater, and slipped down the backstairs and into the foyer through the service door. The duty night porter was yawning behind the desk.

'Let me out through the front, Charlie, there's a love.'

Charlie cocked an eyebrow, he didn't miss a lot.

'Oh, so you spotted him, did you? Been there most of the night, he has. Said he wasn't going to make any trouble, just wanted to be near you. Daft, if you ask me.' He took the keys from the hook behind him, and came out from behind the desk to unlock the swing doors for her. 'Not doing a runner, are you, young Cheryl?'

'I couldn't sleep. Over-excited, I expect.'

'Ah,' said Charlie, holding the door wide for her. 'My daughter, she was just the same. Take care, then.'

The door swung to behind her, and she heard the key turn in the lock. Standing on the steps, she drew a deep breath of the fresh morning air, and then ran down them, across the road, and onto the promenade that bounded the edge of the harbour. She turned away from the marina, superstitious she was not, but she didn't want to run into Oliver this morning, it would be unlucky.

All right, superstitious, she was.

She strolled eastwards along the waterfront towards the bridge over the river from which the town derived its name, with the harbour on her right and the big hotels and blocks of luxury flats on her left, and all the time the light grew stronger. She wasn't sure what the time was, about six o'clock by now, maybe. An occasional car or lorry passed along the road, but otherwise she had the world to herself. It was wonderfully calming.

After a while, she reached the public jetty, which ran out into the harbour and cost people an arm and a leg to tie their boats to, but not as much as the marina. Nor was there a night watchman here, or locked gates. She walked along the jetty to its farthest end and sat down, just beyond the diesel pump, with her feet swinging over the water. It was very quiet, hardly a ripple stirring the mirror-smooth expanse. A flight of birds flew across the sky, calling wildly. The light grew.

Out from the marina, a single yacht emerged, the faint throb of her engine carrying clearly across the water, headed for the open sea. Cheryl could see someone on her deck, doing something at the bottom of the mast. No wind to speak of, but perhaps there would be outside the harbour, and later on. Where were they bound, she wondered? Would Oliver go sailing off like that one day, and if he did, would she be with him? Would she like it, if he did, and she was?

Questions, questions, why ask them? I'm young, thought Cheryl, I have everything ahead of me. Nobody gets it good all the time, but we'll be strong together, Oliver and me, I know it. For that one reason, I need not be afraid. And today, of all days, I can be simply happy.

She closed her eyes. The strengthening sun was beginning to have some warmth to it. Just so had she felt it during those golden Cornwall days that, over this last couple of weeks, had seemed to go so far away. Hang onto them. They are reality, not all this fuss and trouble.

The crying gulls, the blowing seapinks, the blue water crashing in white foam on the rocks, these were what Oliver loved. Not this town, these buildings, the sterile security of the marina. The freedom of the wind, the empty land, the wide sea ... I am doing exactly the right thing, thought Cheryl, and was finally at peace.

When she opened her eyes again, the yacht was gone, out through the harbour entrance and on her way to wherever she was bound. And so am I. Cheryl got to her feet. I am bound to wherever I am going, and the entrance to my own personal harbour is at eleven o'clock, and I, too, am outward bound!

After all the trouble and heartsearching, it took about ten minutes to marry Cheryl to Oliver, and then there she was, back on the steps outside the register office with his ring on her finger and a small crowd of people, most of whom she had never seen before, laughing and congratulating them both.

'I suppose it was legal?' Marilyn was heard to say uneasily, in the background, perhaps with memories of Tracy's traditional white-with-bridesmaids in the parish church at Whytham. Oliver overheard her and looked down at Cheryl with a spark of mischief in his eyes. She wasn't sure, even now, just what Oliver's attitude was to her parents, they were at least as alien to him as he was to them.

'Well, Mrs. Nankervis?'

Cheryl looked at her wedding ring – not a brass curtain ring, a broad band of diamond-cut gold – and up at her brand-new husband.

'Very well, thank you, Mr. Nankervis.'

'Then smile, you're on TV!'

Cheryl hadn't noticed the television crew, nor had she expected it, although she had steeled herself to face reporters and photographers. A microphone like a large furry animal waved in front of her face.

'West of England News!' someone cried.

No, Tracy's wedding was *never* like this!

Candy, spotting attention, ran to push herself in front of Cheryl. She wore her pink party frock and a wreath of tiny roses, and carried a ball of flowers on a ribbon. She looked adorable. Debbie, in a borrowed Laura Ashley dress of dark maroon cotton sprigged with flowers, some of which were pink, carried a Victorian posy and wore a big picture hat, and looked sensational. She stooped to take Candy's hand.

'Come here, scene-stealer, your turn will come later!'

Cameras whirred, lights flashed, everyone smiled and looked happy.

Oliver looked distinguished, but all wrong, in a suit.

'Don't worry,' he said. 'I did a deal. They'll all go away in a minute and leave us in peace if we give them value for money.'

Oliver's parents smiled and joined the group with Marilyn and Bob. Susan, Cheryl noticed, wasn't there, nor her husband, nor Annabel and Sebastian, whom she had never met. Debbie laughed and swung Candy into her arms and filled the gap with joy. Thank God for Debbie. Tracy, Tom, Louise and Micky watched on the sidelines. It could have been any wedding, anywhere, without a doubt in sight.

No Helen, either.

Cheryl smiled, answered questions, looked happy, *was* happy. Unbelievably so.

Oliver hadn't wanted nor, Cheryl thought, expected a proper reception, but her mother and Mr. MacDonald, ably seconded by Debbie, had worked miracles at such short notice. There was a buffet, the promised flowers in profusion, and a string trio of three young people from the Music School playing classical music quietly in the background, filling in the space that might have been left around the talk of the thirty or so guests. At such short notice, Cheryl considered it was amazing, and was cross when Oliver's stepmother was kind about it. Marilyn said, wistfully, that she would have liked a bit more notice – and a bit more information, too.

'Rubbish Mum, it's terrific! Don't worry about a thing!' Cheryl found that she resented the way that Oliver's stepmother made her own mother so awkward and unsure of herself, it made her over-compensate, prepared to defend the chicken salad, giant prawns and sherry trifle to the last ditch.

"His sister Susan isn't here, and she wasn't at the Registry Office either,' said Marilyn. 'Oh Cheryl, are you sure that you're going to be all right?'

'Of course I am,' said Cheryl. Susan's absence was bound to arouse comment, of course, but remembering the ugly little scene in reception last night, and Susan's friendship with Joanna Rendell, the reason was probably not far to seek. It would be just like Susan to boycott the wedding as a gesture of sympathy with her friend. Three Nankervises out of four wasn't bad under the circumstances, and Debbie at least looked as if she was wholeheartedly enjoying herself.

The cake, lovingly iced by Mrs. Peasgood's niece far away in Suffolk, stood proudly on a table by itself. Cheryl's bouquet, rainbow freesias and cream roses tied with long gold ribbons, was placed beside it. How Debbie had contrived in such a short time, Marilyn couldn't imagine. Florists, in her experience, needed several weeks notice. Even buttonholes for the men and corsages for herself and Tracy and Louise had appeared as if by magic. What it must be to have money! She dismissed this sour thought as unworthy, and thanked Debbie with real gratitude.

'I hope that Bob is going to make a speech,' said Debbie. She had fallen easily into calling them Bob and Marilyn. Marilyn wished that she felt as much at ease with Debbie.

Speeches had not been planned, but the cake somehow made them obligatory. Bob spoke briefly, a replay of the same speech he had made for Tracy's wedding, but without any personal allusions to his new son-in-law because he didn't know any beyond the obvious. Oliver's best man who, alas for Marilyn, had turned out to be one of *those* Ravenscourts after all, spoke with equal brevity and very wittily, and flirted with both bridesmaids equally. Oliver said a few words of thanks for everyone's hard work and support. The cake was cut, handed round, and eaten, and that was that, really. The guests were too ill-assorted for the party to last, Oliver's family had little to say to Cheryl's, and Oliver's friends formed a clique on their own. A lot of Cheryl's friends weren't even there, having sided with Jonathan; most of them had been friends of his before he even met her. Only Jeanette and Mr. MacDonald had come to her wedding, and although the waitresses, of course, knew her well, that was a minus factor, not a plus, in these circumstances. Soon after two o'clock, Cheryl and Oliver were able to pile their wedding presents into the back of the MGB, say goodbye to everyone, and escape to the quiet privacy of their own flat. It was the first time they had been so definitively alone together since they came back from Cornwall. It was a great relief.

Cheryl made coffee and they sat and drank it, Cheryl on the studio couch in deference to her wedding finery, and Oliver, who had already exchanged his elegant but unfamiliar grey suit for jeans and a T-shirt, on the floor. The flat had very little furniture. Cheryl looked around her at the untidy cardboard boxes containing Oliver's worldly goods, at her own modest possessions and the pile of as yet unopened presents, and then at Oliver, and looking up, he caught her eye and smiled.

'Hi,' he said, quietly, and she returned the smile without speaking.

He had promised that he would tidy up, but he hadn't done a very thorough job. He had set up the hi-fi system on an upturned box after emptying the contents, mainly books and CDs and tapes, onto the studio couch, but had made little attempt to do anything more constructive. Cheryl reached out an idle hand and picked up one of the books, flicking over the pages. It proved to be a diving manual, full of technical information and awful warnings, with spectacular diagrams illustrating what happened to you if you broke the rules. She looked at a decompression table blankly, and felt her own ignorance rising like a thick mist around her. She knew nothing whatever about diving, and here she was, married to a diver.

'Have you ever had the bends, Oliver?' she asked, because the bends was something that everyone had heard about. He laughed.

'Good heavens, no! The worst that's ever happened to me is nitrogen narcosis, and that's the way it's going to stay.'

Cheryl looked startled and sounded apprehensive.

'Whatever's that? It sounds dreadful!'

Oliver smiled at her, fully understanding.

'Actually, I suppose you could say it's quite fun. Nitrogen breathed in air under pressure at great depths makes you intoxicated – like being drunk, one name for it is rapture of the deep, you must have heard of it. A bit of a health hazard, though, when it happens under the sea, so you have to be strong-minded about it, while you still have some mind left to be strong with. Some people are more susceptible than others. I'm not, particularly.'

Cheryl stared at him, round-eyed.

'What do you do?'

'Get the hell out of it. Thirty or forty feet up, it simply goes. Odd, really.'

'I wish an ordinary hangover would do the same,' said Cheryl. 'Do you really go down that far?' It sounded a tremendous way.

'If it's necessary.' He indicated the book in her hand. 'That's what all those tables are about. You need to take care.'

'All this decompressing and recompressing,' said Cheryl, drawing her brows together in an effort to understand. 'Anyone looking at all these tables would think that every hour you spend diving, you spend another decompressing on the way up.'

'All of that,' said Oliver, and grinned at the sight of her face. 'It's all right, you know – there are very few accidents due to compression these days, in the sort of work that we'll be mostly doing, and the team I'll be diving with is very experienced.'

'You didn't go through all that decompressing routine down in Cornwall,' Cheryl accused him.

'Short dives, for fun – they're different.'

She had known that she was entering a new world, among people different from those that she had known before. Until this moment, she hadn't taken it seriously. She looked at the decompression tables in front of her, very much aware of risks and anxieties of which she had never dreamed. Oliver put his mug down on the floor beside him and got to his feet in one lithe movement.

'I forgot,' he said. 'I put a bottle of champagne into the fridge last night. Shall we drink it?'

'At two o'clock in the afternoon?'

'Why not?'

'How decadent! You get it then, and I'll get changed.'

He had acquired two glasses from somewhere with the bottle – probably the only two, said Cheryl, that they possessed.

'Unless there are some in those parcels, of course.'

'Nice if there are, but who needs possessions, really? They only tie you down.'

Cheryl looked around the room.

'We seem to have quite a few, just the same.'

'People will give you things – fortunately, or we wouldn't have a bed.'

'My mother thinks we're out of our minds, marrying on nothing.'

'Did you want worldly goods to share?'

'I only want you.'

'Then you got a bonus,' said Oliver, draining his glass and reaching for the bottle. 'Me, and a bookcase, and a second-hand studio couch complete with bedding. Have some more champagne. Then I can think of something much more fun to do. I've missed you.'

Along the waterfront at the Queen's, Marilyn and Bob, Louise, Tom, Tracy and the children would be loading up their luggage and driving home. The Nankervises would have gone back to their beautiful, soulless house and Debbie, too, would be heading off back to London. There would be just the two of them from now on, as they had begun. Cheryl leaned towards him and they kissed, slowly and with relief.

'Let's finish the champagne later,' said Cheryl.

Later on – much later on – they spent what was left of their wedding day washing down the dust of unpacking with the last of the champagne, and trying to cover up a strange sense of ... well, almost shyness, thought Cheryl, a little puzzled by it. Being married was quite different from not being married, not in the essential way, which was as wonderful as ever, but in ways that were difficult to pinpoint. It was other people who had made the difference, she supposed. Once you started seeing yourself as others saw you, you were lost. It was an uncomfortable thought.

It was even later in the evening before they got around to cooking supper in the tiny kitchen. Steak and salad, very simple, which they ate sitting on the floor beside one of the low windows, using the sill as a table. Looking out at the twinkling lights of the harbour and the smooth expanse of shining water under the darkening sky, Cheryl felt the world, which had been whirling round her for long enough, slowing at last to a steady circling.

'It really is beautiful,' she said, on a sigh. 'Well worth the three flights of stairs.'

'And practical,' said Oliver, unromantically. 'You'll have no excuse for not having dinner ready when I get back, you'll be able to sit up here and watch for the boat coming in.'

'When I'm not on shift.'

'That's a point, of course.'

Cheryl had finished her supper. She leaned her arms along the window sill and looked pensive.

'I can understand sailing, I suppose, but what makes you want to go diving?' she asked. 'What is it about it? Is it the romance of it, or the danger, or the challenge, or … well, what?'

Oliver set his plate aside and moved up beside her, his arm across her shoulders.

'All of those, I suppose, and there's something about the sea, and ships, even wrecks, and not just romantic ones like the *Hesperides*. They get to you.'

'Do you think she'll ever be found?' asked Cheryl, and felt him stir beside her, a lift along his nerves that transferred itself to her as a faint tingle of excitement.

'That's been the dream of every diver around here for a long time.' He dropped his voice and recited, softly,

'*For she lies deep, the* Inisfail – *ay, deep she lies an' drowned,
Farther'n' ever a wave'll stir, deeper'n' a lead can sound,
 Fifty mile from Fastnet Light, an' homeward bound.*'

'That's poetry,' said Cheryl, surprised.

'Don't you find the sea and ships poetic? I love you, Chel Nankervis!'

They kissed.

And that's who I am, thought Cheryl. I'm not Cheryl Wainwright any more, those days are over. I'm *Chel Nankervis* now, and I've thrown in my lot with a man born under a wandering star. Where will we go, what will we find there, when will we ever come home again? Maybe we shall ride out the storms and perhaps even climb the dark tower but what does it matter so long as we're together?

Marilyn and Bob drove home more sadly than is usual after a wedding. Jerry Nankervis and his second wife, who was unused to not having her own way, quarrelled over Susan's behaviour, and Debbie's, and failed to agree over their daughter-in-law.

In a converted barn in Surrey, an unhappy woman sat alone and thought her own thoughts.

Joanna Rendell dried her tears although her heart was breaking, and Jonathan Holmes, blank-eyed and silent, went out to cover the story of a warehouse fire for the *Herald*.

But Chel and Oliver loved each other, and for them the tide ran strongly, out to the wide sea.

PART TWO

REAPING the WHIRLWIND

I

Chel knelt on the floor, her arms leaning on the low attic window sill. She was definitely *Chel* by this time, her old, single self only a memory.

The spreading waters of the harbour, almost land-locked like an inland sea, lay glittering under the sharp winter sun, the dignified Georgian buildings of the town's better-class waterfront curving around the shore towards the bridge to the east, and looking, in this bright light, almost Mediterranean. To the west, the houses became humbler, greyer, generally older, gradually thinning out until the green countryside took over, backed by low hills purple with shadows, until it reached the distant cottages of the waterside village of Emberton, with its historic shipyard and thriving summer holiday trade – and Oliver, her adored and unpredictable husband, along there somewhere where the boats were ... as he had always been, as he would always be.

It was Oliver, and what he was, that was presenting the present problem – as was frequently the case

Chel wrenched her mind away from that.

Beyond the village, the land fell away, narrowing into the distant low spit of sand and shingle that shielded the entrance to the big harbour. Once, on the end of that spit, a Roman watchtower had stood; now a tumble of huts and buildings and a crowd of small boats marked the more modern phenomenon of a sailing club. Within the shelter of the spit, even this late in the year, yachts lay to their moorings on orderly trots, not so many, not nearly so many, as there had been during the spring and summer months, a lot of them were now laid up at the shipyard.

Damn! There she went again, treading thin ice to no good purpose. Deliberately, knowing that she should face facts but hesitating to do so, Chel let her eyes rove past the harbour entrance to where the rocky cliff began to rise on the other side. Beyond that cliff lay the Bornhope Rocks, where many a good ship had gone down, from the tiny fishing boats that worked the treacherous winter seas to the historic East Indiaman, the *Hesperides*. Many people had tried to find the *Hesperides*, so far none had succeeded. One day, maybe, some diver would be lucky but it wouldn't be Oliver.

Chel sighed. The trouble with this beautiful view was that it was so full of mantraps. The shipyard, the hidden Bornhope Rocks, the commercial dock immediately below her, where the diving boat *Cascabel*, owned by Oliver's old boss Bill Rowlands, lay to her moorings. And the big town marina, to which Oliver had returned in triumph after his epic, record-breaking round the world voyage earlier this year. Everybody loved him then. Well, nearly everybody.

Me too, Chel thought. Particularly me. And then I went and married him although I really hardly knew him, and no, I *haven't* regretted it. They all said that he would never settle, did I really think he had? Was I the fool, to think he loved me enough to give up his footloose, adventurous life? Could he really love me enough to change so fundamentally? Can anyone – *does* anyone?

I haven't changed, I don't think I have.

It was his stepmother's fault, she thought gloomily. Everything had been fine – wonderful, even – until she put in her poisonous little barb. A dangerous woman, Dorothy Nankervis, or so Oliver's natural mother had warned her. A spoiler. Chel believed her, although it was possible that Helen's attitude was unreasonable. The trouble was, she liked Helen, even if Oliver didn't. For Dorothy, who come to think Oliver didn't like either, she had only dislike, mutual and returned in full, possibly with interest. But Oliver didn't seem to like his stepsister Susan that much, either. In fact, when you came down to it, there weren't all that many people that Oliver *did* like wholeheartedly. *The Cat that Walked Alone* ... feral, half-wild tomcat, prowling on the fringes of the world, untamed and untameable.

She couldn't claim that she hadn't been warned, however. Just about everyone had made it their business to warn her. *You'll never hold him, he might stay for a while but one day he'll be gone, and hardly remember to send you a postcard to tell you what he's doing, all Oliver wants is to be alone.*

But be fair, a lot of that had come from her own ex-boyfriend, Jonathan Holmes, or from Susan, whose best friend Joanna Rendell had been mad for him, or the Dreaded Dot whom she seriously suspected hated him – or from her own parents, who didn't trust him, had wanted her to marry Jonathan, had done their best to bring her to her senses. Their phrase.

Shit! thought Chel, inelegantly. And bother Dorothy Nankervis! Couldn't she mind her own business for once?

Pigs might fly.

It shouldn't have worried her, Oliver packing up diving with Bill Rowlands' team when the winter closed in, and going to work at the shipyard for his friends Bob Chase and Merlin Ravenscourt. They were good friends, after all – Merlin had been best man at their hasty wedding – and Oliver of all things hated to be idle, kicking his heels in this tiny flat, waiting for a break in the weather, would have driven him mad. It *wouldn't* have worried her, thought Chel defiantly, if it hadn't been for what the Dreaded Dot had said. *It's not a good idea to make an enemy of her,* Helen had once told her. Chel didn't think she had gone so far as that, but there was no doubt that Dorothy didn't like her. She would do anything to make trouble for Oliver. It was silly to take notice of a word she uttered.

It had been about a month ago, she had been at work. Dorothy never approached Oliver, but she had once or twice dropped into the Queen's for a cup of coffee in the lounge – checking up, Chel supposed, although she herself said kindly that it was just to see how little Cheryl was getting along – *little Cheryl*, head of her department and on top of her job. Chel thought it was done mainly to cut up her peace, and mostly the effort was wasted, but this time had been subtly different.

'He's been home seven months now. It must be something of a record,' had said the Dreaded Dot, and added, smoothly, 'Do you enjoy sailing, Cheryl dear?'

Chel was well aware that Oliver had, generally speaking, more sympathy with boats than with people, whereas she herself, apart from odd trips on the diving boat while he worked for Bill Rowlands, and a little rather inexpert windsurfing, knew little about them and had, until recently, cared less, but she wasn't going to admit that to the Dreaded Dot. No way. She had turned the question with a noncommittal answer, received with a knowing smile, but it had returned to haunt her later. There was no reason why it should rankle as it did, it was Oliver, not she herself, who hankered after security.

In human relationships, or so he had once, rather uncharacteristically claimed. Not necessarily in anything else. It was simply bad timing that, shortly after his stepmother's visit, he had parted from Bill and changed direction. The Taverners' Shipyard had, in the past, given him delivery work. Chel had been unable to work out whether that was significant or not.

'Oh, bugger everything!' said Chel, aloud, disliking herself for her doubts. 'He never promised, or even offered, a settled home, he was always a free spirit and I can't say I didn't know. What do I want, anyway? Oliver, or just to be married with my own home?'

So much for adventuring, the idea of which she had found so exciting only a short time ago. The first hint that the smooth, even half-way conventional, surface of their new life might be developing a rut, and she was wringing her hands before anything had even happened. It was only when she tried to push the whole useless question out of her mind that it occurred to her, out of the blue, what was really the matter.

She liked this flat, of course she did, but it was nothing special. They had had fun here, but it had never been more than a stepping stone. What she was really afraid of was that Oliver would go off and leave her behind, as everyone had so frequently assured her that he would.

She was being stupid. There was no chance of his going off round the world again, for instance, it cost money and they hadn't any, and in any event, she didn't think he even wanted to go.

Delivering yachts to the Mediterranean or the Canaries, or even the Azores, however, was something that he could do. You got paid for that kind of thing.

Well, all right, so what? Those places weren't so very far away, it couldn't take all that long to sail there and fly back, or whatever it was that delivery skippers did.

We've not spent more than a night or two apart since we were married, her mind protested, absurdly.

So think yourself lucky, Chel admonished herself, and anyway, it hasn't happened yet.

She got to her feet, stiffly for she had been kneeling there, lost in thought, for too long. She had been packing, she remembered, when the glittering view had seduced her and she had taken her dive into introspection. And that raised another hurdle, bulking large as an elephant in the hitherto untroubled reaches of her marriage.

Her wonderfully happy and successful marriage, Chel told herself firmly. And it was Christmas – well, almost. They were invited to spend the holiday with her family, and rather against her better judgement, had agreed to go. Even now, her parents hadn't really come round to the idea of Oliver, they put up with him because they had no sensible alternative, but they didn't feel comfortable with him, still believing that she had been swept away by all the glamour and excitement and lost her head, and would therefore come to regret it. In one way it was almost true, so she couldn't really blame them too much. She couldn't see him fitting into her home life with anything but difficulty either, and his attitude to religious festivals was little short of pagan. Going to midnight mass on Christmas Eve and singing carols by candlelight was as much a tradition in her family as the turkey and Christmas pudding, and the Family Service on Christmas morning itself, with children and grandchildren all assembled, was a well-established ritual. Oliver seemed to view the festival more in the light of the Saturnalia which it had replaced in the calendar, and this quite apart from the fact that his personal experience of family life had left him only with a determination to have nothing further to do with it. She shuddered at the thought of the festivities to come. It must be the first time in her life, she realised, that she hadn't looked forward to Christmas with wholehearted anticipation.

Oliver had already packed, his old sailing holdall was by the door, ready for their departure as soon as he got home from work. Time to be busy with her own packing. Chel swung her suitcase onto the studio couch on which they sat, slept, and loved each other, and had just opened the lid when there was a knock at the door. She opened it and found, to her astonishment, Susan outside on the landing.

Susan had never visited the tiny, top-floor flat since the day they first rented it. Whatever the exact content of her quarrel with Oliver that had kept her from the wedding, it had gone deep and remained unforgiven, so it was a considerable surprise to find her there.

'Hullo,' said Chel, in surprise. Susan looked uncomfortable – unusual for her.

'It's Christmas,' she said, obviously. 'Tom said I was being silly, so I came to wish you a happy Christmas, and bring you this.' She held out a gaily wrapped parcel. 'I don't know if it's a wedding present or a Christmas present. You'd better open it.'

The parcel was flat, about two feet wide by eighteen inches high and an inch thick. Chel took it, nonplussed and, as always around Susan or her formidable mother, slightly suspicious.

'It won't explode, you know,' said Susan, watching her. Chel laughed.

'Thank you,' she said belatedly. 'Come in... I'll make us some coffee, shall I?' She didn't want Susan in the flat, but she could hardly slam the door in her face when she came bearing a gift. Susan came in and looked about her, critically.

'You've made it quite nice,' she said, sounding surprised, and Chel, who had seen Susan's family home, all wall-to-wall carpets, upholstered, over-stuffed suites and polished reproduction furniture, felt unreasonably patronised.

Susan sat on the edge of the studio couch as if she feared it might bite, her eyes, as Chel described it to Oliver later, all over the place. The flat was even now remarkably basic, but since Oliver and Chel were still head over ears in love, it tended to be full of evidences of the fact, silly little gifts and flowers and cards. Chel's pink panther sat cosily on the bookcase with his legs and long tail dangling past her collection of whodunits and Oliver's books on sailing and diving. Susan didn't sniff exactly, but the end of her nose definitely twitched.

'He treats you more like a mistress than a wife,' she commented. 'Aren't you cold, with only that small gas fire?'

Chel laughed. She wanted to reply, flippantly, *we've got our love to keep us warm!* but thought she had better not.

'It'll wear off, I expect.' She picked up the parcel. 'What is it? I love parcels, even when they just turn out to be the laundry.'

'Open it and see,' said Susan, and watched her while she did so with a curious mixture of superiority and a slightly pathetic eagerness. Chel stripped off the bright paper and cardboard in which it was wrapped, and stood there with the contents in her hands, jolted.

It was a picture. A watercolour, nicely framed behind non-reflecting glass, very Susan-ish, but it was the subject rather than the presentation that left Chel temporarily lost for words. She wouldn't have expected it of Susan.

Across a crisp blue-green sea, with spray flying from the waves, *Lawley's Girl* sped like a bird. There was movement there, and freedom, and the tang of salt in the air and a suggestion of gulls crying. Susan watched Chel looking at it and said, almost apologetically, 'We had it done from a photo. I thought you would like it.'

'I love it,' said Chel, meaning it. 'So will Oliver.' Probably. Possibly. She had first met him aboard this boat, Susan could have chosen nothing that would have given more pleasure. She was both surprised and touched, and sorry that she seemed to have misjudged her. 'It's the nicest present we've been given,' she said, to clinch it.

'Oh well ...' said Susan, and added, awkwardly, 'I'm sorry I couldn't come to your wedding.'

Couldn't or wouldn't, it hardly mattered. Susan wasn't an important factor in their lives. Chel went to make the coffee, giving the picture a passing glance as she went. It made her feel guilty that she couldn't like her sister-in-law better.

Susan might have been made to feel ashamed of her behaviour over the wedding, or she might simply have decided that the existing state of affairs was silly between fully-grown adults, but whatever her motive, Chel soon found that it hadn't altered her outlook. One of her less attractive traits was the gift of always being unanswerably and invariably right, and voicing her unanswerable and invariable rightness with a directness that took very little note of other people's feelings. She seemed to feel that her apology and her gift had restored her right to criticise, and that her advice should be valuable to Chel – in fact, Chel found herself wondering after a while if Susan's apology hadn't been largely due to the fact that by refusing to speak to Oliver, she had been unable to give Chel the benefit of her experience, but perhaps that was cynical.

Susan didn't approve of Oliver working at the shipyard. It would, she pointed out, hardly make Bill Rowlands consider him reliable, however good at his job Oliver might be.

'You should make him settle down,' she said. 'Diving, if he must, but surely by this time, something more ... more usual would be better. He's nearly thirty after all, is he going to bum around for the rest of his life? Showing off – that's all it is. Oliver always did show off.'

Oliver's mother, Helen, had said a similar thing, but more tactfully. Chel sighed internally, and decided to ignore Oliver's recent career change, it might be easier.

'Don't be so stuffy,' she said. 'Diving is a perfectly respectable profession.'

Susan, too, chose to ignore the tempting red herring that at present, far from diving, Oliver was refitting yachts. She said,

'Oliver has a good brain, if only he would use it. He has a degree, he should be doing something more constructive with his life.'

Chel decided it would be futile to point out that underwater salvage and offshore navigation both required a high degree of skill and intelligence, so that Oliver could hardly be accused of letting his brain go to mush.

'Oh well,' she said, and tried to turn the subject, but Susan had come with the intention of saying certain things, and she was determined to say them.

'I don't know how you put up with it,' she said. 'Don't you worry, knowing what he's doing and how dangerous it is?'

Chel had come to believe, with Oliver, that the danger was in direct inverse ratio to the degree of care and preparation, but she had worried – of course she had. She wasn't going to admit it to Susan, for from Susan would only be a short step to Oliver himself, and she was aware that Susan wouldn't hesitate to use any confession she made as a lever to make Oliver conform.

It would suit Susan's ideas of her own social status far better not to have a brother, even just a stepbrother, who was little better than a gypsy. She described him to her friends, Chel had discovered, as *a bit of a playboy, really,* but it cut very little ice with anyone who knew that Oliver was in more-or-less regular employment, and happily married. Both of these detracted badly from the romantic factor and lowered the glamour-rating to almost nil, and the record-breaking voyage round the world was yesterday's news by now.

'It's no different from a lot of other professions,' she said sweepingly – and inaccurately. 'Anyway, Oliver is careful – fanatically careful. If he wasn't, Bill would never have taken him on. One idiot on the team would endanger them all, that goes without saying.'

Susan gave a ladylike snigger.

'He has brainwashed you, hasn't he? Do you think, then, that he's going to stick with diving in the end?'

'I've no idea,' said Chel, as aloofly as she felt was wise, hoping to discourage Susan, but she had more chance, she realised gloomily, of plaiting fog. Susan was impervious to hints and went on doggedly with what she had come to say.

'It was all very well for Oliver to drift around the world, going from job to job when he was single, but marriage is a responsibility and you should make him face up to it. What will happen when you start a family? I presume you intend to.'

Chel burned inside, but answered as lightly as she could.

'One day, maybe. There's plenty of time for that, after all. We'll have fun first and raise the family after – why not?'

'You're as bad as he is,' said Susan, with disapproval.

'It's our business, anyway,' said Chel, tired of this determined criticism, and tired, too, of the way her own mother, Susan's mother, and now Susan, kept harping on babies, as if they were some magical formula that would – God forbid! – tie Oliver down at last and make him conform.

'Daddy would like a grandson to carry on the family name and the firm,' said Susan.

'One day, *Daddy* may have one,' said Chel. Oliver's father was a very high-profile solicitor, she couldn't imagine any child of hers and Oliver's following in those footsteps.

'Don't leave it too late, that's all,' said Susan, and Chel laughed, and pointed out that she was only twenty-four and Oliver, far from being nearly thirty, a mere twenty-eight. Susan simply tossed her head, and said firmly,

'Diving and potholing and sailing round the world – hardly a recipe for a quiet old age!'

Potholing was a new one. Chel wondered if he had ever potholed and thought it unlikely. She wanted to giggle, but decided not to.

'Oh, rubbish,' she said.

'All right,' said Susan. 'Believe he has a charmed life if you want to – but I think you should accept that you have a duty to the family to make him settle down.'

'And what,' asked Chel silkily, all desire to giggle suddenly fled, 'of my duty to Oliver?'

'Or his to you?' countered Susan, and seeing Chel's face, laughed. 'Oh, come off it, Cheryl – I didn't make up one silly squabble in order to have another! Let's cry quits and be friends.'

She left soon after, leaving her coffee half-drunk and with insincere thanks for the hospitality. Instant not good enough for her, thought Chel, pouring the scummy dregs down the sink in their minute cupboard of a kitchen. Well, good luck to her! Silly witch!

Oliver, returning from the shipyard some time later, greeted the news of his stepsister's visit without enthusiasm, and eyed the picture with suspicion.

'*I fear the Greeks, even when they bring gifts,*' he quoted.

'Don't you like it?' asked Chel. 'I love it.'

'Who did it? That fellow in the Arcade, I suppose – what's his name, Gibbons? *Your pet's portrait, or a picture of your home, to hang on your wall and be an heirloom for your children!* Good old Susan!' He broke off and laughed. 'Yes, I do like it – it may not be great art, but it was a kind thought.' He picked it up and held it against the wall. 'Where would you like it hung?'

'And what would you know about great art, anyway?' mocked Chel, going for a hammer and a nail. 'You know quite well that you're a philistine!'

It wasn't until much later, when the journey to Suffolk was behind them, and they were nearly asleep under the duvet in her parents' spare bedroom, and midnight had struck long since, that she told him what else Susan had said.

'She implied – she didn't come right out with it – that your family were concerned that your way of life – our way of life – was too risky and uncertain for a married couple.'

'Do you think it is?' asked Oliver.

Chel had her cheek against his and her arms round him, she was so close that she felt him leap onto the defensive, although nothing in his voice gave him away.

'I've never been so happy in my life, and I can't imagine you any other way,' she said truthfully, and didn't add that she made the most of what they had in case it shouldn't last. Oliver laughed in the darkness, quietly.

'Anyway, there's nothing particularly dangerous, or even non-conformist, in refitting yachts,' he said.

Chel stirred against him, voicing, almost against her will, something that had often gone through her mind and been dismissed with scorn. Possibly it was being, for the first time since her marriage, in the house where she had grown up that brought it to the surface. Being home seemed to make her more definitively herself again, and further away from Oliver than she had felt since she first met him.

'If it wasn't for me, would you sooner be off sailing again?'

'Oh well,' said Oliver. 'That's a different question. If I did that, I would have to leave you behind – and I don't want to do that. Perhaps, in that respect at least, you've done exactly what they want.'

It wasn't quite the answer she had hoped for, and Chel frowned.

'I don't want to make you feel tied down,' she said.

'You don't,' said Oliver, and kissed her with tenderness. 'You're just being silly, and I should like to know why.'

'It's just that I love you so much,' said Chel. 'It seems indecent, somehow, to be so happy doing exactly what we want.'

'What else would we be doing?'

But that was an unanswerable question, although Chel sleepily thought that it ought to have an answer.

They woke late, to a flurry of snow that heralded a white Christmas, and a combination of her family's determined welcome and Oliver's excellent manners ensured that, in spite of Chel's fears, a truce was maintained until they left again for home. Perhaps it wasn't quite the usual lighthearted family jamboree, but Chel could see no fault in Oliver and they returned to Embridge for New Year's Eve more deeply in love even than before.

But the new year brought yet another wedge to drive between Chel and her roots, for when the New Year's Honours List was announced, everybody knew that Oliver had been awarded an MBE. He accepted it on the day with embarrassed grace and fled back to the comparative obscurity of the shipyard as quickly as was decent, but inevitably, repercussions had to follow. Chel, for whom keeping the secret had been painfully near to impossible, nearly burst with pride, but her parents, writing to comment and congratulate, sounded almost scared.

In Oliver's own family, his father and sisters were openly proud, as if they had expected nothing less, his stepmother had smiled enigmatically and looked at Chel as if expecting her to drop her fork on the Palace floor and follow it with her aitches. It may have been all of this that precipitated the next event in their lives. Too much attention focussed on himself had always made Oliver nervous.

'How'd you fancy spending the summer cruising in the Greek islands?' he asked, one bleak February morning.

It was Sunday, at breakfast time; Chel was on the afternoon shift that week. She nearly dropped her mug.

'What did you say?'

He grinned at her. 'You heard me. Well?'

'Give me time to take it in,' said Chel. 'How? I mean, what do you mean?'

'Flotilla sailing,' said Oliver. 'You know, *see the beautiful islands from the comfort of your own boat* – chartered for the duration, of course. I did it once, the year before I went off round the world – skippering the lead boat for one of the tour operators in the Saronic Gulf. They had a crisis with one of their skippers in the middle of the summer, and I happened to be handy. It was quite good fun, I suppose, but I didn't want to do another season, too much hassle. But the boss of the firm I worked for turned up at the yard yesterday and saw me there, and he asked if I'd consider taking it on again – but in the Ionian this time, and officially, and I thought perhaps you might enjoy it. I told him I was a married man these days, and that you already worked in catering, and he said they were looking for a hostess anyway, so why not you, too? So what do you think?'

Chel realised with a shock that she was being offered a job, not a holiday as she had at first supposed, and that if she accepted, far from making him settle down, she would be throwing up her whole career to follow him into the blue. Their respective families would just love that! She could, of course, claim that it was good experience in a different branch of the tourist industry, but she feared they wouldn't buy it. Even so, a bubble of excitement rose up in her.

'What would I have to do?' she asked.

'Oh, advise on shops and facilities,' said Oliver, vaguely. 'Organise barbecues and evening entertainments, generally look after people, that kind of thing.'

'I've never been to Greece. I've only ever been to France with the school, years ago, and to Tenerife with some friends.'

'I've been there though. You'll soon pick it up.'

'I don't know anything about sailing.'

'You'll find out all you need to know pretty soon. There's the delivery cruise first, when the boats are sailed from the over-winter port to their summer bases – that'll soon sort out the men from the boys, believe me. And the punters manage all right.'

'The punters probably know something about it to start with.'

'You'd be surprised.'

Chel considered the proposal with a tingle of slightly apprehensive anticipation. It might not be an adventure to Oliver, but it looked like one to her.

'Would it be just us on our boat?' she asked.

'Us, and an engineer to stick any broken bits back on the fleet.'

'And all three of us would be living on board?'

'Most of the time. Yes.'

They discussed it for most of the morning. Oliver found some photos of his last trip and they went out to a travel agent to pick up a brochure on flotilla holidays. By the time she left to go on duty, Chel was beginning to be enthusiastic.

'What about the flat, and everything?' she asked.

'We can keep it on, if you like. I expect we can sublet it for the summer.'

'We'd have to pack all our things away.'

'It isn't as if we're overburdened with things.'

'Let's do it, then,' said Chel, and knew as soon as she saw Oliver's face that he hadn't believed she would agree. Whether the decision was wise or not, she had no idea, but she was suddenly immeasurably relieved that she had made it

II

They sublet the flat without trouble, and flew out to Greece in the middle of March, to the accompaniment of cries of despair from their respective parents.

'Deep-sea diving was bad enough, but at least I thought he was going to stick to it,' lamented Chel's mother, and her father muttered something about *instability*. The Nankervises, of course, were less surprised having expected something of the sort from day one, but Chel knew that she had disappointed them – yet again. But Oliver's habit of not caring about them or what they might think was infectious, and she didn't let it keep her awake at night.

They spent an idyllic summer cruising the Ionian Sea. Chel hadn't imagined that anything could be so much fun. She learned a great deal about living in a foreign country and more than a little about yachts and sailing, those new horizons that she had glimpsed when she first ran away to Cornwall with Oliver opening up before her like the gateway to a promised land.

They spent their first wedding anniversary sailing with their flotilla from Abelike Bay on the island of Meganisi to the tiny village of Sivota on Levkas, the evening celebrating at an unscheduled party in a local taverna right on the waterfront, where crayfish awaited the pot tethered to the jetty and tender lamb roasted fragrantly over a charcoal fire. It ended in the olive groves under bright Mediterranean stars, in a warm darkness vibrant with love, free from other people, just their two selves, deeply, unbelievably happy.

The months sped by too quickly, long, hot days spent in sailing, snorkelling round rocky coves, barbecues on soft warm nights with fires sparking in the darkness on curving beaches of white shingle ... wasps, dolphins, new places, new friends, new experiences. Chel finally mastered windsurfing one bright day in the Dragonera Islands, and Oliver who, to her astonishment, spoke it fluently, began to teach her Greek. She learned not only to love the country and to know about sailing, but even more about her husband – skilled, knowledgeable and highly professional, somehow not quite as she had expected but infinitely dear. She knew now, for instance, that the fearlessness in the face of danger that was so characteristic of him wasn't so much due to a lack of recognition, as she had frequently speculated, but because he knew himself equal to meeting it, and because the sea was so deeply in his blood that he looked on it not as a potential enemy so much as an unpredictable lover. He belonged to it, and if it ever claimed his life he would only be going home. The thought chilled her but it swiftly passed. It was after all something that had always been obvious. Looking back long afterwards, although she knew that there had been hard bits, unpleasant bits, and even downright frightening bits, that whole summer had seemed bathed in sunshine and alight with laughter. She and Oliver worked together as if they had done it for years, her own skills with people and knowledge of the tourist industry complementing his seamanship perfectly. Pure magic, time out of time.

Are you planning to stay out there? wrote Chel's mother in the late summer, unable to imagine a daughter of hers living such an exotic life, and still choking on Oliver's MBE.

'Well, are we?' asked Chel.

'Do you want to?' Oliver smiled at her with lazy warmth.

The September sun was hot on her back, the Ionian Sea sparkled deep blue, ringed with mountains and dotted with dark islands. On the brown hillside behind them, the cypresses stuck up like black fingers against the whispering silver surge of olive trees. The chirp of the cicadas was like a purr of contentment. It seemed as if summer was eternal.

'It's a lovely place,' said Chel, cautiously, reluctant to commit herself until she knew what he wanted himself. The lazy smile broadened into a grin.

'The sun isn't always shining, not even here, you know.'

'I know that,' said Chel indignantly. 'I'm not stupid!'

Having fished for her and caught her, Oliver laughed and took pity on her.

'I hate the idea of knowing what I'll be doing this time next year,' he said. 'Let's just take it as it comes.'

Chel had fallen in love with Greece and the Greeks, and maybe that was why she had such a deep and painful pang of loss, but she couldn't be sure. She had laughed when Madame Zsa-Zsa, back in Cornwall, had told her that she had the gift of clairvoyance, but the twist of misery that she felt seemed unreasonable. It seemed linked in some way to what Oliver had said, but before she could start analysing it, if that was even possible, Oliver was getting to his feet, reaching a hand down to her and still laughing. He didn't care about the future.

'Come on sweetheart, duty calls,' he said. 'Skippers' meeting time.'

'Aye aye, Admiral.' She took his outstretched hand and allowed him to pull her to her feet, proceeding naturally into his arms. Whatever it was – nostalgia, regret, foreknowledge – took wing as they kissed, warm, lingering, and full of promises.

'I love you,' said Oliver, and Chel answered ritually, 'I love you, too.'

They flew home again at the beginning of November, after Oliver had predictably turned down any suggestions that they should return the following summer. She sat beside him on the flight back to England with a lost feeling of homesickness, although they were going home, her mind filled with memories of blue seas, bleached earth under olive groves terraced to the skyline, little white houses dreaming beside dusty quaysides, village tavernas where time didn't matter, smiling, friendly people, hazy mountains, burning skies ... and with a totally irrational feeling that in Greece they would have been safe. She was appallingly airsick for most of the way. At least, she thought it was airsickness, but it didn't seem to go away after they landed.

'You've picked up a dose of Greek tummy,' said Oliver, who never picked up such things himself, but the doctor said no, she hadn't. She had brought back a souvenir of Greece, yes, but it wasn't precisely a bug.

'He says I'm about five weeks pregnant,' she said, and watched Oliver go scarlet to the tips of his ears. At first she thought that it was anger, but it turned out to be embarrassment, and a shy delight that was peculiarly endearing. It had been a total accident.

'Our next great adventure,' said Chel. 'Are you pleased?' She wasn't sure that she was, herself, she had long wondered if Oliver had been testing her over the flotilla, and now she would never find out. She would be relegated, whether she wanted it or not, to the domestic life that other women had to lead. She was disappointed, but Oliver smiled and said that of course he was pleased, and she could get no more out of him. She suspected that his principle reaction had been surprise bordering on shock, but he had taken it well.

Their families, when they heard about it, undermined her confidence even more.

'Now he'll have to settle down,' was Susan's predictable reaction, flavoured with a lifetime of envy for everything that Oliver was, or did.

'I hope you know what you're doing,' Chel's mother said, over the telephone.

'But are you pleased?' said Chel. Somebody had to be, after all.

'Of course I'm pleased,' said her mother. 'Does Oliver realise what he's taken on?'

'I've no idea,' said Chel, with unexpected honesty. 'I suppose so.'

'Well, make sure before it comes as an unpleasant surprise, won't you?'

'He's pleased about it too, of course he is!' said Chel, guilt about her own feelings making her sound indignant, but her mother only remarked that that wasn't quite what she had meant.

That year, they spent Christmas in Embridge. Chel, although the idea of the baby was growing on her as time went on, found the first months of pregnancy fairly awful and couldn't face travelling, or even, to begin with, looking for a new job, and Oliver made no secret of the fact that he was glad of an excuse to stay home among their friends.

She found he wasn't terribly supportive when she was unwell. He had hardly had a day's illness in his life himself, and his sympathy was perfunctory and without real understanding. Cut off from her own family, and with only temporary part-time reception work at the Langland to occupy her time, Chel found that she was gradually coming to depend on Susan, who might be interfering but was practical and meant to be kind, and had two children of her own so presumably knew all about it. Moreover, she found that pregnancy had the annoying effect of making her weepy and emotional, and Oliver was embarrassed by weeping women. She began to see more and more of Susan, but Oliver was out most of the day, filling in time at the shipyard again, and only said that he was glad if they were getting along. Oliver was going back to the diving team when the season re-opened; the money was good, which had become a consideration, possibly for the first time in his life. He hadn't said, and Chel hadn't asked, if this time it was a permanent arrangement. She was learning fast.

Easter fell that year at the end of March. Bill Rowlands, who had spent the winter in painstaking research, took his team out over the Bornhope Rocks on the day before Good Friday to start a serious search for the *Hesperides*, and Oliver, going down with the second dive of a series designed to sweep the search area, landed right on her.

It was only by the wildest coincidence, for she had been searched for many times before and could have been anywhere in a wide area, hidden in a gulley, buried in sand, or even completely broken up and unrecognisable. It was such an amazing experience that when he arrived home, halfway through the afternoon, he was so ablaze with excitement that Chel thought he had been drinking. When he had finally calmed down enough to explain, she was as excited as he was.

'Terry and I went down in what we didn't even think was one of the most likely places,' he told her, shining-eyed, with excitement vibrating off him like an electric current. 'It was pretty murky down there, being so early in the year, and we finned about a bit and saw nothing but weed, and a huge sill of rock with a great hump of sand drifted alongside. After a while I sat down to have a quiet look round in case we had missed something, because it's easy to do that if you don't think there's anything there – and we didn't.' He drew a breath. 'Then it suddenly dawned on me, I was looking straight down the barrel of a bloody cannon! It was tucked under the sill, pointing at me for all the world as if it was going to fire! And not only that – I was actually sitting on another one! I thought I was seeing things!'

'And it really *is* the *Hesperides?*' asked Chel.

'God alone knows, only time will tell – but it was a wreck all right, and one that hasn't been recorded before. The sand has silted up right over her, I imagine – what's left of her. She must have gone down right on the rim of the reef.'

'When will you know?' demanded Chel. Oliver grinned at her reflection of his own excitement.

'The short answer to that is, when we find out,' he said. 'If we find something that's identifiable with what we know about the *Hesperides*, then we can be morally certain that's what we've found, but that could take months.'

'Oh Oliver!' Chel looked aghast. 'As long as that!'

'Of course, we could find something tomorrow.'

'You're teasing me!' said Chel.

He laughed at that.

'A bit, perhaps, but not that much. But mind, not a word to a soul.'

'Why not?' asked Chel, round-eyed. He put his arms round her and gave her a hug.

'Because, my little innocent, if she's the *Hesperides*, she is very, very valuable, a genuine dyed-in-the-wool treasure ship, and until Bill has a title of some sort to her, she's as much at the mercy of pirates as she was when she came sailing home, nearly two hundred years ago.'

'So, how do you get a title to a wreck?' asked Chel, and then, with a vague recollection of the divers they had met on their pre-marital trip to Cornwall, 'Do you buy it, or something?'

'In a case like this, you lease the sea-bed on which she lies.'

'You're kidding!'

'No.' He shook his head, but his eyes were dancing with mischief and she wasn't sure if he was teasing her or not. She put her arms round his neck and pulled his head down to kiss him.

'Aren't you the clever one? Will you go back tomorrow for another look?'

Oliver shook his head.

'We won't go near her again until the legal side is tied up. We shall very ostentatiously look for her somewhere quite different.'

'How sneaky of you!'

Oliver returned the kiss with interest.

'What a year this is being! Little Theodosius, and now the *Hesperides*! What next, I wonder?'

'He's just as excited as we are,' said Chel. 'I can feel him jumping about – you can too – feel!'

They ended up on the studio couch, laughing.

'I do love you,' said Oliver.

'Me too,' Chel started to say, dodging her head aside as she laughed, but she was no match for Oliver. He silenced her agreement with a kiss that left her in no doubt that he had spoken the truth, while his hands sought her eagerly. Like some tentacly deep-sea creature, Chel decided irreverently, and then there was nothing but the moment, heady and sweet as wine.

Chel hadn't seen Jonathan Holmes for over a year, had almost, in fact, managed to banish him from her mind.. She assumed that he was no longer sitting wimpishly around waiting for Oliver to come to grief, but beyond that she seldom gave him a thought. Nothing is so dead as last year's romance. But a few days after Oliver found the *Hesperides*, she ran into him in the town.

She had been shopping, and was on her way back to the car when she heard a voice calling after her down the street, and when she turned round, there he was, running towards her.

'Cheryl! Stop a minute!'

Chel had become so used to being *Chel* that for a moment she didn't recognise herself, but then Jonathan caught up with her, breathless and smiling, and apparently both pleased and surprised to see her. It was, of course, almost two years since that poignant avowal of undying love, and if he had pined thereafter, there was no sign of it now. He looked fit, happy and prosperous, and Chel didn't notice that he flinched a little when she turned and he saw the tell-tale bulge of Little Theodosius.

'Jonathan!' cried Chel. 'What a lovely surprise! I've not seen you for so long, I thought you must have moved away.'

'I've been kept working very hard,' explained Jonathan. 'How's things, Cheryl? I heard you'd gone to live abroad. So what's this, another royal summons, or a holiday?'

'We've been back for almost six months,' Chel told him. 'We only went for the summer. Oliver's back with Bill Rowlands now.'

'Oh?' said Jonathan, and added casually, 'Rumour has it that Rowlands is searching for the *Hesperides,* and is pretty sure of finding her. Is that right?'

Chel remembered that he was a journalist, probably still working on the *Embridge Herald,* and tried to look suitably dumb.

'I wouldn't know,' she said. Jonathan cocked an eyebrow at her.

'That sounded very non-committal. You would tell an old friend, wouldn't you sweetheart? If there was a chance of a scoop?'

'It's nothing to do with me,' said Chel, a little defensively, for her conscience whispered that she owed Jonathan something, after all. 'If they find her, I expect they'll tell the media when they're ready.'

'Oh, come on – you could surely let an old chum in on an exclusive.'

'I told you, it's nothing to do with me.'

Jonathan had known Chel intimately, and he wasn't a journalist by accident. He looked at her.

'They wouldn't have found her already, would they, Cheryl my sweet?'

'Don't be silly!' said Chel. 'And don't go printing that in your paper, either – I told you. I can't tell you anything about it.'

Jonathan let the subject drop, saying casually,

'Let me buy you lunch, just for old time's sake.'

He was so nice and natural and easy that it seemed stupid to refuse. She couldn't imagine that he would do anything to hurt her, quite forgetting how she had hurt him. Over steak-

and-kidney pie and chips in a pub, he entertained her with tales of his doings over the past year, and didn't once mention either Oliver or the *Hesperides*. They parted later on friendly terms, and Chel went home to the flat.

When Oliver heard about the unexpected meeting, he showed little interest. He had no recollection of ever having met Jonathan, although naturally he had heard about him, and he trusted Chel. It would be some time before news of the finding of the *Hesperides* would be made public, and at present it was no business of stray journalists. He listened to Chel telling him about the meeting and promptly forgot it. For the moment.

But Jonathan went back to the *Herald* office in a very thoughtful frame of mind. She was as transparent as glass, pretty Cheryl with her bright aura of happiness, and he knew her so well that he had no difficulty in seeing right through her evasions. Perhaps it was cheating to take advantage of the knowledge gained in their old intimacy, but it could do no real harm. What did he owe her, after all? Rowlands could look after himself, none better. And as for Oliver Nankervis, he had been riding for a fall for a long time. Jonathan had no objection to tripping him up.

And Cheryl had cheated him. What was that old thing? – *an eye for an eye.* He thought of her as he had last seen her, so blatantly contented, so apparently unaware of anything beyond her own happiness, cocooned in it like an egg in straw, and he realised that he wouldn't be all that sorry to put her eye out. Public humiliation – which was what she had handed him, running away with Nankervis when half the town knew that she was as good as engaged to himself – had had a very bitter taste. He switched on his computer, sat down at the keyboard and began to write.

III

A few days later, Chel woke under a cloud. She had no idea why, she had gone to bed the previous night feeling perfectly cheerful, but the moment she opened her eyes she felt black depression settling clammily about her. It was early, beyond the window she could see a bright, clear sky still pale with dawn, and the street below was quiet except for the hum of a milk-float in the distance and the purr of a solitary car driving along the waterfront. She lay on her back and felt misery, in sticky waves, piling up over her.

Little Theodosius, a habitual early riser, turned over with enthusiasm inside her, and she clasped her hands over him, feeling the rounded shape of his little head under her ribs, and wondered if he was Little Theodosia after all. His grandfather would be very disappointed; they always discussed the baby as *he,* but there was no guarantee. She hadn't expected that it would be possible to feel so close to a child that she hadn't even seen, but she was beginning to love him with a protective tenderness that was new, and went a long way towards reconciling her to his existence. Oliver's child ... but this morning, not even the wriggling life of him – or her – could cheer her.

There was no point in lying here feeling like this. She would get up and put the kettle on, and make herself some coffee.

Oliver didn't move as she slid quietly out of bed, and it was symptomatic of her mood that she resented it. It was only half-past five, the alarm clock on the bookcase told her, why should she be the only one awake? She padded into the tiny kitchen on bare feet and leaned against the sink while she waited for the kettle to boil, thinking the dreariest thoughts about life and death, and the hazards of bearing children, until she laughed at herself in spite of her depression. She was a perfectly healthy young woman, married to a man whose physical perfection was positively aggressive, and there was no reason why she shouldn't bear a healthy and beautiful baby with no trouble at all. To speculate about anything else was simply giving in to her own subconscious, and unforgivably morbid.

But the cloud refused to lift. It remained firmly overhead, shadowing the bright day.

Chel made her coffee and drank it sitting on the hearthrug in front of the gas fire that Susan had despised, and the minutes ticked by. Oliver slept on. She picked up a book that lay on the arm of their one armchair, and tried to be interested in it, but her mind kept slipping off and after a while she gave it up and let her thoughts take her where they would.

Perhaps because her pregnancy, which so far hadn't been easy, and the half-recognised responsibilities attached to bringing a child into the world, had made her vulnerable, she found herself thinking of the future, not with her usual optimism, but with apprehension. All the comments that people had made, dismissible in themselves but adding up to a lurking threat, came back to her, bringing her face to face with the fear that had always been in the background, unacknowledged. She knew that during her brief marriage she had known remarkable happiness. They had had fun, they had done things that other people considered mad, they had been totally self-sufficient, just between the two of them. Because she had allowed Oliver to run free, because she had gone with him wherever he led, he had given her two wonderful years, and against all the odds their marriage had worked. She didn't think it was just because she had given in to him, in spite of what Susan and her other in-laws, and even her own family, believed. She had wanted to go with him to do what he did, and she had never once glanced aside at the humdrum domesticity of other young married couples with envy. In fact, it could be said with more truth that he had given in to her, he could have gone further and faster without her, but he had never let her feel that she was holding him back.

But now? Did he understand that a child would change things? Had he realised it wouldn't be either practical or permissible to skipper a flotilla round the Greek islands with a toddler crawling around the deck? Did he know what sort of responsibility a baby would represent, and would he even accept that it was so?

And if he wouldn't ... would he stay with her, and get his kicks from treasure-hunting under the sea, or would that, like so many other things in his unsettled, restive life, lose its charm when it became something from which he couldn't escape?

... and herself and her child, the fetters that held him ...

Security, mind you, not prison and a ball and chain.

Bugger! thought Chel, suddenly afraid.

Of course, women did take children on small boats. They sailed to Australia with their entire families, and gave lessons on the way, she had read about them.

She thought, quailing a little, that you had to be a special kind of woman to risk your small children on the wide, dangerous oceans, and that she was quite ordinary, with no exceptional courage. Her experience of the sea was confined to the land-locked Mediterranean, and even that had occasionally frightened her out of her wits, in spite of Oliver's cool competence and great experience, and the knowledge that what they were doing was peanuts by his standards. What would the Atlantic be like? Or the Pacific? Her blood chilled at the thought of them.

She hadn't cared for herself. She would have gone with him to hell and back, but for Little Theodosius?

Chel thought miserably, we should never have had a child without discussing it first. What will I do, if he sails away and leaves me?

Not this year. The *Hesperides* would keep him this year, and presumably the baby. But after that?

He loved her, she knew that. How could she help it, when every hour of every day was sweetened by her certainty of it?

But he couldn't help what he was, and that was a rootless gypsy of the wind.

He would never change. That, at least, was sure. Whatever demon drove him, it wouldn't let him rest. He would go – and although he might always come back, she would in a sense have lost him – not to another woman, but to wind and sea, risk and danger, and the heady wine of absolute freedom, and she suspected that each time he returned, he would be a little less her own.

Looking at the clock, she found to her surprise that she had spent over an hour in trying to read and giving in to fruitless distress, and it was after seven, the paper would be downstairs. She might as well go down and get it – them, rather; today was the day for the *Herald*.

She stole softly down the three flights of stairs, and when she arrived back in the flat, Oliver was wide awake, and wondering where she had got to.

'What's the matter with you? Insomnia?' he asked, when he saw her come through the door.

'Mmm – we woke early, and couldn't get back to sleep. But at least I wasn't sick.' Morning sickness, for Chel, had gone on and on. The Dreaded Dot had shaken her head and said darkly that a sickly pregnancy meant a sickly baby, and that it was so important to take care of herself and such a shame she had to work, but Chel, assuming this to be a dig at Oliver rather than criticism of her own resumption of part-time work, had ignored her. It flitted through her mind for a brief instant now, and then she said, 'Would you like coffee? I can soon make some.'

'I'll make it if you like,' offered Oliver, yawning, but Chel said that she was awake anyway, and might just as well do it herself. She tossed him the papers and went back into the kitchen with the milk. As she made the toast for breakfast, she began to feel more cheerful, until a sudden angry exclamation from Oliver took her to the kitchen door in alarm.

'Bloody hell!' he said, explosively. 'Where the blazes did this come from?'

'Where did what come from?' asked Chel. He was reading the local paper – Jonathan's paper, the *Embridge Herald*, and he held it towards her as she appeared in the doorway.

'Read it for yourself,' he said. He looked angry. Chel took the paper and read the headline across the front page with an unfamiliar sinking feeling.

LONG-LOST TREASURE SHIP DISCOVERED AT LAST? it queried, and went on in the same vein. *The rumours that Bill Rowlands' local team of professional divers have been searching for the wreck of the East Indiaman* Hesperides, *sunk on the Bornhope Rocks in the great storm of 1810 while loaded to the scuppers with treasure, gained ground over the past few days with a further rumour that she has actually been found ...*

'Oh dear,' said Chel.

'It's your bloody friend Holmes!' said Oliver, whisking the paper out of her hands again in order to go on reading. 'Where on earth has he dug all this up?' He looked up at her in swift suspicion. 'You didn't say anything to him, did you?'

'No!' exclaimed Chel, indignantly. 'Of course I didn't! What do you take me for?'

'You met him, and I'll bet he asked. Didn't he?' The accusation in his voice immediately antagonised Chel in her present mood. She answered with rancour.

'I told you, I didn't tell him anything! What are you calling me, a liar?'

'Oh, don't be so silly,' begged Oliver, tactlessly. 'I know you wouldn't mean to, but journalists are so bloody devious, you might have said it without meaning. '

'Oh, thank you!' flashed Chel. 'What have I done to make you think me such a fool? He asked me, yes, and I said I didn't know – which is true, according to you – and that's *all!*'

'He's a friend of yours – '

'Oh Oliver, I haven't seen him for years!' shouted Chel. 'What is this, an interrogation? Fetch the bloody torch and shine it in my face, why don't you? Anyone – *anyone at all* – you, even, could have said something, why does it have to be me? The only person I know of who's even mentioned it is *you*! '

'Now look here – '

'No, *you* look here!'

For a moment, Oliver looked so furiously and unfamiliarly stormy that Chel was frightened, but after glowering at her for a tense second, to her relief, he laughed.

'Good God, Chel, don't look so scared!' he said. 'I'm sorry, of course you wouldn't say anything on purpose, and even if you had I wouldn't be about to hit you, so there's no need to look as if you thought I would.'

'You called me a liar,' said Chel, unappeased, but Oliver had abandoned the fight.

'I only asked a simple question,' he said, and grinned at her disarmingly. 'All right, I could have put it better. I've said I'm sorry. Can we be friends again?'

Chel had never been proof against that particular grin, and she softened perceptibly, but she wasn't going to give in just like that.

'I'll fetch the toast,' she said, and went back into the kitchen.

It had made a bad start to the morning, and although Chel was sure that she had said nothing to Jonathan that he could have remotely construed as an admission that the *Hesperides* had been found, she couldn't help feeling an unreasonable sense of guilt. She tried to recall exactly what she had said, and failed. The little scene had shaken her, she had never seen Oliver angry with her before.

Oliver wasn't diving that morning. Bill Rowlands had gone up to London very early the previous day to see the Crown Estate Commissioners about the lease of the sea-bed around the wreck site, and would be returning on the midday train. *Cascabel* was due to sail from the commercial dock at half-past two. Oliver had an appointment at the bank at half-past twelve, and had planned to leave after an early lunch with Chel, but it was one of those days when nothing goes right. This time, it was Chel who set about rocking the boat, and from some twisted perversity born of a sleepless night, her first real quarrel with Oliver, and her own private fears, she did so to some purpose.

Her depression of the early morning, which had dispersed a little over toast and coffee, had returned as the day went on and had made her, for some reason that she couldn't pinpoint, acutely conscious of Oliver. Wherever she looked he seemed to be in the corner of her eye, dark, elegant and beautiful, tuned to a hair and glossy with well-being. It was as if she couldn't see enough of him, an intensified reflection of their heady falling-in-love days, but with a cutting edge that they had lacked. The feeling that something was coming to an end was very strong. She couldn't understand why, but she found herself talking and behaving as she had never talked or behaved in her life, as if in an attempt to postpone some unknown disaster by fixing the immediate future so that it was graven in stone. The morning, as a result, developed into a running battle between them, for of all things Oliver hated to know what would happen tomorrow. It gave him a mental claustrophobia that Chel couldn't even begin to understand.

She began the wrangle with that time-honoured old flag of battle, *Mum says*.

'Mum says we ought to think about settling down, and not go on in this hit and miss way,' she said – angling, perhaps, for a clue as to his intentions, but she wasn't very clear about it herself.

Oliver, however, found this funny.

'And ought we?' he asked, grinning.

Chel found the grin irritating when she was trying to start a serious discussion.

'We ought to have some kind of plan,' she insisted. 'After all, you'll be thirty this year.' She sounded like Susan. How awful!

Oliver looked at her quizzically, deaf to alarm signals.

'That's a bit young to retire,' he suggested.

'I wasn't suggesting you retired,' said Chel. 'Nor was Mum. She thinks you ought to get a settled job of some kind, even if it's diving.'

Oliver perched himself on the edge of the bookcase, one leg swinging in a way that fuelled her irritation to boiling point, and looked at her thoughtfully.

'And what do you think?'

'At least while the baby is small,' said Chel, defensively.

Oliver continued to sit and made no comment, and after a pause she went on.

'Babies need a lot of attention. We shan't be able to carry on as we do now.'

'Why not?' queried Oliver, reasonably. Chel tried to explain, and the argument, if argument it could be called, went round and round and came full circle, with Chel saying,

'Mum says I ought to talk about it seriously with you.'

'It seems to me, you are,' said Oliver, less equably now, 'and a load of rubbish it sounds too. Have I ever yet failed to take care of you?'

'Well ... no.'

'Then why do you think I'm going to start now? Why does she think so, if it comes to that?'

'Does that mean you're going to stay with Bill?'

'Chel –' began Oliver, and broke off. 'Why this sudden passion for tying me up in knots? Don't you and your mother trust me, or what?'

'She doesn't think you understand about babies,' said Chel.

'For God's sake, Chel, babies don't run the world!' said Oliver, and impatience flickered briefly. 'They go where you choose to take them, stay where you put them – if they're fed and warm and loved, from what I've seen, the selfish little bastards don't care for much else.'

'Who says they stay where you put them?' demanded Chel. 'You couldn't take a baby all round Greece, like last year –'

'Did I say I wanted to?'

'– and growing children like a settled place to keep their treasures, and a home to come back to.'

'My parents thought that, and for your information, they'd not got it quite right.'

'You're different!'

'In what way?' flashed Oliver, leaping to the attack with a speed she hadn't expected, and which disconcerted her so that she broke off what she had been saying and stood with her mouth open.

'I'm no different from anyone else, for God's sake!' he told her, with a crisp intolerance that was new. 'I've got nephews and nieces, my friends have children. What sort of oddball do you and your mother take me for?'

'Mum says –'

'Look, cut out what your mother says for a minute. We never had any of this carry on before, what's got into you all of a sudden?'

'We ought to plan ahead,' said Chel, and heard her voice rising and tried desperately to control it. 'Even this flat isn't suitable for a baby.'

'So why do you think I'm going to the bank?'

This question, which should have been reassuring, enraged her because of the way it was flung at her.

'You never told me you were thinking of moving!'

'You never told me you wanted to dig a hole and climb into it – you told your mother instead!'

'It concerns me, doesn't it?'

'Oh, and it didn't concern me?'

'I don't know anything,' said Chel, on a sudden wail of indignation. 'Ever since I gave up working full time, I don't even know what money we have, or anything.'

'Have I ever let the bills go unpaid?' roared Oliver, properly angry now.

Battle was really joined. The first serious disagreement they had had since they met, and because Chel was feeling low and miserable and Oliver, for all his apparent unconcern, had thought about their changing circumstances with misgiving and a resolve to do the best for her that he could, and resented that anyone should think otherwise, it began to develop overtones of mortal combat.

'I wish we'd never started this bloody baby!' snapped Oliver, in the finish. 'You never used to whinge like this! It's more trouble than it's worth before it's even born!'

'How can you say that?' shouted Chel. 'You're selfish and cold and unfeeling, and you don't understand!'

'Oh, shit!' said Oliver. He looked at the clock on the bookcase and said, 'Look, I must go, I'll be late at the bank. I'll talk to you when I get back this evening, and perhaps we can discuss it without all the theatricals.'

'No, Oliver!' cried Chel, leaping to her feet. 'You can't just go, not like –' She broke off, the slam of the door interrupting her, and ran to open it again. Oliver was already halfway down the stairs and still travelling, and quite suddenly, out of nowhere at all, a horrid conviction that he was never going to come back swept over Chel. There was no reason behind it, but it came to her with certainty, and the knowledge that this was what she had subconsciously been dreading all morning. It shocked her.

'Come back!' she called, but he had already gone out of both sight and hearing.

IV

Chel went back into the flat, shutting the door behind her, and crossed to the window. From this vantage point, she could see Oliver moving at speed along the pavement, almost running, going away from her, leaving the unresolved quarrel behind him.

They had never had a serious quarrel before. It had to be that, and nothing else, that was causing this terrible desolation. She couldn't possibly know the things she thought she knew, and already the certainty was fading. She sat down on the studio couch and tried to be objective.

Men didn't like rows with women. Oliver, she already knew, disliked rows with anyone, and had been known to travel vast distances in order to get away from them, and her subconscious had remembered it. Simple.

He wouldn't do that to her, would he? She was his wife, she was carrying his child.

No, of course he wouldn't. He would be back inside the hour, between his appointment at the bank and going on to work. He would cool down in the fresh air and start thinking, and she could try to do the same. They would each apologise and he would kiss her again as if he loved her. It would be all right. Nothing dreadful was going to happen.

Chel leaned back on the couch and tried to pull herself together. It had just been a day for misunderstandings. The silly quarrel was both their faults and Oliver would be generous enough to admit it. They could sort it out.

Could they? Would he give up any part of his precious freedom to accommodate a child, or had she been right earlier? It was disconcerting to find that she still didn't know. Even when he was shouting at her he hadn't committed himself.

She would keep him for this summer, he would be diving on the *Hesperides*.

And after that?

The thought of *after* made her oddly cold. She was aware of something on the edge of awareness, pushing to get in. Her heartbeat was the only thing in the world, and behind it, knowledge rose like a dark cloud.

No!

It was like slamming a door. The cloud was shut out by the door, and she hoped that it was locked away there. It was because she was pregnant of course. Everyone knew that being pregnant gave women strange ideas.

The minutes ticked slowly by and Oliver didn't come back. Perhaps there had been a lot of people in the bank, perhaps he had another errand that she hadn't given him a chance to tell her about.

The clock on the bookcase went on ticking. Half an hour, three quarters, an hour ... and that door in her mind stayed firmly shut.

It dawned on Chel, slowly and at first with indignation, that he must have gone straight down to the dock after all. He wouldn't be back for hours.

Her first reaction was simply to be furious with him, but very soon those hours came out of the back of her mind and ranged themselves in the foreground ... hours of this impotent fury, hours before she could tell him what she thought of him, hours in which to store up a harvest of rage and resentment ... hours of wondering what he would say, and do, when he returned, hours of wondering if the quarrel could be resolved and peace restored, or if she had alienated him beyond forgiveness, as Susan's friend Joanna was supposed to have done.

Hours in which to sit and search her own conscience and recognise how she had mishandled him to her own distress.

At least four of them.

He might not come straight back. The pubs would be open by the time they all came ashore. He could be away most of the evening.

He wouldn't do that to her. Not when she was pregnant. Not ever. He wasn't like that.

He was just busy proving that he *was* like that.

She could go down to meet him. The thought crept in and was dismissed. She wouldn't do that, let him go his length if he wanted to, she hated him anyway, he was selfish and elusive and he didn't care about her.

Chel began to cry, useless, miserable tears, first of fury, turning to self-pity, to more general depression and finally, to deep despair. The next few hours bulked in her mind like a year. They seemed interminable.

'It wasn't just me,' wept Chel, aloud. 'He isn't perfect either! I was only trying to be reasonable, he didn't have to jump down my throat and twist everything I said!' They had been so self-contained that there wasn't even anyone to whom she could easily turn. Since as long ago as their second meeting, she had only ever needed Oliver, when it came down to it. Not family, his or hers, not Susan, not friends – just Oliver, who had stormed out and left her.

Her own scorn in the end helped her to regain her balance. She had known right from the first that making a scene was the quickest way there was to get rid of him, what on earth had come over her? To calm herself, she made herself a cup of tea and sat on the floor by the window to drink it; below her, the waters of the harbour sparkled under the early spring sun, scattered with islands and a handful of sailing boats, a soothing and familiar scene. To the right of the immediate foreground, the commercial dock, busy and workmanlike, hummed with its usual activity, she could see the space against the pier where *Cascabel* was usually berthed. There was no point in getting into a state, she wouldn't see Oliver again until the boat was back. She could watch until she saw the crew come ashore, and within ten minutes of that he would be home. There was nothing to fret about, nothing to cry over. He couldn't neglect his work for a hysterical wife, and only the fool she had made of herself would have expected it.

A group of youths with shaven heads, and with nose and earrings, dressed in black leather and chains, walked along the promenade kicking an old tin among themselves and laughing noisily, the first of a seasonal plague. Most of them, thank goodness, jetted off to Spain and the Canaries nowadays, but Embridge was no more immune from the attentions of the stay-at-homes than any other south coast town. These days, though, there was seldom the serious trouble that the large-scale invasions of the sixties and seventies were supposed to have caused. Chel was too young to remember that, and she watched the group almost with approval. Oliver had been a biker in his wild younger days, she thought with fleeting warmth, although she didn't quite see him as bald. She imagined him as unruly rather than vicious, whatever his horrible stepmother tried to make her believe.

Quite suddenly, she felt extremely tired, and after her early start to the day and all that drama, no wonder! She would lie down with the headache she had given herself and sleep the next few hours away, and when she woke, he would be home.

She awoke with a start a long time later, her mouth dry. She had had a dream, a dark dream that now she hardly remembered. There had been some sort of tower, black and ragged against a glowing sky, and some foul thing that lived there, and a door in a wall that stayed obstinately closed. She had torn at the door with her fingers until they bled, because there was something behind it that she should have done, and if she didn't do it the thing in the tower would get out ... but it was already fading. There was a quayside and evening light that might have been in Greece, and then nothing.

252

The light in the room was dim. The gleam from the streetlamp below probed through the low windows and cast yellow reflections on the sloping walls and the ceiling. She lay for a moment aware that something had broken her dream, acutely conscious once more of the swift beating of her heart. Along the promenade, the traffic ground to and fro, and faintly in the distance she could hear a siren wailing, dying away. Perhaps whatever it was, police car or ambulance or fire engine, had gone past directly beneath and that was what had disturbed her. Yawning, she sat up stiffly and rubbed her eyes.

It was very dark outside, she must have slept for ever. She peered at her watch in the gloom and was startled to find that it was nearly half-past eight, and her already galloping heart missed a beat and gave an alarming thump. It was too late to go down to meet Oliver, if she had ever meant to do so. He should have been back ages ago.

Too late rang in her ears like an epitaph. At the back of her mind, her hands scrabbled at a door in a wall, breaking her fingernails and her heart together.

She tumbled off the couch and ran to the window, dropping on her knees to look out. Down by the pier, *Cascabel* lay against the quay with no lights showing, and further along, the diving company's little office was in darkness. They were all ashore then, and dispersed to their homes ... all except Oliver.

In an instant, all the day's accumulated miseries and fears leapt back into the room with her. She scrambled to her feet again, switched on the light, and stood looking at the emptiness.

He could have come back, found her asleep, and gone out again, but if so he had left no sign. No little note to say where he had gone, nothing ... nothing at all.

Chel swallowed. This was something new – he must have gone off for a drink with the rest of the crew, that was it. She had thought of that possibility earlier, of course she had. He would be back home soon, and she would maybe be wise to have supper ready and a smile on her face.

The kitchen felt cold. Chel tipped a few potatoes into the sink and began to peel them, but slowly, and after a few minutes the knife slipped from her hand and she went back into the other room. How stupid of her to have this feeling that something was dreadfully wrong. Men quarrelled with their wives every day of the week, and went out to drown their sorrows, and everyone survived the experience. All right, they had never done it themselves, but there had to be a first time. She folded her arms round Little Theodosius for comfort, and the deserted room mocked her.

It was nearly nine o'clock now. If *Cascabel* had come in on time he must have been ashore ages. It was a hard punishment for something that had been at least partly his own fault, and Chel began to feel resentful again. Resentment kept her going for ten minutes, but there was no proper fuel for it, and it died.

Oliver wouldn't do it. He might, she supposed, go off and have a quick drink, just to make a point, if he was still angry enough, but he wouldn't ... he wouldn't stay away for all this time out of spite. Although it would be comforting to convince herself that he might, she knew perfectly well that he wouldn't.

'Oliver, where are you?' asked Chel, aloud, but it was a mistake. The sound of her own voice only underlined the desertion of the flat. She sat down on the edge of the studio couch.

The minutes ticked slowly by. Half-past nine now, and she had no idea what to do. She could go down to the payphone in the downstairs lobby and phone round their friends, she supposed, he might just have dropped in somewhere and forgotten the time – anything – nothing was actually impossible, however unlikely. Her reluctance to put this theory to the test sprang, she discovered, from the thought that he might not be with any of them, and if he wasn't ...

Oh God, Oliver, what are you doing?

Chel got to her feet at last, searched in her purse, and took out all her small change. She would phone Bill Rowlands, it was just possible that something had come up over the *Hesperides* and they were meeting to discuss it, and that for some reason Oliver had failed to let her know. They had no phone of their own, after all – Oliver hated the very idea of being too available and, in spite of the inconvenience to herself, had steadily resisted the idea of either of them owning a mobile, claiming the payphone downstairs was more than enough – and if anyone had knocked on the door with a message she had been so heavily asleep that she easily might not have heard.

But there might well be a message downstairs in the shop, they were quite happy to take business calls and it stayed open late. Of course there would be! Pleased with this thought, Chel ran out of the flat and was down two flights of stairs before she realised that her knees were shaking.

Supposing there wasn't?

There wasn't.

The telephone for the use of the tenants was in the narrow hall just inside the street door to the flats. It wasn't an ideal position, as it was rather dark, cramped and cold, and constantly invaded by people going in and out. Chel, searching through the directory for Bill's home number, heard a clock on a nearby church striking the three quarters, and dropped the book at her feet.

'Oh God!' It came out on a sob.

She thought of Susan, of Oliver's parents, of anyone in this big town to whom she could turn for help. Bill Rowlands was forgotten. Almost of their own volition, her fingers punched in the first number that came into her head in this emergency.

His voice answered her almost at once, easy and untroubled.

'Holmes here,' he said. 'Hullo?'

'Jonathan!' Relief that he was at home flooded her voice, swept over her, and almost reduced her to tears. 'Jonathan, thank God you're there – it's Chel – Cheryl.'

'Cheryl!' He sounded startled. 'Good God – what –'

She interrupted him. 'Jonathan, help me. Oliver's gone mi –'

'Gone?' Jonathan interrupted, sharply. 'Gone where?'

'I don't know,' said Chel, desperately. 'He should have been home hours ago, but he isn't and there's been no message. I don't know what to do.'

'Now then,' said Jonathan, soothingly. 'He'll have gone to see a mate and forgotten the time. Blokes do things like that. *You* know.'

'For *this long*? Don't be silly!'

'Did you forget that he told you he'd be late? Come on, Cheryl, don't panic.'

'I'm not panicking,' said Chel, hoping it was true. 'Oh please – help me.'

Something in her voice reached him over the wire and a pulse leaped in his throat. She was in trouble and she had come straight to him, but he could think about that later. His own voice as he answered her was calm and steady.

'Have you tried the police? Perhaps there's been an accident.'

'Between here and the dock?' Her voice shrilled. 'How could there be? I'd have heard the fuss – someone would have told me –'

'Well, he's not been abducted by aliens,' said Jonathan, calmly.

'Something's happened to him!'

'Steady on there,' said Jonathan. 'You've just told me there's no possibility of an accident between there and the dock, and if he had one diving, you'd have known by now. Now listen

– just listen, and then answer me slowly. Are you sure he was coming straight home? Quite, quite sure?'

'I thought he was!' Chel wailed, and bit her lip.

'All right, calm down. But he might have gone somewhere else? Think, take your time.'

'He might, but not for all this time, Jonathan. Surely he couldn't.'

It didn't seem to occur to her that going somewhere else introduced the missing scope for an accident, and Jonathan didn't point it out. He said,

'No, possibly not, but you can't be sure. Have you any ideas where he might have gone? Have you tried asking anyone?'

'No,' said Chel. 'And no. I don't know where to begin.' Her voice rose on a note of desperation again, and she clenched her teeth on a need to scream at him.

Jonathan hesitated, sensing the unreleased scream and reluctant to ask his next question, with all its implications.

'Does he carry any identification on him – driving licence, credit cards, something like that?'

Oliver never bothered when it was just a matter of covering the hundred yards or so from the flat to the dock. Dressing and undressing in the confines of the boat, things tended to get lost, he said, and where was the point?

'I don't think so,' said Chel, in a whisper.

Jonathan thought. He didn't believe that anything very deadly could have happened to Oliver Nankervis of all people without half the town knowing, and himself, very probably, among the first, but Cheryl was obviously in a state. He thought, with his journalist's objectivity, that there was a story here, more of a story than appeared on the surface.

'Just stop there,' he said. 'I'll be right round. And don't worry, he'll probably be back before I get there.' He rang off.

He hadn't meant to be taken quite so literally, but when he opened the street door, Chel was sitting on the bottom stair, her arms round her knees, shivering.

'He isn't back,' she greeted him.

'OK.' Jonathan slipped off his own warm jacket and put it round her shoulders. 'Look, I'll tell you what we're going to do. You get your coat and I'll drive you to the police station – no, listen to me. If anything's happened to him, they should know, and if they don't the hospital may. If we don't find him at either of those places, and why should we? then the odds are that he's fine. We'll leave a note, just in case he comes in and wonders where you are, or you'll end up spending the entire night looking for each other – that's better! Smile, nothing terrible's happened.'

Chel sniffed and wiped the back of her hand inelegantly across her nose. She didn't feel at all like smiling, but her emotions had gone into a jelly and were beyond her proper control.

'We had this stupid quarrel,' she said desolately.

'Ah,' said Jonathan.

They looked at each other, Chel biting back tears and Jonathan trying not to look knowing, and both of them failing.

'It wasn't like that at all – it isn't like that,' said Chel, and got stiffly to her feet.

The police at the station weren't particularly concerned over the husband of a tear-stained pregnant woman who had failed to return home after a domestic, they'd heard it all before. They patted her shoulder, told her it often happened and was nothing to get upset about, and gave Jonathan a long, all too knowing look.

'Just let us know if he isn't back in a day or so,' said the desk sergeant, in a fatherly manner.

'A day or so!' Chel had found mere hours too long, and her face was aghast.

'Oh, he'll be home at closing time, never you fret,' said the sergeant. 'Have a nice cup of tea now, and try not to worry.'

Chel declined the tea and returned to the car with Jonathan.

'I suppose you haven't thought – no. Silly me,' said Jonathan, and could have kicked himself. Chel peered at him in the darkness.

'Thought that he'd jumped on a boat and taken off to the ends of the earth again? Yes, of course I have – but how could he? Why would he?'

'Just a thought. Forget I spoke.'

Chel wished she could forget it. Of all the things that she had tried not to think, this was the most likely and the most frightening. Because you couldn't put it past Oliver, he had done it before. In fact, it seemed to be a conditioned reflex in the face of threatened domestic controversy. But surely, he loved her, they were married, they were going to have a child. Oliver had a problem with close relationships, true, but not with her, never with her.

They drove to the Embridge General Hospital in silence.

The Accident & Emergency department was busy, but the nurse on the desk listened to their story. She rubbed her nose thoughtfully.

'Nankervis?' She shook her head. 'We haven't had a patient of that name here, I'd have remembered.'

'Oliver Nankervis,' said Chel, hopelessly.

'I can double check for you,' offered the nurse, doubtfully. She went off and Chel leaned exhaustedly against Jonathan. She didn't want Oliver to be here, of course she didn't, but it would be better than the Azores, and if he wasn't here, what else could she think? What else could he possibly be doing? Perhaps she would never see him again.

Jonathan put his arm round her.

'Cheer up, I expect he's home by now and wondering where *you* are.'

A more senior nurse appeared and came over to them. She was accompanied by a police constable.

'Mrs. Nankervis?'

'Yes,' said Chel.

'Mrs. Oliver Nankervis? Has your husband a middle name, can you tell me?'

Chel felt only a dreary surprise at such pedantry.

'Yes. Jason. Does it matter?' Helen had chosen it, she knew, with what seemed now uncanny prescience. No doubt the Dreaded Dot had shuddered over it.

'Sit down.' The nurse pulled out a chair invitingly, and Jonathan put Chel into it and sat down beside her, taking her hand in his firmly. The nurse said,

'Mrs. Nankervis, can you describe your husband?'

Chel said, suddenly cold with dread,

'Six foot tall, dark hair ... sort of dark, greyish-blue eyes ...' Her voice tailed off uncertainly. *Wild, exciting, a free spirit.* The police constable held out something in his hand.

'I'm sorry, Mrs. Nankervis. Have you seen this before?'

It was Oliver's watch. The glass was broken, but the time stood accurately at eleven fifteen. Chel turned it over, and there were Oliver's initials on the back.

O.J.N. and a date. She wondered who had given it to him. Joanna, perhaps.

'Yes, it's his,' she said.

She sat with the watch in her hands, absent-mindedly rubbing her thumb over the cracked and starred glass, oddly relieved to have the question settled. It was Jonathan who asked, 'What happened?'

'I'll fetch Sister,' said the nurse, exchanging a glance with the policeman.

Sister was straightforward, coolly sympathetic, and had kind eyes that promised nothing. Mercifully, she wasted no time trying to break things gently.

'Nobody knows yet what happened,' she said. 'Somebody found him, in the alleyway behind those houses in Meridew Street. It's dark down there, but she thought she heard something and went to look. He had been rather viciously attacked, I'm sorry, but it wasn't robbery, he still had money on him and that watch. But no identification, and nobody recognised him or we would have informed you long ago. I'm sorry,' she repeated.

Chel's nails had dug into the palms of her hands until, she found later, they left a series of crimson half-moon shaped bruises on her flesh. The thought of Oliver hurt and unrecognisable, abandoned like so much rubbish in a dark alley, was completely unacceptable. To her own amazement, her voice came out without a tremor.

'How bad?' she asked.

Very bad, it seemed. Broken ribs perforating both lungs, internal injuries to the stomach and intestines, a shattered spine, renal failure and a lot of superficial bruising, as if, Sister did not quite say but Chel and Jonathan clearly understood, he had been brutally kicked while he lay on the ground. He had arrived here in a state of collapse from shock and dying from suffocation, among other things, and been sent straight to the operating theatre. That had been at half-past eight, or very shortly after. The surgeons would go on working on him so long as he survived, but Mrs. Nankervis should understand ...

Mrs. Nankervis should wait. Should – not could. The hospital would inform Oliver's parents if she wished, now that they knew who he was.

'I'll stay with you until someone else comes,' said Jonathan, and although her strange new calmness felt quite unassailable, Chel was glad of the offer because the world was suddenly a very lonely place. They sat on a black vinyl sofa outside the closed doors to the emergency operating theatre, and the quiet of the night settled round them like a blanket. A nurse brought cups of unwanted tea, smiled reassuringly, and shook her head in answer to Jonathan's questions. The patient was still alive, that was all she knew.

The night crept by on leaden feet and Chel sat on the hard black bench with her arms curled protectively round her unborn child. They would tell her if he died. She tried to imagine him hurt as described and utterly failed. The failure was obscurely comforting, demoting the appalling truth to the level of a film on television that made only a token impact on the emotions.

Jonathan appeared far more upset. He took her hand and patted it helplessly.

'Cheryl, I'm so sorry...'

He was there beside her when she needed someone, as he had once promised he would be. Chel found suddenly that she wasn't a bit grateful after all, the patting was irritating and when she turned to look at him and saw his friendly, familiar face all broken up with sympathy, she removed her hand firmly.

'I'm all right Jonathan, don't fuss.'

The hours crawled on. Oliver's parents arrived, his father white with shock, his stepmother weeping. They looked censorious, Chel thought, to find Jonathan there. Even so, he would have stayed if she had asked him.

She didn't.

'Oh Cheryl, you poor child!' cried Dorothy Nankervis, and tried to take her in her arms. Chel leaned back on the seat and kept her hands well out of reach of further patting, and Dorothy had to be content with kissing her, which was bad enough, leaving a wet smear of her tears on Chel's cheek. Chel bunched herself into a protective corner. Too much sympathy, she dimly realised, would bring her to the ground with considerable pain and loss of dignity. Even her present untouchable isolation had to be better than that.

Finding that she wouldn't talk, the Nankervises spoke quietly to each other. Oliver's father patted his wife's hand, Chel noted sardonically, and she sobbed and sniffed into her handkerchief.

'He was so difficult always, poor Oliver, but I would never, never, wish this on him Jerry, you know I wouldn't. I always tried.' Very edifying no doubt, particularly when one considered how she appeared to dislike Oliver, but not at all helpful. Chel wished that they would go away.

More hours had gone past. Whatever were they doing, Chel wondered. He must have been in the theatre now for almost eight hours.

A quiver of apprehension ran along her nerves like the first icy breath of a long winter. It wouldn't do to think of Oliver on the operating table, broken and bleeding and dying. She thought childishly, *perhaps it won't happen*, and then found that Dorothy was looking at her with red-rimmed eyes limpid with concern.

'Cheryl darling, you look exhausted. Let me take you home to rest. Think of the baby.'

'I'm quite all right,' said Chel, coolly.

'Jerry can let you know the minute there's any news.'

And while he did so, trying to shield her and break things gently, Oliver could go off on his last long voyage without her there to say goodbye.

'No,' said Chel, and only added 'thank you' as a belated afterthought.

It was very dark outside. From where she sat, Chel could see along the passage to a window that was a black rectangle against the clinical white walls, but she knew that beyond it lay a clear starry night, with a hint of frost in the air. A beautiful night ... there had been other clear starry nights before this one,

263

nights in Cornwall on that premature, magical honeymoon they had stolen together, and nights spent under the golden ball of a Mediterranean moon, warm and soft with summer. Nights – and days – of laughter, days of adventure and of love. Chel took them out and looked at them all in her mind, and at her memories of Oliver, tall and strong and aflame with an enthusiasm for living that swept her along beside him like the surf of the sea he loved. Oliver couldn't die, not kicked to death in some dark alley for no apparent reason. It couldn't end here in this great impersonal building smelling of disinfectant. That wasn't how a dream should finish, and she felt a sudden unexpected burst of rage as if he had cheated her somehow.

People came and went quietly, offering more tea, useless comfort, and the endless hours crawled on. It was a lifetime since Oliver had run downstairs calling that he would see her when he got back.

Her anger with him had gone as suddenly as it had come. Now she could only think how life with him had been such fun! She remembered him, pink to the gills with embarrassment and pleasure over the baby that he might never see, and the two sides of the picture grated together almost audibly. She couldn't believe that Oliver would never see his baby.

Shortly after seven, there was a sudden disturbance in the quiet dawn, the doors of the theatre were pushed open and there was the bustle attendant on getting a trolley out into the passage and Oliver was taken right past them, barely alive and on his way to intensive care. At least, Chel supposed that it was Oliver, but for a moment wasn't absolutely sure. The dark hair, tousled and damp, was familiar, but the planes of his face seemed to have fallen away, leaving the bones starkly outlined and she hadn't realised that a human being could be that colour, a sort of ashy grey, his skin glazed with sweat under the overhead lights. She had armoured herself this far, she realised, with the conviction that he was unsinkable, but seeing him, even in a flash like that, she knew that he was not.

She could feel herself unexpectedly breaking up inside, like the *Hesperides* on her long-ago reef, so that it was only with an effort that she was able to hold on to her self-control.

A middle-aged man in green overalls, with a mask pulled down under his chin and a consciously kind face white with exhaustion, came out and spoke to them.

'I'm sorry,' he said. 'We've done all we could.'

Nearly eleven hours, and at the end of it, *I'm sorry*. Chel couldn't believe it, and Oliver's stepmother gave a moan of distress.

'But all that time –' Chel realised with a shock that it was her own voice, uselessly pleading.

'I know,' he said, and she thought that he really did, for he went on to explain. 'We have to try. There's always a chance, and if we can't save your husband today, there's always a hope that we can learn something that will save someone else tomorrow. We have to try,' he repeated, and Jerry Nankervis asked, soberly, 'How long?'

'Not long. An hour, two maybe. You can stay with him.' He hesitated, and then, with instinctive understanding, added the only thing that might make this remotely bearable. 'There are no responses, he'd be paralysed if he lived, from the neck. Not much of a life for a man like that.' He gave Chel's shoulder a gentle squeeze and went on his way.

Two more hours ...

Intensive care, in a chilly April dawn, had soothing blue lighting and an air of purposeful activity, and even if Oliver was expected to slip quietly away, they had given him every chance. It was some while, in spite of what the surgeon had said, before they were admitted, and by then he had been linked to a life support machine and given help with his severely impaired breathing. He was extensively, brutally injured, and in deep shock, hanging on to life by no more than a tenuous thread. Dorothy broke down at the sight of him and had to be taken outside again, but Jerry stayed beside Chel, not touching her but sharing her vigil. They had never been friends, but as they sat together through that awful night, watching the man they both loved slowly die, she felt closer to him than she had ever felt before.

In the quiet ward, in a silence broken only by bleeps and soft footsteps, Oliver struggled for breath with his ebbing strength and Chel sat beside him, her hands lying still in her lap, safe just for this endless hour in the quiet eye of that storm that had come so suddenly out of nowhere, bursting their fragile bubble of laughter and love. It was, she realised, the greatest understanding she could give him, to let him go without wanting to hold him back. The last unselfish gift that she would ever make to him, and the hardest. She felt the pain as if it was a monstrous incubus shaped to her fit.

Please God, let time be endless, just for today.

Oliver had been wrapped in a foil blanket to retain what little body warmth he had, spinning out the final hours for as long as might be. His hair had stuck to his forehead in a sweaty fringe, and after a while, Chel reached out a tentative hand and brushed it gently aside. He was icy cold, and fear rolled itself into a tight ball under her ribs. He was going, he really was – Oliver, who hadn't wanted to die, who had wanted to go on living – but on his own terms, not these, Oh God, not these. She let her hand rest against his cheek, keeping contact until the very last moment, feeling all the love that she had ever had for him making a hard lump in her throat, horribly aware of the nervous disintegration taking place under her touch, her will to make her head rule her instinct in shatters, her own mind blank with shock and a voiceless whistle for the wind.

I love you, I love you, I love you. Take my love with you, out on this ebbing tide.

The hands on the clock went slowly round.

Twenty-four hours now since he had run down the stairs of the flat, whole and strong and apparently invincible. It felt like a hundred years, long and laden with tears. Chel was unaware of feeling tired, but she must have been more exhausted than she knew, for she began to be stupidly convinced that while she was here with him, he couldn't die. It was grotesque, unthinkable, but while she was here he would continue to labour for breath, and the natural processes of healing would slowly go on.

She was keeping him alive. The conviction was terrifying when she knew that he would prefer to die. The persistent blip of light across the screen of the monitor unit became the biggest reproach in the universe. She withdrew her hand from physical contact with him for a moment, and was certain that the blip grew weaker.

If she let him die, would it be the same as killing him?

Oh God, no!

It had to be her imagination. They were close, yes, but not, surely not, that close. *Please God, not that close!*

Five hours. Six hours.

Oliver was now four hours beyond his allotted time, the wavering blip still struggling with fragile determination across the screen. The surgeon had come in with a colleague and stood for some time at the foot of the bed, talking to the ward sister in low tones. Eventually, she came over to Chel and Jerry.

'His sister is here outside,' she said quietly. 'You should go and get some rest, she can stay with him for a while. We can ring at once if there's any change.'

'I don't want to leave him,' Chel tried to insist, but they gently detached her from his side and sent her away, urging her to think of the baby. Jerry took her home with him, to a meal she couldn't eat and a bed on which she couldn't rest. She lay on it, tense and wakeful, and thought, if it wasn't for the baby they would have let me stay, if it wasn't for the baby it would never even have happened, I hate the baby, I hate it – and suddenly she wanted Oliver so much that it was agony.

Getting off the bed, she moved restlessly around the room. It was a pleasant enough room in its impersonal way, but she didn't belong in it. It was for guests, and she could never be anything but a stranger in this house. Had Oliver ever lived in it? She couldn't imagine him here.

They hadn't wanted her to marry him, and now at the moment of his death they were snatching him back. Unable to bear it any more, Chel ran to the door and opened it. If they wouldn't take her back to him, she would walk the whole way.

In the downstairs hall, someone was speaking on the telephone. Oliver's stepmother, her voice hushed, paying lip-service to convention, her tears miraculously dried.

'... no, I don't think I shall be able to come. He won't live out the day, and then I suppose there'll have to be an inquest and there will be all the arrangements to make for the funeral. We can't expect too much from the Wainwright girl, I'm afraid, it will all fall on Jerry, and I shall have to deal with the flowers and the catering, all those things. It's likely to be well-attended, and there'll be a lot to do. Oh God, and the media again! How will poor Jerry bear it? And Oliver was so improvident always, heaven knows what sort of a muddle he'll have left behind him.'

Chel was on the stairs, furiously angry and dreadfully frightened. In that brief moment she had seen terrible things, post mortem and inquest, the inevitable verdict, the long cortege of funeral cars winding its way to the crematorium, herself weeping in an agony of loss and everything over for ever. Nor had she realised until that moment that when Oliver died, he would have been murdered. She was screaming.

'He won't die, he won't, and I'm his wife, it's nothing to do with you! You hate him!'

Dorothy put down the telephone with a brief apology.

'The child is getting hysterical, I must go.'

'Take me back,' said Chel, brokenly. 'I want to go back.' Before she had even finished speaking, the telephone rang, and it was the hospital.

V

A nger was some sort of defence against reality, it gave her something on which to spend her emotions. Chel sat beside Oliver's father in the car and wondered how long his stepmother had been on the phone, how long the hospital had been trying to get through. If Oliver died before she got there, she would never forgive her, never. The idea of unforgiveness was a rock to cling to. You weren't dead if you could feel unforgiving, and there would be nothing else to go on living for.

The bare, functional ward with its meaningless technical equipment and the high, narrow bed was like an oasis in infinity. Everything – living, love, laughter, seemed to her to have gathered there ready to take flight. Oliver was so close to death that the blip of light on the monitor screen was beginning to run into a continuous line. It couldn't be long now, said Sister to Oliver's father, somewhere in the background. They, and Susan who was still here, looked at Chel with pity, and Oliver's father, at least, had tears running down his face.

Yet half an hour later, to the surprise of the hospital staff and Chel's considerable alarm, the blip had picked itself up and resumed its weary struggle across the accusing screen.

'It must be something about you, dear,' said Sister, but didn't mean it.

Later, an apologetic policeman asked her if she had any idea why her husband should have been near Meridew Street. Chel, who didn't even know for sure where Meridew Street was, found this impossible to answer. One of those narrow little terraces up behind the dock, the policeman told her, but it meant nothing. He could have been taking a short cut into the town, but she had no idea why he should when he ought to have been on his way home. Nobody knew but Oliver, and he was too ill to be asked.

The question mark wove itself ghoulishly into the memory of their quarrel, and remained as inconclusive, and Oliver went on clinging to life with the same courage and tenacity that had taken him round the world. Chel had come to hate the spring of love inside her that seemed to be, bizarrely, strong enough to support them both, to hold Oliver here against all reason or all mercy. She was quite unable to walk away and leave him to die, but he would hate being paralysed, perhaps more than anything else in the world. Nobody who loved him could wish that for him, unless like Susan and her mother they had no imagination. The conviction left no room for hope, either for his death, which she dreaded, or for his continued survival which would be so much worse. Not knowing what to do, she sat beside him waking, slept in a chair beside him, had dreadful dreams laden with guilt and woke again to grief and pain. Everyone was very kind and gentle to her.

The crawling hours had become crawling days, threatened to grow into crawling weeks, and Oliver ceased to hold onto life merely by the gossamer thread that bound him to Chel, and began to fight back on his own account. He was far too ill to realise what had happened to him, and his own will to survive began to take over, slowly bringing him back from the dead.

But there had to be a price. The little baby died.

He arrived in the world too soon, and was whisked straight away to an incubator. He was tiny, outwardly perfect, dark as his father with the same winged eyebrows that Oliver had from his natural mother, Helen. Chel turned her face away from him and couldn't look. She had said that she hated him, she had been eaten up with hate for everyone. Hate poisoned you, and she wished that she was dead, she wished Oliver was dead. Two hours later, they brought the baby to her and put him into her arms, and a kind vicar christened him, very quickly, Jeremy, before his little heart ceased to beat, cradled there, after only ten short minutes – dead in his father's place, she thought, through a mist of shock and physical exhaustion, the poor little baby who had everything to live for, life, love, happiness, a future, sacrificed for the man who wouldn't want to live. Too tired and miserable to care any more, she turned her face to the wall.

Once it became obvious that Oliver would live when he had been marked to die, an entirely new element came into play. It was now worth trying – imperative to try – to see if anything could be saved from the wreck. The distinguished orthopaedic surgeon who was consultant to the new spinal injuries unit was brought in, and he in his turn brought in an even more distinguished neurologist. What they had to say was very encouraging, or so said Dorothy Nankervis, taking the forefront of the stage.

'Because they say poor Oliver isn't completely paralysed after all,' she said brightly, and Chel's heart gave a tremendous thump and began galloping like a startled horse, but Dorothy went on, reaching out to take Chel's hand as it lay, listless, on the arm of her chair. 'No, it was all part of the shock – traumatic, they called it. He may be paraplegic, they can't be certain yet – but he can still move his fingers, and he's beginning to breathe properly. Why, they had him off the ventilator for five whole minutes yesterday! Isn't that good news?'

Chel withdrew her hand, and Dorothy smiled more widely to show that she wasn't taking offence.

'It doesn't sound much.'

'My dear, you must learn to be grateful for the mercies that you have, however small they may seem to you.'

Did Oliver have to be grateful too? Chel couldn't bring herself to imagine how he must be feeling, what he must be thinking. She turned her face away, afraid that his stepmother would read too much into her expression. Her throat ached with pity for him.

'I want to see him,' she said.

'And so you shall, of course, just as soon as you're well enough.'

'Me?' asked Chel, choked, and swallowed hard.

'You poor children,' cooed Dorothy Nankervis. 'We don't want poor Oliver upset, now do we?' She reached to pat Chel's hand, which retreated instinctively like a tortoise's head scenting danger. 'You must try not to grieve, darling, the poor little baby was never right, was he?' *I told you so*, read the subtext. Chel hated her.

Helen had flown back from America, where she had been attending an exhibition of her own delicate and individual sculptures. She came to see Chel and sympathised over the loss of the baby, trying to hide her own distress but with her mind very obviously with her son. There was talk of a possible need for a kidney transplant when Oliver was strong enough, his father and his young half-sister, Debbie, were both tested for compatibility, but it was Helen who had proved the best match. If he would accept such a gift from a mother he appeared to dislike, and believed had deserted him, or even wanted it from anyone.

He might just prefer to die anyway.

But then, he probably didn't know ... oh, poor Oliver. Poor Oliver.

Chel moaned with pain, but there was nobody there to hear her. She sat in her hospital room and wished that the stupid quarrel had never happened. Without it, Oliver would surely never have gone near Meridew Street, whatever it was that he had been doing there. If he hadn't gone there, their child would still be growing inside her – growing towards life, whatever Dorothy said. That poor little baby, whose tiny coffin would lie soon in the churchyard at St. Mary's in the Meadow – *her* church, it would be. Chel had never been inside it, couldn't imagine it. She resented Dorothy Nankervis, who had arranged everything, although since both she and Oliver had been too ill to consult, she should maybe have been grateful. But Dorothy hadn't wanted her to have Oliver, and now she had stolen his child. Chel wept. The tears came easily.

Debbie came to see her, obviously uneasy, wary as a cat on eggshells. She didn't live in Embridge and seldom came home, for whatever reason. Chel had met her only once before, at the wedding. She remembered a confident, attractive young woman who had set out to charm Chel's own reluctant parents and largely failed, and had then taken over the halting wedding arrangements and in less than twenty-four hours transformed them into something that, if you didn't look too closely, almost seemed to work. That in itself had been a minor miracle, given the fact that, although Jerry Nankervis was reputed to be behind Debbie, neither set of parents had wanted the marriage in the first place, and that the two sides had nothing else in common. But now, two years on and away from the family circle, operating independently, she seemed a different creature. The streaked blonde hair, denim jeans and black leather jacket were recognisable, but her manner was less studied, probably nearer the truth. Ten years ago, her half-brother must have carried with him a similar air of dangerous rebellion, but it was to be hoped that a kinder fate lay ahead of Debbie.

'I'm sorry,' she said, awkward and embarrassed, standing just inside the door.

Chel made some meaningless stock response, but Debbie's appearance had shaken her. Debbie was a comparative stranger to her, although she had always felt that she might like her better than the others if she ever got the chance to know her. Unlike Dorothy, or Susan, or even Jerry, she wasn't looking at Chel with pity, she simply looked miserable and out of her depth. Also, for some reason Chel couldn't define, defiant. A faint, a very faint, flicker of interest warmed her breaking heart. Of Debbie, she might have made a friend had things been otherwise.

'I've just been to see Oliver,' said Debbie. 'He sent you his love.'

Chel looked down at her hands, twisting them together in her lap without noticing.

'He must wonder where I am.' It was her worst nightmare, that he might think she had run out on him. She hadn't, until now, even tried to voice it. Debbie didn't move from the door, but she said,

'He knows what happened. They told him.'

They must have had to, Chel thought miserably, to explain her absence. It said much for her state of mind that it had never occurred to her. Poor Oliver. Oh, poor Oliver, poor Oliver. She felt the easy tears starting to her eyes yet again, and her hands gripped tightly together. Debbie said, 'I don't think he understands, not really. He's doped to the gills anyway. You mustn't ... well, worry or anything, not about that. I brought you these.' Abruptly, she held out a tight bunch of violets, stepping forward at last to drop them onto Chel's clasped hands. 'A bit inadequate, I'm afraid.' Her voice took on a hard, mocking note. 'What do you give to the person who has nothing? Saccharine platitudes and bunches of violets. Hate me, if you want. I'm sure you hate the rest of us.'

Chel looked up in sudden surprise, her fingers curling round the delicate stems. The scent of the flowers rose up, a breath of sensual beauty in the dark of the abyss.

'I don't hate you, why should I?'

'Because all I've got to give is stupid violets!' She sounded angry. She would have liked to work miracles, had it been possible. '*All the king's horses and all the king's men, couldn't put Humpty-Dumpty together again* – don't mind me, I loved him too. It's not allowed.'

Jerry's daughter, of course ... but Dorothy's too. Oliver's half-sister ... and Susan's. Too young to be tactful, or even graceful, but Chel instinctively felt that she, perhaps alone among the well-wishers, fully appreciated the extent of the tragedy. Debbie, come bearing violets, young as the springtime herself – Chel caught herself up. Her voice, when she spoke, was wooden.

'The violets are very pretty.'

'Glad you like them.' Debbie hesitated, poised ready to fly but feeling it ungraceful to leave too soon. She had nothing to say to this weary woman, this stranger looking ten years older than her age, her sparkle quenched and with lightless eyes. She wanted to get away, to forget her. And to forget Oliver, too, so sterile and unfamiliar in that horrible bare room, with all those tubes and machines and things that dripped and bleeped and kept him in purgatory. She hadn't known what to say to him, either, but in his case it hadn't mattered much, he was hardly listening. It would be good to get back with her friends. And go out on the town, thought Debbie precisely, and get thoroughly drunk, because if she stayed sober, the memory of what she had seen today wouldn't let her sleep. She couldn't do anything, anyway.

'I have to get back to London,' she said, at random. She didn't have to take sides while she stayed away, that was the best way, she'd learned that early. But Cheryl – *Chel,* Oliver called her – needn't know that. She went on. 'Must dash. I'll see you again.'

She was gone, and Chel was left with the violets. She was too tired to untangle the threads of her sister-in-law's visit. Somewhere in the background, she thought that perhaps she ought to try... but it was too much effort. She dropped the little posy into her lap and covered her eyes with her hands, forcing back the tears. *What do you give the person who has nothing?* You allow them the blessedness of death.

But not she, no. She had given life.

It was Jonathan who told her what had happened that never-to-be-forgotten night, everyone else had – mistakenly, for the many possibilities haunted her – decided it was better to protect her from it for now, but naturally none of them had thought to warn Jonathan. Oliver's recollection of events was mercifully hazy, but the little that he did remember, and the subsequent police enquiries, had made it possible to piece most of the story together.

'It all started with that girl,' said Jonathan. 'The one who found him, remember? She didn't hear anything at all, she knew what happened and she went back. It was bloody brave of her under the circumstances, and if she hadn't he really would have died.'

Chel postponed feeling grateful until she had heard what Oliver thought about his prospects, she hadn't yet been considered fit to see him, which was a bad joke. Nor, to be honest, had she wanted to. Once she could face what happened, then perhaps she could also face Oliver. Perhaps.

'Tell me,' she said, now.

It seemed that *Cascabel* had come in from sea rather later than planned due to her late start, but in spite of this, Oliver had borrowed a fiver off one of the others and gone off towards the town. This much they had learned from Bill Rowlands. Chel, filling in the blanks correctly, deduced from this that his memories of the morning had still been uncomfortably clear, and that he had intended to find somewhere open to buy a peace offering, probably bottle shaped if she knew her Oliver. He had cut through the cluster of streets round the dock area, not by the alleyway but via Meridew Street itself. Halfway along, there was a tunnel which led through the terrace of shabby houses into the alley, narrow and somewhat noisesome, that ran along behind them.

'People keep dustbins in it,' said Jonathan, wrinkling his nose distastefully. 'It's rather an unsavoury spot. Dogs like it. Have you ever been there?'

'No,' said Chel.

'Don't bother then,' said Jonathan. 'Every town has its blot, that's ours. It's the sort of place where you can scream the place down, and people will just put their fingers in their ears. She – that girl who said she found him – was screaming the place down.'

'And Oliver wouldn't dream of putting his fingers in his ears,' said Chel with a swift, unreasonable surge of resentment. 'Tell me the worst. He went to help her, didn't he?'

An echo sounded in her head. *Beware of acting without thinking* ... who had said that?

'Of course he did,' Jonathan was saying, 'I think – I hope, anyway – that I would have done the same – but I might have thought twice when I found what it was all about. She lives in Meridew Street. Her story is that she was working late at one of the supermarkets on the edge of town, caught the bus in, and walked home from the town centre – it was a fine night, and if she was chancing her arm – which if you ask me, she was – if you live there, I suppose you feel differently. Then again, she may not be telling the entire truth here. But anyway, she says she cut through the alley to go in through the backyard entrance to her home, and as she walked along, minding her own business, she met this crowd of mindless hooligans coming the other way. They weren't local, I'm glad to say. We have 'em, but they're generally a fairly reasonable bunch. This lot were the scaff and raff from some no-go, inner city area, come south to make trouble somewhere respectable where they could shock old ladies and gentlemen and crowds of holiday-making grockles, and make themselves feel big. They'd been around all day, lots of people had seen them, sowing the seeds of trouble here and there, one jump ahead of the fuzz, having fun. By this time, they were just drunk enough to have taken the brakes off ... if there ever were any, that is.'

'I think I saw them,' said Chel. 'It must have been them – earlier, walking along by the harbour.' She had watched them almost with affection, she recalled, and felt a shock of revulsion.

'Quite likely. Anyway, to cut a long – and to my mind, slightly suspect – story short, they met this young lady walking demurely home to Mum, butter won't melt and all that, and got ideas. Oliver arrived when they appeared to be weighing the possibilities of a gang bang – I say appeared to be, because they never got the chance to take a vote on it. From what the girl says, he sailed into them with the wind behind him and walloped two of them into next week before they quite knew what had hit them. But there were seven of them, and only one of him.' He paused. 'She ran away in the confusion, and whether she invited it or whether she didn't, who can blame her? But later, when it had gone quiet, she thought she ought to go back, just in case. She found him dying there among the dustbins, and ran screaming to the pub on the corner, where there's a phone. But it wasn't until Oliver was able to say what he remembered that she actually told the truth – or her version of it. She says she was afraid the police might not understand, which I personally take to mean that she can't honestly say she didn't ask for what she nearly got. And of course, by the time she got over her modesty, the birds had flown – or trained, or biked or whatever – back to their gloomy little lairs.'

'So they'll never be caught,' said Chel, and was amazed at the wave of pure rage that swept her, and the raw fury in her own voice. Jonathan looked at her speculatively.

'They have been caught,' he said. 'Does that make you feel better?'

'I'll tell you, when they've been tried and sentenced,' said Chel, viciously. 'How did they catch them?'

'Oh, enough people had seen them during the day, I told you. Some officious old biddy had even taken the numbers of their bikes, providentially. The police up-country pulled them in, and the girl identified them. It was as easy as picking up sticks.'

Chel thought of poor Oliver, exhausted by the simple effort of breathing, ignorant of his dramatically altered life, and resolutely didn't think of her dead baby. Her fists curled into tight balls.

'I'd like to kick *them* to pieces!' she said, between her teeth, and looked so blackly furious that Jonathan hardly recognised her. A sob caught in her throat. 'Bloody, *bloody* animals!'

'They're caught now,' said Jonathan, but if he had intended that as consolation, it missed its mark.

As soon as she felt that she could trust herself not to be stupid and upset him and herself together, Chel was taken down the long corridors smelling of disinfectant and was able to speak to her husband for the first time since he had stormed out of the flat, almost three weeks ago now.

Oliver was still under continual observation in intensive care, but he would shortly be transferred – ironically, to that same spinal injuries unit that he had sailed round the world to help provide, now preparing for its official opening – although unofficially it had already been operational for some months. The nursing staff were thrilled with him for having been tough enough to survive and thought that he was lovely, but Chel thought that he looked frail, exhausted and extremely ill, flat on his back in a plaster cast to his chin, and supported by terrifying electronic equipment and yards of plastic tubing. He was still sedated, since the passing of traumatic paralysis had meant the return of sensation and the onset of considerable pain, but he was rather drowsily awake and perfectly aware of her, even managing a faint smile at the sight of her.

'Chel.' His hand stirred minutely towards her on the sheet, and Chel reached out and took it. He felt hot and unfamiliar, and his eyes were full of drugged shadows.

'Hullo,' said Chel, in a breaking voice that tried its best to sound bright and cheerful. Her trust in herself had been misplaced, and she could feel the all-too-ready tears hovering ominously. Oliver's fingers pressed her own, so lightly that she nearly missed it.

'They told me about the baby. I'm so sorry.' His voice was little more than a thread of sound in the quiet room.

'Oh well,' said Chel, unsteadily. 'We can have other babies. There'll never be another you.' It seemed a monstrous betrayal of her son, but she had too much dread of her own distress for absolute honesty. Oliver seemed to take the remark at face value, he gave a very slight sigh and his eyes looked away from her.

'Good thing, too,' he suggested. 'One of me is going to be more than enough...' The words were said with an attempt at lightness killed, stone dead, by their ominous truth.

'I love you very much,' said Chel, because she could think of nothing else.

'And I love you,' said Oliver.

A silence fell between them – an awkward silence, the first they had ever known. Oliver broke it eventually. He was still not looking directly at her, his eyes were unfocussed and hazy, fixed on frightening possibilities.

'I've been told my back is broken. It is going to be all right, isn't it?'

The sudden urgency in his voice frightened her, it pleaded for a reassurance that she wasn't qualified to give, even if she hadn't known, if he did not, that *broken* was an understatement.

'Of course it is,' she said, helplessly.

'You wouldn't lie to me.' It was a statement, not a question, but tense and uncertain. 'I couldn't bear to be paralysed, Chel – I couldn't.'

'You mustn't worry,' said Chel, crossing her fingers, because what Oliver meant and what she was about to encourage him to believe were two different things. 'You know you can move your fingers, and that's just the beginning, I promise.' She laid her hand against his cheek gently, as she had done when she thought that he was dying ... as he had been, but he had lived.

I didn't do it on purpose, Oliver, I didn't.

Oliver had closed his eyes, his lashes making dark fans against his pale cheeks. She choked back tears and watched him miserably. Restricted by the heavy cast, his breathing seemed so slight as to be non-existent. He didn't seem like Oliver at all. She sank her teeth into her lower lip and forced back the tears.

Back in her own room, she sat for a long time feeling bleak and unsure of herself, and cried for a little because it was better to cry than to think about the awful thing she had done to Oliver, and the emptiness that was all that remained of their hopes and dreams. There couldn't possibly be any more babies with Oliver like that, either, and at that moment she didn't even care.

VI

Chel was discharged from hospital the next day, and took her heartbreak home to the flat. Oliver's parents had urged her to go to their house for a while until she felt more like herself, but the invitation had struck her as forced, and although Oliver's father was kind – very kind, considering how little he approved of her – there was something about his wife's kindness that made her feel herself a moral obligation rather than a welcome member of the family. The Dreaded Dot still thought of her, quite obviously, as *the Wainwright girl*, only her sense of duty made her pretend to be kind. Chel didn't want to feel shut out of the family circle like that even if she had no wish to join it. She further refused her own mother's offer of a few day's companionship while she "found her feet", whatever that was supposed to mean. She had a desperate inner need to get away from all of them and to work out her grief in her own way, knowing that until she could do so, she would never come to terms with what had happened.

Only, once in the flat, it seemed less simple than she had thought, and there were many times when she wished that she had felt able to accept her mother's kindly meant offer. The sunny room under the roof where she and Oliver had been so happy was now so appallingly empty. She spent a lot of time sitting on the studio couch, rocking herself to and fro and cuddling the Pink Panther, but he was no real substitute for her handsome husband or for her little son, no cure for the huge ache inside her. Disaster had come so quickly – she needed Oliver to help her to get over it, she told herself, but their separation could easily last a year or more, and even then it wouldn't be Oliver she would have, but a severely disabled stranger. She turned away from that thought with the first stirring of real fear.

It would have been easier if Oliver had died. She didn't allow herself to think this in so many words, but the monstrous thought was there, hidden underneath a great pile of fears and inadequacies that haunted her through the lonely days. With hindsight, she suspected that she had always known that their shining happiness couldn't last, but she had been wrong – everyone had been wrong – about the direction from which the end would come. However would independent, active Oliver, who so loved his freedom, cope with being disabled? However would she cope with him? What kind of things would they have to learn, how restricted was their life going to be? There were no answers yet to any of these questions, but one day there would be, and they would have to be faced. She had a dreadful feeling that they might be answers she wouldn't like at all, and that Oliver would actively hate.

The thought crept in and wouldn't be turned away that if she hadn't insisted on marrying him, those answers wouldn't matter. It wasn't that she didn't love him any more, she told herself desperately, it was simply that the helpless invalid in the hospital wasn't the same person. She had only known him while the sun shone and now it was gradually going out altogether. She would never in a million years have tied herself so finally to a cripple. The bitter knowledge that this kind of thinking was at best politically incorrect, at worst downright cruel, made her ashamed but couldn't change the truth. She would never have done it. Finish.

Susan was no help, although her intentions were good. Her kindness was more genuine than her mother's, but unintentionally insensitive in spite of that.

'You'll have to give up that flat,' she said, in her brisk, competent way. 'You can't live in an attic with Oliver disabled. You'll have to find somewhere else before he comes home.'

This was another thing that Chel wasn't ready to think about, she didn't want to tear their home to pieces, feeling unreasonably that it would tear the remnants of their happiness to pieces too. She wished Susan would be quiet and go away, only Susan could be so unanswerably right and so unutterably wrong both at the same time. Because it was the only familiar thing left to her and Susan seemed so set on wrenching it away, she began to be stupidly obsessed with the flat. If only they could be together again in the place they had made so specially their own, everything would come right. Her awful depression would vanish like mist on a summer morning, Oliver would miraculously recover completely and confound everybody, everything would be as it had been before.

'He'll never get up three flights of stairs,' said Susan, as if that was the only consideration, but it wasn't, of course. There was also the question of money.

Chel and Oliver had never had a joint account, it had never occurred to them as an option. They didn't even use the same bank. Throughout most of their married life they had both been earning good money, they had happily pooled their resources for food and rent and continued, as they had always done, to use the remainder as personal disposable income. When they went out together, it had generally been Dutch treat. Anything that remained at the end of the week, and there hadn't been very much in Chel's case, remained in the balance of their individual accounts. Chel had frittered a lot of her balance away on things for the baby, there was a frighteningly small amount left. The rent was due on the flat, she couldn't afford that, let alone the expense of moving, and anywhere suitable for someone severely disabled, as Oliver might well turn out to be, would be miles beyond her means.

Oliver lay immobilised in the spinal injuries unit, slowly recovering from shock and injury, heavily drugged and for the moment quite unable either to sign his name to a cheque or to recognise the need to do so. Chel had only the vaguest idea of what a power of attorney was, and would never have gone to Jerry Nankervis for help even if she had fully understood.

Oliver's family already despised her. She couldn't confess that she was nearly destitute in front of them, any more than she could betray Oliver by telling her own parents that he had left her penniless in this crisis – if he had done so. For all she knew, there was money in his account. It was so stupid of her neither to know nor to have access to it if it was there.

Her part-time job had gone during the crisis. It would be too humiliating to have to go to Social Security. She went instead to Mr. MacDonald at the Queen's Hotel, and took a job as a chambermaid, at a chambermaid's wages, with the promise of something better if it arose, which was all that he had to offer her. But it paid enough to live on, and at least the awful Maeve was no longer there to jeer at her after all this time. She pushed the future out of her mind. Without actually lying about it, she allowed her family, and Oliver's, to believe that she had her old, pre-Greece job back. The work was tiring and uncongenial, but at least it helped to fill the days and made them – almost – bearable.

It was the nights that were not.

'Why don't you give up that flat and live-in like you used to do?' asked Susan, returning to the attack from a different angle. She was a shrewd young woman and was beginning to have her suspicions. 'It would save you money, and you wouldn't be on your own so much. It'll be months before Oliver is out of hospital.'

She would say that.

'No, I don't think so,' said Chel. There was no provision for chambermaids to live in, and it didn't occur to her that Old MacDonald would consider her a special case. The desire to cling on to the flat blinded her to anything beyond her own attic windows.

'I don't think you should be so much on your own,' said Susan, firmly. 'You aren't at all well, you should see your doctor.'

'I'm fine, don't fuss,' Chel said irritably, but when Susan had gone she cried for loneliness and was furious with herself for doing so.

Oliver didn't appear to notice that his wife looked tired and ill. Coping with pain, frustration and apprehension about the future took most of his fragile strength. He said little and asked no questions, but he seemed to like having her there with him. She spent a lot of time that summer just sitting beside him, her mind blank with weariness, unable either to give or to receive comfort and bitterly ashamed because he was showing considerable courage in the face of calamity and she knew that she wasn't. There was nothing she could say to him that wouldn't worry him, and he mustn't be worried. Communication between them virtually ceased.

Because for one reason or another she wouldn't let those who should have been closest to her into her confidence it was quite unexpected people who offered her the help she desperately needed. Bill Rowlands called round to see her to bring back Oliver's personal gear, his professional dry suit, his more casual wet suit, the mask and aqualung equipment which had all been left in the storeroom attached to his office.

'It's worth a bit,' he said, embarrassed. 'It doesn't look as if Oliver will be needing it again, and you could probably sell it – I could find you a buyer.'

Chel looked at it piled in a corner of the room and knew she would never have the heart. Diving and the *Hesperides* were the essence of Oliver as she had first known and loved him, and wouldn't ever know him again. Bill, a man of few words and kindly disposition, turned away from her obvious distress.

'But what I really came to say ...' he said, awkwardly. 'I know things must be difficult for you ... we think it really is the *Hesperides* down there, from what we've found so far, and if it is... well, Oliver won't dive on her of course, but he's the one who found her and he'll be entitled to a share eventually, so if it would help ... well, you could borrow against the expectation, if you needed to.'

Chel tried to imagine a bank lending money against a hypothetical treasure ship, and failed.

'It's very kind of you to tell me,' she said. 'But ...' And Bill replied, looking fixedly out of the window at the glittering expanse of harbour below, 'I meant, from me.'

Oh God, thought Chel, exasperated, I'm going to cry again! She swallowed hard and blinked a few times, but even so her voice wobbled badly as she repeated, 'It's very kind of you, Bill. Thank you.'

'Oh well,' said Bill, still looking intently down at the harbour. 'It was lousy luck. The offer's there if ever you need it, just let me know.'

Jonathan meant no more than kindness too, at least to begin with. In a way he felt responsible for what had happened, if it hadn't been for him, Cheryl would never have met Oliver Nankervis, although he would strenuously have denied anything more. Also, he loved her. He hadn't realised it at first and was inclined to despise himself when he did. After the way she had behaved he would have expected himself to have more pride, but there it was. Love hadn't been rooted out as he had confidently thought, it had gone underground, and like ground elder in a flower bed, was waiting there deep-rooted, to take over again and choke everything.

A wise man would run for cover, he told himself. What do you think you are, some medieval champion defending a damsel in distress? Sir Lancelot Rides Again! Chivalry rules, OK! But his Lady Guinevere was in real trouble, and he soon found somebody had to be her champion.

Like a raging bushfire that starts with a tiny spark, it began so simply. He was driving past the back entrance to the Queen's when she came off duty one lunchtime, and it was the most natural thing in the world to stop and offer her a lift for the short distance back to the flat. It seemed even more natural to accept her invitation to come upstairs for a few minutes.

'How's it going?' he asked. She looked pale, but that was natural, he supposed. She had plenty of people to look after her. He was aware of resenting this without understanding why.

'Oh,' said Chel. She was ahead of him on the stairs, he couldn't see her face. 'All right, I suppose.'

Jonathan had never been into the flat before. He looked around it critically and rather surprised. Oliver Nankervis's family must be loaded, he had bitterly imagined her enticed by money and luxury, so whence then this light and airy frugality? Was it possibly true after all then, what nobody had ever really believed, that Oliver had repudiated his father's wealth? If that was so, he was even crazier than people supposed. Jonathan looked thoughtful.

Chel came out of the kitchen carrying two mugs of tea. He saw her looking at him looking at the room and felt himself redden.

'I'm glad you're all right, then,' he said awkwardly.

She had known Jonathan for longer than anyone else around her now, she trusted him. The words spoke themselves before she realised they were even in her head.

'I'm not, that was a lie. Jonathan, what am I going to do?'

On the top of the bookcase, adjacent to the Pink Panther, Oliver and the Queen smiled at each other, the Queen with practised warmth, Oliver with his delightful easy charm. He had the world at his feet then, thought Jonathan sourly, and Cheryl in the hollow of his hand. Well, that was yesterday's news.

'Tell me about it,' he said.

They sat on the studio couch, and she told him something of the Nankervises attitude towards her and the general awfulness of everything, and cried a little. Jonathan listened and tried to comfort her, and it felt strange to have him there where Oliver habitually used to sit. He was kinder to her weakness than Oliver would have been.

'I'll always help you if I can, you know that,' said Jonathan. Chel didn't see how anyone could help her, but it was kind of him to say it. She dried her eyes, ashamed of herself and obscurely consoled.

'I know you will,' she said, "I'm so glad you're here. I've been so lonely.'

He saw her quite often after that, just for a few minutes, half an hour, here and there. It became a pleasant habit to meet her from work and drive her home, dropping her off outside the little tobacconist's shop, by mutual unspoken agreement never going upstairs to the flat again, he was out of place there. He was the only person to whom she told the truth about her job.

It must have been about three weeks before he realised that he had never stopped loving her, and by then it was too late.

The invitation came as an unwelcome surprise.

The Embridge & District Area Hospital Management Committee requests the pleasure of the company of Mrs. Cheryl Nankervis ...

Chel read it with horror, realising that she was being asked to take Oliver's place at the opening of the new unit, which she should have expected, but hadn't. Chel had spoken to the Queen, of course, on a happier occasion, but that had been with Oliver beside her, and the idea of having to be presented, on her own, to even rather lesser royalty, frightened her unreasonably. And there would be speeches, although God forbid anyone would expect her to make one, and newspaper reporters – who would undoubtedly want to speak with her. And a formal tea in the hospital grounds, and then the royal party would inspect the new facilities – provided, in a large part, by her husband's courage and enterprise, and Oliver, poor Oliver, would be there, unable to escape from what could only in the circumstances be a dreadful ordeal. She wondered how she had ever come to overlook the likelihood of it, and panic set in, full scale.

'I can't do it,' she said.

'Of course you can,' said Susan, to whom the bald negative was addressed. 'You owe it to all the people who gave sponsorship, even if you don't feel you owe it to Oliver. Don't be silly!'

'I've nothing to wear,' said Chel. Every instinct resisted what she already realised was an obligation she couldn't decently ignore. She felt the panic rising.

'Oh, nonsense!' Susan marched over to the cupboard in which Chel and Oliver kept their clothes and flung the doors open, rattling hangers along the rail. 'You must have – there's this, look, it's perfect, and this classic style never really goes out of date!' She whisked the ivory silk dress and jacket that Chel's mother had bought her for her wedding out of the cupboard, the same one that she had worn to the Palace for the investiture. Happy occasions, both. The soft, shimmering material of its circular skirt fell into rich folds that gleamed under the light. It had been ridiculously expensive. Chel remembered remonstrating unsuccessfully with Marilyn over its purchase. In a very real way, it hadn't been so much for her adornment as to show the Nankervises something in which they had not been interested anyway. She recalled the only times she had ever worn it and felt the too-ready tears sting behind her eyelids. Memories like that were no help at all.

'It's far too grand,' she said perversely. 'Anyway, I wore it to the investiture.'

Susan gave it a brisk shake.

'Don't talk rubbish, Cheryl, whoever is going to remember? And it's the Prince you're going to meet, not the local mayor!'

Bad move, Susan. At the time of her wedding, the local mayor had been Jonathan's sharply astringent mother. Chel winced at the recollection.

'No, really, Susan ...'

Susan gave her a scornful look.

'It's the perfect thing,' she said with decision, and flung it over the back of the studio couch before plunging back into the cupboard. 'And there was a hat that went with it, wasn't there? You must have a hat for royalty.'

The hat was in a box, a little crushed, but in Susan's capable fingers it hurriedly resumed its shape, even inanimate objects hesitated to argue with her.

'These flowers will have to go,' she said, looking at it critically. 'We can find something else a bit more sophisticated and re-trim it. I've got a yellow velvet rose somewhere, you can have that. It's a pity your hair is so gingery.'

Resentment flared momentarily.

'I like the flowers,' argued Chel. Her mother had chosen them.

'Oh Cheryl, they're so *ingénue!*' cried Susan.

'So am I,' Chel muttered, but not too loudly. She felt as if she had been flattened by a steamroller, there was no possibility of rebellion. The rose had it, and the ivory silk. Defeat on all fronts.

Chel went to the official opening with a vibrant golden rose tucked into the ribbon round her hat, accompanied by Susan's best leather clutch bag, her toes pinched in new shoes that had cost her a good part of her week's wages. She thought Susan genuinely didn't realise that because of them she would be walking to and from work until next pay day, she wouldn't understand that anyone connected with her family could be unable to afford both new shoes and bus fares, Susan had never wanted for anything in her whole life. But here, she did Susan an injustice. She didn't know the full truth, but she did suspect something and was angry, not for Chel's troubles so much as for her refusal to accept help and advice, specifically from herself.

'Cheryl's so dreadfully *bourgeois,*' she said despairingly, to her husband. 'One daren't offer her anything, she's so proud she'd take it as an insult, not a gift!'

Tom Casson was sorry for Chel. He found the Nankervis family hard to live up to as well, sometimes.

'The poor girl only wants to be left alone,' he said.

Unaware of this unexpected ally, Chel curtsied to the Prince, listened to speeches, and found it comforting to see Jonathan's friendly, familiar face smiling at her from among the assembled pressmen. The Nankervises had protected her from the press when Oliver was first injured, today, finding her unguarded, they were mobbing her. She was glad of Jonathan's presence in the throng, drawing their fire where he could, helping her through the ordeal. He found an opportunity during the official tea in the hospital grounds to have a quick, private word with her.

'You're looking very beautiful.'

Chel had a cup of tea in one hand and a cucumber sandwich in the other. She put the sandwich into her mouth and shook out her skirt with her freed hand, speaking through the crumbs, inviting him to share an absurdity.

'All this fuss! It seems so unnecessary when the place has been up and running for months already.'

She had reason to be thankful for that, but neither of them said so. Jonathan grinned at her with understanding.

'Not quite the scruffy Cheryl we all know and love,' he said. 'Do you go on the official tour?'

It was another of those obligations she couldn't avoid. The laugh died out of her eyes, and she said, 'Yes.'

'It'll be interesting, I expect,' said Jonathan, to encourage her. 'You'll be shown all the things they can do, all the equipment and so on.'

'Will you be there?'

'No. Only one TV video man, and he'll concentrate mainly on the Prince. The hospital insisted. But it'll be all right.'

Chel said, 'I could faint or something, and they wouldn't make me go.'

'But you won't.' He gave her hand a squeeze. 'Anyway, you wouldn't want to disappoint Oliver and he'll be expecting you to be there.'

Oliver was the whole trouble, although Chel didn't know exactly why this should be. She toured the unit, acutely uncomfortable and feeling out of place, beside Sir Charles Lawley and in the immediate wake of the Prince, who trailed his entourage of VIPs and interested parties like the tail of a comet. The unit had ten beds, and all those patients well enough to stand it were visited and presented to the royal guest, and offered sympathy and encouragement, permitted to share a princely joke or two. Chel was disconcerted to find that her status as Oliver's wife made her important, and that where others were excluded from the more personal part of the tour, she was expected to accompany the Prince and Sir Charles. Not only that, but she seemed to be a welcome visitor. She had no idea how to respond to the sympathy of people on Oliver's behalf, but was relieved, when she saw herself on the local news later, to see that she appeared friendly and natural; she had thought that she might be being patronising and superior. She was surprised to see, too, that she and the Prince looked like old friends, but that was probably more due to the excellent manners of the Prince.

But it hadn't been easy, and her heart was heavy.

Oliver had known that he of all people wouldn't escape a royal visit, but he hadn't been prepared for the bridal appearance of his wife. Chel had caught his startled look and realised too late that Susan had led her into hurting him, and she was angry, unjustly not with Susan, but with Oliver for being vulnerable where he had previously always been invincible. She found that she bitterly resented the way in which he looked at her and was frightened at the depth of that resentment.

She felt as if a wedge, delicately placed between them, had been given a gentle knock, driving it downwards. Being frightened of the resentment protected her from fearing the consequences if the trend should continue.

Perhaps resentment wasn't such a bad thing after all.

VII

Late spring drifted into the beginning of a long, hot summer, without Chel feeling able to reach any decision on Bill Rowland's generous offer. Decisions of any kind were too difficult, and she had other things to worry about. Not the least of these was Oliver, who should have been safely in the hands of specialists and physiotherapists and nurses, and no immediate problem of hers. There was nothing, after all, that she could do for him at present but to visit him regularly and try to be cheerful. Her part in the drama was safely in the future, months away. And things shouldn't have been so bad. Oliver was no delicate hothouse plant, he was tough and he healed with the efficient swiftness of a dog.

'All the internal bruising and things have gone,' Chel told Jonathan, in answer to his routine inquiry. 'His ribs have mended, and he shouldn't have any come-back from the lung damage so long as he takes a bit of care – not that he's ever done that, but still, I suppose he can learn. He's even coming off the dialysis machine soon.'

'That's all good, then,' said Jonathan.

Chel said, on a wailing note, 'It's his back that's not going right, and to Oliver, that's the most important thing of all.'

'He must have curled round to protect himself, so that it took the brunt of the assault,' the consultant had said, but that was guesswork, Oliver had no recollection of what he might have done. Although he had suffered no particularly serious head injury, it was all wiped from his mind. Sadistic ... the word that went with Chel through the lonely nights and made her cold, came into her mind now. They had meant to inflict the maximum damage, those vicious youths with their distorted pack instinct, and they hadn't cared, when they got bored and the fun was over, whether their victim lived or died. If he chose to live, it was all the same to them.

Jonathan saw her eyes darken with trouble, and said, bracingly, into a pause,

'Well, he's in the best possible hands. Everybody said it would be a long job, you mustn't start to worry now.'

'How can I help worrying?' asked Chel. 'I wish I could stop – I wish I could put it all out of my mind and leave it to the experts – but how can I? This is my life, as well as his, we're talking about. Suppose he ends up in a wheelchair. I can't get my head round that, Jonathan, I simply can't.'

The marring of Oliver's physical perfection was, for some reason she hadn't defined to herself, almost more distressing in prospect than anything that had happened so far. Scars could be covered up, but she didn't want to imagine him helpless. Still less, did she want to see it a fact. She couldn't say that to Jonathan, she couldn't say it to anybody, they all thought she should be brave for Oliver. She looked at him miserably.

'Come on, they can do wonderful things these days,' he said, trying to comfort her. He put his arm round her shoulders and gave her what passed, to Chel, for a brotherly hug. She thought how nice he was, and how good it was to have him there to turn to.

'It's all going to take so long,' she said. 'Do you know what they're talking about now? They want to put a steel rod into his spine, they think it will help – they put a hook at each end and –'

'No – no, please, Cheryl!' Jonathan threw up his hands. 'Don't tell me, I beg you! Never mind your head, I can't get my stomach round that one. Leave me in ignorance, I get the picture.'

She managed a watery smile. Jonathan's weak stomach had always been a bit of a joke between them. The old joke brought them close together.

'He can take it,' said Jonathan, more gently. 'Oliver is as tough as old boots, look how far he's come already, against all the odds. Cheer up, for God's sake – the worst may never happen.' He paused, obscurely troubled, not just by his own reactions, which he was beginning to understand, but by hers. He had a strange feeling, just for a second, that he had stepped through the looking-glass in *Alice* and the world had turned inside-out, but it was only for a second. 'When are they performing this miracle? When it's all safely over – and it will be, you must believe that – give me a ring and we'll go on the town and celebrate. Is it a date?'

She nodded miserably, thinking he didn't fully understand. It was Oliver – wilful, desperate, different, Oliver, who had agreed to this unthinkable thing. Not she, she had simply not disagreed, when the proposal had been put to them both. *This miracle*, Jonathan had said. Miracles were in short supply today.

'Ring me,' Jonathan reiterated, and against all the odds, a week later she did so. She was crying, too overwrought by events to sound even remotely sensible. All she could say, and keep saying, was *it worked, it worked* because the fear that it wouldn't, that they would be plunged into the nightmare they had only barely escaped once already, had been a burden almost too heavy to bear. The risk of paralysis had been high – unacceptable, Chel had thought, but it hadn't happened. The swing from fear to relief had left her incoherent.

If the worst had happened – if the long road to nowhere had opened under their feet – she thought that she would never have coped, but there had been no mistakes; the fear, the emotion, had all been wasted. Oliver would hardly be allowed to blink an eyelash for some days yet, but he was most certainly not paralysed. The drips and drainage tubes might be back in force at present, but there were flowers in the room and birds singing beyond an open window. For a brief, wonderful moment she had been visited by real joy. Then she had kissed his forehead

298

and left him, with relief, to people far better qualified to deal with that sort of thing, danced out into the sunlight and realised that she needed to share this moment with someone. Oliver's family would only flatten her with dreary cautions, her own were too far away.

But Jonathan, her dear friend, would understand.

And then, she had spoken to him from a payphone in the hospital café, and found herself falling apart, her emotions swinging like a compass needle at the North Pole.

'I told you we'd be celebrating,' he said, immediately. 'Stop snivelling, woman, what have you got to snivel about? Where are you?'

His pragmatic approach steadied her. She wiped the back of her hand across her streaming eyes and sniffed, inelegantly.

'Still in the hospital, hiding from you lot,' she said.

'Nah – local news now. I rely on you!' He laughed, pleased for her. 'Stay where you are. I'm going to take you out and treat you to the best lunch in town.'

'On expenses?' asked Chel, who had learned to be cynical even over Jonathan.

'On me,' he replied, firmly.

'But you're working?' It was half a statement, half a question.

'That's right – and you're news. But first of all, you're a friend, OK? I'll be with you right away –' The phone disconnected before she could argue.

Chel went outside to stand on the pavement in full view, vaguely uneasy without quite knowing why. She kept forgetting that Jonathan was a journalist and that she was married to a man who was News, but that wasn't why Jonathan was so nice to her. Or was it? They were old friends and he had never written one word said to him in confidence in the *Herald*.

A brief recollection of the quarrel she had had with Oliver over the *Hesperides* came back to her, but she pushed it away.

Apart from the fact that the memory was painful, she had said nothing to Jonathan on that occasion that he could have remotely construed as information. She knew she hadn't. In any case, he wasn't the sort of person who would make copy out of privileged information given him by a friend.

If he was a friend, she hardly deserved it. She had told him she loved him, and left him without a backward glance.

She stood irresolutely outside the hospital, wondering for the first time what it was that Jonathan wanted from her. No man could be completely altruistic towards a girl who had done to him what she had done, surely. He would have to be a saint, and Jonathan had never been that. He liked her company, he might, she supposed, want her to sleep with him again ...

A stab of pain, so unexpected it was like a swift arrow from nowhere, caught her and made her wince. She had tried not to think about it since Oliver was hurt and she lost the baby, but it suddenly came home to her, how much she missed the physical expression of passion, how much she missed Oliver. He had been a wonderful lover.

Had been.

Would they, could they, ever make love like that again?

I don't know. It's one of the answers that nobody will give. Why won't they tell us about such important things, unless they don't know the answers themselves? Doctors and hospitals never tell you anything, it's going to be all right, it has to be. He won't dive again, but you have to be one-hundred per-cent fit to do that anyway. That's nothing. Nothing. Nothing at all.

Her heart began to thud against her ribs. If Oliver couldn't make love to her ever again, what would happen to their marriage? She was a normal, healthy young woman with normal, healthy instincts, and her husband had taught her the secrets of paradise. You couldn't forget something like that, when once you had learned it. If it was lost, you might have to go looking for it.

There was no room in her heart for anyone but Oliver.

He wasn't paralysed.

But he had been terribly injured.

Whatever would I do?

She hoped that she knew the answer to that, but how could anyone ever be sure?

Joy had been as short-lived as that. She stood there waiting for Jonathan, and all her fears and problems came back and waited with her.

Jonathan had last heard her voice awash with relief over the telephone, and he took his cue from that. He arrived to pick her up in the mood to celebrate, and in the same way that he reflected her, Chel almost instantly reflected him. She remembered that she had something to be glad about, and it was such a novel sensation these days that she gave herself up to it.

'So it was a complete success?' said Jonathan, as they drove towards the town centre.

When she wasn't alone, Chel could be sensible and objective.

'As much of a success as it could be. After all, it isn't as if he has an undamaged spine any more.'

'But it'll mend,' Jonathan said, and Chel agreed that she supposed it would.

'And at least he's not likely to be permanently in a wheelchair,' she added. Jonathan looked at her quickly.

'That bothered you, didn't it?'

She hadn't known that she had made it so obvious. She looked down at her hands.

'You know what he was like. It seemed unnecessarily cruel.'

To him, or to you? Jonathan wanted to ask, but it wasn't really the sort of question that she would answer. Probably she didn't know herself. But it did occur to him that she hadn't known Oliver Nankervis at all well when she married him, and less impressionable women had been carried away by physical beauty combined with great courage before now, and who would blame them? It was a heady mixture.

'Where are we going?' asked Chel.

'Mario's.'

She laughed. It was a happy sound.

'Have you come into a fortune?'

'You have,' Jonathan reminded her. 'A fortune of good fortune.'

Mario's was a very select little Italian restaurant in the town square. It was both expensive and superlatively excellent, and had for some years now enjoyed a reputation as *the* place in town in which to eat. It had been way out of reach of Chel and Oliver and they had never gone there, but she saw now that it was his kind of people who sat at the tables. Well off. County, business, professional. Smart. Not that Oliver had been any of those things personally, of course, but his family were some of them. Chel was thankful jeans were still universally fashionable, and her shirt had come from Greece and not some catalogue.

She began to enjoy herself, with the illicit pleasure of an urchin scrumping apples. Nobody among these smart, confident people knew that her parents ran a village store. The Nankervises had often made her feel that it was written all over her forehead in neon letters, but obviously it wasn't. The Italian waiter was as deferential as if she had been a duchess. She smiled at Jonathan over the top of the menu, and he smiled back.

Today was a good day. The best day for ages.

She only became gradually aware that she was being stared at. It was an odd feeling, because she couldn't actually see the person who was doing the staring, an invasion of privacy that made her uncomfortable. She looked at Jonathan across the table.

'Someone is looking at us. Can you see?'His eyes flicked past her shoulder and swiftly looked away.

'Oh, shit!'

'Who, then?'

'Sssh, she's coming past. Don't look as if you care.' He grinned at her conspiratorially. A tall, elegant woman with piled dark hair brushed past their table without turning her head and walked unhurriedly to the door. She stood there for a moment, looking out into the square as if she expected to see someone, and then turned again and walked as unhurriedly back. Her eyes swept over Chel without interest, and she passed out of sight behind them again.

'Oh, wow!' breathed Chel, reverently, and gave an involuntary giggle.

'Joanna bloody Rendell,' said Jonathan.

'Real cloak and dagger stuff too,' said Chel, giggling again.

'She wanted to make quite sure it was you,' said Jonathan. He spoke soberly. He didn't think Chel realised that without Oliver to protect her she was at the mercy of Joanna Rendell and that set. She had no idea of the damage that gossip could do. She never had had any idea. He said, 'Does Oliver know that I see you sometimes?' so abruptly that Chel stared at him.

'He wouldn't care,' she said. It was no sort of answer. Jonathan looked at her, calculating. She hadn't told him, then. Because he was too ill, or because she hadn't thought it that important, or because she didn't want him to know?

'Don't be silly, Jonathan,' said Chel. 'Nobody could make it into anything – you only came into the flat once!'

Joanna Rendell was a spoilt little bitch who had had her nose put firmly out of joint by Cheryl. It was his fault, he hadn't given other people a thought, he had only seen Cheryl's unhappiness. He should have been more careful.

'I shouldn't have brought you here,' he said.

She had lovely eyes, sea-green and in the past, inflexibly honest. She wasn't stupid, either. He watched her pleasure ebb away.

'How I hate *people!*' she said bitterly, echoing Oliver as she had understood him.

'People are as they are,' said Jonathan, more pragmatically.

Her appetite had gone. She pushed the food around her plate with a fork and felt depression banking up like fog on the horizon. She didn't want to giggle any more.

Jonathan wanted to coax her and comfort her, and make her smile again, but he knew he mustn't. He said, 'We'd better see less of each other. Your sister-in-law, Mrs. Casson, is a friend of that Rendell cow.'

Chel had gone red. She spoke angrily. 'Why? What have we done, that we need to be ashamed of?'

Nothing, of course, but he knew that he had had thoughts that he ought to be ashamed of, and that the last thing in the world he had meant was to hurt her any more than she was hurt already. Not Sir Lancelot so much as Sir Galahad, the poor high-minded fool, he told himself. The Great Sacrifice and all that jazz. Quaint, really quaint.

Joanna Rendell, with neither word nor look, had made Chel feel guilty. She remembered that her husband was in hospital, and all those unanswered questions. She remembered that Jonathan had been her lover before ever she knew Oliver. She remembered all the things that she knew about Oliver's past, and her heart sank.

'Come along,' said Jonathan. 'I'll settle the bill, and take you home.'

'But I will see you again, won't I?' said Chel, when they were back in the car. Jonathan drove a little way without answering, and she went on, urgently. 'I don't think I can face it without you, Jonathan. I haven't got anybody else.'

'You've got a husband,' Jonathan reminded her – reminded them both.

'Oliver!' said Chel. 'I can't talk to him, he's too ill. Anyway, what is there I can say?' It was an admission that she hadn't meant to make. Jonathan took due note of it.

'Well, all right, but we must be more careful.' He paused. That had a furtive sound. He imagined himself sneaking up to the flat, and didn't like the picture it presented. He made a face at the windscreen.

'You're my friend,' said Chel.

True, not true? He loved her, but did that make him a friend when she was married, and her husband was shut away in hospital for months to come? Sir Galahad would no doubt have known, but Jonathan didn't. It was all too complicated. If she needed him, perhaps that was all that mattered now.

'I'll always be there if you need me, you know that,' he said.

Susan was round at the flat by tea-time, indignant and critical.

'What's this I've been hearing?'

Chel would have liked to slam the door in her face, but she was in before there was time to react.

'I don't know,' she said. 'What have you been hearing? Cup of tea?'

'No, thank you!' Susan flounced past and turned to face her. 'You had lunch at Mario's with that journalist you used to go about with.'

'That's right,' said Chel. 'It's a nice place, isn't it?'

Her heart had begun to thump nervously and her palms were sticky. Ridiculous to be like that when she hadn't done anything.

'Don't be stupid!' said Susan, with scorn. 'What did you think you were doing? Or is that obvious?'

Chel took time before she answered. She realised that her symptoms were those of fury rather than of guilt. She said, 'Since when did I have to ask permission if I wanted to have lunch with a friend?'

'He isn't just a friend! Poor Oliver – don't you feel you owe him *anything?*'

'No, I don't *owe* him anything at all,' said Chel, hotly angry. 'We give, we don't lend and borrow. You don't owe for a gift.'

'Oh, very pretty! And what do you think he's going to feel, when he hears what you've *given* him this time?'

'Why, what am I supposed to have done?'

'Don't stand there, looking as if butter wouldn't melt! You know very well what I'm saying!'

'No, tell me.'

Susan stared at her, momentarily nonplussed. Chel looked coolly back. She had begun to tremble, but she clenched her fists so that Susan wouldn't see it.

'I was told that you were sitting in Mario's, blind and deaf to anyone but each other, and everyone was staring at you! What sort of behaviour is that supposed to be?'

'Your spy has a good imagination!' retorted Chel. 'If you feel due an explanation, and I don't see why you should, an old friend took me out to lunch to cheer me up. What's so awful?'

'You've been seen with him before.' Susan's eyes narrowed accusingly. Chel was surprised, Joanna Rendell had been busy – or somebody had. The thought that it might be more than one person was an uncomfortable one.

'I expect we have,' she said dismissively, as if it didn't matter.

'Is that all you've got to say?'

Chel shrugged her shoulders, deliberately infuriating.

'Well, yes.'

'He's been seen coming here, lots of times. Couldn't you even have the decency to keep your *affaire* secret, when Oliver is so ill?'

Chel said furiously,

'There is no affair, except in the nasty minds of you and your nosy-parkering friends, and none of them ever saw anything to justify you saying so, because there hasn't been anything! Now, do you mind going?'

'It's got to stop,' said Susan.

'Oh, has it?' Chel threw caution to the winds. 'Go away, and mind your own business! I'll go out with whoever I please, and you can think what you like. Oliver wouldn't – '

'Is this what he can expect in future, then?' Susan interrupted.

They stared at each other, mutually despising. Susan tossed her head and made for the door.

'I suppose it was too much to expect loyalty from someone like you.'

'And I suppose it was too much to expect understanding from someone like you!'

Unexpectedly, this brought Susan up short. She paused with her hand on the door and looked over her shoulder, puzzled. Chel said, slowly and deliberately,

'Oh, I have the morals of an alley cat, and having fun is all that I care about. What else can you expect from the daughter of a *shopkeeper?*'

'Don't be silly, Cheryl,' said Susan, but uncertainly. Chel turned her back. She wanted to scream and weep and laugh all at the same time. She said, 'Goodbye,' without turning round, and after a moment or two she heard the door open and close, and Susan's feet running down the stairs. It brought back the memory of Oliver running, running on swift feet towards disaster. Chel flung herself down on the studio couch and buried her face in the cushions, suddenly shaken with great tearing sobs that brought no relief at all, and far below her, the street door closed with a bang.

VIII

Susan apparently had enough doubts to make her say nothing to her parents, for Dorothy Nankervis remained charitable towards Chel. Charity was a cold virtue, but it was preferable to outright warfare. Chel couldn't have borne that, she knew she couldn't. She could at least shout back at Susan, but Oliver's stepmother rendered her speechless and inadequate.

In any case, they all had other things to think about now. Those answers that Chel had dreaded were about to come thick and fast.

'Your husband is doing splendidly,' the consultant told her, a fatherly arm around her shoulders. 'He was a remarkably fit young man, he should go on making good progress. Of course, there's a lot of damage we can do nothing about. You do realise, don't you my dear, that any recovery is necessarily going to be incomplete, although we can't yet say how far it will go.'

'But he'll be able to walk again,' said Chel, swiftly, for wasn't that what this was all about?

'Oh, I think so. Yes, definitely I think so. Not ten mile hikes, of course, and he may be a bit ungainly. There's too much physical damage, and that back of his will always be a weak point.' He looked at her compassionately, knowing that she had been hoping for so much more, it was only human nature after all. 'You must make up your minds to it, both of you, that with all we can do he may still be permanently disabled. You'll be given all the help possible.'

'Thank you,' said Chel.

There, it was out at last, in so many words and with no room for either misunderstanding or argument.

Permanently disabled. It sounded so final. It was final.

She had married in haste, albeit in love, a man who was now permanently disabled. She turned the words over in her mind and wondered what they meant exactly, and found that she didn't really want to know. Like Susan's blithe assertion that a disabled man couldn't climb three flights of stairs, it was just words.

She did nothing about the flat. It didn't seem urgent, when Oliver couldn't be home for months yet. Anyway, she didn't see what she could do. She let it slide.

Oliver's family found her elusive, but in spite of what they considered her unreasonable behaviour, they were still concerned about her. Jerry Nankervis particularly felt responsible for his son's wife, and he wasn't sure that all was well with her. He understood more about unhappiness than his wife or step-daughter, and she seemed very lonely to him. Susan had said that she seemed curiously reluctant to look for somewhere else to live.

'That flat's cheap,' she said, in her downright way. 'I'm not sure that she can afford anything else.'

Her father looked at her worriedly.

'Are you certain? Surely Oliver must have been insured. I'm sure I remember him saying so.'

'He's a fool if he wasn't,' said Susan, adding with one of her rare flashes of perception, 'He may have been insured against death. People don't necessarily insure against being disabled. They don't believe it can happen to them.'

Jerry Nankervis continued to look worried.

'You must ask her,' he said.

After her last encounter with Chel, Susan could see that wasn't a good idea.

'You ask her, Daddy,' she said firmly. 'It'll come better from you, she's so touchy.'

Chel didn't mean to be touchy, most of the time, and didn't know that she appeared so. She simply didn't want his family to have any more reasons for calling Oliver irresponsible.

310

'Oh yes, the insurance,' she said, when her father-in-law approached her. 'He paid a self-employed stamp while he was at the Shipyard, but I don't know about when he was with Bill ...' She let the sentence end in thin air, knowing that she was babbling, but whenever one of Oliver's family came near her these days, she came out in a cold sweat in case they mentioned Jonathan. No amount of telling herself that she had nothing to feel guilty about seemed to help. Anyway, there was one thing. She still hadn't told Oliver.

'I didn't mean that sort of insurance,' said Jerry. 'Oliver had a private insurance policy, didn't he?'

'Oh, that.' Chel wrinkled her nose. 'I wrote to them, of course, and they wrote back and sent a claim form that said we had to produce a doctor's certificate to say that he was totally disabled, but he isn't. Then they said they wanted to know the percentage, or something, and nobody will tell me that yet, and then they just said to let them know when I knew. And I can't. I asked at the hospital, but they said they don't know, and there's no way of telling. He won't go diving, or sail round the Med, but he'll probably be able to do something ...' Her voice, which had been deliberately casual, tailed off again. Jerry looked at her. She got her lunch at work, and he wasn't to know she could no longer afford to run the car, or that bus fares and rent accounted for so much of her wages that her evening meal was a snack that she was often too tired and depressed to eat. He could see, though, that she was pale, and surely thinner than he remembered, and had a waif-like air that was certainly new. Oliver's wife had been a bright, energetic girl, with some of that same dare-devilry that he had himself. She was nothing like that now. Compassion stirred, a genuine emotion.

'Cheryl,' he said. He wanted to ask her outright if she had enough money, but he didn't know either her or Oliver well enough. Not touchy, Susan had been wrong about that. Resentful. Perhaps they had all been hard on her in the past.

His ex-wife Helen loved her, and Dot notwithstanding, Helen's opinions carried a lot of weight with him – too much, maybe, for the health of his present marriage, but he didn't think about that. He said, 'My dear, find me those letters and the policy. This sort of thing is what solicitors are for, you know. Let me handle it for you.'

She could accept that. It didn't cross the fine line she had drawn between their help and their charity. Even Oliver would surely accept professional advice from his father if it was offered, and he needed it.

Jerry went home and shook his head over it all.

'That poor girl,' he said. 'I wish I could think of a way to help her.' He didn't think he specifically meant financial help. He frowned. His wife sniffed expressively.

'Any girl who married Oliver was asking for trouble,' she said. 'Well, she's got it. She should have been content with the lovesick journalist.'

'Nobody could have foreseen this,' objected Jerry.

'It was up to Oliver to provide for her, it's not up to you. He refused anything from you long ago.'

Oliver had tried to provide for his wife, in his own happy-go-lucky way. His father looked down at the handful of papers that Chel had given him, shutting an old hurt, that his wife's words had revived, back into its box, out of sight and feeling.

'We must do what we can,' he said.

Although she might not say so, the question of what was to happen in the future worried Chel a lot. Oliver had said nothing about it – in some respects Oliver was still in shock, and what he couldn't yet face up to, he instinctively dismissed from his mind – but just not talking about them didn't make the problems go away. The day was going to come when he was well enough to leave hospital, but there were those three insurmountable flights of stairs.

Permanently disabled, permanently disabled, permanently disabled....

There's always the insurance, Chel told herself, desperately trying to shut unwelcome facts out of sight, and we might get something from the Criminal Injuries Board. Oliver's father will see to it, there's no need to worry. It's going to be all right.

The thought of the insurance quietened a growing fear and consoled her a little. There was no consolation to be found in the sentences given to the seven yobs whose mindless brutality had wrecked Oliver's life.

The two whom he had attacked before they could attack him were acquitted on all charges, including the attempted assault on the girl, and their solicitor talked about bringing a claim against Oliver for his brutal and unprovoked assault on them. The other five received two years each for grievous bodily harm, and were acquitted of the attempted assault due to lack of reliable evidence, which meant, said Chel, in sudden unexpected rage, that they would go free, with the remission that they would probably get, not very long after Oliver was out of hospital. It seemed that Oliver was the one who was going to do the paying, one way or the other, for anything that they had intended or done. Her fury was futile, pathetic and deep, and Jonathan, who had broken his own rule and come to the flat to tell her the news before some other, less sympathetic, journalist ran her to earth to press her for her opinions, was angrier on her behalf than he would have believed possible.

'And they call that justice!' said Chel, bitterly, with the tears running down her face. 'How can anything be so unfair?'

Jonathan had his arms round her, the first person whom she had allowed to come that close since the tragedy happened. He hugged her tightly, feeling helpless.

'Oliver doesn't deserve it, he doesn't!' sobbed Chel. 'I wish he'd left that horrible girl to be raped – he doesn't deserve all this to happen to him! What was he expected to do, wait until they had her knickers off?' She buried her face against him, and Jonathan, at a loss, tightened his arms and wished that she wasn't the wife of a national hero in the forefront of the news until he ached with it. It was an impossible position to be in.

Chel was going on speaking, retreading the same dreary old ground, tormenting herself.

'They killed our poor little baby, and they might as well have killed Oliver too for all he's got left to be alive for, and they bloody get away with it! It's not fair!'

Jonathan didn't think it was fair either, and nor was he certain that the law wasn't on the side of the two who had, for one reason and another, not attacked Oliver themselves. Or even, which was slightly worse, on the side of the ones who *had* attacked Oliver, since once the element of rape was removed, he became the aggressor. Which probably explained the sentences, the law being an ass, at least in some respects. He said nothing of any of this to Chel, however. He led her to the studio couch and made her sit down.

'Come on, Cheryl, I know poor old Oliver got a life sentence, but judges don't hand out real life sentences even for murder these days, it's the way things are.'

'But *two years?*' pleaded Chel, piteously. 'And I expect they won't even do that much. Jonathan, I'm not vindictive, I swear I'm not, but that can't be right, or just, or – or anything.'

'Don't cry,' said Jonathan gently.

'I'm not crying.' Chel scrubbed angrily at her cheeks with the palms of her hands.

'Cheryl –'

'So they said they didn't mean to kill him, but if they didn't mean to, why did they attack him like that? They could have just knocked him down and run, there were enough of them!' Chel heard her own voice rising insecurely and broke off, swallowing hard. 'All right, so they didn't murder Oliver – but our baby is dead because of what they did, and if that isn't murder, what is?'

'Cheryl, I'm so sorry,' said Jonathan, helplessly. 'And you are crying.'

'I know I am,' said Chel miserably. Jonathan put his arms round her again, the gesture was meant to be comforting. She leaned her head against him and tried to be comforted.

'Don't,' he said. 'Don't, Cheryl. Oliver of all people wouldn't thank you for it, and you'll have other children.'

Chel thought of Oliver as she had last seen him, in plaster up to his neck and unable to move, and her heart sank like a stone to new and unbearable depths.

'No,' she said, with what had suddenly become certainty. Jonathan patted her shoulder, feeling angry and useless and rather ill at ease. After a while, Chel said, from the unexpected haven of his arms, 'Oliver could live for years and years – he was always so fit. What is he ever going to do with all that time? He can't dive, or swim, or sail, he'll be lucky to be able to walk! He's still young – twenty-nine, Jonathan, that's all!' She drew a breath. 'We're going to be punished every day of our lives for a crime that wasn't even ours. We've already paid more for it than they ever will. They've taken Oliver's livelihood and left us with nothing at all – no idea what the insurance will give us, in spite of all those premiums Oliver paid, and if it was a million pounds how could it possibly *compensate*? And if they say it was his fault in the end, how do you think he's going to feel? He only went to help someone in trouble, that's all, and he's going to end up crippled and destitute!'

He was the first person she had trusted with even a hint of her financial difficulties, but this didn't occur to her. Jonathan had been at the trial in his official capacity as a reporter, he refrained from telling her that the young men had grinned at their sentences, and gone off apparently unconcerned to start serving them with thumbs-up signs to their girlfriends and well-wishers in the public gallery, but he knew he would have to include it in his report. Other reporters weren't going to respect Cheryl's feelings. A sudden wave of anger that things like this could happen to someone he loved swept him. He had only his pen to defend her, but by God he could wield that to some purpose!

'Don't worry, they won't get off as easily as that,' he said. 'I'll damn well see that they don't!'

'How can you?' demanded Chel, on a wailing note that wrung his heart.

'I'll write a piece that'll sizzle the paper it's printed on, and send it to every major newspaper in the country.'

'What good will that do?' sobbed Chel, bitter and unconsoled.

'Two things,' said Jonathan, with ill-suppressed emotion. 'It'll make me feel better, and believe me, it'll make them feel a whole lot worse. Never underestimate the power of the press, Cheryl, the British have a very well-developed sense of natural justice, and there's more than one way to make it work. Please don't cry any more. It doesn't help, truly it doesn't.'

'I can't stop,' wept Chel.

Jonathan was a good journalist, and he kept his word to Chel. The story was a gift to a man of his talents, and by the time he had spread himself on the details, such as the scandal of the annual invasion of respectable family seaside resorts by gangs of troublemakers, the girl threatened with rape and screaming for help, whom the law (predominantly male) had declined to believe, the lonely wife working as a chambermaid to make ends meet, and even the *Hesperides*, he had made it into headline news. Tragedy always goes down well, and his vitriolic denunciation of a system of justice that allowed a man to be crippled while his attackers laughed at their punishment and threatened, with impunity, to sue him, had great popular appeal. All the big national dailies took it up gleefully and played it for all it was worth. Chel began to understand the phrase *hounded by the press* at first hand, turning down several more than generous money offers for her story, to the point she began to be relieved the flat had no direct phone line, but more than that, the sentimental British Public took her and Oliver to their hearts.

Nothing more was heard after that about claims against Oliver for assault, it was rumoured that there was so much public feeling that the lads' solicitor had warned them not to press the action, or perhaps it had only been bravado in the first place. On the other hand, the story refused to die a natural death. It caught the public imagination. People called things like "Disgusted of Dorchester" wrote indignant letters to the newspapers about *this terrible miscarriage of our so-called justice*, the judge who had passed sentence came in for a great deal of criticism, and left-wing tabloids trod a gleeful knife-edge of libel that rendered Oliver's father speechless with fury, with clever, politically correct articles about rich people who left it to the State to take care of their families when they were down on their luck.

The people of Embridge took the matter even more personally. Two years earlier, Oliver had been their hero and they hadn't forgotten. A swiftly-formed committee of well-wishers launched an appeal with the help of the *Herald* and the local radio station, and donations came pouring in. Chel, appalled at what Jonathan had started so skilfully, was very much afraid that Oliver would be hurt or angry, or both, but he didn't appear to be – a fact that surprised her so much that she should have suspected it, had not relief over-ridden everything else. He seemed far more concerned with the wave of sympathetic letters from total strangers that swamped them both.

'Good God, Chel,' he said. 'What have you done to me? I hate writing letters at the best of times.'

Chel paled at a new thought. 'We can't answer them all!'

He grinned at that, a shadow of his old warmth but at least by now a recognisable shadow.

'With the best will in the world, I don't think I'm even going to try. Could we put an ad in the papers, do you think?

317

Something along the lines of *Mr. and Mrs. Nankervis thank the Great British Public for their sympathy –*' He broke off abruptly, and Chel tried to smile but it was a poor effort. Oliver looked at her carefully. 'All right, sweetheart?'

'How can you ask me that?' asked Chel, and Oliver reached out to her, curling his fingers gently round hers.

'Because in a lot of ways, you've got the worst of it,' he said. 'I let you down good and proper when it came to it, didn't I?'

'Don't talk rubbish,' said Chel.

'No bloody money!' said Oliver, who thought that he bled somewhere deep in his soul every time he thought of his beloved Chel as an object of national pity, largely due to his own unthinking, care-for-nobody career. Even so, it was with a flash of resentment that he also thought she could have spared him the humiliation of seeing his wife described as a chambermaid, she had enough qualifications to do better for herself than that, but he wasn't strong enough for emotional scenes, and let it die unspoken. They were in it together, after all. At least, he thought they were.

Chel was thankful that he was still too ill to care what people said in the outside world. She said, 'You couldn't know what was going to happen,' but Oliver only looked sick.

'I knew very well we had nothing behind us for a rainy day,' he said. 'And what do we get? Bloody thunderstorms!'

'There's your private insurance.'

'Yeah, so there is.' The derision in his voice was the measure of her own disillusionment with people who issued insurance policies. 'It probably said in the small print, *thou shalt not get thyself mugged.*'

'Oh, don't.' said Chel.

The other members of Oliver's family were less forbearing. Not only did they receive the undiluted impact, from which

Oliver was protected, but Jonathan had hit them where it hurt.

'The little so-and-so!' exclaimed Susan, indignantly, reading the *Herald* at the breakfast table. 'Not content with flaunting her lover all over town, now she gets him to write lies about us!'

Tom was more realistic on the subject of Chel's dealings with the press. He appreciated that it was next to impossible to stop them saying what they wanted to, and it would certainly take bigger guns than Chel had in her armoury.

'Keep your sense of proportion,' he advised his wife, now, with a warning glance at their two children, deep into their cornflakes and listening with all their ears. 'I don't suppose she had much say in it. And you don't know that about Holmes.'

'Joanna says –'

Tom hurriedly pushed back his chair and reached for his briefcase. The introduction of Susan's great friend and crony into the conversation could only make it more complicated, and he headed for the door at speed.

'Can't talk now, I'll be late for work. See you this evening darling.'

Baulked of her listener, Susan rang her half-sister Debbie, who worked in London as a graphic artist.

'Have you read the papers this morning?'

Ringing Debbie was a mistake. Not only was she working, but she had always been very partisan towards Oliver and anything he decided to do, inclusive of his marriage to Chel. She said, 'I don't see anything to make such a fuss about. Everybody knows newspapers always exaggerate everything.'

'They're making collections in the High Street!'

'No, are they?' Debbie sounded amused. 'I hope you mean to give generously!'

'It's so humiliating! Don't you feel it?'

'It's how Oliver feels that matters, isn't it?' Which Debbie didn't really want to discuss, or even think about. Certainly not with her sister.

'Oh, Oliver!' cried Susan, exasperated. 'Poor deluded fool! He thinks that little tramp can do no wrong! God knows what he's going to say when he finds out.'

'About what?' asked Debbie, circumspectly. Her immediate boss was looking at her with raised eyebrows, she picked up a pencil and began to doodle on the edge of a note-pad as if she was taking notes.

'About how she's sleeping around with that journalist she used to live with.'

Debbie had drawn a plump, rounded heart with a feathered arrow through the centre, and three globular drops of blood. Now she wrote under it, in elegant Old English script, *Oliver loves Cheryl.*

'Do you actually know that she is?'

'It's obvious, isn't it?' Susan sounded scornful. Debbie said apologetically,

'Not to me, it isn't.'

'But I told you – '

Debbie was a great deal more streetwise than Susan, for all her youth. She understood, for instance, that things are not always black or white, there are several shades of grey in between.

'Don't you think you should be careful how you tell people? With all this media interest?'

'It's all right for you, you manage to keep clear of everything!' retorted Susan, and since this was her main aim in life in much the same way as it was her brother's, Debbie didn't deny it. Instead, she said, 'I feel sorry for her.'

Susan tossed her head dramatically, which was wasted on someone who was miles away.

'Then come home for once and try to be a sister to her! Maybe you'll understand then. She just isn't one of us.'

Debbie had liked Chel, what little she had so far seen of her, and she didn't consider herself *one of us* either, and she knew quite well that Oliver didn't, and so did Susan. Having been brought up by a ferociously determined Good Samaritan, she decided after only a moment's pause to pass by on the other side.

'Oh, don't be such a snob, and let her alone!' she said.

'Heaven knows, I don't want to sit in judgement on her,' said Susan piously, 'but you aren't here, you don't know what it's like. Mary Clarice is helping a friend to run that nice little teashop on the seafront, and she says she's seen Cheryl and that journalist drive past to that flat of hers nearly every day this past month. And Joanna saw them in Mario's together, and when I taxed her with it she was really rude!'

Debbie had written *Cheryl loves Oliver*, and now she added an ornate question mark, and a jagged crack across the pencilled heart.

'And as for all this business in the newspapers,' went on Susan, but Debbie had had enough of it. She had work to do, if Susan hadn't, and she objected to having her feelings harrowed.

'It's the silly season,' she pointed out, interrupting. Her refusal to be impressed was more to annoy Susan than anything else. It was a pose she had copied from Oliver since her childhood, although she didn't realise it. 'People read anything, and then forget it.'

'You're hopeless!' exclaimed Susan, and banged the phone down.

But Debbie was a long way away. Chel didn't even suspect that there was anyone in Oliver's family who more than tolerated her. Susan's attitude became even more frigid and Dorothy said, steel beneath the saccharin, 'We just don't do things like that, Cheryl dear.'

Chel felt humiliated, as she had been meant to do, like a child that doesn't know what it has done wrong in front of visitors. She would have preferred an angry confrontation, at least it would have given her the chance to defend herself, for truth to tell Jonathan had disconcerted her too, she hadn't expected quite so much crusading zeal. She went red in the face and fidgeted, and Dorothy patted her cheek with a patronising pretence of forgiveness.

'Never mind dear, you'll know another time, won't you?'

Chel had meant to ask Jonathan if it was possible to stop what he had started, but now she decided that she wouldn't. Oliver had never cared what his family thought anyway, and it was much easier to let events take their course. She would just keep out of the Nankervises' way more in future.

So the awful year went inexorably on, and Chel drifted miserably along with it, horribly aware that things on every front were going from bad to worse. Her depression showed no signs of lifting, the space in her heart left by little Jeremy's death gaped like a wound, and to make things worse she was beginning to understand that things were deteriorating between herself and Oliver. She had no idea how humiliated he felt over the appeal fund because he didn't confide in anyone, but as he began the slow struggle back to health she was beginning to be very frightened of how they were going to manage in the future. In holding the fear away from her, she was unaware that she had begun to hold Oliver away from her too, but Oliver was aware of it. Her arms still ached with emptiness, but more for the dead child now than for the man who still lived, and she didn't realise that either, but he was beginning to. Nobody had told him about Jonathan, Chel because she just hadn't and now it was a bit late, and Susan because she didn't quite dare, but in some elusive way Oliver knew that someone was there, a shadow behind the shadows. He never asked, without putting it into words he decided that it was easier not knowing. Because they were both holding things back, it became more and more difficult to talk to each other.

Chel would have been very lonely during these months if it hadn't been for Jonathan. Oliver's family had eventually appeared to forgive her, or at least tacitly agreed not to place the blame for all the talk and embarrassment caused by the newspapers exclusively at her door, but their magnanimity only increased her resentment, and a coolness had sprung up between her and his father that was unexpectedly hurtful. Of his stepmother, who so prided herself on her good works, she suspected that she had inadvertently made a real enemy, for all her sugar-sweetness, and sometimes she remembered Helen's long-ago warning about doing just that with a flicker of apprehension. And as for Susan, she always seemed to Chel to be watching her with dark suspicion, ready to catch her out and make a big deal out of it. She and Jonathan were very circumspect these days, as if they really did have something to hide. They all resented her lack of confidence in them, she thought, but she didn't see how she was to blame for choosing to protect Oliver from their criticism, however much it had backfired on her.

She lay awake at night in the flat where she had been so happy, remembering how she had been convinced that Oliver would never see it again. She wondered now how she had been so sure, and felt a sick apprehension when she thought of the dark cloud that had hung over her that dreadful day from the very moment that she had woken. Sometimes she wondered too, miserably, if she had really made him live, or if she had just imagined that she had. There was something here that she didn't want to know, and she tried to make it go away. She felt quite often that it was impossible to face the future and thought a lot about what she had done in the past that had brought her to here and now. She was young, and Jonathan was being so good.

She had snatched at a future of undreamed excitement and adventure – and come down to being nurse to a cripple. There was no way out. She should never have married Oliver, and if she hadn't, the way of escape would be open.

The thought formed itself clearly for the first time, and then lay on her spirits in the darkness like a smothering fog that wouldn't go away, and the empty flat echoed with despair.

IX

The insurance company, opposed by the implacable determination of Oliver's father and harried by popular opinion, abandoned the argument that as it had been suggested that Oliver had brought his misfortune on himself, the insurance was null and void, and agreed to make an interim payment on the understanding that the balance would be withheld until the full and exact extent of his disablement should allow them to decide on the final amount. Added to the appeal fund and carefully invested, it would give them a reasonable income – which was lucky, for it was becoming increasingly obvious, even to Chel who didn't want to see it, that for a while at least there was no question of her continuing to go out to work. It became necessary to face the fact.

'It's no good, you can't keep sweeping it under the carpet,' said Susan, who had taken on herself the role of family spokeswoman. She did speak kindly, for in spite of her lifelong jealousy of her stepbrother she wasn't unfeeling. 'It may sound crude, Cheryl, but Oliver won't make it up the kerb for a while, never mind three flights of stairs, and even if you want to hang on to his diving gear for sentimental reasons, you'll have to get rid of that car and find something a bit more practical. You never use it, anyway.'

The only thing in this speech which was either new, or with which Chel could legitimately argue, was the bit about the diving gear. She wasn't hanging on to it for sentimental reasons, she simply didn't dare to ask Oliver what she should do with it. She looked at Susan irresolutely.

'So, what should I do?'

Susan patted her arm kindly.

'Sell your lease, or give notice on this flat, whatever you need to do to be rid of it,' she said. 'Daddy says he'll help you with the deposit on a nice little bungalow, and that will leave you with enough to pay a mortgage and make poor Oliver comfortable.'

Oliver, like herself, had been perfectly content with the flat. Chel looked at their few possessions and felt familiar misery. She didn't even bother to despise herself for it these days, it was too much a part of her.

'I suppose I could,' she said. 'I'll see what Oliver says.'

'I'd just get on and do it, if I was you,' said Susan, instantly. 'Oliver never has known his limitations.'

He had plenty of limitations to know now, poor Oliver.

'And that car will have to go,' reiterated Susan, sweepingly. 'You'll have to ask him about that, I suppose, but I don't see how he can object. After all, there's no chance he'll even ride in it again, in his condition, and he certainly won't drive it.'

They had had fun with Oliver's MGB, and Chel loved it, but of course Susan was quite right. It would make an expensive souvenir with Oliver in a wheelchair, even if that was only temporary.

'You need a nice sturdy, comfortable estate car,' said Susan firmly. 'I know the very one for you.'

She knew the very bungalow, too. Not too far from her own home, or her parents', although in a rather less exclusive street, close to the shops and on level ground all the way.

'We shall be on the spot if you need anything,' she pointed out triumphantly. 'And it's handy for shopping and there's the park quite near, too. You can take Oliver there quite easily while he has to be in a wheelchair, there's no hills to push him up.'

'Susan –' began Chel, but turned her head away with the sentence unfinished, so that Susan wouldn't see her face. The thought of having to push Oliver around in a wheelchair, however temporarily, made a sharp pain somewhere deep inside her, where self-pity and fear hadn't quite penetrated yet. Susan didn't notice.

'And it's not too far from the hospital, either,' she finished, with satisfaction.

'Oh,' said Chel. She didn't much like the area where Susan lived, which she mentally classified as *boring middle-class suburban*, and when she saw the chosen bungalow, she didn't much like that, either. It was small, red-brick and very ordinary, with the front garden paved over and hydrangeas, which Chel thought dull, planted neatly round the edge, and other plants emerging in a regimental way through square holes here and there. The back garden was very little better, long and narrow and overlooked, mostly down to lawn. There was vacant possession because the previous owner had died six months earlier, and the surrounding bungalows – this was a definitely bungaloid area, Chel observed cynically – all seemed to be occupied by elderly people. None of this, she thought, would be very cheering for an invalid who was still young, but most of all she didn't like the feel of the place. There was no explaining this to Susan, of course. She thought of the bright airy little flat high above the harbour, where the seagulls wheeled past and the salt spray patterned the windows in a gale, and where you could sit and watch the boats go in and out, and the whole beautiful moving tapestry of the harbour, and she thought that the bungalow was soulless and depressing, and that Oliver would probably hate it.

'It's so convenient,' said Susan, pleased with her choice.

'It's miles away from the sea,' said Chel.

'There's only flats and terraces along the harbourside,' said Susan. 'And it's all uphill to the town. And no proper gardens.'

'There's some bungalows up on the cliffs,' said Chel, fighting a rearguard action, but Susan only laughed and told her not to be silly.

'Property costs the earth up there, far more than you can possibly afford, and there's not even a corner shop worth mentioning, and nobody near that you know. Be practical, Cheryl. Live in the real world.'

Chel privately thought that nearness to the sea would make up for the lack of a garden, and that Oliver would prefer, if he had to be pushed anywhere, for it to be along the waterfront rather than round the tameness of the municipal park, but she hadn't the energy to argue. She gave up and went with the tide. Oliver's father was paying, so let him choose.

In spite of what Susan had said, Oliver had to be consulted of course, but he couldn't be said to be of much help. So far as he was concerned, the flat was already a long way in the past, the bungalow probably as far away in the future. He told Chel to do what she liked, but added, possibly a little conscience-stricken, 'I'm afraid I can't do much to help you.'

About the car, he was even less helpful. Although he knew as well as Chel or Susan that it would be quite useless to him in future he couldn't bring himself to give any definite permission to sell it, but three thousand pounds worth of assets couldn't be left rusting in a garage. The MGB had to go, traded in against a smart new Japanese estate car with excellent suspension and a replacement front passenger seat specially designed to make getting in and out simple for the disabled, and Chel moved from the flat into the red-brick bungalow.

It was undeniably a lot more comfortable. Wall-to-wall carpets and fully-lined curtains were part of the package, and Oliver's father had paid to have it fitted out with everything that Chel could possibly need to make looking after Oliver easier. There were grab rails everywhere and an electric hoist in the bathroom, an adjustable bed that responded to the touch of a button, an expensive wheelchair that Chel feared Oliver might well refuse to use, that folded down easily to fit in the car, even a special orthopaedic armchair, and clever gadgets to allow Oliver to reach for things or pick them up from the floor when Chel wasn't around to help. Chel wandered around the house when she was alone, looking at them all and fingering them, unable to relate them to Oliver at all.

It could have been all these strange and unfamiliar things that made her feel so odd, she told herself. The house seemed to brood around her and she was very much aware of her own heart beating. If she hadn't known it was silly, she might almost have thought she was afraid, but there was nothing here to frighten anyone. She touched the shining chrome rails in the bathroom and thought for a while, painfully, of Cornwall. Why Cornwall she didn't know, unless it was because that had been the happiest time of her life, and this ... well, it wouldn't be. She felt the soft west country wind tugging at her heartstrings, the moors and the flowery clifftops and the squeaking bats of Vellanzoe, where Oliver's roots began, and she could almost hear the sea whispering as the tide crept in over rocks and sand, and the sad, wild cry of the seabirds.

'*Don't!*' she said aloud, folding her arms tightly against her ribs to contain the pain. 'Please, don't –'

Something in the house stirred – a feeling, not a sound – and settled back with a sigh that lingered on the mind rather than the ear. She had a disconcerting feeling of not wanting to look over her shoulder.

The beat of her heart was so fast and hard that it made her breathless. She had to take a firm hold on herself and tell herself that there was nothing there before she could even turn her head. But of course, only the dauntingly clinical hoist and a blue-flowered shower curtain hanging beside the bath met her eyes.

The bathroom was the worst room in the house, except possibly for the second bedroom where Oliver would have to sleep. Chel went hurriedly back into the hall. She had forgotten her brief vision of sea and moorland.

That first night in the bungalow wasn't a pleasant one. From one cause or another, she had never slept entirely alone in a house before, and that might have been why she kept waking up and listening, stupidly afraid of what she might hear. Once, starting suddenly out of a troubled dream, she opened her eyes and could have sworn that she saw a light, cloudy and red, drifting across in the darkness. She shivered under the duvet; it was very cold, and there was a horrid feeling in the room. For some unexplained reason, she was very, very frightened.

The light seemed to hover at the foot of the bed for a moment or two, then continued its drift and went out somewhere over by the wardrobe. It must have been the reflection from a passing car, although she had heard nothing and Endicott Road wasn't a busy thoroughfare even in daylight. The horrid feeling had faded, but she was still uneasy. She lay in the silent house and wished that she was somewhere else – back in the flat, anywhere. This wasn't a very nice house. She realised that there were tears running down her cheeks on to her pillow and it seemed a natural thing to do to go on crying. The silent grief poured into the room and filled all the corners.

Eventually she went into the kitchen and made a cup of tea to wash down two aspirin, creeping back to her empty bed in a chilly dawn to sleep heavily and with no dreams at all.

The second bedroom that Chel found even more depressing than the bathroom had been fitted out to accommodate Oliver when he came home, and looked more like a hospital ward, she thought, than a room in a private house. He would still have a lot of pain to endure, and would be more comfortable on his own, had said Susan, firmly backed by her mother. Chel's own mother, coming from Suffolk to inspect the bungalow and see how things were going, wasn't so certain. She had visited Oliver and her private conviction was that he stood in dire need of a lot of that cuddling which her daughter lavished on the Pink Panther. But the bedrooms at the bungalow had never been designed to take twin beds comfortably, and Susan was right so far. She held her peace, remembering how close Chel and Oliver had always been, and trusting to Chel's humanity and good sense.

Chel hadn't hung the picture of *Lawley's Girl* flying over the green and white sea. As Dorothy hadn't failed to point out, it would be too cruel. Over her new mantelpiece hung a reproduction of Constable's *The Hay Wain*, and Susan's wedding gift, together with Oliver's diving equipment and books and various other souvenirs of their old life, was tucked away in the loft. Susan was horrified at the reproduction, calling it the acme of council-terrace bad taste, but Chel liked it and didn't see why she shouldn't enjoy it. It reminded her of home and happier days, and she had no hope of owning the original after all, and for that matter, neither had Susan.

In fact, everybody was very kind, very generous. It was almost like getting married all over again, and Chel knew that it was silly of her to feel that it was all a monstrous charade, leading nowhere. She tried to hide how she felt but she knew that she had disappointed everyone again.

'It's such a dear little bungalow.' Even her mother had said that, admiring the fitted kitchen and the smart new bathroom, so modern and practical.

'It's all right,' said Chel, tepidly. Her mother looked at her.

'It's very kind of Oliver's people to help you. Don't you think it would be nice if you tried to sound more grateful?'

The Nankervises, thought Chel unreasonably, seemed to have everyone's approval, while she had nobody's. And there was no explaining things to her mother when she couldn't even explain them to herself.

It was anyway impossible to describe how she felt about the bungalow. It was nothing to do with its architecture, or the area, although left to herself neither would have been her choice. It had very little to do, she was now beginning to believe, with the clinical air of all the special equipment. It went deeper than that. It was an unhappy house. Although she knew it was fanciful of her, Chel felt that its depression was blacker than her own. She was already miserable there, but nobody would sympathise if she said so. They were all beginning to take the view that she would be miserable anywhere, and it was time she got over it.

Well, perhaps they were right. Only it wasn't that easy. If only it were. Didn't they think she wasn't tired of this dragging weight of depression, these foolish easy tears, herself? She began to develop a policy of living just from hour to hour, only as much as she could cope with at one time. It made things marginally more bearable if she didn't look too far ahead, or worse, too far back.

Yet it was hardly all doom and gloom. Oliver's physical condition continued to improve. He could get about by this time with the help of crutches, although it wasn't for very far, and was in a slow and painful shuffle that Cheryl could hardly bear to watch. She had been told very plainly now that although Oliver wasn't paralysed in the strictest sense, extensive neurological damage had impaired his control over his own ability to walk properly, and there was some doubt as to whether it could ever repair itself. It was obvious that this was true, and that he had a struggle to overcome it. Chel hated it, for herself as well as him, because it was ugly and embarrassing and so at variance with his former grace. The plaster cast was gone at last, but for some time to come he would need to wear a spinal jacket to support his back. He had accepted this in silence, but it added to the already bitter burden of his humiliation. Combined with the crutches, it made him very self-conscious, particularly with anyone he didn't know. He thought it was far more noticeable than in fact it was, and took to wearing loose heavy sweaters to disguise it. But apart from mental blocks of this kind he was getting better, there was no escaping it.

Chel had been deliberately shutting her eyes to the necessity of telling Old MacDonald at the Queen's that she wouldn't be able to stay in her job, for she needed it to help her through the long days, quite apart from the money it brought in. She was back in reception now, although not in her previous position as head receptionist and trainee manageress, and sometimes she was almost able to imagine that she had her career back again. She didn't want to relinquish it. The money wasn't so essential these days, of course, but valuable because it was her own. She soothed her conscience by telling herself that girls like her were two-a-penny, and in any case she had months yet in which to give fair notice, and it came as a distinct shock when she was told that she could have Oliver home for Christmas. She had trusted so implicitly in the original estimate of a year at least before he was fit to leave hospital that it had never occurred to her that his own natural resilience might cut the time down, certainly not by so much. She went cold all over with the shock.

'It's a little earlier than we had thought for,' the consultant said, thinking that she would be pleased, with Christmas coming, to have her husband back with her. 'There's very little more we can do now but wait and see, and your husband has had no unforeseen complications. We'll try it over the holiday and see how it goes, shall we? If it proves to be too much, he can always come back for a few weeks, but I think it might do him good to be at home now.'

In a way, of course, Chel was pleased. She still thought of Oliver as someone she loved, but she was a lot more frightened of what he stood for. She knew, because she had been repeatedly assured of it, that she wouldn't be left to cope on her own. The health visitor from their doctor's practice would be in regularly, the doctor himself would be in and out, Oliver would go for regular physiotherapy sessions at the unit, but the fact remained that a lot of the time there would be just herself and him. He looked so frail these days that just looking at him made her nervous. What would she do if something went wrong, or she did something that hurt him and there was nobody there?

She gave in her notice in the middle of December and began to learn how to look after Oliver when he came home. There seemed an awful lot to know, so many seemingly simple things he couldn't for the moment manage unassisted. She had, too, to learn about diet and the danger signs to watch for in a chronic kidney patient. She knew that she would have to lavish all this care and attention on him for a long time yet, and began to be frightened of the responsibility she would be taking on. Knowing was far worse than imagining. She lay in the lonely bungalow at night and thought *I can't do it*, and knew that she must. She couldn't leave her husband in hospital for ever, however scared she was.

His family all told her how happy she must be at the prospect of having Oliver home for Christmas.

'And you really must make an effort to pull yourself together now,' added Susan, as ever a bracing Greek chorus to events. 'Oliver needs you. You've had plenty of time to get over your miscarriage, and how can you possibly help him if you're so wrapped up in yourself? It'll do you good, you need something to keep you busy.' And keep you out of mischief, she might have added, but the words hung unspoken between them.

Oliver would keep her busy all right, but then so had her job, and more pleasantly.

Susan's words fell on stony ground. Chel began to hate her for her good sense, and hated herself for hating her. It was as if she was two people, one of whom could stand back and watch the other making a fool of herself being stupid and hysterical, but powerless to do anything to prevent her. She was learning at first hand that the worst thing about depression is that it defeats its own recovery, and understood and resented the fact that Oliver must have equally first hand knowledge of the same thing.

She sat in the unhappy little bungalow on her own and cried for hours, and despised herself for doing it. Oliver, whom she had once loved more than she loved her own life, might have had his wings very thoroughly clipped, but he was alive wasn't he? She still had him with her. Not like the lost baby, who had only been put into her arms to die.

She didn't want Oliver, not as he now was. It was a dreadful thing to admit. She wanted him whole and strong and thumbing his nose at life in the old lighthearted way, so that she could love him without reserve as she had in the faraway past.

She had once thought that she would go with him to hell and back, she recalled. Well, here they were, well on the road. She had an awful feeling that it was going to be a one-way street.

It wasn't fair, it wasn't fair, it wasn't fair!

Only Jonathan, of all the people around her, seemed to realise the height, depth and breadth of her unhappiness. He saw her regularly and worried about her a lot, wishing that there was something he could do to help her – but the only thing he could think of was quite out of the question. Public opinion, if not Chel herself, wouldn't allow it. He alone it was who asked,

'Are you sure you're ready for this, Cheryl? You're not at all well yourself, you know.'

'Susan says it will do me good,' said Chel.

'Susan! What does she know about it?'

'Well, I think she does know, a bit,' said Chel, trying to be just. 'She had post-natal depression too, after her first baby. It went though, when she started another.'

A remedy barred to herself for obvious reasons until some indefinite time in the future, and anyway her hands would be full with Oliver. A baby on top of all the things she would need to do for him would be unthinkable.

'I think you should ask them to put it off for a bit,' said Jonathan firmly, but Chel said, how could she? And then, because he was an old friend and the only one who really seemed to care about her, she laid her head against him and put her arms round him, and said, 'I don't know what I would do without you. Don't leave me, will you? Don't stop seeing me. I need you so much.'

Jonathan put his arms round her, too, holding her gently, his nice face serious and concerned.

'Oliver might not like that.'

'Oliver won't care,' said Chel, with more optimism than certainty. 'Why should he?'

Jonathan could think of several reasons, not the least being the reaction of a newly disabled husband to a sound and healthy ex-boyfriend, but he hadn't the heart to say so. She was so bleakly and obviously unhappy. He wanted to believe her when she said she needed him.

'All right,' he said, against his better judgement. 'If he really doesn't mind. You can rely on me.'

Chel had come to take him for granted, too self-absorbed to see more than that he was a friend who didn't criticise.

'I know I can,' she said, lifting her face to his, and like a fool he kissed her.

The kiss went on and on, urgent and unsatisfying, a triumph of need over circumspection. There was no necessity to be gentle with Jonathan, Chel's lost and lonely hunger expressed itself with a passion far too violent for her husband's new frailty, spending itself with a physical strength that was as voluptuous and rippling with power as a stretching cat. Jonathan was warm flesh and blood, not stuffed pink fur. She hadn't known until she started how far she was ready to go, and it was he who pulled back first.

They stood there, hands on each other's shoulders, and looked at each other without speaking. After a while Jonathan swallowed. Lancelot and Guinevere had brought down a king between them. He said, 'Cheryl, are you sure you want me to go on seeing you?'

She wasn't sure of anything any more. She said, 'Yes.'

He drew a breath, his ideas in chaos. He must sort them out later, he knew, but even that thought couldn't quench the sudden spring of hope that leapt inside him.

She must know that they were playing with matches in an ammunition dump. She was standing there waiting for a promise that he knew he shouldn't give, as simply as a child asking for ice-cream. She was married, married, married – and her husband wasn't some John Doe of little account, he was Oliver Nankervis, whom the whole world loved.

He needn't kiss her again. She did need a friend. She didn't need another slap in the face. He said, 'All right.'

Knowingly or unknowingly, and neither was clear on that point, they had passed the fork in the road. If there was a signpost then they ignored it. They walked in the shadow of a dark tower and the lightning crackled over the distant hills.

X

Chel had been scared enough of having Oliver home, but he had looked a lot less daunting in a hospital ward than he did in the outside world. Getting him into the new car was a nightmare, driving him back to the bungalow felt like toting a load of high explosive. As she guided his slow progress into the house, Chel was a lot nearer to more tears than any feeling of pleasure in having him home.

Apart from the wheelchair, which they didn't talk about, there was only one chair in the house in which he could sit at present, the orthopaedic armchair specially designed for people with back problems. No more passionate interludes on the old studio couch – ever, Chel realised with a jolt. It had gone to the tip, helped on its way by Susan, and even if it hadn't, those days were quite possibly gone. It was surprising the things she hadn't let herself know, a defence mechanism, she supposed, like Oliver's refusal to accept that he might never walk properly. A wave of familiar hopelessness, mixed with panic, swept over her. She couldn't do it.

Oliver found sitting down nearly as big an undertaking as standing up, he was as dead a weight on Chel's arm as he was on her spirits. The nurses had managed him with ease, but her own attentions made him catch his lower lip between his teeth and draw a sharp breath.

'I'm sorry –' she said, and heard her own voice, cross, and bit her lip in vexation.

'It's all right.' Polite, not genuine.

He was safely into the chair, and he hadn't come to pieces in her hands. Thankfully, Chel sat down in the armchair opposite, largely because her knees were shaking. They looked at each other, wary, their long separation and their changed circumstances making a chasm between them, but just for a second the very faint echo of rueful laughter trembled in the air around them.

'Hullo,' said Chel.

'Hi,' said Oliver. His eyes went round the room, taking in the expanse of pale grey fitted carpet, the flowery curtains, the new sofa and armchairs that Susan had helped to choose – no, be honest. That Susan had chosen. There was nothing in the room that was familiar. 'A bit different from the flat,' he commented.

'Yes,' said Chel, and was about to add, do you like it? but was forestalled by the doorbell. If communication had been going to be re-established, it was postponed.

The caller was Susan, come to see if Chel was managing all right, and if there was anything she could do. She would have done better to keep away and leave them to sink or swim as best they could, but her slightly officious kindness prevented her from seeing it. She stayed for some time, organising them both for their own good and getting on Oliver's nerves, leaving finally with a promise to look in tomorrow.

'Does she come here often?' asked Oliver, when she had gone, contentiously because he was tired and edgy, and Chel reacted instinctively to the tone of his voice.

'She's been a great help to me while you've been ill,' she said, too quickly, too defensively.

'Oh,' said Oliver. The word hung in the air during a pause that went on too long, and finally Chel said, diplomatically because whatever she thought privately about his stepsister, she couldn't face the idea of starting a new life with a scene, 'She is very kind at heart, when you get past the front she puts up.'

Oliver let this pass, only saying, 'I hope she doesn't make a habit of just dropping in.'

The day staggered on somehow. Chel made a cup of tea and tried not to feel as if her once-beloved husband was a stranger whom she had to entertain, and Oliver wished she would stop fussing him. She cooked a light evening meal and he made an effort to eat it, they watched a little television, and then the district nurse came in and the two of them helped him to bed. Well, to be more accurate, Chel told herself, they put him to bed. He had trouble even in removing his own socks, and hated every minute of it. Hating it made him angry, and his anger rubbed off onto Chel. She caught herself snapping at him when the nurse had gone, and left his room with tears stinging behind her eyes. It wasn't going to work, she knew it wasn't! He was too much changed, and they had nothing in common any more. Any last hope that being on their own together would help them had been dashed.

But perhaps tomorrow would be better.

The night was endless. The unfamiliar room and a growing sense of isolation kept Oliver from sleeping, and wakefulness meant pain, and the pain, even when blunted by drugs, wasn't quite under his control yet. Chel lay on her own in the big double bed that she had bought before Susan changed her mind for her, tense and acutely conscious of his presence in the house, wondering if she should get up and see if he needed anything at every slight sound, a sense of overwhelming responsibility growing like some fearful mushroom in the dark. She slept only lightly, in short bursts, jerking awake to lie listening, a prey to stupid fears. If the house was quiet, she was ridiculously frightened that he might have died, once she even got up to check, creeping into his room by torchlight to find that he had slipped into a shallow sleep from which her careful inspection roused him to pain once more.

'I'm sorry,' she whispered. "I was just checking you were OK. Go back to sleep now.'

In the quiet darkness, something that had once been theirs and which they had mislaid over the past months came stealing back, unsure of its welcome and ready to fly at a word. Oliver stirred painfully, his voice reaching her thin with weariness.

'I'm not sleeping too well these days, actually.'

Chel's sense of pity, of compassion, turned in its sleep and fluttered an eyelid.

'Can I get you anything? Are you thirsty, would you like a drink?'

'Please.'

She poured water and held the glass for him so that he didn't need to sit up, her hand supporting his head; his hair tickled her wrist, and she could feel the warmth of him against her palm. As she laid him gently back against the pillow, just for a moment her hand sought his and held it.

'All right now?'

'Yes ... thanks.'

She released his hand, not recognising the lie for what it was, and straightened the duvet in an unconsciously tender gesture, feeling horribly useless and at a loss, and after a moment or two when he didn't move or speak, crept quietly away to her own bed.

The day began early, because Oliver was programmed after so many months of it to wake at hospital hours, and it began badly. The fleeting understanding that had returned in the night fled before Chel's tired impatience and the touchy bad temper that stemmed from Oliver's weary, over-familiar discomfort. By the time he was up and dressed, all the tensions were back, Chel's sense of inadequacy had deepened to flat despair and Oliver had begun to feel insecure and rather unwanted. The situation might have eased as the morning went on, but any chance of that was swiftly undone by a visit from Dorothy.

She came at a bad moment: Oliver hadn't realised that having his wife doing for him those things that he had come to take for granted from trained nurses would make him feel so unreasonably ashamed. Where he had thought that he had begun to plumb the depths of being disabled, he had suddenly found that the pit was apparently bottomless. The last thing either of them needed was his stepmother.

She came in with a wide, encouraging smile.

'Now then, and how are you two young people managing this morning?' she said brightly. Oliver looked at her woodenly from his chair by the fire, and Chel said nervously, 'All right, thank you.'

Dorothy gave her a scented embrace and a peck on the cheek before sweeping past to Oliver. She didn't kiss him – Chel had never, that she recalled, seen a demonstration of affection between them, but said, 'That's good, you'll soon settle down! Now Oliver, are you quite comfortable? Nothing you need? You must just ask, you know, we're all here to look after you.'

Since the only things that Oliver felt in need of were legs that didn't try to twist under him, and a spine that stayed upright without help and preferably didn't ache, he didn't bother to answer. Chel said, twittering,

'Coffee – I'm sure you'd like some coffee, wouldn't you?'

Dorothy patted her arm.

'There's a kind girl, I'll help to get it ready. Oliver will be all right for a few minutes, will he?'

'I can sit in a bloody chair without supervision!' snapped Oliver, and his stepmother smiled at him forgivingly as she followed Chel from the room.

'Poor Oliver is going to make life very hard for himself if he's going to fight every inch of the way,' she said, once they were out of earshot in the kitchen.

Chel had already realised that. She rattled cups and saucers onto a tray and didn't reply. Cups and saucers ... in the flat it had been mugs, and Oliver's parents had never drunk from them. A bleak feeling of loss suddenly assailed her.

Dorothy was busying herself, uninvited, with the kettle. Her voice went briskly on, finding out all the sore spots and poking at them.

'*God moves in a mysterious way,*' she said, in a warm voice that was also somehow insincere, placing a sympathetic arm around Chel's shoulders, so that the hairs on the back of Chel's neck prickled warningly. 'I won't hide it from you, Cheryl, when Oliver married you instead of dear Joanna, we all thought that he had ruined his life, but see how lucky it's turned out to be! Poor Joanna – so sensitive, always, and she hasn't been brought up to cope with things the way you have. She would never have managed, and it would have hurt her quite unbearably to see Oliver like this. She loved him so much, you know.'

And what do you think it's doing to me? Chel wondered, but didn't ask. She was well aware of what Oliver's stepmother thought of her. Her voice when she spoke was flat and colourless, giving no clue to the seething resentment and misery beneath.

'Excuse me, the kettle's boiling,' she said.

Christmas that year was a non-event, poignantly haunted for Chel by the pathetic little ghost of the lost child who should have given extra meaning to the festival. Her parents, abandoning the boys and Louise to Tracy and her little family for once, stayed in a nearby hotel to help Chel and Oliver through it, but the occasion had no sparkle, and in the days that followed nothing got noticeably better. Chel found Oliver an incredible drag on both her energy and her uncertain spirits, more of a tie than any baby could have been and at least as much work. He seemed to have set his mind on being impossible. She had to be constantly on the watch, since he was both wilful which she recognised, and desperate which she didn't, in case he did something stupid and fell and hurt himself, knowing that if he did he might never get up again, and they would be precipitated into a worse nightmare than the one they were in already. Her days and weeks were becoming regulated by the routine of caring for an invalid, but the worst thing of all was the impossible task of keeping him occupied, now that everything he had cared about was permanently denied him. He did nothing to help her, and quite often she felt that he was actively obstructive, making of the little house the prison that he had always so much feared. He was too morbidly aware of the spinal jacket under his sweater and of his own violated pride, too convinced that he was an object of pity or even of revulsion. She couldn't persuade him to leave the bungalow.

'You never see things like me being pushed around,' he said, when she tried to persuade him to let her take him to the park. 'Elderly people and kids, the odd broken leg maybe, but not freaks like me.'

Useless to remind him that thanks to skilled surgery he wasn't deformed, or that most people wouldn't have cared if he had been, even less possible to inform him, however kindly, that his comparative youth and still-striking looks would only attract sympathy. Pity, she sometimes suspected, was more of an ogre to him than revulsion. Anyway, Chel had stopped feeling kind some time ago. The few flashes of reawakening understanding had been smothered by the sheer weight of her worry and depression, and his unreasonable determination to react like a wild animal resisting captivity.

'You might think of me sometimes,' she said, in futile frustration at being unable to reach him, but Oliver ended that argument before it had fairly begun by switching on the television. He had never been a great reader, unfortunately, and the television was growing into a huge bone of contention between them; he used it like a drug to block off the terrible desert of boredom and frustration in which he found himself, and he would watch anything and everything – half of it, she was convinced, he neither saw nor heard. It drove her mad. She tightened her lips now and escaped into the kitchen.

Although he went twice a week to the hospital for physiotherapy, Chel wasn't freed by this to come and go because she had to take him and bring him home again. He was too frail as yet to leave on his own, she felt that in order to secure her own release from the bungalow she was obliged to find somebody to sit with him – Susan, his stepmother, friends. The man who had sailed single-handed round the world and loved the lonely oceans and the quiet deeps of the sea, felt himself being driven slowly along the path to complete insanity by the constant presence of well-meaning people, and longed desperately to be left alone.

For Chel, release was becoming more and more important, far too important for her to worry what she might be inflicting on Oliver. She fled the bungalow with the feeling that she was escaping, hurrying down the short drive on swift feet, huddled in her coat against the January cold. At first she walked – to the local shops, in the bare and wintry municipal park, up and down the deserted and windswept residential streets, long, long walks with no aim but to fill the empty hours and keep out of the house. Then the day came when she had a reason to take the car into the town centre.

It wasn't a very good reason, in fact it could almost be called a trumped up excuse. She needed a few things for Oliver from the chemist, that was true enough, but when Susan offered to fetch them for her she lied, and said that she needed some new shoes. It would have been so simple to say that she wanted to have a look round the big stores in the town centre to give herself a change, and probably they would none of them have blamed her – but she didn't say it. She drove away towards the centre, and stopped at the station to use the payphone there.

She hadn't seen Jonathan since the week before Christmas. Both of them had revealed rather more than they meant to reveal, and they were a little shy of each other as a result. Honest enough to admit that not the most complacent husband could accept that kiss as innocent, they were at the same time reluctant to define just what it had been. Jonathan had demonstrated too clearly the power and weight behind the press and public opinion. It was a fact that they were both afraid of it.

'I needed to talk to you, that's all,' said Chel.

They walked along the promenade with a decorous space between them, each of them so aware of the physical presence of the other that they touched without touching. Two friends who had met by chance – but it hadn't been chance, and Chel wasn't even sure that they were friends in any true sense. It wasn't talk she needed from Jonathan, nor friendship he wanted from her. He said, sympathetically,

'Family being difficult, are they?'

Chel pushed her hands into the pockets of her coat and hunched her shoulders against a cold wind damp with salt spray. Grey wavelets ran up the muddy foreshore to a tideline tangled with seaweed, and grey clouds to match scudded overhead in the teeth of a rising wind. She felt better in the open air.

'They always are,' she said. 'They're such – such *stuffy* people! They don't understand about anything, and they preach at me.'

'How is Oliver?'

Chel said, after a strained pause,

'Different.' Jonathan said nothing, and after a little while she said, 'It's very cold today, isn't it?'

'Shall we find somewhere for coffee?'

She shook her head and they walked on in silence. The air was full of surf sounds and the crying of seagulls, and the pungent smell of the weed. Chel wanted to tell him how hard she was finding it to reconcile Oliver to the constant presence of his family, and how impossible this made it for herself, but when she tried to put it into words that was impossible too. Because the frightening thing about Oliver was that he *wasn't* different in any but the most superficial sense. Underneath he hadn't changed at all. He had always preached freedom, he worshipped it still – and yet he must realise he had himself become the ball and chain that bound her hand and foot. Walking along like this beside the wide estuary that flowed out to the sea brought him – as he once was – so close to her that the pain of it rendered her speechless.

Altogether it wasn't the most successful of meetings, but it broke the ice. After that, they met quite often.

Chel had lied to get away the first time and on her return she found it impossible to say in front of Dorothy Nankervis that she had run into Jonathan, however casually she could pretend it to be, because she knew that Dorothy wasn't stupid enough to swallow it. When Dorothy had left, after a sort of third degree into her doings that made Chel wonder if she had second sight, it was then impossible to tell Oliver about Jonathan without it looking as if she had been trying to hide it from his stepmother. The deception that had thus begun almost inadvertently became very difficult to undo. But Oliver wouldn't care, Chel told herself, and anyway, what he didn't know couldn't hurt him, could it? Seeing Jonathan, not regularly of course, she wouldn't do that, but every now and again would keep her sane. To Jonathan, she could talk freely. He was her kind of person.

'And they just aren't,' she said, one afternoon when they had taken refuge from the cold in a tiny café. 'They make no secret of it, they despise me.'

'What, Oliver too?'

'I don't know what Oliver thinks, not any more.' Chel looked at him sombrely across the cafe table. 'He's never been like them. You'd think he was a changeling.'

Jonathan was happy to criticise Oliver's family, and glad of anything that might interest her.

'What about Deborah?'

But Chel would listen to nothing good about any of them.

'What about her? After she'd got her own way over our wedding and upset my mum, she more or less kept out of my way. I expect she despises me too.'

'Don't bet on it,' Jonathan advised her. 'The family are popularly supposed to have sent her to boarding school to keep her away from Oliver's influence. She might be a good friend.'

'They none of them want to be friends with me.' Chel's voice had taken on a grieving note, because although she wouldn't admit it, not even to Jonathan, she missed her own family a lot these days. She said, listlessly, 'I never knew that about Debbie.'

'There's a lot of things you probably don't know,' said Jonathan. 'There's a great thick file on Oliver and his family kicking around in the office. Good and bad – he's news, his father's a prominent citizen, his stepmother sits on committees, Mrs Casson is big on organising things for charities. You'd be surprised.'

Chel didn't think that she would be. She had become hardened over the past months to the endless and sometimes spiteful curiosity of the media. She had come away from what she had believed to be her husband's deathbed and found a posse of them waiting for her at the hospital doors, and after that nothing surprised her. And she knew at first hand that there was more than one way of presenting the truth. It was because she knew it that her relationship with Jonathan had such a bittersweet taste.

Jonathan was looking at his watch. He had stolen a few minutes between assignments to be with her, but they were over now.

'I must go. Have you finished your tea?'

'Just a few more minutes won't hurt, surely.'

Jonathan was fairly certain by now that her marriage was over in all but name, and that time, if left to itself, would return her shaken but basically unharmed to his arms. Even so, he knew that the longer they stayed in each other's company, the more risks they ran. A run-in with Oliver Nankervis's family was not what he wanted for either of them.

'I don't think I'd better. I've got to get down to Gracechurch to interview a man whose cat plays the piano –'

She interrupted him with a little spurt of laughter. 'No, really Jonathan!'

He grinned at her.

'It's true. His neighbour objects and is threatening to strangle kitty, and both of them are shouting about taking legal action. You must admit it's piquant. Just so long as they don't put it under a headline saying *Kitten on the Keys*.'

'I bet they will.' It was wonderful to be talking nonsense. It was wonderful to be talking at all, if it came to that. She smiled at him. 'All right, I wouldn't like someone else to scoop your scoop. You go, and I'll finish my tea and follow in a moment.'

In case we're seen, in case we're seen, in case we're seen –

Oliver and what he might think, say or do, was beginning to loom in her life like a Big Brother figure straight out of *Nineteen Eighty-four*. Jonathan saw the light die in her eyes and knew why and was angry.

''bye then.' There was no kiss. There mustn't be another kiss if they wanted to contain the fire the first one had kindled. It smouldered very quietly at present, warming them both but harming nobody. It was safest like that. He left her with a smile and a cheerful wave, and the café door clicked shut behind him.

Chel sat there on her own for another ten minutes. Outside it was still bitterly cold, with a hint of sleet in the wind, so that the windows were all steamed up on the inside and it was impossible to see out. It was warm here, safe and ordinary. She hadn't wanted safety or ordinariness, but she would settle for them now. It wasn't the ordinary that made your heart break, it was the dreadful irredeemable loss of perfection.

A girl's family sent her away to separate her from her own brother's supposedly bad influence, and that sounded more like

Dorothy than Jerry. A man threatened to sue his neighbour over a cat with musical ambitions. Two sides to life, one so alien that it left her chilled, the other warmly bizarre, funny, commonplace and therefore comforting. The Greek islands versus a kitten on the keys and a sleety wind. The shadow and the substance, the unknown and the known. Oliver's world and hers, and never the twain shall meet.

'Excuse me, miss, it's five o'clock. We're closing now.'

Chel jumped, surprised to find that she was still sitting in the café. The waitress looked at her curiously, swinging the key on its tag.

'I'm sorry, I was just going.' She got up hurriedly.

Out in the street, the biting wind still blew, and the dusk was coming in early under a leaden sky. The brightly lit shops looked friendly and familiar. Chel walked past them, dawdling in spite of the cold on her way back to the car. This was life, people hurrying with their heads down, busy and intent, longing to be home and out of the weather. Bright shop windows, buses going past loaded with other women who were going back to warm, cosy homes. In that horrible bungalow there was nothing but a kind of slow death.

She got into the car, and drove slowly back to Endicott Road.

Susan had Joanna Rendell with her, Chel found on her return, which she thought in irritation was something that only Susan could have thought of. The visit was not being a success. It was obvious that Oliver's stepmother, for once in her life, had hit the right nail on the head, although Joanna's sensitivity didn't prompt her to hide the fact that she found Oliver's disablement not so much emotionally unbearable as acutely embarrassing. She too pointedly tried not to look at him, and her manner when she couldn't avoid speaking to him was over-reminiscent of the late, great Joyce Grenfell in her famous kindergarten-teacher sketch. As if, thought Chel indignantly, he had somehow been turned by misfortune into an idiot. When the unwanted visitors were ready to leave, Joanna put her arms around Susan out in the hall and snivelled into her shoulder.

'Oh, I can't bear it,' she said, in the thread of a voice, just as Dorothy had predicted, and Chel said, nastily and too loudly, 'Well, you don't have to, so cheer up.'

Susan gave her a look.

'That wasn't very nice, Cheryl.'

Chel saw no reason why she should be so particularly nice to Joanna Rendell, who had caused her a lot of trouble one way and another in the past, and had very possibly just caused her some more. Her disinclination was aggravated by the fact that she felt plain and dispirited these days, while Joanna Rendell had apparently dressed deliberately to get the last ounce of drama out of the situation. Pale and lovely and romantic. Until she actually realised how Oliver was going to be, Chel had a grim suspicion that she had been rehearsing a touching, romantic scene. Romantic! There wasn't anything particularly romantic about a prickly, bad-tempered cripple who could barely get to the bathroom on his own! You needed to be more than pale and lovely to cope with the sort of life she had with Oliver these days, and Joanna Rendell could put that on her pale and lovely needles and knit it! She wasn't aware that her mouth had thinned to an unattractive line, but Joanna gave her a tear-drenched look, and choked, 'Poor Oliver!' in a heartbroken little voice, before leaving in a hurry and without saying goodbye.

'She's very upset,' Susan offered, preparing to follow her friend.

'Aren't we all?' said Chel, aggressively.

Back in the sitting-room, Oliver had a lost look and black shadows under his eyes. Mourning his lost love, thought Chel spitefully, prodding her own bad mood, and briskly clearing away the teacups left by the unwelcome visitors. Oliver had never given her any reason to suppose that he regretted Joanna Rendell, and he didn't do so now, but she looked at herself in the mirror later, taking due note of the hard look that seemed to have grown into her features of late, and the drab lankness of her once-pretty hair that she had no heart or incentive to care for any more. Probably he was sorry that he had married a red-haired shrew out of a shop. You found out what people were really made of when you hit the hard times, and he had nothing much to be proud of, either. She made a face at her reflection and it leered back at her.

She hadn't had an unbroken night's sleep since Oliver came home, and that night was no exception. She woke in the cold hours before dawn, not certain what had disturbed her, reaching before she was fairly awake for her dressing gown with what was fast becoming a well-developed instinct. Exactly like having a baby – except that babies were easily comforted compared to Oliver. No normal baby ever had such miserable, tormenting nightmares, or such brutal pain to contend with, and nobody short of a fully qualified hospital nurse should have to cope with anyone who did. Subconsciously aware of a grievance, Chel felt her way to the door without bothering with a light and went out into the hall.

There was no sound. Fully awake now in the cold January night, she paused and listened. Her door and Oliver's were both ajar at night so that she could hear him if he called her, not that he ever did, specifically, but if he had done so for once, he was quiet now. She switched on the dim hall light and crossed over to his door, hoping that it was something quick like a pillow on the floor, and nothing long-winded that needed pills, time and sympathy, and halted on the threshold, riveted to the carpet with shock, as another smothered sound reached her – a quick intake of breath, a choked-back sob ...

Oh no. Chel leaned against the door frame and closed her eyes in sudden, sharp pain. Oh no, I can't handle this – don't

Oliver, don't cry, don't cry whatever you do. Please, *please*.

She told herself that he probably hadn't called to her anyway, that he didn't want her, would hate her to see him crying. She stayed outside the open door for what felt like hours and listened to his choked and private grief, and felt a million miles separated from him, creeping back to her own cold bed eventually, shivering and frightened and not knowing what to do.

In the morning, apart from the fact that he was more listless even than usual, the incident might never have happened. Chel wondered if she had dreamed the whole thing, and then, knowing that she had not, thought bitter thoughts about Joanna Rendell for all the wrong reasons. It wasn't for lost love that Oliver had wept... or if it was, it wasn't Joanna's love.

XI

It was Oliver who came across the advertisement, in the personal column of the *Herald*, and drew Chel's attention to it in a rather desperate attempt to make conversation.

'I never knew people like that advertised,' he said.

'People like what?' enquired Chel, crisply. She was waiting to clear away the breakfast, and while he had the newspaper all over the table she couldn't get at it properly. She wanted to get the job done, and her impatience showed in her voice. He looked up swiftly, and their eyes met. He held her gaze for a moment and then looked away, slowly crumpling the pages together.

'Palmists – clairvoyants generally. You don't imagine it, somehow. That gypsy we saw in Cornwall, she was more the kind of thing ...' He wasn't reaching her, he saw. He let the words tail off into silence. Chel wasn't certain what she had read in his look, and it made her aggressive.

'Why shouldn't they? If they do it for a living.'

Oliver had dropped the paper onto the floor, which left the table free but gave Chel one more thing to do. Oliver was becoming rather good at making extra little jobs for her. He sat back in the chair, listless and aching. It wasn't one of his better days, but she hadn't noticed. The empty husk of their marriage was becoming rather pointless, but they both clung to it for fear of the alternative. He said, 'Perhaps we should consult one. It might be a relief to know where all this was going to end, or don't you think so?'

Chel picked up the *Herald* with an elaborate sigh and began to put the pages more tidily together with far too much rustling of paper. She tucked it under her arm and picked up the marmalade and some plates, turning for the door.

'Don't be silly, why should it *end* anywhere?'

'I hope to God it does,' said Oliver, but she had already left for the kitchen.

She had snubbed Oliver, but back in the kitchen she had second thoughts, knowing what might happen couldn't be worse than living through it, if it was going to be anything like the present, and she was much less sceptical about fortune-telling than she had once been. Desperation could drive you to the strangest lengths, she decided, and instead of going back to finish clearing the table, she unfolded the paper.

She found the advertisement quite quickly.

MICHAEL PARTRIDGE

Clairvoyant & Palmist

Guidance on all personal & business problems

As seen on TV

The name was vaguely familiar, perhaps she had heard of him before, or even seen him if he had been on the eternal television. His address wasn't far from their old flat, it should be quite easy to find. She remembered Madame Zsa-Zsa in Cornwall telling her that she had psychic powers and would need help, she had thought it funny, she recalled, but that had been a long time ago and in a different life. Perhaps she would give this Michael Partridge a ring ... and then again, perhaps she wouldn't. Then the door bell rang and it was Oliver's stepmother, she could see her car out in the street through the kitchen window, and half the breakfast things were still all over the table in the living-room. Bloody Dorothy! She crumpled the paper even more thoroughly than Oliver had done and tossed it aside before going to answer the door.

She might never have given Michael Partridge another thought if Jonathan hadn't stood her up one afternoon.

Although they always arranged their next meeting when they parted from each other, Chel and Jonathan didn't always succeed in keeping these trysts. There had been a couple of occasions when Chel had needed to stay at home because Oliver was unwell, and their relationship hadn't yet deteriorated to the point where she would leave him to the mercies of Susan or his stepmother if he was having a bad day. If she had fallen out of love with him, it would be cruel to let him know it yet, and anyway, if she did let him know, let the world know, she wasn't ready herself to face the uproar that would surely follow. It wasn't possible just to walk out on a national hero disabled in going to the rescue of the traditional damsel in distress, unless you were prepared to face some quite unpleasant consequences, and that was a fact of life for Jonathan just as much as for herself. He had his career to consider. They had to be very, very careful, measuring desire against expediency every moment of the time.

The restraints placed on their relationship made it that much more precious, and the stolen meetings sweeter when they came. Chel went to them with her heart singing for joy at the simple feeling of freedom, and when one day he failed to meet her by carefully calculated chance in the Amusement Arcade on the seafront, she was disproportionately disappointed.

It did happen, of course, that he could be sent unexpectedly on an assignment, because that was the nature of his job. In the old days, she had been able to go with him some of the time, in fact that was how she had come to meet Oliver, but not any more. She remembered this as she wandered along the aisles between the slot machines, hoping that he might at any moment come rushing up, out of breath, to explain why he was late. It was clearly understood between them that a failure to appear on either side wasn't to be taken as anything but inadvertent, but this didn't help. She was very disappointed.

After a while, she wandered to the entrance and stood looking out at the busy street that ran between the houses and the water. There was no sign of Jonathan's battered old banger among the cars that drove past, and her excited mood began to evaporate into dull depression, familiar and exhausting. The harbour itself was sullen and still under the winter sky. Eternal chill, and herself caught in it. Perhaps things would improve when the weather improved. She was tired, oh so tired, of being unhappy. Day after grey day of worry, responsibility, guilt – and no way that she could see of ever breaking free.

For a fleeting moment then she remembered that once before she had run away. With Oliver. For a brief time she had been perfectly, unreasonably happy. How silly, how naïve, to think that anything so beautiful could ever survive. From the moment that they returned from Cornwall to this boring town, things had begun to go wrong. She had become to some extent estranged from her family, she had earned the scorn of Oliver's for such simple things as her christened name, she had lost the baby she had come to want so much, in the end lost, too, the career that she had loved, and with nothing to show in return.

We should have stayed away –

Chel jerked herself back from the edge of a dangerously evocative dream, telling herself firmly that thoughts like that were just silly. What was done was done. As things now stood, Cornwall was as inaccessible as Greece, and that was that. And then, for no reason that she consciously recognised, she remembered Michael Partridge.

He only lived a few blocks away and Jonathan was obviously not going to come, and on top of that it was starting to rain. Michael Partridge wouldn't see her at once, of course, but perhaps she could make an appointment. After all, she had to do something to pass the afternoon, and she certainly wasn't going back to the bungalow before she needed to. She was meant to be at the dentist.

Sometimes it seemed as if her life, these days, was made up of nothing but lies and deceptions. Sad for the honest, happy days that had apparently gone so irretrievably, Chel left the shelter of the Arcade and walked along the road in the direction of the commercial dock.

Michael Partridge opened his own front door, and he was a bit of a surprise because however she had expected a palmist to look, Chel hadn't imagined one as a tall, youngish man in a dark grey business suit. Something more exotic, on the lines of Madame Zsa-Zsa with her shawls and diamond rings would have been more comfortable, because Michael Partridge didn't look the sort of person who could be laughed off. He looked credible, if such people ever were. Chel felt scepticism rising and squashed it firmly. If she was going to be sceptical, why was she here at all?

A good question.

'I don't want to know my clients' names,' Michael Partridge told her. 'With some of them, knowing that much could influence me and affect what I told them. You can call me Michael. Won't you come in?'

Chel hadn't thought that he would see her so promptly, and as she followed him into a pleasant, chintzy sitting-room, she said so. He laughed.

'If I said that I had been expecting you, you wouldn't believe me.' He looked at her again, more searchingly. 'Or perhaps you would. Sit down.'

She sat on a sofa, and he sat half-facing her and took her left hand, holding it casually as he went on talking. One of the many reasons she had shied away from believing herself clairvoyant was because she had always thought of such people as eccentric and peculiar, even a bit crazy, but Michael Partridge was none of these things. He could have been a bank manager discussing a loan – except, of course, that her own bank manager had never held her hand.

'People come to see me for many reasons,' he said. 'Some just out of curiosity, of course, but often because they have problems that they feel have grown too big for them to handle. Now your problem, I feel very strongly, is a personal rather than a business one. You think that it's connected with affairs of the heart, but I don't think it's as simple as that. Let's try and find out what it really is, shall we?' He didn't take his eyes from her face, but his fingers touched hers, exploring her wedding ring. 'You're married. That usually means trouble with another woman, or in this case, I believe, another man. Turn up your palm.'

She turned her hand over and he looked down at it, casually tracing the lines with his forefinger. She sensed surprise in him, just as she had with Madame Zsa-Zsa. His fingers closed over hers and he was laughing into her eyes. 'You have made a mess of things, haven't you? Put that hand away, we don't need it.' He let it go, and leaned back in his chair. Chel folded the rejected hand neatly over its fellow and waited. There was very little in this session to remind her of the flamboyant fairground gypsy, no window-dressing, no atmosphere. But she felt power flowing through the room like a tide, and herself resisting.

'You have to go with it, you know. Stop fighting and let it speak to you, and you'll find you don't need me.'

'I'm afraid to,' said Chel. His matter-of-fact acceptance of the incredible made it quite easy to say.

'Why are you afraid?'

'I don't really know.'

'Then ask yourself. You sit there with all the powers you're ever going to need in your own two hands, and you come to me for help because you say you're afraid. What are you afraid of?'

Chel said, 'Of knowing without knowing why.'

'You won't change it by wishing, or make it go away. If you have it, you have it.'

'I can't make it work for me.'

'You haven't tried. Or you have tried, and you don't like what it told you.'

'Help me, Mr. Partridge – Michael, I mean – I need someone.'

He looked at her for a moment, as if he was weighing her financial viability, and then took her hand again, letting it lie loosely in his.

'Your life is like a train that's gone off the rails. Oh yes, I can tell you all about it. But what I'm going to do with you instead is to help you to learn to help yourself. At this very moment, you're experiencing a power surge that can help you to change your life.'

'It comes from you.'

'We won't argue. Do you have anything with you that either of these men in your tangled little life has handled?'

'I'm not sure.' She felt in her pockets, and came up with a screw of paper on which Oliver, some time in the previous winter, had scrawled the name of a reference book he wanted her to get for him from the library, and a pen she had borrowed from Jonathan on their last meeting and forgotten to return. Michael Partridge placed these unpromising exhibits on the sofa between them.

'I have no way of knowing which of these belongs to which of them,' he reminded her. 'You take one of them in your hand and hold it, and think about the man, and if we're tuned in to each other I shall tell you if it's husband or lover.'

She chose the paper, but it was impossible to keep her mind entirely on Oliver, as impossible as it had been to think of nothing, nearly three years ago now. She did try, but Jonathan was so close to the surface that he kept pushing in. When she thought about Oliver, it was all dark things, but Jonathan was light and the possibility, however remote, of escape.

Michael Partridge held out his hand and she dropped the twisted note into it. He held it for a moment, thoughtful.

'The man who wrote this can't be the man in your thoughts, surely.'

'It must have been in my pocket for almost a year,' explained Chel.

'Husband, or lover? A bit of both here, I think. You had a very successful marriage on your hands once, young lady, and to a brilliant man. What went wrong?' He looked at her seriously. 'You feel that the world's come to an end, don't you?'

'His world has.'

He laid the paper down.

'I need something more recent, this is no good. This could have been written by a dead man.'

He felt Chel jerk beside him and looked at her inquiringly, but she shook her head and he reached for the pen and held it.

'Now this is different. I get this person very strongly indeed. A nice young man, very sincere. You mean a lot to him. He doesn't strike you as very deep, perhaps, and there you're wrong for he could surprise you. Is he what you want, are you sure?'

'If I knew that, I wouldn't be here.'

'Then it's high time you learned to sort yourself out. Look, you don't need me to tell you any of this.' He put the pen down again and sat back, crossing his legs. 'You've got to do it for yourself. You're in grave danger that you don't even recognise because you refuse to open those beautiful witch's eyes of yours. There are people watching you – which I think you know without the help of clairvoyance – and at least one of them dislikes you very much indeed, and means you harm. You must take your courage in both hands and pull your head out of the sand, for unless and until you do, nothing is ever going to come right.'

'I didn't know my head was in the sand.'

'Yes, you did. Now stop wallowing in an unavoidable loss – oh yes, you are – and use your head. You can't have anything both ways, least of all life, and you're going to have to make a decision. Running with the hare and hunting with the hounds is never an option.'

'I know that, but can't you help me *how* to decide? Or when?'

'You have the power. Use it. Go on, use it.'

'I don't know how.'

'Let your mind relax, and let it flow.'

She tried, but she had been fighting it for too long and she thought she didn't succeed. All that came to her was a feeling of intense despair and a blank wall that couldn't be scaled, and that was built, she felt, surely unreasonably, of the same red brick as the bungalow.

'I can't do it.'

'If that's true, it's because you won't let go and stop trying to blank it out. You'll get there, in the end.'

He wouldn't tell her any more, and he refused to take her money.

'I don't make people buy what they don't need,' he told her. 'If you don't know what to do now, you soon will. And take care.'

He escorted her to the front door and opened it for her, polite and businesslike, but as she stepped out into the street he took her hand again, and said, almost as if it came without his wishing it,

'*Many waters cannot quench love, neither can the floods drown it.* Goodbye, and good luck.'

And that was true, she told herself as she walked away. She had been caught in a flood of many waters all right, but somewhere under the torrent her love for steady, reliable Jonathan, who drank real ale and played rugby with his mates on Saturdays, had gone on burning, bright and steady. She had only to take hold of her courage.

She woke in the middle of the night, bitterly cold and unreasonably frightened, to find someone standing at the foot of her bed. Not anybody she knew, or even anyone she could see very clearly, just a dumpy outline of deeper blackness in the dark. The dim light that came through her slightly ajar door from the uncurtained hallway just touched the edge of the shape of a little old woman. Chel knew without really seeing it that she wasn't an old-fashioned person, or a medieval nun, or anything traditionally ghostlike and therefore half-laughable of that kind, but rather alarmingly of the present time. She just stood there and said nothing, and her unseen eyes in the dim cloud that was her head looked at Chel with pity.

Chel lay still with her heart beating fast, rigid under the comfortless and chilly duvet. She couldn't look away, but neither did she want to look, and then a cloud must have gone across the moon for the light in the hallway dimmed and the dark figure faded. In the corner of the room, a nimbus of light began to grow in its place, a misty cloud with a red spark in its heart. It floated quietly across the room, hung for a moment in the air, and was gone.

There was no sound. Exactly like the last time. Only last time there had been no shape. Or at least, no moonlight and no door ajar to show it.

Chel couldn't breathe. She was so frightened that her natural reflexes had become paralysed with the shock and it was an effort to force air into her lungs. She didn't believe what she had seen, and whatever it had been, she never wanted to see it again. It was like some ghastly warning from the other side, she thought, trying to make herself laugh, but something inside her shuddered and said, *don't!* She reached out and switched on the bedside lamp, and was relieved when the room sprang into clear view, comfortable and pretty as it had always been.

Her heart was still hammering her ribs. She sat up and pulled the pillows up behind her so that she could lean back, but she wasn't comfortable even then. Even in the bright-lit room she was still afraid, and if Oliver called out, or even so much as moaned in his sleep – come to think, most of all that

– she felt that she would scream. She could feel the scream rising up ready in her throat.

But the little house was silent in the still, cold winter night.

XII

Of course, Oliver's family visited on other occasions too, not just when Chel wanted to go out. They were genuinely trying to help, but she felt, probably unjustly, that they disapproved of her wanting to go out at all and liked to keep an eye on her. It did nothing to make her feel better. Unrecognised, depression was beginning to give way to resentment. Resentment seemed to grow on the bungalow walls like mould.

There was no shortage of sensible advice, and several bracing platitudes on offer – all irritating rather than comforting, for both Chel and Oliver were well aware that help under the circumstances could only come from within.

'You have to face up to it,' urged Jerry, coming dangerously close to the heart of the matter. 'Life goes on.'

Oliver, who wished that it didn't have to, and who couldn't even face the idea of facing up to anything at all, had nothing to say to this, and his father gave him a sympathetic and consciously gentle touch on the shoulder that made him cringe.

'Never mind son, it's early days yet.'

Early days? My God, thought Chel blankly, are there going to be so many more of them like this? And knew that unless she did something to stop it there were, and unconsciously drooped a little under the knowledge that knowing something should be done was one thing, doing it, or even knowing what it was, was quite another. Dorothy gave her a cool look and followed it with a wise smile.

'Poor little Cheryl,' she said kindly. 'Now come along, let's all have a nice cup of tea.'

As matters deteriorated, Susan was becoming unbearable. Chel couldn't imagine how she had ever begun to like her. She usually left Tom to entertain Oliver, with whom she had never had much in common, and like her mother tended to buttonhole Chel in the kitchen. Chel was beginning to dread the mere suggestion of tea or coffee these days.

'You should encourage Oliver to take up some hobby,' said Susan firmly. 'It can't be good for him to sit and brood like this, you must try to help him.'

Surf riding, windsurfing, sailing, diving ... no – no, don't think about it!

'Such as what?' asked Chel, coldly.

Susan kindly overlooked the tone of her voice.

'You could encourage him to read more. Or draw, or something. Oliver was always rather good at drawing when he was at school. Or get him one of those electronic chess games. That would give him something else to think about.'

Poor Oliver, who could break out in a sweat with the simple effort of sitting still! Chel at least had that much understanding.

'He isn't ready yet for things like that.' She didn't bother to ask herself why she should be so sure, simply stated the bare fact as if it was something everyone should know. Susan looked at her with scorn.

'Don't be so silly! It's more than ten months now since he was hurt. He's been home nearly five weeks.'

Chel shook her head.

'He won't look for ways to make the best of it until he can accept it.'

'Then you should make him see a psychiatrist,' said Susan decisively. 'He's turning himself into a head case just sitting there with the television. My God, Oliver never watched television!'

And where was the use of saying that? Chel asked herself silently. If it hadn't been television it would have been something else, equally irritating. Nobody, not even Oliver, could live in a vacuum.

Susan looked at her sharply.

'Do you still see that journalist?' she asked suddenly. Chel froze on a moment of indecision when she almost said *no,* but something in the way Susan had spoken warned her.

'We're bound to meet sometimes,' she said casually. 'We have a lot of mutual friends.' Almost true, she comforted herself. They did have a lot of mutual friends, or at least, they once had done so. 'As a matter of fact, I ran into him only the other day – why do you ask? Did you want him for something? You can always get him through the *Herald* office.'

Susan said, pushing for a reaction,

'Joanna said she saw you having tea with him.'

Chel felt a surge of anger. Always *Joanna*! She said, more coolly than she felt, 'Yes, it was trying to snow, we went in to get out of it.'

Susan gave her a frustrated look.

'Don't you think it would be kinder to Oliver not to see him at all?'

Chel managed a look of artistic surprise.

'It's not the crime of the century, is it, just drinking tea with a friend?'

'It could be misunderstood,' Susan warned her. Chel laughed.

'Only by little-minded people with nothing else to think about,' she said, provocatively. 'Do all your friends go around stirring up trouble where there was none before, or is it special to Joanna Rendell?'

This was bringing warfare a little too far into the open for Susan, who favoured a more subtle approach.

'Don't be silly, Cheryl!' she repeated crossly, and Chel gave her an infuriating grin. Being angry with Susan and her spying friend Joanna gave her a splendid feeling of coming alive again. She could feel the anger tingling right through her like an electric current, bringing back light and warmth.

'Well, you be careful, that's all!' said Susan, and immediately wished she hadn't, because it made Chel grin again. It was true that it had sounded childish. She turned her back and busied herself in making the tea.

Chel wasn't afraid of Susan and her friends because she had convinced herself that she had no reason to be. Her thoughts were her own affair, they couldn't read them, and she had done nothing so far which anyone could use to do her any harm. Except not telling Oliver, but that was as much for his own good as anything. Although she had no idea of it, what she thought was so coloured by Oliver's views of his family that she was more scornful of Susan than she should have been.

Michael Partridge had warned her of danger, but that she had forgotten. He had shown her hope for the future, and that she remembered. The hope and the revitalising anger together made her completely overlook the fact that the only person she knew of who might consider she had reason to dislike her and wish to harm her, disliked and resented Oliver far more.

Things couldn't go on the way they were for much longer. There were too many people who imagined themselves to have an interest, and the leaven of well-meaning interference was already working like yeast in the sour everyday dough. Chel had tried her best to be discreet and to keep her affairs – *affaire*, maybe – to herself in order to protect Oliver until, as she told herself, he was well enough to know the truth, but she had overlooked one thing. She could keep out of the way of the Nankervises more or less, because to a great extent she knew their lifestyle and their friends and the places where they were likely to be. But Helen Macken, Oliver's natural mother, had lived in Embridge too, twenty years or more ago. She had the same charisma as Oliver had once had when he chose, and her friends wouldn't forget her, or she them. Chel, running through the rain to meet Jonathan outside the cinema, was observed by a passer-by. When they met, the outstretched hands, the laughter, the deliberate holding apart that spoke so eloquently of its exact opposite, were all observed by a shrewder and less prejudiced eye than Joanna Rendell's. Helen, back in New York that was her second home these days, received a letter. Unable to drop her commitments and come home, she telephoned to Oliver's father, and Jerry, who had as little to say to his ex-wife as Oliver had these days to Chel – and maybe for similar reasons – failed to understand that the confidence was for his ears alone, and discussed it with his present wife.

To be fair, Dorothy didn't so much intend to make mischief, as see a way to end a situation that had gone on quite long enough, or at least, that was how she rationalised it to herself. The cheap little shop-girl that Oliver had so thoughtlessly married to inflict upon them all had been a thorn in her flesh for a long time. She had liked the idea of a connection with the Rendells; although there was no chance now of that marriage ever taking place, this if anything only served to deepen the disappointment she felt. It was too bad about the Wainwright girl, really it was.

But thank goodness, poor Oliver, so badly disabled and so dreadfully frail these days, was obviously no longer happy with his ill-bred wife, and her behaviour in putting the family's private affairs in the public domain had been so vulgar that it was really unforgivable. Fortunately, no child of the marriage survived. It was time to bring it tidily to an end, and to fetch Oliver back to his father's house where he belonged and where he could be properly cared for during the remainder of his life. They could give him his own rooms and pay a nurse to look after him. Some nice middle-aged woman who would let him lead a quiet, soothing and celibate existence. A man in his condition really didn't need a hurly-burly girl to make his life a misery with her thoughtlessness, and her affairs with other men.

'You leave it to me,' she said. 'Yes, really Jerry, it would be much better. I can handle it all much more tactfully than you will and see that nobody is hurt. The little Wainwright girl can marry her journalist when the divorce is through, and she'll be far happier than she has ever been with Oliver. It'll all be for the best, you wait and see.'

Oliver's father, who knew something about these things, had a suspicion that the happiness that Chel had known with his son had possessed a more special quality than Dorothy would ever appreciate. He looked at his smart, capable wife and tried to find an argument that would serve against her crusading zeal, but there wasn't one. Oliver *was* unhappy, although under the circumstances it was hardly surprising. Cheryl, apparently, was seeing the Holmes man in secret. If there was nothing left of their marriage it was better ended. But ... there was a *but*, although he was unsure where it led.

'Let me talk with her first,' he said, obscurely troubled, but his wife told him that he would only make things worse, not better.

'It needs a woman to handle something like this. It needs a delicate touch. How can you ask the child if she's seeing her old flame? You'd only lose your temper.'

It was like Dorothy, he thought, to avoid calling a spade a spade, or in this case an ex-lover an ex-lover. The old-fashioned phrase she had used instead, for some reason that he didn't understand, set his teeth on edge. Helen had simply called the man *Jonathan.*

He had begun rather to like his daughter-in-law at one time, it was a shame.

Helen had said, *help her,* and it took a good deal to make Helen talk to him at all. But perhaps Dorothy was right, the best way to help her was to set her free. As for Oliver, nobody could free him.

'Make sure of your facts first,' he suggested unhappily.

'I'll see what Susan can tell me. She and her friends seem to know all the gossip in this town.'

'She would have told us.'

Dorothy Nankervis put on a pious expression. 'Not if she wasn't sure. Susan would never make trouble.'

Susan hadn't been sure. Not sure enough, at least, to risk upsetting Oliver, of whom she stood rather in awe these days. And Chel's explanation had been very specious.

'She does see him, I know,' she said, when questioned. 'But I believe Oliver must know she does. I've taxed her with it, of course, but what can one do? I can't call her a liar to her face.'

'I'll speak to them both,' said her mother. 'That naughty girl is going to be in the papers again if she isn't careful. Really, the pair of them are so thoughtless! She should consider your father's position.'

Chel would have been astonished to hear Susan defend her.

'Hardly Mummy, not just for this,' she objected, but Dorothy took no notice. It suited her purposes not to do so.

The fact that she chose a bad time for her confrontation was hardly her fault, there were very few good times in that bungalow. But it was particularly unfortunate that she chose a moment when there was, for a brief while, some lightening of the general doom and gloom.

It was one of the days when Oliver's pain seemed really to be easing at last, which always helped, and a visit from Bill Rowlands in the morning had brightened it further. Oliver's friends had frequently visited the hospital, but they didn't come to the bungalow very often, possibly because hospital visiting was normal, but visiting a tragically disabled colleague at his own home was slightly embarrassing, and they no longer knew what to say to him, their own lives had moved on. Chel had been quite glad, they were all so aggressively healthy and fit that the contrast with Oliver was hurtful, but Oliver had missed them and suspecting the reason for their tacit desertion had made it harder for him.

Bill had brought the preliminary report on the first season's work on the *Hesperides*, taking the refreshingly sane and normal view that since Oliver had been the one to find her, he would naturally be interested. The two of them had discussed it exhaustively and Oliver had become quite animated. Chel had listened to the talk with interest, and the three of them had laughed together over a cup of coffee, and nobody had tried to pin her into a corner while she was making it. It was so novel that when Bill finally left, the feeling he had generated remained and Chel and Oliver were able to go on discussing the *Hesperides* in a perfectly friendly way. For the first time since he had left hospital, Oliver ate all his lunch, almost without noticing that he was doing it, and Chel had begun to wonder if it might be possible to talk about other things too, when his stepmother arrived.

She had decided on a cosy approach that immediately frightened Chel and set Oliver on the defensive.

'Now, I've been hearing things about you two young people that we need to talk about,' she said, settling in an armchair by the fire as if she meant to stay all afternoon. Chel looked at her in sudden dismay, and Oliver said, 'Not about me, you haven't. I don't do anything.' He still sounded fairly lighthearted, but now there was a brittle undertone. Chel looked down at her hands, giving no help. Dorothy said, 'Your mother had to ring your father all the way from America, Oliver, to ask him what was going on. Isn't this a bit thoughtless of you both? After all, we've had quite enough fuss in the newspapers, haven't we Cheryl dear?'

The playful tone for some reason made Chel more afraid than a straightforward accusation would have done. She stole a glance at Oliver under her eyelashes, and found that he was looking back at her. She couldn't read his look, and in any case his behaviour these days wasn't always predictable. He had taken one of his powerful painkillers after lunch, they slowed him down as they took effect – and was it awful of her to sit here, calculating hopefully that it would happen now, and he would miss the point of what she feared was coming?

When neither of them said anything, and the only reaction she got was a look from Oliver that she described to herself as deliberately stupid, Dorothy said,

'I'm talking about Jonathan Holmes, my dears.'

Oliver's stupid look, if anything, deepened, and Chel said,

'Oh him – yes, he's been very kind. What about him?' Attack was the best defence, but *oh Oliver, Oliver, I'm so sorry. I didn't mean you to know this way.*

Dorothy said, with a bright smile that covered her surprise at this straight-talking response,

'We all appreciate, dear, that you need friends of your own kind, but don't you feel that one of your nice girlfriends would be a better choice? Oliver, we all know that it's hard for Cheryl, but we don't want talk, do we?'

'What do you mean, talk?' asked Oliver. For a moment, Dorothy looked taken aback. She couldn't admit that she hadn't believed what Cheryl had said to Susan – how complicated it all was! – but Oliver's lack of reaction was disappointing. And the Wainwright girl too – why, she didn't even have the grace to look guilty! Surely, Oliver couldn't have known all along? Could he? She hurriedly regrouped her arsenal.

'Well, *that* sort of talk, Oliver dear. Don't pretend to be stupid, please. You owe it to the family not to stir up any more scandal.'

Oliver gave her a long, cool look that was suddenly very far from stupid.

'I didn't know we had stirred up any scandal,' said Chel. She should have kept quiet.

'Oh come Cheryl, you've never done anything else since we knew you –' Dorothy broke off and forced herself to smile again, counting up to ten. 'Now, you know what I mean, both of you. Don't pretend that you don't. I've come here to help you, but you must help me, too.'

'I don't think we need your help,' said Oliver, with a lift of his brows.

Chel was breathing very slowly and deeply, trying to control her heart which was thumping in alarm. It was one thing to decide for herself that her marriage was over and must come quietly and decently to an end for the sake of all concerned, but quite another to have a spiteful woman smash it with a sledgehammer. But Dorothy Nankervis, of course, seized on this perfect opening with glee, ill-disguised as concern for their welfare.

'If Helen Macken knows in New York that your marriage is shaky and your wife seeing another man, Oliver dear, and feels it necessary to ask your father to speak to you both, then I think that it's becoming obvious that you *do* need help, and badly.'

Oliver's face was all at once so expressive that Chel looked away, but it was only for a second. A shuttered look closed down on it, and he said only,

'How very busy of Helen. I didn't realise that she was that interested.'

Chel momentarily forgot her own position, and was furiously angry on Helen's behalf – poor Helen, who loved Oliver so much that she would willingly have given a part of her physical self to save his life. Her triumphant rival couldn't even resist kicking her when she had been down for years, for surely Dorothy knew how much Oliver resented interference – and suddenly Chel remembered that she was facing a woman who was married to another woman's husband, and several other things that Helen had once told her. Sweet, reasonable, helpful

Dorothy Nankervis, who got her own way and left her beaten enemies stripped of everything. And wasn't content with that, it now appeared. How could Oliver's father have preferred her to beautiful, intelligent, creative Helen? The thought came into her head that Dorothy's aversion to Oliver had its root, branch and flowering in the fact that he was Helen's son and Jerry was his father – but that was surely unreasonable. The woman would have to be sick.

'Helen didn't ask *you* to speak to us!' she said. 'Anyway, who says our marriage is shaky?'

'That's a very good question,' agreed Oliver. Finding that they were both looking at her with interest, Dorothy became unaccountably flustered, and said,

'Well, nobody exactly said that, of course.'

'Then what did they say?' demanded Oliver, pushing home the advantage.

He's protecting me, thought Chel, horrified, and the shock went right through her. She didn't deserve it. Or was he simply protecting himself? She began to feel physically sick.

Dorothy was still smiling, but it seemed to Chel that her eyes had narrowed in a calculating way, or perhaps it was just her overheated imagination.

'So many people have seen Cheryl going about with that journalist from the *Herald* –'

'Jonathan,' agreed Chel. For some reason, this interruption put Dorothy off her stroke. She opened her mouth and shut it again, and looked at Chel with distaste. Oliver said, casually, 'Joanna came here, which means about as much, or as little. So what?'

'That's different.'

'Well...' Oliver looked thoughtful. 'It would certainly be difficult for her to meet me anywhere else.'

'But Jonathan Holmes doesn't come here!'

Chel waited for Oliver to speak, but he said nothing, seeming to have suddenly lost interest. She made the only possible response, but it would have come better from him. From her, it sounded like the last ditch stand of someone who knows themselves to be very much in the wrong – which of course, it was.

'Do the family spies watch the door twenty-four hours a day?'

The fact that Oliver had, to all intents and purposes, abandoned ship, hadn't escaped his stepmother. She didn't care for anything the Wainwright girl might say, whether she knew it or not she was on her way out. She gave a sharp, unmirthful laugh.

'Perhaps they should!'

Oliver looked vague, and doubled back on the conversation. It might have been the painkillers kicking in, or it might have been deliberate, the jury was out.

'So what was this help you felt you had to give us?'

His stepmother stared at him. Chel saw that he had disconcerted her again. She should try living with it, she told herself grimly. She might realise then why being tied to this house was so exhausting, and why seeing a normal man every now and then was necessary. Oliver returned the stare almost drowsily, heavy-eyed as if his eyelashes had been tipped with lead. Dorothy bridled – she was one of those rare, old-fashioned women who could still do this.

'Am I to understand that Jonathan Holmes is a welcome guest in this house, then?' Incredulity was beautifully suggested.

'I think,' said Oliver, very slowly and clearly, 'that I shall go and lie down.'

'I'll help you,' said Chel, jumping to her feet. Her help wasn't necessary any more, but the welcome diversion was too tempting to resist. Perhaps he meant it to be, who knew any more with Oliver? She turned to Dorothy. 'You will forgive me, won't you, if I don't see you out? He always rests about now, only you came.'

Dorothy rose to her feet, knowing for certain now that she had been right, but needing to get away and rearrange her arguments. She sniffed.

'I think I know when I'm not welcome in a house!'

"Oh no,' said Oliver, with gentle ambiguity. He leaned on Chel for a moment, getting his balance. The physical closeness was like a momentary alliance against a common enemy. His stepmother picked up her handbag and stood up, not quite knowing how she had lost control of the discussion but only that she most certainly had. She didn't make the mistake of taking umbrage, but smiled at them again instead. She wasn't unsatisfied with what she had achieved – for their own good, of course, for their own good. One had to be cruel sometimes in order to be kind.

'Now, if you want any advice or help when you've thought it over, you know where we are,' she said kindly. 'I understand – we all understand – that it's difficult for you both, that's what we wanted you to know. Now can you manage, Cheryl dear, or shall I help you?'

'We can manage, thank you.' Oliver had taken his weight from Chel and transferred it to his crutches, she returned the warm, charitable smile with a polite nod. 'Excuse us, won't you'

As they crossed the hall together, she was aware of Dorothy standing baffled in the sitting-room doorway, and as she was helping Oliver onto his bed, she heard the front door close. But she had stayed long enough, thought Chel, dully. The barb she had so deftly planted already leaked slow poison. She picked up the blanket that lay folded on a chair and put it over Oliver without speaking. He looked up at her with the same heavy look he had given his stepmother, but either he had been putting it on, or he was deliberately fighting off the drug in order to speak to her.

'It might be an idea if he did come,' he said. 'It might shut them up.'

Chel paused, the ribboned edge of the blanket in her hands, before she stepped back and said, 'Jonathan, you mean? You don't want to see him, do you?'

He looked exhausted suddenly, the dreariness descending again like a fog.

'Why should I care? What can he take from me, after all?'

She began to speak, but there was nothing to say. She patted the blanket in a smoothing motion.

'Is there anything you want before I go?'

'No.'

There was something unsatisfactory about what had just taken place, but she didn't know what to do about it. She wasn't even certain what it was. She waited a moment, but he didn't move or speak, and she began to feel silly standing there. She turned and left the room, leaving the door ajar behind her in case he called.

By this time, Chel hated the red-brick bungalow, although she still had no clear idea why. It wasn't only the dark shape in the night, for she couldn't be sure that hadn't been imagination and a trick of the light. It was more that she felt it malevolent, against them, its walls seeping with unhappiness and dissension, and although he never said anything, she didn't think that Oliver liked it much either, although possibly for rather different reasons. She thought that it made a very suitable background for the disintegration of their happiness, and occasionally wondered what sort of people had lived there before them. Not happy ones, she was certain of that.

She had the opportunity to find out one day soon after Dorothy Nankervis's unwelcome visit, when an unseasonably mild February day beguiled her out into the garden to do a bit of weeding. Oliver was resting, he wasn't asleep, but he was safely out of the way, and he could yell out of the window if he wanted her. Not that he would; Chel often thought that she might have found him easier to live with if he had been less obstinately independent, at least he would have been less of a worry, but this afternoon, for once, she wasn't going to care. She couldn't be a nurse twenty-four hours a day, particularly an unwanted one, and it was time people began to realise it, and if he wanted her after all, well it wouldn't hurt him to find her not there for once. She hadn't gone far – she *couldn't* go far.

She pitched into the tangle of last autumn's weeds with vicious energy, and Mrs. Honeysett bobbed up on the other side of the fence, and cried, 'Hullo, dear!'

Chel almost jumped out of her skin. She had lived in Endicott Road for some time now, but had never yet spoken to any of the neighbours. There had been twitching blinds occasionally as she went by, and she had sometimes seen elderly people walking slowly past the front fence and peering over, but nobody had called and nobody had gone out of their way to smile, or to say good morning. It had been part of the dreariness, she supposed that it was because she and Oliver belonged to a different generation. So she gave only a rather helpless and startled, 'Oh!' to Mrs. Honeysett's greeting.

Mrs. Honeysett was also taking advantage of the weather to clear a bit of ground. She was a small, spry little lady in her late sixties, and she liked to talk. She was pleased to catch Chel in the garden.

'I didn't quite like to call,' she explained. 'Your poor hubby is in a wheelchair, I understand, I thought he might not like it. Such a shame for you both! We were so pleased when we knew that young people were moving in here, I said to Will – that's my hubby dear, and a bit of a cripple himself, what with his arthritis, but then, we're none of us getting any younger – I said to Will, it'll cheer the place up, and about time too after poor old Mr. Stevens.'

Oliver wouldn't cheer up a mortuary in his present mood, Chel reflected, and wondered if Mrs. Honeysett actually knew who he was. But she was off again, and Chel had, perforce, to listen.

'It seemed so strange at first, this isn't a place for young people, but of course when we heard about your poor hubby, we understood. Can he get out at all? We never see him.'

So they didn't know, Chel decided. Susan or the Dreaded Dot must have been gabbing, but typically, had managed to drop her and Oliver in it while preserving the family privacy! She was so taken up with indignation, and the oddity of hearing Oliver described as her *poor hubby*, that she nearly forgot to reply. It was the sort of joke that might have set them both giggling in the old days, now she didn't think he would see the funny side at all. Oliver had lost his sense of humour along with his freedom to come and go.

'Oh well,' she said, hastily recovering herself. 'It's early days yet, he's not long out of hospital. And the weather's been so bad.' Which was all true, and gave away nothing.

'Well, I hope you both mean to stay,' said Mrs. Honeysett. 'We need a breath of young life in this elderly place! Of course,' she added, pulling a face, 'we're elderly ourselves by some people's reckoning, but we don't feel it, you know. I'd like to move, but hubby won't do it.'

Chel recalled the mention of a Mr. Stevens. They had bought the bungalow, she recalled, from a Mrs. Howarth who had inherited it from her father and didn't want to live in it. She asked, 'Was Mr. Stevens the person who lived here before us?'

'Oh yes, dear! He and his wife lived here for years, ever since the road was built – such a sad couple, we knew her quite well, although, of course, nobody saw *him* much.'

'Oh?' asked Chel, in the tone of voice, she hoped, of someone who would like to hear more. Hardly necessary, with Mrs. Honeysett, as it happened. She went on, pleased to have an opportunity for gossip.

'He was a sad invalid, you know – practically bedridden, and between you and me, a bit of an old tartar! He used to run that poor woman in circles, nag, nag, nag – I don't know how she used to bear it! But of course, he had a dreary life, poor old soul, always in pain and really quite helpless. She used to cry a lot, you know, when he wasn't looking, but she cooked and washed and ran all the errands, and the housework and everything, and never a thank-you, for he took it all for granted. Nothing but criticism, she got, for all her hard work! It was Jessie do this, Jessie do that, from morn until night, and he said such horrible things to her if things weren't exactly as he liked them, well, if he'd been *my* hubby... But there, I said to Will, you shouldn't speak ill of the dead, and it's the hard times as show you what people are really made of.

'She used to talk to me over this fence sometimes, when it got too much for her, just like I'm talking to you, and there would be tears in her poor old eyes, and she'd say, *he was such a lovely man, Gilda, such a lovely man.* Lovely! He was a bullying old slave-driver with a tongue like vitriol, but I suppose he must have loved her underneath it all, for when he drove her away in the end, the old man took his own life. Yes, he found the bottle of her sleeping tablets, that she left behind her, and finished the lot. He couldn't live without her, see. Poor things.' There was genuine regret in her tone, and Chel liked her for it even while she thought, in fascinated horror, that Mr. and Mrs. Stevens didn't appear to have left the place where they were so unhappy. The situation that Mrs. Honeysett had just described exactly matched the feeling in the house – except that, if she took off, Oliver would probably hang out the flags.

Ghosts ...? Real ones, not just queer lighting and a bad conscience?

It was a funny thing, and Chel hadn't thought about it before, but it was a very cold house too, for all its central heating. She hesitated, and then asked, 'So Mrs. Stevens ... she's still alive then?'

'Jessie? No dear, she died not long after. A massive stroke, they said, but of course she'd gone away by then so I only know what her daughter told me. It was all too much for her, poor old soul. She felt responsible.'

Chel swallowed. No, it wasn't possible. Not even imaginable in broad daylight. It would have been nice to have discussed it with Oliver, but they didn't really discuss things any more. She thought that he would probably sneer at her for a fool if she suggested the house was haunted.

And yet ...

It was interesting just the same, even a little disquieting. Perhaps she would mention it to Jonathan.

Mrs. Honeysett had bobbed back down behind the fence to get on with her gardening, where Chel could hear her humming to herself like a swarm of musical bees. Thoughtfully, she went back to her own weeding.

She went back into the bungalow later, and stood in the hall, not listening or anything – just feeling. The place was quiet, and in spite of its pretty carpets and curtains, chilly and a little depressing. A lot of it, of course, would be due to themselves. She sighed inwardly, and wondered what had gone so desperately wrong, knowing that whatever it was she couldn't entirely blame the bungalow for it. It had begun way back in the summer, before she had even seen the place. Perhaps it had been losing the baby, or maybe it was simply that she and Oliver had rushed into marriage without really knowing each other, and had nothing to fall back on when the hard times came, she didn't know. She shrugged her shoulders and turned to go into the kitchen. Oliver would be awake again soon, if he had even been asleep, and she could do with a hot drink herself. Time to put the kettle on.

Dreary routine, nag, nag, nag – *Polly, put the kettle on.* Only, Oliver didn't nag. She did all the nagging. Maybe, outside Mrs. Honeysett's obvious partiality, Mrs. Stevens had, too.

Chel sat down at the small kitchen table and rested her elbows on it, the heels of her hands against her eyes, holding back sudden tears. She hadn't wanted to cry for a long time now, and wasn't sure what had started her off. She thought, if we had been less happy, it would be easier to bear the present. How could so much love vanish so completely and so swiftly? Useless to wish the old days back, and the man she had loved so much, the days were gone and the man with them. The future would be very different.

Poor Mr. and Mrs. Stevens. Perhaps their love had died on them, too. *He was such a lovely man* ... and Oliver had been a darling.

She didn't cry, after all. She made the tea when the kettle boiled and took a cup in to Oliver, and she didn't mention Mrs. Honeysett's confidences.

XIII

A few days later, Jonathan accepted the invitation so unexpectedly given. Because he didn't know what had led to it and was still playing his hand very carefully, he came determined to keep his friendship impartial, with as much to say to Oliver, whom he genuinely admired, as to Chel. Chel made no secret of her pleasure in seeing him, not sure if she was being disingenuous or honest, to be truthful, but Oliver, his awareness sharpened by mental and physical suffering, knew perfectly well the moment he saw them together that it was true, Jonathan was still in love with his wife. Like Chel, he had reached some time ago the conclusion that their love had been built on sand and hadn't survived the first real storm of a long winter, and because he had little enough to distract him these days, he had thought a lot about Jonathan long before his stepmother took a hand. Jonathan was the one who had originally thrown Chel straight into his arms, well, more fool Jonathan ... at the time. But now? Oliver didn't know. He sometimes felt as if he knew nothing for certain any more, and never would again.

His suggestion had contained a certain amount of bravado. He had regretted it afterwards when it was too late to retract. All else apart – and he had only been guessing about some things until he saw them together – Oliver had for a long time felt himself to be in an invidious position in so far as Jonathan Holmes was concerned. Apart entirely from the fact that Jonathan was his wife's ex-lover, and there being some doubt about the *ex*, it was also Jonathan who had revealed their straitened circumstances to the world, and paraded their private grief for the curious to gape at, and it was Jonathan who was, if indirectly, largely responsible for the fact that Chel was now in her own home and free from financial worry ... and it was

Jonathan who had made Oliver himself an object of pity and charity.

He had never tried to tell Chel how he felt, he had never told anyone. The whole thing, from the silly quarrel in the flat right through to the appeal fund had been totally annihilating and deeply humiliating. There had been nothing he could think of to do but to let events pound over the top of him and hope to scrape up a few rags of dignity when it was over. He had hoped at one time that it might be over. Tonight, watching Chel laughing with her old friend, speaking to him in a way that he hadn't heard from her himself for a long time now, he knew for certain it wasn't over at all, and Chel was going to leave him, soon or late, and nothing he could do would stop her. He had opened the cupboard door himself. It was only his blame if the skeleton was now about to fall rattling into the daylight. And perhaps anything was better than not knowing what it seemed the whole town knew, anything was better than pity.

'Oliver?' Chel's voice interrupted his thoughts, speaking a little too sharply, and he realised that she had said something to him and that he hadn't heard a word.

'I'm sorry?'

Chel looked at him with a touch of irritation.

'You're very quiet,' she said as if it was a crime, and Oliver replied, nastily,

'So what? Your friend is talking enough for two.'

It was the first time that the lurking shoals beneath the surface of their life together had been allowed to cause a ripple in public, even in front of his stepmother they had somehow kept a united front. Chel's hurt flickered in her eyes. Oliver had never used that deliberately snubbing tone to her before and she wished that he hadn't chosen to do so in front of Jonathan. But perhaps he was in pain, she excused him to herself, and was piercingly aware, suddenly, that she was sick and tired of making excuses for him.

Jonathan stepped smoothly into an awkward moment with a remark about a story he had recently covered for his paper, but a demon of perversity had got into Oliver, and before long Chel was wishing that she had left him alone with his private thoughts. Within ten minutes, he had twisted the conversation round on its tail, and given himself the perfect opportunity to ask Jonathan how he reconciled his principles with his journalistic duty to invade the privacy of other people.

'People always ask that,' said Jonathan. 'If it's in the public interest for the public to know the truth – then principles don't enter into it.'

'Really?' said Oliver. 'How interesting.'

'I mean,' said Jonathan, realising that he had been trapped into a damaging ambiguity, 'it then becomes a matter of principle in itself.'

'But don't you find that there are times when the Public's Right to Know is better defined as sheer bloody nosiness?' asked Oliver, with deceptive interest. 'In rape cases involving juveniles who may not be telling the truth, for instance, or where someone is suspected of a murder, when there's no recognisable evidence – like that poor sod on the News the other night, who's supposed to have disposed of his wife but equally, of course, may not have done. Guilty or innocent, he'll never get a fair trial. Or brought down to its lowest, how can it possibly be my *right* as a member of the public to know that Mrs. Bloggs of Emberton got done, once in her blameless life, for shoplifting?'

'To suppress the facts would be to distort the picture of life as a whole,' suggested Jonathan.

'If they *are* facts, maybe. That's the point. Are they, or are they just the overactive imagination of some journalist looking for a story? To sell newspapers, because let's face it, that's what it's all about, isn't it?'

'Oh, come on Oliver!' said Jonathan. 'These things happen, we all know they do. They're a symptom of a sickness in our society – and in cases of rape, particularly, the facts must be made public to protect other possible victims. That should be obvious.'

'Sacrifice for the Greater Good?' asked Oliver, derisively.

'If you like. How would you like it if it was *your* child involved?'

There was a silence that seemed to go on for ever. Chel caught her breath in pain, but Oliver's face didn't change. He said, 'So, what if it's none of it true? The child crying rape just wants to get back at a teacher and the media have kindly shown them how it's done, or the man hasn't murdered his wife at all, and yet she never turns up? What if poor Mrs. Bloggs was worrying about the dinner and collecting the kids from school, and quite genuinely made a mistake? Each of these people is branded for life in the eyes of the general public, and more important, in front of their friends and neighbours. Each of them, whether they deserved it or not, has to some degree either been denied justice or placed under a cloud – mud sticks as easily to the innocent as to the guilty, remember. How the hell does that come under the heading of the Public's Right to Know? Or is it more honestly defined as the public's right to be entertained by malicious gossip?'

'In any situation, or profession for that matter, nobody can be right all the time. Did *you* never slip up? Be honest. Obviously mistakes are made – it would be unrealistic to deny it – but very seldom by reputable journalists. We only report stories, we don't manufacture them.'

'Bullshit!' said Oliver, rudely. 'Who are you trying to kid? In any case, that isn't the end of it. Take a case where your so-called Public's Right to Know comes into conflict with the invasion of the privacy of your friends – as it might be Chel and me, for instance. How do you get your convenient conscience to wriggle you out of that one?'

'Oliver!' cried Chel, distressed. Both men ignored her. Jonathan said, 'The proper administration of justice has to be of interest to every man and woman – and child, for that matter – in this country. How else are we to maintain our reputation for one of the best judicial systems in the world – which is in effect the protection of our children, and the future of our free society?'

'It didn't occur to you that we might prefer that you didn't support the cause of justice at our expense?'

Jonathan met his eyes.

'I don't accept that what I wrote did you anything but good,' he said. 'It brought an injustice to the attention of the general public, which they then set out to redress in their own way – with generosity and openhandedness, the only way they know. How did that hurt you? Tell me, and I'll apologise.'

Oliver drew a breath to do just that – and let it go again.

'If you can't see it, why should I waste my breath?' he asked.

Chel entered the discussion, speaking quietly and cold with shock – or was it shame? She wasn't certain.

'If you didn't like it, why didn't you say so at the time? I suppose we could easily have given the money to a suitable charity – thanked everyone and made a gesture of it. I expect everyone would have cheered you to the echoes.'

'And you would still have been in want,' said Oliver. 'Or more probably, my father's pensioner. But perhaps you wouldn't have minded that.'

'Oh, my God!' said Jonathan, getting to his feet. 'I think I'd better go, this is no place for me if you're going to take that line. Oliver, if I did the wrong thing I can only say I'm truly sorry – but I didn't see it that way, and I still don't. If you want to know, I agree with the general opinion – you got a raw deal, and I was glad to be able to help you.'

'Help me?' roared Oliver. 'Bloody hell, have you seen me get across the room? I don't say *walk*, you will notice!'

Jonathan winced. It was impossible to miss the intense pain in the words, but pain on its own excused nothing. Other people had a perspective too, and this situation had gone beyond mending.

'I can only repeat, I'm sorry,' he said, stiffly. He stood for a moment, looking down at the man who had stolen the girl he loved and seemed intent on breaking her heart, and his lips tightened. He didn't care any more, he really didn't care about the possibility of a full-scale scandal. He hadn't fully understood how difficult Cheryl's life had become with this pathetic travesty of a hero until he had been invited here, apparently on purpose to be insulted. If Cheryl ever came to him, as he was sure, now, one day she would, and begged him to take her away, he would do it, so help him, without a second thought. That time maybe wasn't yet, but he could see it coming. He could afford to go now and leave Oliver Nankervis to wreck his own marriage. He certainly didn't need help.

'Good night,' he said.

Chel followed him to the front door. Oliver could hear them talking together in the hall in low tones, Chel's reluctant laugh, a brief pause which he had no difficulty in filling in with some accuracy and considerable pain. Then the front door closed and Chel came back into the room. She stood in the doorway and looked at him.

'Did you have to do that?' she asked.

'Do what?' asked Oliver. He had watched her come back in through the door with a smile on her lips, and her face softened with love as it had once been for him, all her new, bitter hardness melted away as if she had never woken from her daydreams and found herself tied to *a cripple*. Chel as he had loved her, as she could never be again. Her expression had hardened even as she saw him. His own infirmity mocked him from the shadows, Jonathan was whole and sane and strong. 'Did that creep have to make it so obvious that he only came here to stare at you?' he asked, with an edge to his voice that held a warning

Chel might have done well to heed. She ignored it. As always nowadays, he had spoiled everything, shattered her peace and on top of that, sent Jonathan away upset and worried.

'Why did you have to be so rude to him?' she countered, resentfully. 'He's my friend, and *you* suggested he came here. Why shouldn't he look at me?'

'Because it's my house, you're my wife, and I don't like him doing it, just for starters. Hell's teeth, Chel, what do you think I am? He bloody comes round here, making sheep's eyes at you under my nose, and you think it's all right? If he comes a second time, he can bloody well bugger off again!'

'And then, I suppose, we shall just have each other?' said Chel, sweetly. 'That will be nice, won't it? After all, we get on so well together.'

'And whose fault is that?'

'Try *yours!*' flashed Chel. 'You and your constant snarling, staring at the television or sitting there staring at nothing, making people feel you don't want them, only opening your mouth to say something rude and ungrateful –'

'I don't!' denied Oliver, indignantly.

'You did tonight. You should have heard yourself, seen yourself! All you ever think about these days is *you* and what you want – you don't ever want to see your family or friends, you don't want to do anything, you've always got a headache, or a backache, or some other miserable excuse, you won't go out – you keep me tied in this horrible house like a prisoner because you won't go anywhere or do anything! All just because you're too bloody proud – no, *conceited* to let people see you as you are, and if I do go out without you, in desperation, your horrible family spies on me!'

"If it's a horrible house at least you can't blame me for that!' shouted Oliver, the row escalating beyond the bounds of logic in one swift leap. 'It was you, not me, chose the dreary dump, and if this is what you think a home should be, I owe you an apology! For me, I loathe it – and I loathe the prying old women that peer over the gate and the bloody cement front garden – so where's the bloody garden gnome? Don't mind me, fetch him out – he'll look sweet among the sodding hydrangeas!'

For a second there, Chel almost laughed. The laughter trembled in her voice and sweetened the acid that burned in her heart.

'Oliver, don't be silly!'

'And while we're on the subject of failings,' continued Oliver, throwing discretion to the four winds. 'What about your own behaviour? Drooping around the place with a face like thunder, snivelling in corners, moaning about how nobody understands you and how hard done by you are – do you think that's attractive to other people? Everyone who comes through that door gets a little moan or a snivel or a scowl, did you realise that? You talk about me, damn it, haven't I got enough to depress anyone? I lost everything, all at one go, and for keeps – you're just nursing an unhealthy grief over your dead – no, make that *our* dead! It was my child too, or perhaps you've forgotten that.'

Laughter had gone, not an echo remaining. There were still tender places that wouldn't be touched, let alone punched like this.

'You don't understand!' cried Chel, distressed and outraged. 'Men don't bear children.'

'Oh, bloody hell!' said Oliver. 'How can anyone talk about anything to you? You're obsessed with babies, and you only listen to yourself!'

She was furious at the injustice without stopping to think there might be more than the obvious behind it.

'The last time I tried to talk to you, you slammed out of the house and left me to be miserable on my own –'

'– and you haven't stopped being miserable since!'

After all she had put up with from him it was too much.

'I hate you!' cried Chel, screaming at him. 'You're not just crippled in body, you've let yourself get crippled in mind! I hate you, I hate you, Oliver Nankervis!'

There was a silence that seemed to go on for ever. Oliver broke it.

'Crippled ...' he said, musingly. 'That about says it all, doesn't it Chel? What happened to *I love you very much?*'

'The same thing that happened to *I love you, too,*' said Chel. She seemed to be looking at him through a mist, but it wasn't of tears. Tears for Oliver had dried. 'I suppose it just died,' she added bitterly. 'Like everything else that was ours.'

'If it's any consolation to you,' said Oliver, after a long pause, 'I hate you, too. I hadn't realised how much – or how long.'

'Oliver –' She wished she hadn't said so much then.

'It's as easy to get divorced as it is to get married these days, and God knows, that was easy enough. You go ahead. Everyone seems to be expecting it and I shan't defend it. I think the phrase you want is *irretrievable breakdown of the marriage,* but my father will set you right.'

'Oliver –'

'You don't want to be tied to a *cripple*, after all,' said Oliver. 'Oh yes, I had noticed that I embarrass you.'

'How can you say that?' Indignation made her voice shrill. Oliver gave her a disturbing look that contained also a frightening resentment.

'When you shut me away in that soulless room at every opportunity – ?' He stopped, visibly pulling himself up. 'Jonathan Holmes will be able to give you much more fun, and at least he can provide for you without charity. You can raise a large family, since children are so important to you, and concrete the entire garden if you want. I'll send you a gnome for a wedding present. You could have a whole family!'

Chel wanted to say his name for a third time, but could think of nothing to follow it. She said nothing. Oliver sat still, the light from the lamp beside him slanting across his face and leaving his eyes as dark pools of shadow that revealed nothing. She thought how much she had loved him once and felt completely empty. Not a spark, not a glimmer. Nothing. Romance hadn't outlived disaster, it had been kicked to death on a soft April evening, and left nothing behind it but ... well, nothing.

There was nothing to keep her here any longer, no guilt, no sense of duty. He wanted her gone, and for once she could do something to please him.

It seemed strangely unreasonable. The end of passion, of deep love, heartbreak, anger and despair, all of them disintegrating together leaving just two unhappy people who had become strangers with nothing in common. She couldn't wait to get away – away from this prison. But not just like that, not as easily as he was making out. She hesitated.

'We can talk about it tomorrow,' she started to say, thinking that they would both be cooler then and could be civilised about it. At that point, she still wanted to be civilised, but Oliver said,

'No. Go now.'

'But I can't –' she began, and he said flatly, 'I want you gone.'

She couldn't just go. He wasn't only the person with whom she had fallen out of love, he was a responsibility. He could hardly walk, or dress or undress himself without help, he couldn't do the simplest thing unless somebody was there with him. However little she cared about him – and at that instant she was sickened by the very sight of him – she couldn't be that callous.

'I can't leave you here alone,' she said.

She could sense his rage like a tangible thing, a black beast caught in a cruel trap, frustrated and blinded by its own fury, and because he was no longer whole, she found it terrifying, distorted and out of place as if he had in some way forfeited the right to such turbulent anger and thus walked on some frightening tightrope of sanity with no safety net to catch him when he fell. Without realising it, she took a step back.

'I don't want your pity,' said Oliver, spitting the words at her. 'Take it away from me – take anything you want – just go, go, go!' He was shouting at her, with an edge that scared her on a totally new level that she barely understood. If he went into hysterics, she would join him, they would scream together until their world ended. She could feel the tension building already. She took another careful step backwards to the door, towards retreat, escape.

'I can phone your father – Susan – they're both close, either of them would come –'

'I don't need you to do anything for me,' said Oliver, brutally, and they stared at each other, deadlocked, across the width of the room.

This had ceased to be just a row, Chel realised coldly. They were not simply shouting any old thing in order to hurt each other, he at least was in deadly earnest. How could she stay – but equally, how could she go?

'Be reasonable, Oliver,' she begged, and added weakly, because although it sounded silly, it really mattered. 'What would people say, if I just walked out and left you?'

'Just get out of my sight, and out of my house,' said Oliver, with such quiet deadliness that although there was nothing he could do to her, no way in which he could physically hurt her, she did as he said.

None of it seemed real. With the odd feeling that she was acting a part in a play, she went across the hall and into her bedroom. Hers – not theirs. She hadn't shared a room, let alone a bed, with Oliver since the flat days. It remained unreal as she took a suitcase from the top of the wardrobe and began quickly to pack it. She did it mechanically, taking only what she would need for the immediate future, her mind still wrestling with the problem of what she should do. It would feel strange to be free – free of Oliver who had become such a burden, free of this dreary, unhappy bungalow and all the boredom and frustration, walking through the open door to – what? Where?

... how?

Chel closed the suitcase and slowly picked it up, and stood looking round the room that she would never have to sleep in again, still frightened, still not sure what she should do. Her heart was beating hard and swiftly, a regular rhythm but fearful. She wanted to run, to get away from this horrible place and Oliver, who was frightening her, to get into the car and drive away as fast and as far as she could. She hated the bungalow more than she had ever hated it tonight, and yet a sense of duty bound her to it after all, bound her to Oliver.

Please let me go!

She put her suitcase down by the front door and went reluctantly back to the pleasant but characterless room where she had left him. He was still sitting there beside the light, with the cordless telephone in his hand. As she came in, he dropped it with meticulous attention onto the carpet. The sharp sound as it clipped the edge of the hearth cut across the tension in the room.

'Did you ring your father?'

'Just get out, before someone comes. Spare yourself a row.' He didn't sound sarcastic, but he must surely have meant it that way.

'I can wait –' Chel started to say, but he cut her short.

'Ten minutes – my God, can't you even give me that much? Ten minutes on my own, what can possibly happen to me?'

It might have been exasperation that sharpened his voice but she wasn't quite sure, and still she hesitated. Oliver said, on a breath so quiet that she hardly heard him, 'Get out Cheryl, get out of here – get out, or I swear to God that I will somehow find a way to kill you!'

'You need to take your painkillers in an hour –'

'Out!' shouted Oliver, in helpless, frustrated rage. 'God damn you, *get out!* For God's sake, *go!*'

Chel went.

She went, as Oliver had known she would, straight to Jonathan, the one safe haven in a town that she knew would be unfriendly and critical. It was very late by the time she reached his flat, but she was far too overwrought to worry about details like that. She ran up the stairs and rang his bell.

Jonathan hadn't gone to bed, he had been sitting with a drink, thinking of her. He came to the door and stared in blank surprise when he saw her there, as if his thoughts had conjured her from air. Chel took one look at his friendly, familiar face and broke down completely.

'He threw me out,' she said, on a gale of sobs. 'He made me go, and I could only think of you.'

Jonathan looked at her howling on his doorstep, he looked at her suitcase, he looked at the carefully opening door along the landing, and he took her arm in one hand and the suitcase in the other and drew her inside. His door shut firmly, and the audience, disappointed, melted away.

Inside the flat, Jonathan pushed Chel down into an armchair, thrust a roll of kitchen paper into her hand, and perched on the arm beside her. She sat there for a while, gasping with convulsive sobs and dabbing at her eyes, while he waited for her to get herself under control. When the sobs had become sniffs and the paper towels were merely being crumpled into damp balls, he poured a stiff drink and gave it to her.

'All right,' he said. 'Tell me what happened. Quietly, from the beginning. I take it you had a row after I left?'

'Yes,' said Chel. She looked back on it now in bewilderment. 'It was an odd sort of row... very quick, and ... and as if we'd rehearsed the words.' She paused, not liking the sound of that. 'He doesn't want me any more so I came to you.' Her voice broke a little and she bit her lip. 'I couldn't think of anywhere else to go.'

Jonathan looked at her steadily for a moment, his thoughts chaotic. Then he got up and poured them both another drink.

'Did you leave him there on his own?'

Chel shook her head and gave another pathetic sniff.

'No, how could I? He rang his father – he was on his way, he'll be there by now.'

'Are you sure?'

'He said so,' said Chel. 'Oliver never lied to me in his life. He begged me –' A new wave of tears swept over her and she put down her glass to grope again for the roll of paper towels. 'He only wanted to be alone. I did my best, Jonathan, I swear I did. I tried and tried – but he's changed so much now, he's like someone else, and he hates me, he said so.'

Knowing that something would happen one day made it no easier to believe in when it did, Jonathan discovered. He was afraid to trust the senses of hearing and seeing, while a great bursting firework of glorious hope tingled like golden rain, sparking through his blood. He said slowly, unable to take in the fact that Oliver Nankervis, the great hero who was everybody's darling, had finally shot himself in the foot, 'He's been very ill.'

'Do you think I, of all people, don't know that?' Chel demanded angrily, fighting with a surely unreasonable feeling of guilt. She couldn't possibly have stayed, could she?

She could have waited outside until someone came. She wept again, helplessly. She couldn't even leave her husband without making a mess of it.

'Look, don't cry,' said Jonathan. 'Drink up.' He put the glass back in her hands. 'Come on, cheer up now. It'll all blow over by morning. He was just in a bad mood tonight, look how he did his best to pick a fight with me.'

But Chel shook her head.

'No. I think he was looking for an excuse. And Jonathan ...'

'What?' prompted Jonathan, after a moment. Chel let out a long sigh.

'I'm glad,' she said. 'I feel ... set free.' And perhaps guilt was for nothing more than that. Jonathan looked down at the dregs in his glass.

'Two years ago, you thought the sun shone out of his arse.'

Chel looked back on that time with wonderment.

'I must have been mad.' She hesitated. 'I'm sorry, Jonathan. I made a big mess of everything, didn't I?'

Jonathan drew a breath.

'Will he divorce you, do you think?'

'He said so.'

There was a silence, while they both considered the implications of this. Then Chel looked down at her empty glass and gave a little laugh.

'What is this? It tastes horrible!'

Jonathan took it from her.

'Scotch, and I think we've both had quite enough.'

Their fingers touched. Chel looked up, startled, and their eyes met. For a moment they held each other, warm brown and clear sea-green, and then the glass dropped between them onto the carpet and their hands clasped. Chel closed her eyes. Everything that she had lost, and it had been more than anyone except perhaps Oliver would ever know, gathered into one great incandescent flare of urgency and desire. When his arms went round her, she melted into them as malleable as wax, empty with a hunger that nothing, nobody could ever fill. She was crying again.

'Don't,' said Jonathan. 'Don't, my darling, don't.' His lips were on her lips, her forehead, her wet eyelashes. Her tears were salty as the Dead Sea. He tried to laugh, but it didn't come out right. 'Oh God, Cher, oh God, don't cry, it's all over, it's over my darling, over.'

They had made love before, a long time ago now but many times, and their bodies were mutually familiar ground. When their ways had parted, other feet had walked beside Chel down her particular fork in the road, another man had loved her, she had learned to hear music that Jonathan would never hear. He hadn't led a celibate life either, but the love of his heart he had kept for her. Everything that she had known and would never know again, everything that he had stored up in his heart, made their reunion good for them. And when the last spark flickered out in the darkness, Jonathan was able to sleep, believing at last that the waiting time was over and Sir Lancelot had found the Holy Grail after all.

Chel lay beside him, drowsy but not sleeping yet, feeling the weight of his head in the hollow of her shoulder and the warmth of his bare skin against hers. There were girls she had known who tried to say that a man was only a man, and in the dark they were all the same, but it wasn't true. She would know anywhere that this was Jonathan, not Oliver. His hair was curly, rough against her skin, where Oliver's, thick and almost straight, had brushed silkily and tickled. Jonathan slept in a compact ball where Oliver had tended to sprawl, he slept more deeply too, his breathing slow and soft. They even smelled differently. Jonathan carried no salt tang of the sea with him, he was warm and masculine and blessedly ordinary, faintly scented with aftershave. She had married a merman, she thought sleepily, a gypsy of the wind and water. She had stepped through the gate of a Never-Never Land that had no true reality and been held there, in thrall to a dream ... but now she was free. Sleep, delicious and complete, crept closer, and a great first wave of relief that swept over her from top to toe. She was free, she could sleep at ease again, Oliver was in the past. She would be able to live her own life, choose for herself what she would do, very soon.

A faint echo of something long forgotten stirred at the back of her mind and was gone like a wisp of smoke. A comfortable feeling of things falling back into place ran over her in a pattern, like wavelets now, running up smooth sand ... it would be all right, there would be no dreadful, destructive scandal. A gentlemen's agreement ... a return from the Never-Never Land ...

She fell asleep quite soon, and it was no longer thinking of either Oliver or Jonathan but of her baby, Jeremy. For once it was without the hard, painful longing that had hurt her for so long, that page in her life must be turned. Before she left for Suffolk in the morning, she would put some flowers on his tiny grave and say goodbye. It would be a harder goodbye than the one to his father, but it must be said or she would never be whole again. Oliver had been right about that at least. . And *goodbye* didn't mean that you had to forget. Just not hold on.

Yes, she would go home. For Jonathan's sake, she would do that. She would wait there for the storm to blow itself out so that she could come to him without hurting him ... she would go back to the rolling dunes and the silver marram grass, and the tossing grey North Sea that was her birthplace. Back to the slow-running rivers and the flat fields and the crying gulls over the marshes ... home.

For many waters cannot quench love.

XIV

In the small hours of the morning, Chel woke up. It was dark in the room, and quiet except for the noise of distant traffic on the town by-pass, but she had a distinct feeling that she had woken because someone had called to her. Who would do that in the middle of the night? Not Jonathan – not with that sense of deep urgency that remained so persistently with her, and anyway she could feel him still curled against her, relaxed and heavy with sleep. The warmth of him gave no comfort. All at once she found that she was frightened, sweating under the bedclothes in the cold night and with no idea why.

Oliver came into her mind only moments later, it was Oliver who had called her. It must have been in a nightmare, for he was way over on the other side of town, safe with his father and his triumphant stepmother, glad to be rid of her as she was to be rid of him.

She couldn't get him out of her mind. However she tried to control it, her head became insistently full of him, Oliver, Oliver, always Oliver. Quite suddenly, she knew that she would be wrong to ignore it.

Being careful not to disturb Jonathan, she got out of the warm bed to grope for his bathrobe in a below-zero chill that made her teeth chatter. She would ring the bungalow, and if nobody answered – and they wouldn't – she would know that he had to be at his father's house, and it was all in her mind. If by chance anyone was there with him and did after all pick up the phone, she could hang up. She certainly wasn't going to tangle with his stepmother at this hour of the morning, that really *would* be the wrong thing to do.

Jonathan stirred as she moved away from him, but slept again. She tiptoed out into the other room and lit the table lamp beside the telephone, trying to be as quiet as possible. It was all wrong, too, to be creeping out in the night to phone her husband on her lover's phone, and although she thought Jonathan probably wouldn't have stopped her, she did think that he might mind. With hands that for some reason were shaking, and not from the cold, she picked up the phone and dialled her own number.

The line was engaged. Of the options she could have expected, Chel hadn't expected that. She stood there with the phone in her hands, staring at it, her mind whirling. Had the fall perhaps broken it when Oliver dropped it on the floor? Had he simply forgotten to disconnect, had he deliberately left it that way ... or was he, possibly, frantically ringing round all their friends, trying to find her?

Wishful thinking. Chel squashed that weasel thought before it had barely twitched its whiskers. A year ago he might have tried to find her, tonight he had been glad to see her go. And anyway, he knew exactly where she was, if he had any intelligence. As he had.

She stood shivering beside the phone, and the engaged tone went on and on in her ear. After a while, she put the phone back on its rest, but she went on standing there and looking at it, and knew quite certainly that something was dreadfully amiss, and couldn't imagine either what it could be, or how she could possibly know.

Something had happened to Oliver in that horrible little house. It came to her as clearly and believably as if someone had spoken to her, telling her. But he wasn't there, was he? She knew he wasn't there. Oliver had never broken a promise made to her.

But he had made no actual promise ... nor even any statement of intent. She had taken it for granted, because she wanted to.

... and in that tiny bungalow, where every sound could be heard all over the house, she had never heard his voice speaking while she was packing.

Her blood ran suddenly cold, roaring in her ears.

If she got dressed now, she could drive over to the bungalow. If she was ever to live at ease with herself again, she knew that she would have to.

It would take her too long to get over there. There wasn't that much time to spare. She had no idea how she knew that. She picked up the phone again, and without hesitation dialled Susan's number. Her hand trembled as she did it.

Susan herself answered the ring, after a long interval that had Chel on a knife-edge of suspense, sounding sleepy and cross.

'Who is that?'

'Susan!' Chel was amazed at the wave of relief that swept over her. 'Susan, it's Chel – look, please can you get round to the bungalow, right now, and see what's happened to Oliver? I tried to phone him, but the line's busy, and I'm afraid ...'

Saying the word brought the truth of it home to her. She *was* afraid. Deadly, selflessly afraid, as she hadn't been for months, but there was no time to stop to ask herself why.

'Look Cheryl, it's three in the morning,' Susan was saying. 'If your line is engaged, it'll only be because he's trying to ring you. Just put the phone down and try again, for God's sake, and let me go back to bed. You'll wake the children.'

The precious moments were ticking by.

'Susan, please,' begged Chel, urgently. 'Something's wrong, I know it is – please go. It won't take you ten minutes, and I'm coming as fast as I can – please – '

It was like talking to a brick wall. She could feel Susan's reluctant indecision right down the wire.

'Susan, *please!*'

Something in her voice must have got through to Susan at last, for she said unwillingly,

'Oh, all right, but I think you're being silly and hysterical. Why aren't you at home, anyway?'

'It doesn't matter now,' said Chel. 'I'll tell you – I'll explain. Just hurry!'

She banged down the phone and returned to the bedroom, and found Jonathan sitting up in bed and waiting for her.

'Cheryl? What's up?'

'Something's happened to Oliver,' said Chel. 'I'm sorry, Jonathan. I've got to go.' She was halfway across the room by that time, but Jonathan stopped her as she passed him, reaching up a hand to catch her by the arm.

'Oi, stop a minute! How do you know?'

Chel stood a moment, looking down at him. She didn't know how she knew, she just did. She said so, impatiently.

'I just do. I can't explain.'

Jonathan continued to look up at her for a moment, his face giving nothing away, and then released her.

'All right,' he said. 'Get some clothes on. I'll come with you.'

'There's no need.'

'I'm coming,' repeated Jonathan. There was no time to argue with him, in a few minutes they were running across the street to Jonathan's car, parked close outside.

'Drive quickly – please drive quickly –' said Chel, but it was unnecessary; her urgency had already communicated itself to him.

It was one of those nights when nothing goes right, and it was three red lights and a fortunately sympathetic policeman later that they turned into the end of Endicott Road. It was deserted for its entire length, not even Susan's car parked there, and the bungalow was in darkness. Jonathan stopped the car, and before he had the brake on, Chel was out and up the drive. He followed her more slowly.

The front door was locked. Chel, fumbling in her bag for the key, felt all fingers and thumbs and Jonathan took it from her hand and opened the door himself. They stepped into the hall. It was freezing.

Chel stood there shivering, hugging herself with her folded arms, knowing that the place was empty. The telephone was on its rest, and everything was as it should be, except for the bitter draught sweeping through the hall and a new feeling in the place – almost of triumph, she thought confusedly. It was pleased with itself. Her pulses raced.

Jonathan was going round peering into all the rooms. He came back to her.

'There's nobody here, and a window has been broken in the small bedroom. What do you want to do now?'

Chel stood irresolute.

'Ring your sister-in-law again,' urged Jonathan. 'Set your mind at rest, and then we can go home.'

Although she knew that it was a sensible suggestion, Chel was sure that it would be a pointless waste of more precious time. She dialled the number for the second time that night, and listened to it ringing at the other end.

Tom answered it, sounding cross, and she could hear one of the children grizzling in the background. Susan, he said, wasn't back yet, and what did Chel think she was doing, playing silly games like this in the middle of the night? Chel hung up on him, and stood quietly. Trying, however impossibly, to divine what had happened here.

'What now?' asked Jonathan.

'Sssh ...'

She was aware of a lees of desperation and misery so deep and consuming that they had swamped everything else. Bitter resentment, a thousand times deeper than her own. And underlying it, that echo of gleeful satisfaction, because someone had cheated and defeated ... no, not death. Life. A chill ripple began at the crown of her head, ran over her skin and right down to her soles.

She pulled herself together, afraid of a sudden feeling of not quite belonging to herself. She tried to concentrate, to think.

'Why would anyone have broken the window?' she asked, more of herself than of Jonathan. He shrugged his shoulders.

'How do I know? Because the door was locked, and somebody needed to get in? It doesn't look as if it was a burglary.'

No, burglary wasn't the evil that had taken place here tonight. If Jonathan was right, then it was probably Susan who had broken the window. But had she then found Oliver here, or was it simply Chel's own mind playing tricks on her?

Susan wouldn't have broken a window if she had thought the house deserted. She would simply have gone away again. It seemed unlikely, on the other hand, that Oliver would do it, unless he had completely lost his cool and thrown something.

No. That wasn't right

'Come on, Cheryl,' said Jonathan, going towards the door. 'There's no point in staying. It's cold, and there's nobody here.'

Chel said nothing. She pushed open the door of Oliver's room and looked in. The draught from the broken window made the curtains wave about and cast odd shadows on the walls, splinters of glass lay inside on the sill. The room had an impersonal look, as if nobody lived there. Oliver had never impressed it with his own personality, perhaps, she thought with a shock, because his personality was too disintegrated by what had happened to impress itself on anything. It certainly hadn't been the Oliver she knew who had lain awake and suffered and wept his heart out in secret in this room.

If he had called to her before, he had gone now.

'Cheryl!' called Jonathan, impatiently.

He was right, there was nothing to stay for. Irresolutely, she followed him out onto the drive, pulling the door to behind her.

A light went on in the house next door, and a window was flung open. Mrs. Honeysett's head, adorned with a flowered scarf and curlers, poked out.

'They've gone, you just missed them,' she called. 'They took him away in an ambulance. It woke us up.' She sounded injured, but broke off abruptly as Cheryl stepped out into the moonlight. 'Oh, it's you love!'

Chel's voice had failed her, but Jonathan asked,

'Do you know what happened?'

Mrs. Honeysett peered down at him.

'No, but they were in a great hurry. Hardly here before they were gone, and lights flashing everywhere, like they do on the telly when there's no time to waste. If you're asking me –'

But Chel and Jonathan hadn't waited to ask her anything. To her disappointment, they were both running down the drive.

It was like a replay of the worst night of her life, but with none of the slow awfulness, none of the blanketing shock. Everyone in casualty, this time, could tell Chel what had happened.

And as on the previous occasion, there were the nightmare questions.

What time did you leave the house, Mrs. Nankervis? Did your husband give you any idea that he might take his own life? How many of these tablets were there in this bottle when you last looked?

Chel was appalled. Oliver had taken an overdose, not of the painkillers that might have meant an accident, but of his sleeping pills, and followed them with half a bottle of whisky, which could only be cold-bloodedly deliberate, however she tried to excuse it. Or bloody-minded deliberate. Either way, the implications were so awful that her mind blanked out completely and she stammered, stupidly, 'I don't know – I didn't count –' and the harassed casualty doctor looked at her as if she was a moron.

They had already taken him away to try to save him, and there was none of the sympathy that had been offered on that previous occasion. Casualty was busy, and people had no time to waste on a woman standing there with her boyfriend, while her husband was probably dying. Realising that he was being a hindrance rather than a help, Jonathan suggested, reluctantly, that perhaps he should go.

'Unless you'd like me to stay,' he added, but Chel had apparently forgotten that she had run to him saying that she never wanted to see her husband again, and forgotten too the other things that had passed between them this night. She clung to his arm so hard that she hurt him, but what she said was, 'If you make copy of this for your horrible paper, Jonathan Holmes, I shall never speak to you again!'

The uncomfortable knowledge that she wasn't speaking without reason made Jonathan bite back an indignant retort, but he did look down at her in honest bewilderment.

'I wouldn't say anything to hurt you, and why should you worry about him? That's all over.'

It was a clumsy thing to say, and if he hadn't felt suddenly threatened, he would never have said it. She looked at him as if he was a stranger. She wasn't thinking about him at all, he realised, with a sick feeling of impending defeat. If Oliver Nankervis went and died on them now, she would be lost to him for good, and after that nothing – nothing on this earth – would ever bring her back. Every time she looked at him, she would remember that she had left a sick man alone to be with him, and that man had committed suicide, and nothing would ever make her forget it, not passion, not tenderness, not anything that he could ever give her or do for her. He loosened her fingers and gave her hand a squeeze that was as much to reassure himself as to comfort her.

'Try not worry too much – I expect he'll be all right.'

He stopped and spoke to the casualty sister on the way out, but Chel didn't see it. She was already halfway down a corridor behind an overworked nurse.

Susan, sitting on a bench in a deserted waiting area, leapt on her in a self-righteous fury as soon as she arrived.

'How could you do it, Cheryl? How could you be so selfish? If he dies, it'll be all your fault!'

'You could have left me a message at the bungalow,' retaliated Chel, already distressed and so furious in her turn.

'There wasn't time,' said Susan, dismissing the unanswerable. 'Anyway, if you hadn't been so selfish, it would never have happened! And you left it long enough before you told me, only a little longer and he'd've been dead anyway! How could you do it, when you know he should never be left on his own?'

There was a lie there, but it wasn't a deliberate lie, more a failing in understanding, not necessarily Susan's but her own. Chel felt it fly past her like a feather in a raging storm, uncatchable, untraceable, maybe something to do with never leaving Oliver on his own.

'You knew how worried I was, you could at least have left a note!' she raged. 'I didn't even know what had happened until I got here, and if we hadn't seen Mrs. Honeysett –' She broke off, and Susan tossed her head.

'Well, don't blame me for that! Nothing would have happened at all if you had been there, where you should have been!'

It was a relief to be angry, but neither of them could keep it up for long. They relapsed into an uneasy silence. Susan picked up a magazine from a table and began to turn the pages, far too quickly for her to have been reading them, and Chel sat on the edge of her seat twisting her hands together, her frightened thoughts racing to and fro.

She must have been out of her mind.

The truth crept on her slowly, but it was something that she must have always known. The shame of it, after what had happened on this awful night, was unbearably bitter. However had she come to see Oliver simply as a tiresome invalid, when she should have recognised that he was in deep distress? How had she ever let herself become so used to taking from him that she had never realised that the time had come for her to give? Her own self-absorption over the lost baby, her own depression and the easy palliative of tranquillisers, must have turned her brain completely to mush, if she had ever once paused to think, she would surely have been shocked out of her own self-indulgent misery months ago.

Oliver had desperately needed her, and she hadn't been there for him, and so he had taken his own life. The shock of it was like falling into icy water on a hot day. It took her breath and stopped her heart. It was like dying herself, but without the oblivion.

Oliver, whom she loved. Yes, that was the truth. She told herself brutally, it wasn't love you were lacking, it was sex. What sort of a person are you, if you can't live without it? He's had to, and what did you ever do to try to help him? Does he feel like you did? Did you ever try to think about it from his point of view? And he taught you more than Jonathan will ever suspect there is to know.

... *and left me with this aching regret.*

'He fell,' said Susan, briefly and cruelly, out of a sharp silence. 'All the lights were on, so I broke in and found him on the floor, that's why your phone was off the hook. He knocked it off as he fell.'

'Oh no!' It was the last straw. The one thing that must never happen, the one thing, that even if Oliver survived his overdose, could make her own remorse pointless.

'He could be really paralysed this time,' said Susan, pushing home the point.

If he was, nothing could ever put things right. How could she ever make it up to him, even if he would let her try?

'Don't you care?' demanded Susan. 'Haven't you anything to say at all?'

'Shut up,' said Chel.

She had never even suspected that Oliver might give in to the extent of committing suicide. Not because of pain, or frustration, or even the threat of permanent illness, he had always had far too much courage for the thought to have entered her head, and it would be conceit beyond reason to suppose that he had done so because she had left him. He had loved her once, yes, but to despair? Surely not.

He had let her go – made her go – and made no attempt to hold her.

Why?

Because he had really come to hate her, and only wanted her gone?

Because, after all, he could no longer bear to live within the prison that his body had become, and had already planned to take his own life and escape?

Or because he really believed that she had come to hate him and be ashamed of him because he was no longer whole and fun and exciting, and he had opened the door of what he saw as a mutual prison, and let her fly free where he never could?

And afterwards? Had he seen that he, too, could escape, or had he regretted letting her go?

It all came back to her, however she looked at it. She had killed him, and she loved him, and she could no longer understand how she had ever thought otherwise.

And if he lived ... would he want her back?

Oliver, I love you! She tried to send the thought winging to him, wherever he was, as he had sent his voiceless cry to her, but knew that he had gone too far and it could never reach him.

'You'd left him, hadn't you?' said Susan, accusingly, and Chel made a helpless gesture with her hands.

'We'd had a row. People do.'

'You left him alone, and you knew he was disabled and sick, and shouldn't be left at all.' There she went again. Rubbing it well in.

... but she had. All of that, she had, however she tried to justify herself. She had been concerned only with herself and her own depression and grief over her dead baby and her lost-forever lovely exciting life, and Oliver had made rings round her.

'How could you?' asked Susan, reproachfully.

To say that Oliver had practically pushed her out of the house would only make things worse.

'Please leave me alone,' pleaded Chel, but Susan wouldn't.

'If he dies, it'll be your fault.'

'*Please!*'

Susan shrugged her shoulders. 'I don't understand you. One minute you can walk out on a sick man, and the next you can't even bother to defend your own actions! Hadn't you better make up your mind what it is you want? You're tearing Oliver in pieces, and we all think it's gone on long enough.'

So they had discussed her, had they? The thought was curiously humiliating. Chel retorted, 'It's hardly your business!'

'Of course it is! He's my brother.'

Chel looked at her coldly, despising her for her hypocrisy when she didn't even like Oliver all that much.

'Stepbrother,' she said.

'So what's the difference? Your selfishness might have killed him, just the same.'

'You said that already,' Chel reminded her, wishing she would be quiet, anything, and let her concentrate. If Oliver had reached her, she *must* be able to reach him. She had done it once, and when things had been even worse than they were now. She brought all her will to bear as if by doing so she could bend time and space to her need.

Susan looked at her, centuries of civilisation and the thought of what people would say warring with an inclination to shake

412

Chel until her teeth rattled in her head, and tell her to get out of Oliver's life and stay out.

'I think you should stay right out of it until we know just what happened,' she said, firmly.

The bridge that she had so nearly built shattered into nothingness. It was too much. Chel turned on her like a wildcat.

'Think what you like, but shut up!'

'I think you're being very unreasonable – and cruel. And selfish, if you don't mind my saying so.'

'He's my husband, are you forgetting?'

'Then why weren't you there, looking after him? Where were you, anyway?'

So she hadn't seen Jonathan. With luck, nobody would tell her. The reflection was sordid and shaming. Chel shouted at her. 'Mind your own business!'

Fortunately, before Susan could react to this declaration of war, a nurse came down the corridor towards them. Whatever Jonathan had said had made its due effect, she smiled at Chel with real warmth, and spoke kindly. 'Mrs. Nankervis, you can see your husband now if you would like to.'

Chel stumbled to her feet with a gasp, more shocked at this moment than at any other during the interminable night, and Susan said sharply, 'She'd walked out on him. It'll upset him.'

The nurse looked at her, her face expressionless.

'Hardly dear, he's out cold,' she said, but kindly.

'I should be there too –'

'Mrs. Nankervis?' The nurse stood aside for Chel and smiled at Susan. Chel walked past her without a backward look.

Intensive care was familiar ground, dawn-quiet and dim, and the night staff were kind. Her husband had been very lucky, the night sister told her with a touch of severity, not the least because he had been found while there was still time to do something for him. It had been touch and go, but he was safely back in the world, and although he had fallen, he must have been too drugged to resist and had suffered no more than the probability of a nasty jar when he hit the floor. None of the painstaking reconstruction work had shifted with the impact, the X-rays were perfect.

They had put Oliver into a side ward that had a big glass window in the wall through to the nurses' station. There was a blind, but it was up. The effect was like being in a fish tank, or the vivarium at the zoo, Chel decided, but she supposed miserably that attempted suicides couldn't really be left unsupervised. She walked to the foot of the bed and stood looking at him, the relief on top of the shock making her too numb to think of anything sensible to do.

For a while, at least, there wouldn't *be* anything sensible to do. She had been warned that he would probably sleep for some time, she was going to have to sweat this one out on her own. He lay tidily on his back, his left arm resting on the sheet with a drip running into a vein, and they had put the railed sides of the bed up, like a child's cot, a surely unnecessary precaution with somebody who couldn't get up off the bed with any ease even if he was awake. She hadn't looked after him very well. His hair was too long, an untidy dark fringe to his eyebrows, and his eyes were shadowy hollows in a gaunt face. Oliver had never been more than slim, but now he looked pitiful. Surely, surely, she could have done better for him than that?

He hadn't let her.

He hadn't let her because he had thought she didn't love him any more.

There was a salty taste on her lips, and she suddenly realised that she was weeping. She smeared her palm across her wet cheek, thinking irrelevantly that she must look a mess as well as a fool, standing here like a watering-can. But it wasn't important. She recognised that these were not the bitter, familiar tears of self-pity and frustration, but legitimate tears of release and awakening hope.

A chink of china almost in her ear brought her back to reality and the quiet room. A young nurse stood there, holding a cup and saucer.

'We thought you'd like a nice cup of tea,' she said.

Tea! All the dramas she had been through over Oliver seemed to have been drenched in tea!

Better tea than more tears, maybe.

'Thank you,' said Chel.

She sat and drank it, the cup rattling unevenly against the saucer, and watched Oliver sleeping. There was nothing she could do now until he woke up. She wondered how long it was going to take for the drug to wear off entirely, and what he would have to say to her when it did... if he didn't want her back, there was something of her soul that would die, a little piece of her spirit that would never breathe again, and she would be less, in her own eyes, than she would like to be.

A very long day lay ahead of her.

Chel had a ridiculous and illogical feeling that if she was parted from Oliver now, something dreadful would happen. She had just enough sense left to know that it was purely subjective and had no foundation even in clairvoyance, but it was an effort to push it away and think properly. If it was in any sense true, the something dreadful was going to happen to her, not to him. There was a heap of trouble waiting to be faced, much of it of her own making, and the sooner she faced it, the sooner it would be over. The quiet, busy nurses could do more here than she could do at the moment, she was only in the way. She leaned over the bars to kiss Oliver, his cheek was cool and unresponsive to her lips as if he was a sleeping stranger, not himself at all. It was only with an effort that she could bring herself to leave him.

Susan, thank goodness, had got tired of waiting and gone. Chel took a bus back to Jonathan's flat.

He was out, gone to work presumably, but he had left a note behind him on the kitchen worktop.

Ring me when you get back. Don't worry, it's going to be fine. Jxxx.

She looked at it for some time, wondering what she had ever done to deserve his continuing love. She had deserted him once without a backward look, she was about to do it again, and in between she had made shameless use of him. It was no good pretending that anything remained between them. Clear-eyed from shock, she knew that she had done just that, used him. To ease her pain, to bolster her self-esteem, and finally and least forgivably of all, to stifle her hunger. And he loved her, he *loved* her. Whatever did it feel like to be in love – like that – and be rejected?

She could be about to find out.

Oh shit! thought Chel, what a bloody awful mess! Why didn't someone give me a good shaking months ago? Whatever got into me, did I think the world owed me perpetual sunshine? I had two years, my God, nearly two whole years, more happiness than some people get in a lifetime! Whatever do I think I deserve?

She hadn't unpacked last night, she had simply hurtled into bed with Jonathan as if it was the only thing in the world that mattered. She opened her suitcase now and took out her shower gel and toothbrush, and went into Jonathan's bathroom for a shower.

Later on, sitting at his breakfast bar wrapped in his towel and drinking his coffee, she began to consider the situation more objectively.

She couldn't stay here. Not only did she not want to any more, it wouldn't be fair, not to herself, to Jonathan, and most of all, to Oliver. She didn't want to go back to the bungalow

416

either – in fact, she wasn't going back. She shuddered. Horrid little house! Whatever was in there was insidious, creeping like mould to destroy everything. Oliver had nearly died there, she herself had made herself into a miserable drudge, scarcely human, not at all like her normal self. To go back to that – no, she couldn't do it!

The outer door of the flat banged, and she heard a step in the living room. Jonathan's voice called, 'Cheryl?'

'In here.'

A moment later, he appeared in the kitchen doorway. They looked at each other. Jonathan said uncertainly,

'I saw his sister leave. He's going to be all right, I take it?'

'He's going to live, yes.' She hesitated, and what she didn't say hung in the air between them.

'I see,' said Jonathan. She was slipping through his fingers again, he could feel it. She sat there on his bar stool with her bare shoulders rising out of the towelling, and her hair, wet and shiny like a mermaid's, knotted on top of her head. Cheryl, warm and sweet and vulnerable – and slipping, slipping, out of his reach. It didn't matter if it was love or pity – and he supposed that it was probably pity – that was her motive. She wouldn't deceive her husband a second time, or not with him. He spoke with forced casualness. 'You're going back to him, I suppose?'

'If he wants me – yes.'

'And if he doesn't?'

'I don't know.'

'I see,' said Jonathan, again, scanning her face. He read nothing there but polite regret. No pain, no loss. He drew a difficult breath, last night's illusion – no, the illusion of many months – shattered like brittle glass, clear as ice and cold.

'What if he gives you a hard time of it all over again?' he asked, thinking that if he did, disabled or not, he, Jonathan, would bash him, Oliver, into a jelly. Chel shrugged her bare shoulders, an unconsciously graceful gesture that she didn't mean to be provocative, and Jonathan felt physically sick.

'That we shall see, but I don't think he will – not like that.' She hesitated. 'Jonathan, if I tell you something, will you think I'm mad?'

If they talked, she would stay a little longer. How stupid, how pathetic, could a man become?

'I don't know,' said Jonathan. 'Try me.'

Chel told him about Mr. and Mrs. Stevens and the bungalow.

'We were so desperately unhappy there, and so were they,' she said. 'I cried all the time, and so did she. I nagged Oliver and made him miserable, and so did he, to her, except I think Mrs. Honeysett had that wrong, and it may have been the other way about, who knows now? And when I went, he took an overdose – and so did he, Mr. Stevens I mean, when she couldn't bear it any more and ran away. It's such a sad little house, Jonathan. I think they were unhappy in it for so long that now nobody can be happy there ... I love Oliver, but I really came to hate him, and so did he hate me. Mr. and Mrs. Stevens –' But she broke off there without speculating on Mr. and Mrs. Stevens. She had never met them, but she thought that she, and perhaps Oliver too, knew things about them that nobody else knew, and her heart ached for them, dead though they were.

She had used the word *love* ...

'You mean,' said Jonathan, woodenly, 'that you think the house is haunted?'

'I don't know that,' said Chel. 'What is a ghost? I think ... I think that what they felt was so intense over a period of time that it printed itself onto the house walls like an image onto photographic paper. If that's a ghost then yes, the house is haunted.'

418

She had been afraid that Jonathan might laugh, but he didn't. He looked at her very soberly across the remains of her breakfast.

'You mustn't ever go back there to live, not either of you.'

'No,' said Chel.

Jonathan swallowed. Keep talking. Say anything, it didn't matter. Keep talking, and she wouldn't go away.

'Has anything like that ever happened to you before?' he asked. Chel said,

'No,' and broke off abruptly. Why did her instinct always make her deny it? Because it had happened before, of course it had. She remembered a place called Vellanzoe and a sensation of unbearable physical agony and mental distress ... and quiet fields under the evening sun, the gleam of distant sea, wind that whispered in a roadside copse. The emotion that swept her was familiar, but evanescent as always. There was no road open for them that led back to Cornwall, not now. She wanted to cry and forced the tears back. Jonathan looked at her curiously. It was necessary to say something.

'Once, I did,' she said. 'I heard something ... voices ... and felt something ... in a ruined house, and I was told about something that happened there. But that was afterwards.'

'Are you clairvoyant, do you suppose?' asked Jonathan. He was prepared to consider it, she saw, which surprised her in a journalist, but then, he must have seen and heard many strange things in his job. Perhaps she should believe it herself. If she did, she would have to admit to a great many mistakes, oversights, responsibilities, errors of omission ... *But I didn't know,* she pleaded, inside her head, and her own thoughts answered her disbelievingly. *Didn't you?*

There was a silence. The haunted bungalow had served a turn, but now there was nothing to keep last night out of their thoughts. Chel shivered and drew the towel round her.

'I think I'll get dressed.'

He drew back as she passed him as if she was untouchable. He didn't dare to let her brush against him, aware of her nakedness under the towel as if he could see it. A cold shower was the recommended remedy for his problem, he thought – and that would make two of them naked and wet, and *sod it!* Who did she think he was to be put down and picked up again, and then set aside like a book she couldn't quite get into? He reached out a detaining hand.

'Cheryl –'

She turned at her name, standing like some classical statue with the draped towel slipping off her back. Whatever she thought, something that was almost pain flickered in her eyes. For herself? For him?

'I'm sorry,' she said, very gently. She turned away again and the kitchen door shut firmly behind her. Jonathan looked at the shut door for a long moment, then seized her empty mug from the draining board and hurled it after her with all his strength. It struck the wall and smashed. A little dreg of coffee ran down the tiles.

Jonathan swore. His mother had drummed it into him from childhood that a man didn't cry. He said every swear word that he knew, several times over, and then sat alone in the kitchen until he heard his front door close behind her.

And no, he wasn't crying. It was just that these tears kept sliding down his face.

XV

It took all Chel's courage to go back to the bungalow, but of course, she had to do it. Not to sleep there – never, never again – but it was necessary to arrange for the repair of the broken window, to set the heating so that it would keep the place aired, to collect the things that Oliver would need during what might prove a protracted stay in hospital. It would have been nice if there had been some friend she could have asked to keep her company, but unfortunately there wasn't. She didn't know where they had all gone, hadn't seen the going of them, she had been too wrapped up in herself. She felt empty now ... empty and afraid.

And then, when she got there, it all seemed at first so ordinary and innocent that she almost laughed at herself. Almost, not quite. Because the events of last night had really taken place, and they were not the kind of things that could easily be forgotten.

She rang a local builder who agreed to send a man round that morning, but she had no intention of waiting for him. She would throw Oliver's things into a bag, and then she would leave the key with Mrs. Honeysett. Mrs. Honeysett would probably ask questions, but there was no need to answer them too honestly. They wouldn't be neighbours any longer, after all.

So, what do you have in mind? she asked herself, derisively. Nothing's changed. You're still married to a stubborn, embittered man who hates your guts, or at least, for all you know different. No kind fairy has waved a wand over you both. He's every right never to trust you again, and if he could bring himself to do it, for now at least he's still disabled. Wherever you think you're going, all these aids are going to have to go with you for the moment, and that's not going to be so easy. Have you thought about that?

She pushed the thoughts away. Even if it was all true, here in this defeated little house wasn't the place to think about it. She imagined that she could feel it already, sapping her resolution and draining her optimism. She must get out quickly. The thought skimmed into her mind and out again. She zipped the bag shut and swung it through the bedroom door into the hall, took a last look round the aseptic little hospital ward, and ran out suddenly, slamming the door behind her.

There was just one thing more she had to do before she braved Mrs. Honeysett. No – make that two. Clear out the fridge, ring home. It was strangely difficult to think clearly.

She would give the things from the fridge to Mrs. Honeysett. She didn't know where she was going to go, but it would almost certainly have to be a cheap boarding house for now. The Nankervises – and quite possibly Oliver too – would think she had lost her marbles. The thought, in a grim sort of way, cheered her considerably.

She shut the bag into the back of the car, put the box of perishables on the front door step, and rang her mother with the front door wide open. She knew it was silly, but she was becoming actively scared of this boring little bungalow. The nearer she got to escape, the more scared she was becoming. Hysteria, nothing else. She shivered in the draught from the open door and listened to the ringing of the phone at the other end of the line. *Come on, Mum, come on, come on!*

Marilyn's voice in her ear was so sudden it made her jump.

'Wainwrights' Stores.'

'Mum – it's Cheryl.'

The Nankervises had already been in touch with the news, trust them for that. Her mother was angry with her, she could hear the grimness in her voice.

'Oh good – at last! I've been trying to ring you.' Deep breath. 'Really, Cheryl, I thought better of you – and Oliver too, if it comes to that! What got into you both?'

Ghosts? Chel thought that she had better not say that, not over the telephone. Those waters were too deep. She took refuge in the age-old excuse of child to parent.

'I don't know.'

Her mother made a tutting noise at the other end of the line, and said, ominously,

'I shall be right down to sort the two of you out! That dreadful woman –' She broke off, and Chel had a sudden, rather comforting vision of her mother squaring up to do battle with the Dreaded Dot, and for the first time for what seemed like forever, almost smiled. But her mother was going on. 'If Oliver is too much for you, you must both come back here until he isn't – what will the pair of you do next?'

'It's been difficult,' pleaded Chel, but broke off in sudden alarm as a gust of wind swirled round the house. The windows rattled, and the door of Oliver's room, perhaps because of the open front door, clicked open again and crashed back against the wall. An atavistic instinct to drop the phone and run swept over her. 'Look, Mum –'

'Yes, I know it hasn't been easy, but ...' Her mother's voice going on and on, trying to understand. But she didn't understand. How could she? Chel was hardly listening, she could feel the hairs rising on her arms and a prickling on her neck as if she was some threatened jungle animal. The front door swung to and fro in the rising wind – of course, there was a through draught, that was it, because of the broken window –

She dropped the phone and made a dive for the front door, catching it just before it slammed. She was sweating in the cold wind, and her hands were shaking. She clung to the edge of the door, leaning her forehead against its cold surface, trying to pull herself together. Behind her in the hall, her mother's voice on the telephone, safe in the shop, quacked on and on.

'Cheryl? Cheryl, are you there?'

Keeping hold on the door, Chel reached out, picked up the phone, and dropped it back onto its rest. Then, unable to control her instincts any longer, she rushed out into the open air, pulling the door to behind her. The crash as it closed woke the echoes.

A quick visit to Mrs. Honeysett, who mistook her agitation for wifely concern and was all kindness and sympathy – of course, she had no idea what had really taken place last night. Then, on to the next hurdle. It was no use putting it off.

Even so, she drove much more slowly than usual, and turned into the Nankervises' drive with a sick feeling of dread. This was going to be a sticky one, and she couldn't either mislead them or hang up on them. They knew.

Susan's car was parked in the drive, she saw with a sinking heart, and behind it a bright yellow VW Golf that she didn't recognise. Oh please, not Joanna Rendell! At the thought that it might be, Chel almost turned and drove away again, but Susan had seen her arrive. She flung the front door open. She looked furious.

'Oh, so it's you at last!' she said, ungraciously. 'You'd better come in.' It sounded almost like a threat.

The door to the drawing-room was wide open. Beyond it, people were shouting, Debbie's voice, high and angry, over-riding her mother's sharp with displeasure.

'- well, I'm sorry if it's a bad moment, but how was I to know since none of you told me? And how you *couldn't* –'

Susan pushed Chel out of the way and stepped past her into the room.

'So what good would it have done if we'd rung you in the middle of the night? And this morning, you weren't there. Stop being so silly!'

Debbie rounded on her without noticing Chel at all – a new, unfamiliar Debbie, incandescent with fury, generating a distinct aura of angry jungle cat. Chel was transported straight back to that dreadful morning in the flat. Debbie had never looked more like Oliver.

'Are you trying to say that when you all drive my brother to suicide *it isn't my business?*'

'Deborah!' Dorothy cut her short. Debbie hesitated, her stride broken, and caught her breath on a stumbling sob.

'At least I love him,' she said. 'None of you do!'

'Love, love, love!' cried Susan, sounding like the chorus to an old Beatles number. 'How useful that word is! If you ask me, you don't have any conception of what it even means!'

'Maybe not!' flashed Debbie, returning the insult with lightning speed. 'Maybe not – but I shall come nearer to it than *you* ever will, at least I *care!*' Then she saw Chel standing in the doorway, and broke off abruptly. 'Oliver – is he all right?'

'He'll live, but you know that already. That's all there *is* to know yet.'

Debbie covered her face with her hands, and her shoulders rose and fell to a deep breath. When she took her hands away, her anger seemed to have evaporated, she looked drained and pale, and about sixteen years old.

'I wouldn't have come here and caused a scene if anyone had told me.' Her voice was pleading. 'I'm so sorry, Cheryl. Really.'

There was no sensible answer to that and Chel made none. Her failure, for some reason that she couldn't pin down, bothered her. There should have been an answer, and if she had found one it might have resolved something, led forward – but the idea faded before she had time to think it through properly, as Susan tilted her chin, shooting a defiant glance at her sister.

'Oh, so you admit that you came to make a scene? And there's no point talking of caring to her, Deb. She doesn't, and she doesn't mind who knows it.' Shooting them both down together, Chel thought wryly, and was strangely comforted, but again without knowing exactly why.

'Susan, that was unnecessary, dear,' said Dorothy, but perfunctorily, paying mere lip-service to convention. Neither of her daughters took any notice. Debbie watched Chel. Her eyes were shining as if tears weren't far away, and her lower lip pouted dangerously.

'If you dare to hurt him now –' She sounded both fierce and accusing, but stopped herself abruptly. In spite of her efforts, a slow tear brimmed over and ran down one cheek. 'It's all so unfair!' she burst out. 'How can we know – anyway –' She swallowed. 'I think you did the right thing when you married, whatever anyone says, and however it's turned out – if you don't grab happiness when it's there for the grabbing, how do you know it'll still be there tomorrow? Only ... don't ...' Her throat closed on a painful lump, silencing what she had wanted to say. She turned and ran, the door slammed behind her and the cut glass displayed in the china cabinet gave back a steady ringing note that died into silence. Dorothy said, 'I apologise for that little scene, Cheryl, and so does Susan.' Susan made a sound of protest, she didn't look sorry at all. Dorothy continued, smoothly. 'But I have to admit that there was some justification for what Susan said. What you have just witnessed is a direct result of the example that you and Oliver set a young and impressionable girl.'

Debbie had always struck Chel as about as impressionable as marble. She looked, and felt, bewildered. Susan said, waspishly,

'She chose this moment, of all moments, to come and tell us that she's going to live with her boyfriend. If Oliver does it, it has to be right, of course. So –'

'Now, wait –' Chel began to protest, but Susan didn't.

'All her life, she's behaved as if he was God or something,' she said scornfully. 'Only look at her – the rebel without a cause!'

Outside the window a car engine started up, roared, and faded away towards the end of the drive with a fierce crunch of tyres on gravel. Dorothy looked as if she was going to cry, and as if for once her feelings were genuine.

'I'm sorry for Oliver, don't misunderstand me please, but if ever anything goes wrong in this family, there he is somewhere at the back of it – even now, when you would have thought ...'

Chel had counted up to ten. Now she interrupted, but unsteadily. 'How can you possibly blame Oliver for what Debbie does? Lots of girls live with their boyfriends these days, and anyway, Oliver and I didn't.'

'You went off together,' said Susan. 'Don't split hairs.'

'Deborah was brought up to go to church, and to have a proper respect for the marriage vows,' said Dorothy. She looked at Chel as if inviting her to talk her way out of that one, but Chel elected not to get involved. She said, angrily, 'It's the times, it's not Oliver. And if you want to know –'

'We don't!' Susan cut her short. 'It's you two, preaching the gospel of snatch-as-snatch-can, you'd think she could see with her own eyes it doesn't work! And on the subject of Oliver, by the way ...'

In retrospect, there had been a certain amount of affection in Marilyn's tirade. From Dorothy and Susan there was nothing but reproach, and a great thing made of *poor Oliver*, which Chel considered unfair. Oliver's only advantage over her, when it came down to it, was his physical disadvantage, and it was he and not herself who had told lies and taken a stupid overdose, she hadn't forced it down his throat. She made the mistake of saying so, and precipitated another unpleasant row which brought up the unwelcome question, 'And where were you last night, anyway?'

'That's my business – and Oliver's,' said Chel.

'And will you tell Oliver?' demanded Susan.

Chel thought that Oliver didn't need telling. The fact that he already knew was half the trouble, but she wasn't going to say so to these two critical and unforgiving women.

'Yes,' she said. It saved argument.

'You've been nothing but trouble to this family!' Susan stormed. 'You drive poor Oliver to suicide and teach Deb immorality –' She broke off, perhaps feeling that she had gone too far, and indeed, had gone out on a limb, for surely even Susan couldn't mistake her streetwise sister for an innocent young *ingénue*, but her mother took no notice this time, directing her attention to Chel.

'You are so heartless and cruel!' she exclaimed, and there was really no answer to that.

By the time Chel left the house, she was in a seething rage and as a result, drove away without any thought as to where she was going to go. There was no sign of Debbie, if she had any sense she was probably well away on the road to London by this time, and Chel didn't blame her really, only the thought that it would have been nice if she had been waiting round the corner couldn't help but slip into her head. She hadn't considered Debbie, except as a peripheral character, until this morning, but now a lot of random incidents were beginning to click into place, nothing in themselves but suddenly adding up to a surprising conclusion – Deb couldn't be lumped with the rest of Oliver's family. She had a foot in both camps. Whether the discovery was important or not, Chel couldn't decide, and thinking about it she simply drove where instinct took her, and was surprised to find herself outside the shop beneath their old flat.

That was a Freudian slip, if you like, she thought, startled. And it wouldn't do, either. The flat was as far out of reach now as the life they had lived there. What she needed was a cheap B&B somewhere, preferably a ground floor room with twin beds, *en suite* shower. If Oliver ever – she jerked her thoughts away from the dangerous ground.

But this familiar end of the waterfront was as good a place to start as any. There were several inexpensive boarding houses overlooking the harbour, and they weren't likely to be busy in

February. Locking the car securely, she began to walk back towards the dock.

They weren't likely to be open in February, either, as she soon discovered.

It was bitterly cold. The weather, which had been chill and sleety for weeks now, had taken a turn for the worse, this time Chel thought it was really going to snow. Huddled into her coat, she walked along with her head down against the wind, and beside her walked ... not ghosts so much as memories. There was *Cascabel*, moored in her old place against the quay. Nobody on board, not on a day like this – thank goodness, she couldn't have faced Bill or Terry or any of them, not today. And up there somewhere was Meridew Street, where Oliver had come to grief. She had never seen it, didn't want to ever. And there was the corner shop where she had done her shopping and beyond it the alley that led to the block of garages where Oliver had kept the MG. But this was their old life, they could never come back. It was like walking on ashes after a great fire that had burned away the people they had been, leaving behind two strangers.

With nothing to say to each other? Chel didn't know. Her heart felt like lead. She went up the steps of the first boarding house she found still open, and rang the first bell of many on that long, cold day.

She found a room in the end, after a long search that left her chilled and tired. It hadn't been possible to get exactly what she had wanted, the cheapest places closed in the winter months. She had to settle in the end for a first-floor room in a small hotel which wasn't particularly cheap but had a nice view of the harbour, what Oliver would make of the stairs she had no idea. Anyway, it had to be better than the haunted bungalow even if he had to be carried up them. There was a small lift for luggage and laundry, perhaps he could squeeze into that ... she shook her head at the icy view. She had almost made a joke and laughed, and none of it was funny. She felt suddenly exhausted, and sat down on the edge of the nearest bed.

She was probably being stupid even to imagine that they would ever live together again.

This time, the thought refused to be pushed away. Perhaps because Chel was tired and cold and had eaten little breakfast and no lunch, or maybe because there was nothing left that had to be done, all of a sudden, full realisation of where she stood hit her for the first time.

She could say she still loved Oliver until she was sick of the sound of the words, but nobody would believe her, and nothing could alter the fact that her marriage was firmly on the rocks. Because Oliver might be disabled – well, all right, he *was* disabled – but he still had rights and opinions and feelings and nothing she or anyone said would make him do what he didn't want to do, and never had done so.

Stubborn ... stubborn and wrecked and breaking up in the storm.

As if on cue, a buffet of wind, sweeping unimpeded across the waters of the harbour, hit the building with a force that made it shake. Chel got to her feet to draw the curtains across against the weather, but paused with her hand on the fabric. She stood at the window and looked out.

There was nothing to see outside by this time but the early darkness of a winter's evening and the lights blinking into life down on the quay, oddly unfamiliar from this angle, but she felt restless, unsettled. The last twenty-four hours had lasted a year, and had taught her so many things that she would sooner not have known, and now, in this impersonal, lonely room, where nobody knew where she was, there was nothing to do but tell them over to herself, endlessly. She didn't even have a book to read, to come between herself and the truth.

She leaned her forehead against the cold glass. For a start, it wasn't enough simply to love Oliver, it was going to take more work than that. Someone should have told her so right at the beginning, and then she would have known that she had things to learn. She might not have wanted to learn them, but she wouldn't have had any illusions; it was illusions that tripped you up, every time. The illusion, for instance, that there were no differences between a man who could sail a boat around the world and dive in the depths of the sea and a man who couldn't, except for the fundamental fact.

What a baby she had been! How swiftly now she must grow up, if she wanted her marriage to mend and thereafter to last.

And as for Jonathan, what was done was done. She couldn't mend that.

It might happen again. Or she might want it to. If Jonathan had laid a finger on her this morning she would have scratched his eyes out, but that was nothing to go by, that was just a gut reaction. If she and Oliver tried again to make a go of things, the same old problem would still be there, and she didn't know what to do about it. Because she wasn't ready for the life of a nun and she had no idea, and she didn't think Oliver had either, if he was ever going to be able to offer her anything else.

If she hadn't convinced herself she was in love with Jonathan, and if he hadn't really been in love with her, it wouldn't have hurt either of them. There would be, she supposed, men who would like to go to bed with her with no strings attached, who would give her what she needed and pass on, but what a dreary, shaming prospect! And what about Oliver? He wouldn't trust her now, even if he wanted to.

And that was to see things only from her side. It wasn't only herself who had made the last year so difficult, and it was no good trying to take all the blame. She had been self-centred and probably unkind, but he had been impossible. There was something basically wrong with Oliver, and she didn't think that it was only that he resented her preoccupation with her lost child because he didn't think he could give her another, although that was clearly part of it. Sex was one ingredient, it shouldn't make the whole of a marriage. Nor should children, having them or not having them. She and Oliver had had a good marriage once, and just as losing a branch wouldn't kill a healthy tree, the loss of children or even of a totally fulfilling sexual relationship surely shouldn't have wrecked it so quickly, or so thoroughly. It wasn't as if she had been having it away with Jonathan for months, she had been stupid yes, but at the start, very naïve. Innocent, if the word could be applied to the situation.

The stuff of which heroes are made doesn't dissolve in less than a year, so the hero was still there somewhere, Oliver wasn't just the wilful and unmanageable invalid who had helped make life hell for both of them, but also an intelligent man of great physical courage. He had been a wonderful person, vital and fun, powerful and confident in himself, so what could change someone like that to the point where they were next door to unrecognisable?

She told me I was dangerously wilful and selfish, and wouldn't start to grow up until I learned to recognise fear.

Who had said that? Oliver of course, but that was a long time ago. Was that what was the matter, that he was afraid and couldn't admit it?

Afraid of being disabled? But that was done, you weren't afraid of things that had already happened. Of illness, then, of pain? They would pass. They were already passing, however slowly. Of the future, then?

Well, maybe. What could it hold for him, compared to the things he had hoped for, lived for? Afraid of limitations, then. And if she admitted that she had made him live to face it, not once now but twice, she also had to admit a responsibility. He wouldn't agree, but she knew that it was so.

It came to her then like a breath or the sigh of the sea in a shell, a whisper on the edge of consciousness. *That was then, this is now, so there has to be more, there has to be a lot more. There's a whole new life out there to find, all you need, both of you, is the courage to reach out and take it. You've barely*

432

started, you've seen nothing yet, you're young – and you're alive ... follow ...

But at that point it all ran foolishly into a song they had sung at school about the merry pipes of Pan, and she lost it. Follow what? Follow your nose, follow your inclinations, follow your star, follow the yellow brick road?

I can't live without him!

Which was a foolish thing to say, when she might have to.

This night would be endless.

But morning came, as it always does, and when Chel rang the hospital they told her that Oliver was sleeping. Well out of his coma, but still sleeping although he would rouse easily. He must have taken a huge dose, she thought uncomfortably. This wasn't a cry for help, this was more like a determined attempt to get out and stay out, and if he had regretted it at the last moment and sent that desperate message winging across town to her it wasn't because he had expected to. And that was a weird thing too, and a bit creepy. She had read about things like that and ridiculed them. She looked down at her hands as if they might bite, but as Michael Partridge had said, if you had it, you had it. She was getting used to the idea, she even suspected that she was beginning to call it at will, but she had no idea how she could actually put it to use. She thought how she would discuss it with Oliver and wondered what he would have to say, and then remembered that she was taking too much for granted and her heart sank. The waiting was the worst of all.

She hadn't told the Nankervises where she was going, or even that she was going at all, so that when she was called to the telephone in the early afternoon, she knew that it must be the hospital, and her stomach gave a sickening lurch.

'Your husband is awake, Mrs. Nankervis. Perhaps you would like to come in and see him, and to speak with Mr. Adams.'

'Mr. Adams?' queried Chel. The name was a new one, after this last year she had thought she knew them all.

'Mr. Adams is the Consultant Psychiatrist.'

She didn't like the sound of that, but no doubt she was being naïve again not have expected it.

'Has he asked for me – Oliver, I mean?'

'He hasn't said anything,' said the person on the phone, but Chel didn't realise until she arrived on the ward that it was meant to be taken literally. Oliver was awake, yes, but he wouldn't speak. Not to anyone. He just lay there with his eyes open, staring at the window where the fragile flakes of the year's first real snowfall were fluttering at last from a leaden sky. Only last year, Chel remembered, they had run out into a whirling storm and thrown snowballs at each other before it all melted again and was gone.

'See how he reacts to you,' had said the ward sister, but the fishbowl glass wall was a spying eye and made it difficult and embarrassing.

Oliver didn't look away from the window when she walked up to the bedside. It was very hard to start a conversation when she wasn't even certain that he knew who was standing there. Nor was there a lot to say. Only one thing, in fact, that she either wanted to say or felt appropriate, and when, for all she knew, she had driven him to the edge of the grave, how could she possibly say *I love you?*

So she reached out instead and touched his hand, twining her fingers with his, and after a moment he turned his head on the pillow and met her eyes. His matched the sky outside, dark and stormy and full of chill. Chel tightened her grip on his hand and at last the words came, forcing their way past a hard lump in her throat.

'I love only you, and I'm sorry.'

His fingers returned her grip so hard that her wedding ring dug painfully into her flesh, but he didn't say anything, and after a moment, she said, 'It's true. I won't blame you if you can't believe it, but it's always been true. It's just that I couldn't bear what had happened to us, and I know that's no excuse. I won't leave unless you want me to. I promise.'

She was talking too much, filling the silence with words. She bit her lip to stop herself. His throat moved as he swallowed, but he said nothing, just went on staring at her. She began to feel sick, with a deep, shaking sickness that seemed to fill the world. It would have been all right, she thought confusedly, if she could have taken him into her arms and cuddled him like that stupid panther, but how could she when here he was flat on his back again, and looking as if he would snap at the slightest touch? She said, 'Oliver ...'

The way he looked at her, almost without blinking, was unnerving. As if he mistrusted her sincerity, and why shouldn't he?

'I didn't understand,' she said, babbling on when she knew there was nothing left to say that should be said. But she couldn't stop, the words had begun to take on a life of their own. 'I thought that you were being bloody-minded just for the sake of it. I never thought that you might ...' *Oh God, help me to shut up!* '... be scared,' she said. There, it was out. Her pulses leaped and began to race. She added, as if accusingly, 'You were, weren't you?'

Oliver stirred. For the first time, something that might have been warmth and life flickered in his eyes. She had made it easy for him, if pride had forbidden him to admit it, honesty now forbade him to deny it. He made two attempts before he finally got it out.

'I thought you'd despise me for it. I was never afraid before.' He sounded most unlike himself. And of course, now she thought about it, a man who had faced the possibility of death a hundred times in the course of an adventurous life, and not cared when he held his fate in his own hands, could well be afraid of that arid, painful and humiliating life sentence.

But it could have been worse, and it might well get better, if they only worked at it. She said, 'You could have been totally paralysed.'

'Do you think I don't know that?'

'All right. So your luck ran out. Everybody's does in the end. But we're in this together if you'll let us be, it's up to us to make sure that it isn't the end of the world.'

He answered her on a sudden unnerving swing into despair, leaping from his pent-up, miserable silence to the flooding speech of emotional dissolution.

'How can we, what can we do, the way things are? I can't give you any of the things I promised you – I'm stuck with a collapsible spine and two useless legs so that I have to drag myself about and be ashamed to let people see me. I can't even provide for you without charity – and I could live for years and years, making you live through it with me. Chel, I can't do it. I can't.' He rolled his head over so that his face was turned away from her. His voice was rough with suffering. 'Help me, Chel. I don't want any of this.'

Chel had begun to shake.

'But there isn't a choice,' she said, with a desperate sincerity and in a voice she had to fight to keep steady. 'Be honest with yourself, Oliver – be honest with us both. It's done, and it can't be undone, not by anybody or anything. Are you going to live for years and years wishing back the past you can't have, or are you going to look ahead and find something that can be done to make things better? Something that you can put into life, you've had enough out of it one way and another –' She broke off. She was pushing him too hard, she knew it. Oliver's breathing was shallow, as if he had been running.

She told me I took too much out of life, and the time would come when I had to put something back.

That wasn't the first time recently that she had been reminded of the fairground gypsy. For a moment she could

436

almost hear the jangling music of the roundabouts, hear and see and feel the seething crowds, smell onions frying.

Unconsciously, she had tightened her own hold on Oliver's hand and dug her nails into his flesh. He made a small sound of protest, rolling his head back to look at her, heavy-eyed and desperate, but the first glimmer of light shone uncertainly in the unhappy gloom to which they had condemned themselves.

'Get me out of this, Chel,' he said, shakenly. 'Get me away. Take me home.'

'Home?' asked Chel uncertainly, thinking of the bungalow, and it gave her a jolt, after what she had thought only a moment before, when Oliver said, 'Home to Cornwall.'

XVI

In the everyday world outside the hospital, the snow fell thickly, blurring the outlines of walls and shrubs, turning to slush in the busy streets but mantling the gardens with smooth untrodden white that deadened sound, making everything new. Like a fresh page waiting to be written on, Chel thought, but she still had no idea as to what she should write.

The future had an outline now, but only a shadowy one. Although Oliver's expressed wish slotted precisely into her own repeated longing, she had no idea of how she should fill in the details, how to stop herself thinking of Oliver in terms of his disablement, most of all how to overcome the obvious and immovable obstacles. It no longer seemed impossible, that was all, and not for the first time in their lives, it was Oliver's will that had made it so.

But how?

Knowing that she had to start somewhere, Chel drove into the town centre and tentatively put the bungalow on the market. If she started the ball rolling it might gather momentum on its own.

'Cheryl dear, don't you think that's a bit previous?' asked Jerry, when he found out what she had done.

'No,' said Chel. 'We aren't going to live in it any more, and the sooner we sell it the sooner we can move away.'

'Away?' He raised his eyebrows.

'We thought we'd go to Cornwall,' said Chel, tentatively.

There, it was out. A little apprehensively, she watched his reaction.

'Cornwall?' he echoed, as if he had never heard of the place, and the storm broke around her ears.

She very soon found that she was trying to defend an untenable position. Susan's belief, freely aired and accepted, that she had walked out on Oliver, had gained ground with his family, and it was difficult to argue with it when it was true. Her sudden decision, unwisely publicised, to go with him to Cornwall to live aroused more bitter opposition than she had ever dreamed, particularly when she could produce no set plans. It was too far away, the family all cried, too far from the spinal injuries unit, too far away from everyone he knew, too far, most of all, from them. They seemed to have conveniently forgotten his past record, as if being disabled had robbed him of any say in how his life should be lived and made him into someone else. The arguments were wearing and repetitive, sapping her will. That, too, was no new thing.

'Cornwall, indeed!' said Dorothy, as if Chel had suggested Outer Mongolia. 'Really Cheryl, when are you going to grow up and face facts?'

'He won't need the unit any more soon,' she insisted. 'Only for a check-up every now and then. They've told us so. Cornwall isn't on the next continent, exactly.' Mistake.

'Oh really, Cheryl!' exclaimed Dorothy, in exasperation. 'What rubbish you do talk!'

'It's what he wants to do,' pleaded Chel, beaten into a corner, and was checkmated by Oliver's stepmother in one swift, unanswerable move.

'Oliver is not only chronically sick, but in the middle of a breakdown,' she said firmly, which was near enough to the truth to send Chel into full retreat, although Oliver was perfectly all right in her company, even if he went completely to pieces with everyone else. There was a moral there somewhere, but it would have taken someone more foolhardy than Chel to point it out. Had this incessant squabbling gone on all his life? she wondered. If so, it was no longer surprising that he had taken off round the world. The surprise lay in that he had ever come back.

But it was her own insistence on keeping her job and having a place to live that had kept him in Embridge. At the thought,

Chel turned hot all over and felt her cheeks burning. Fool! Fool! Destructive, self-centred *fool*! They could have lived anywhere in the world, it didn't have to be here.

It occurred to her, out of nowhere, that, one way or another, Oliver must have seen life as an ongoing act of betrayal – first his mother, his father, herself maybe, although that had been more a failure of understanding, finally his own physical strength had betrayed him in its turn. She suddenly wondered just how far the damage went, wishing that she had paid more attention to Jonathan when, in those early days, he had tried to tell her about Oliver's family and she had brushed him aside. Debbie ... what had he said about Debbie? She had been sent away to school ... but no. *Sent* was the operative world here. Oliver couldn't possibly have thought she was trying to avoid him, could he? The answer came on cue. Yes, given the Dreaded Dot and her sweet, poisonous tongue, he probably could. Not today's Oliver. That much younger Oliver, blindly resentful and full of anger, hating everyone, destroying himself from within. She thought of Debbie's outburst in the drawing-room, and wondered if it was even just Oliver who had suffered. Susan had been right – in a way anyway – Debbie crying *grab what you can while it's there for the grabbing* was only a short step away from Oliver sweeping herself away with him on impulse. If only life was kinder to Debbie.

... and if he did see life in that way, it was perfectly possible that Oliver had other, hidden talents that he had never trusted enough to use for fear they should betray him in their turn ... she brushed her hand over her face as if she was brushing away a cobweb. Pull yourself together, Chel! One thing's certain – it's time to go.

The only good that she could see in the immediate situation was that Oliver's urgent wish to go back to Cornwall meant that she didn't have to burden him with ghost stories that she couldn't feel he was fit to hear. Every other aspect had a nightmare quality that was in danger of sending her spinning off into full-scale panic. The hardest thing in the world to fight, she was discovering, is well-meaning goodwill, and she had succeeded in leaving herself wide open. Even the bickering – most of it anyway – was directed towards their welfare. Now that her initial anger had cooled, she could see that her randomly chosen boarding house was impractical, and Oliver's implicit faith in her ability to arrange things as he would like them to be arranged was a frightening burden to carry. It was easy for him, he had a lifetime of disregarding his family behind him. She herself stood rather in awe of them if she was honest, and it put her at a tremendous disadvantage. Sooner rather than later, Oliver was going to be discharged from hospital into her care once more, and she still had not the faintest idea of what to do with him. Her planning ability had gone into a skid from which there seemed to be no recovery, and all she was sure about was that whatever she had done in the past had been wrong.

It wasn't that his family didn't try to be reasonable, for they did. It would have been so much easier if they had been *un*reasonable and given her something to push against.

'All right, so you neither of you like it in the bungalow,' said Jerry, influenced no doubt by his wife, and in the voice of one calming the hysterical. 'You had an unhappy time there, it was hard for you both and we all understand that. But for heaven's sake, Cheryl, that doesn't mean you have to go and live at the furthest end of the country to get away from it. Think about buying somewhere that you do like, here in the town – up on the cliff if you think you would like that better, I'll be glad to help you, as I hope you know. Somewhere where you feel you can be happy and settle down – but be sensible, please! You can't go uprooting yourselves and tearing off on the whim of a very sick man.'

It was pointless to say it, Chel knew, but she said it anyway.

'It isn't a whim. I think it's a desperate need.'

'It's Greece all over again,' said Dorothy in her forthright way. 'Don't be so silly, Cheryl, and don't encourage Oliver to be silly, either! That's childish, and you know it! It's high time that husband of yours grew up and pulled himself together! He can't go dashing about the world now that he's disabled, and he must be made to understand it. For one thing, his health won't stand up to it and you must make him see that. For *both* your sakes!'

'If dashing about the world, as you put it, is what he wants to do, then that's OK by me, and I'll take care of him,' ventured Chel with a cautious burst of spirit. Dorothy, who knew exactly where best to plant her barbs, promptly changed tack and became syrup-sweet where she had been brisk and scornful.

'But Cheryl dear, suppose it didn't work out? Suppose you decided to part again? Caring for an invalid isn't going to be any easier in Cornwall than it was here, you know.'

Chel wished she wouldn't use that awful word *invalid* all the time. She felt it pushing them back like a great hand in their faces.

'We'll be all right,' she insisted, but a note of desperation had crept in. Dorothy smiled.

'Oh come now, Cheryl, you can't possibly know that! Your marriage is going through a very sticky patch, you need help and support, and who better to give it than the family?'

'Please stop and think before you do anything,' interrupted Jerry hurriedly. 'I don't see any immediate prospect of Oliver earning a proper living again, and you can't go out to work either, while you have the responsibility of looking after him. Oliver's disability pension won't go far, even added to your invalid care allowance – and you might lose that if you worked, even a few hours a day. You want to build up your investments if you can, any other course would be most inadvisable the way things are, you'll need that money. Your mortgage payments, whether on Endicott Road or on some other property, already absorb a lot of your investment income and you must have something put by for a rainy day. However much we may sympathise – and believe me, we do – we have to advise you to be practical. You can't afford to pull up your roots and go all that way, it really would be best to stay here where we can help you, keep an eye on you.'

Spy on us, you mean thought Chel, and rebuked herself hurriedly. Dorothy, maybe, but she was beginning to think that Jerry genuinely meant what he said. For a fleeting instant, looking at his friendly face, listening to his good advice, she wished that things could have been different. But there was Dorothy – always Dorothy. Dorothy was a spoiler – to be dreaded, as Helen had warned her. But she had to make an effort to put up a fight.

'If we can afford to live in Endicott Road, we can afford to live somewhere else,' she said, reasonably enough she thought. 'You mustn't worry about us, we can manage.'

'And how, I should be interested to know, do you propose to?' snapped Dorothy, tartly. 'Don't be stupid, Cheryl, it really won't help. Oliver is a great responsibility and you can't shoulder it on your own. Have some consideration for him, please!'

'I am considering him,' said Chel, knowing already that it was useless. She might as well talk to the wind.

Dorothy made a tutting noise.

'Cheryl, try to show some sense! You're worrying us to death, and it's cruel too, encouraging Oliver to hope for things that can't possibly happen!'

'Is it so cruel to want to give him back some happiness?' asked Chel, and was annoyed to hear her voice quiver with nerves – she hoped it was nerves. Dorothy gave a scornful sniff.

'The quickest way to make Oliver happy is to make him accept what's happened to him,' she said. 'And the sooner you do it, the better – look at this last upset! What will you do if he takes another overdose?'

'Now then,' interposed Jerry, for the second time. 'That's water under the bridge, Dot. Cheryl, we'll agree to humour you both over the bungalow, for I think we can all see that it's been a disaster for you, but you really must be sensible about the rest. You had better make arrangements to move in with us when Oliver is sent home from hospital, and we'll take it from there, shall we? When we can see how things are going to be?' He took her hand and gave it a comforting squeeze, quite unaware of the horror his well-meant suggestion had caused. 'There now, it won't be so very bad, will it?'

'Really, you two are worrying us all to death!' said Dorothy, having the last word.

The arguments were repeated, with variations, twice a day for the next week, by which time Oliver had begun to take an interest in what was going on around him. Recent events had in no way impaired his enthusiasm for a good fight with his family: no sooner had he caught the drift of the arguments than he had, predictably, crossed swords with Susan. It seemed to Chel, who was present, like a conditioned reflex. *You bite me, I bite you*, on and on for ever. They had to get away. She couldn't live with it, and it did Oliver no good at all.

Susan had become as persistent as a dog with a bone to bury under the best cushion. She considered herself more personally involved than the rest of the family since it was she who had originally picked out the bungalow, and she felt her judgement and competence to be in question. She was defending herself more than her stepbrother, and because they were brother and sister rather than different generations, things very quickly got out of control.

'You're being thoroughly selfish,' she told him roundly. 'It's just silly to say you don't want to live in Endicott Road any more. What's wrong with it, I should like to know?'

'What's right with it?' countered Oliver.

'We weren't happy there,' Chel added quickly. 'It's not really our kind of place. It's not your fault.' She paused. 'Anyway, what's selfish? It's our bungalow, after all.'

'Daddy paid the deposit,' Susan reminded her. 'Anyway, Oliver's ill, he's in no state to judge.'

'Oh God!' exclaimed Oliver, who was heartily tired of this theme. 'I have chronic backache, I'm not falling to bits! So, we'll rent a place instead of paying a mortgage. Now for God's sake Suse, go away and leave us to manage our own affairs!'

'It's silly to want to live in a rented house when you've a perfectly good house of your own,' insisted Susan.

'So? If we want to be silly, need it worry you?' demanded Oliver.

'Yes, it need, Oliver! It's a worry to anyone who has your welfare at heart! We're all fussed to death about you!'

'Oh, I see,' flashed Oliver, in anger. 'Just because it upsets the family if we arrange our lives how we want, we have to go and live in a house we both dislike – is that the way it goes?'

'You don't dislike it, you're just being silly again.'

'Oh yes, we do. We dislike it quite unbelievably, and only someone as unimaginative as you are would ever have talked poor Chel into choosing it in the first place!'

'Oliver, that's not fair! Cheryl liked it well enough when we chose it, it's only you that's put the idea that she doesn't into her head.'

'Excuse me!' interrupted Chel, entering the fight with spirit. 'I'm quite capable of speaking for myself, if it's all the same to you. I do hate it – I always hated it – I just let you over-persuade me in a weak moment, and now I'm sorry.'

Susan flushed to the roots of her hair.

'Excuse me for breathing!'

'Oh, Susan!' Chel was contrite, belatedly realising how her words must have sounded. 'I'm sorry. It was really kind of you to help us at the time, and it was my fault, not yours, for not standing up for myself. But we're both better now, we can manage for ourselves. You must let us get back on our feet in our own way.'

'Very impressive talking, with Oliver lying there on a hospital bed and the pair of you behaving like two stubborn children from the playgroup! You're worrying poor Mummy and Daddy quite unforgivably!'

'Look,' said Oliver, fiercely, 'we never did want the same things as you want – we never have, we never will. Why should you all come forcing them on us now?'

Susan looked at him, and all the things that he was and had seemed to have, that she wasn't and didn't, rose up in the corners of her mind and lacerated her already hurt feelings. Her mouth curled spitefully, she looked for a moment the image of her mother.

'Have you looked at yourself lately, Oliver?' she asked. 'Really looked, I mean? Your days as a carefree adventurer are over. You're disabled, and you might as well accept it. You've got to put all those things you used to do behind you, once and for all. They're over and in the past!' She paused and drew a breath. 'And as for going to live in Cornwall, miles from everyone, it's out of the question! A silly, romantic daydream! You might as well forget it straight away!'

Oliver had gone sheet white, but before he could say anything, Chel leapt to his defence.

'That was a particularly stupid thing to say, and cruel and unnecessary too, and I think you had better go if that's all you've got to contribute!' she stormed.

'Cruel it may have been,' said Susan, defending herself the more swiftly because she knew she had over-stepped the mark. 'Unnecessary, no. What's ever going to get through to you two? All right, it sounds hard and unkind, but face up to it for heaven's sake! Oliver can hardly walk, how do you think you're going to manage on your own, and among strangers? Answer me that. What are you going to do with yourselves all day, with no friends or family to come and see you, to give you a break, some freedom? Or perhaps you're better without the freedom, come to that!' She paused, her glance scathing, her lips a hard line. 'You'll know nobody – nobody you can ask to come and sit with your husband, anyway –'

'I'm not a bloody baby!' interrupted Oliver, in a furious voice that broke in the middle. 'And Chel isn't a bloody gaoler! For God's sake get out, Susan, before I throw something at you!'

Susan flounced to her feet, snatching up her bag as she did so.

'Oh well, if you persist in behaving like spoiled children, there's no more to be said. But your mother is going to have something to say when she gets here, Cheryl, and you had better listen to her. We're all united in this –'

'Then stuff the lot of you!' said Oliver rudely, and Susan left abruptly and without saying goodbye.

Chel tried to slam the door on her retreating back, but was defeated by the automatic closing which insisted on taking its own time. Frustrated, she turned back into the room.

'The sooner we can –' she began, and broke off. 'Oliver!'

'Shut up!' said Oliver, between his teeth, and groped round unsuccessfully for a tissue. 'Oh shit, now I really am behaving like a playgroup brat!'

Chel said nothing. She was still not entirely sure that Oliver hadn't accepted her return simply because he saw no better alternative, and what she now wanted to do might, under those circumstances, be impertinent. She followed the impulse anyway, now was as good a time as any to find out. Crossing the room, she put her arms around him and cradled his head into the hollow of her shoulder. He felt rigid as steel under her touch.

'She's a cow,' she said forcefully, after a moment or two. 'Don't take any notice of her, Oliver. Please don't.'

'She's bloody right,' said Oliver, in a choking voice rather muffled by her sweater, but he didn't push her away. 'Oh

God, Chel, I'm nothing but a drag on you. Why did it have to happen to us?'

Chel was running her fingers through his hair, twisting it into curls that sprang straight again the moment she released them. She had no idea what she was doing.

'I hate her!' she said, with more venom than she had believed herself capable of. 'I hate her, I hate her!' Right at that moment, she meant it.

'She makes me want to go straight out and do the craziest thing I can think of,' said Oliver, and sounded rather alarmingly like his old self as he did so, and Chel said, apprehensively, 'Oliver ...'

'Oh, don't worry about it,' said Oliver, with a controlled quietness that all in a moment frightened her silly. 'I can't, can I? Don't worry, whatever Susan chooses to think, I know it. Oh yes, I know it. None better.'

'Oliver, please,' said Chel, helplessly.

Joining forces against Oliver's family, however inadvisable, gave Chel and Oliver some common ground to stand on again. To begin with, the novelty of this blinded them both to anything but itself, but that phase was short-lived. It didn't wipe out what had gone before, and Oliver was by this time as clear about that as Chel. Because he had to accept that Jonathan was in love with Chel, it had made it that much more difficult to ignore that it had gone a lot further than that. Whatever survived between them, he knew as well as Chel did that they were either going to have to have it out properly, or he was going to be eaten away with jealousy, suspicion and insecurity until they lost all the ground they were so laboriously regaining.

He didn't even know what she did when she wasn't with him. It would take a saint to sit helpless in a chair wondering, and never asking, whatever asking precipitated. Suspicion was like an ulcer, it ate into him, and although he would have liked to be sure of Chel, the truth was that he couldn't be. It had to be faced. Without trust there was no point in trying to rebuild their life together. The only thing that he was certain of was that she wouldn't lie, and if he didn't like the truth, at least he would have the consolation that he had demanded it.

Knowing that was one thing. Putting it to the test was quite another, and the strain of living with all the unsaid things began to tell. Chel watched Oliver's slowly rebuilding confidence begin to fade again day by day and knew the reason, and one day, it inevitably became too much for both of them. There was a pause in their conversation that grew too long, and their eyes met across the pause. Each of them knew what the other was thinking, and because she was the one who could do it, it was Chel who got up and moved away, over to the window where she could stand looking out at the fast-melting snow that she didn't even see.

Her heart was beating so fast suddenly that she couldn't breathe properly. *Many waters cannot quench love, neither can the floods drown it* ... she had deceived herself over that because at the time she had wanted to, but now it was suddenly terrifyingly apposite. For they lived under the weir, and the sluice gates were about to open.

'Let's talk about it,' said Oliver, abruptly.

She didn't turn her head because she was afraid to look at him. There was no graceful way to reply and so she just said, baldly, 'Sex, you mean.'

'Or the lack of it. You know the score, we both do. I could be stuck like this for the rest of my life – and yours.'

He wouldn't even say the word *impotent*. Perhaps he couldn't, but she didn't know what to say to make it easier for him.

'It might not be like that.'

'Is it a risk you're prepared to take?' asked Oliver deliberately, and she did turn round then.

'I don't know. I only know I love you.'

'You and I both know that's beside the point. I suppose I must love you too, and we can think up something, no doubt – but will it ever be enough?'

'I don't know that, either. Anyway, we don't know for certain, it could just be the shock – they said –'

'They don't know, Chel, don't kid yourself. I don't know, you don't know, nobody knows. And even if ... oh hell, Chel, you know what I'm trying to say! We both know that whatever happens nothing is ever going to be the same again. God almighty, how could it?'

Magical unity in the claustrophobic warmth of a tent down in that promised land of Cornwall, in the cicada-loud nights among the olive groves of the Ionian islands, tenderness and joy high above the busy street in their snug little flat, while winter's winds blew against the low windows. Gone, all gone.

'We had it once,' said Chel, steadily. 'Full measure, running over. Let's be glad of that.'

'Thank you,' said Oliver, after a brief, surprised pause. He left just long enough not to spoil what both of them recognised as a moment of rare understanding, and then he said awkwardly, 'About Jonathan Holmes, Chel. I'm not stupid, I'm not blind. You had an affair, didn't you?'

She swallowed, and after some searching found a voice that wasn't quite her own.

'I slept with him once. That night ... but yes, before you ask, I wanted to a lot. We met in cafés and things, where there were people. It was safest. But I didn't love him. Not the way I do you. I swear it.'

Oliver looked down at his hands, resting deceptively still in his lap. He knew the truth when he heard it, just as she did, but he knew too that there was more to it. He spoke carefully.

'There might be other Jonathans. I know you think that there won't, now, but there might... quite easily, there might. What would you do?'

'I don't know,' said Chel, for she hadn't found an answer to this for all her thinking. It wasn't a very good reply and she tried to elaborate on it. 'I told you, I love you, and it's true. I don't think I'll ever stop loving you ... but ... well, it's different, isn't it?'

Oliver said,

'If it's different, I suppose I shall have to try not to mind.' The words nearly choked him.

'No!' Chel came swiftly towards him. 'No, Oliver! I wouldn't do it to you –'

He broke in before she could get any further, throwing up his hand as if to ward her off.

'Don't, Chel – don't say that. You and I aren't going to make promises to be broken, not ever again. Just leave it there – please.'

She slid her arms round his neck, resting her cheek against his hair. Her heart was heavy.

'How can we even talk about it when we say we love each other?' There was despair in the words, even a touch of their old hopelessness. It was so easy to slip back into the old ways when those ways were still so close, when nothing new offered.

'Because we've got to be honest,' said Oliver. 'And perhaps, if I let you go, just a little, you'll stay.'

And that had always been the way it had to be with him. The poignant justice of it caught in her throat as a sob.

'I'll always stay,' she said.

'No promises, remember?'

'All right. No promises.' She bent her head down, setting her mouth against his. Their kisses disturbed her deeply. She wondered what they did to him, because certainly hunger and longing as well as the cautious resurgence of love were in them. He put his hands up, framing her face.

'I love you, Chel.'

'I know.'

Stereotype declarations. But something, where nothing had been before.

No, the future couldn't be easy, not in any way. But they could talk together, and while they could do that they had a chance. And perhaps she could help him, if any spark remained to be rekindled.

But children, no, there probably wouldn't be. That chance had to be gone for ever.

She had thought that she had got over that, but the sense of loss that swept her unawares was like a breath from the Arctic ice, so chilly that Oliver felt it too.

'What's the matter?'

'Nothing.'

'Yes there is. Tell me.'

Chel took a short, irresolute step away back towards the window.

'No, really. It's nothing.' Whatever was the matter with her, rocking the boat like this? The last thing they needed now was for her to go broody and dewy-eyed over babies, how tactless could she get? But it wasn't just babies – not babies in that sense at all. It was Jeremy, the little dead boy who had never had a chance at life. Her throat closed.

Odd moments of perception had visited them both from time to time in the past. Now, as if those days had never gone, Oliver picked her thought out of the empty air.

'It's Jeremy, isn't it?'

An old resentment surged to the surface and she said, 'You told me it was unhealthy to grieve for him.'

Oliver flushed a little, his tone when he spoke was defensive.

'I didn't mean exactly that, and you know it. Come on then, let's have all the skeletons out while we're at it – this is something we never shared, and we should have.'

He sounded angry, and so tense did she feel that it would have been easy to be angry back. She looked down at her hands, twisting her fingers together and remembering his furious voice on that awful night. *Our dead,* he had cried. She hadn't suspected him of such bitterness – or grief, either.

'You never even asked about him.'

'I would have, if you hadn't shut me out.'

'I'm sorry,' said Chel, recognising the accusation as just. The words came out as an unrecognisable squeak. She repeated them. 'I'm sorry.'

After a pause, Oliver said, 'I'm not good for much, admitted, but I still have a fairly serviceable shoulder for crying on.'

'You hate being cried on,' said Chel.

He reached out and covered her twisting hands with his own. His clasp was strong and comforting, and although she knew how frail was his support in reality, she was reassured.

'And do you so enjoy crying?' he asked. She shook her head.

'No.' The word was hardly audible.

'Well then.'

'Oh Oliver!' cried Chel, on a wail that cracked in the middle, and slid to her knees at his feet, weeping as if her once-broken heart would break all over again.

But crying all over Oliver was a strange experience, and a new one. Eventually, the strangeness of it succeeded in drying her tears and she just stayed there, her face hidden against his knees, conscious of an unexpected feeling of peace and release. The child, who should have drawn them together, and who had, from some perversity for which they couldn't hold themselves entirely unresponsible, pushed them apart, had suddenly slipped into his proper perspective. Like poison cleansed from a festering wound, the taint had gone. They stayed silent, Oliver's hand gently caressing her hair, and peace stole into the room with them. After a while, Oliver said slowly, 'What a pair we are. Are we going to make it, do you think?'

Chel raised her head.

'Of course we are!' she exclaimed, indignantly, and then, because absolute honesty was essential in the circumstances, added, 'Of course, we're going to wish sometimes that things were different – as they were. How can we help it? But if ever I feel tempted to look back with regret, I only have to remember what it felt like to face living without you, and I won't need to look any further to know that now is all I want. All I need. So long as you're content, too.'

'In a way, it's easier for me,' Oliver pointed out. 'I have no choice.'

'In every way that matters, neither have I.'

'In a year – two years – maybe things will be different.'

'I shan't care if they aren't,' said Chel.

'You speak for yourself!' said Oliver, with a wry smile.

Another river crossed, another obstacle behind them. Why did she feel, she wondered, as if they were clearing a minefield? True enough, the future would be impossible if there were any mines left. She repeated, with emphasis, the only thing that seemed to matter.

'I love you. It's going to be all right. I love you.'

Ghosts ... Jeremy, Oliver as he had once been, herself so young and heedless and immature... they must all be exorcised. Don't look back, never look back.

'I love you, too,' said Oliver, in the old familiar formula, but when they kissed it was this time without passion, and the stony path that could lead back into the sunlight stretched endlessly ahead of them.

XVII

With all these existing pressures from outside and within, neither Chel nor Oliver looked forward to the impending visit from Chel's mother with anything but foreboding, and as it turned out, they were right.

She looked at the stairs at the hotel and told Chel that she was too stupid to be let loose, she looked at Oliver and told him he needed a keeper, and then kissed them both and told them not to worry any more, before turning her attention to the Nankervises. There was a lot of bottled-up resentment towards them needing an outlet, of which she hadn't been consciously aware, and she went into battle with all guns blazing. The right of Chel and Oliver to arrange their own lives was asserted, proven, and reluctantly accepted – and immediately challenged from a new quarter.

'You must both come home and rest awhile, Oliver's father will sort things out for you,' said Marilyn, with the kindest intentions in the world. 'Just as soon as Oliver is well enough to travel. Then, when all this is behind you and the bungalow is sold, Cheryl can go down to Cornwall and choose you somewhere nice to live, perhaps Louise would like to go with her for company. How does that sound?'

So reasonable, was the uneasy answer.

Chel lay awake a long time that night, trying to work out why she should be so convinced that it wasn't reasonable at all, and what the alternative could possibly be, and to both queries her mind returned a blank. It *was* reasonable, it was kind, it was a heaven-sent lifeline compared to the alternative, and there was nothing else that she could do, was there? She had nowhere to take Oliver herself, but it wasn't peace and quiet and cosseting that was needed now, in spite of what everyone agreed among themselves. OK, so he was totally unfit for the upheaval of moving house, they hadn't another house to move into, and she felt herself as if she had been put through an emotional wringer. Even so, she was convinced that now wasn't the time for more rest, the very word made her skin prickle. Now was the time for moving on.

If only there was someone with whom she could discuss the matter objectively, but everyone around them felt themselves to have such particular interest. There were hidden agendas wherever she looked these days. Family – everybody's family, hers as well as Oliver's – interfering everywhere, all with the very best of intentions. They didn't realise it and wouldn't believe it if they were told, but they were in themselves a bigger stumbling block than all the physical hurdles put together, because if there was one thing that Oliver had always resented deeply, it was his family. Except maybe for Debbie, she now supposed – but Debbie kept her distance and her own counsel, as alienated from them all these days as Oliver himself, and Chel had never known her well enough to break the deadlock now.

Oliver had been conditioned to resentment from childhood, and only now was he beginning to see it. Starting with Helen, whom Chel had come deeply to pity, his close relatives had always brought out the worst in him; at close quarters, would her own family have the same effect? That was a sobering thought. Freedom from family interference was one of the things – the many things, she in her turn was beginning to understand – that he had given up for her.

We should never have settled here. We should have gone back to Cornwall right at the start. Or stayed in Greece, while we had the chance – anywhere that was a long way from all of them. Greece was one of those forks in the road, how many more have we missed?

Her mind felt like one of her native east-coast rivers, slow-moving and silted up with rubbish, in urgent need of a flash-flood to clear it out. They were killing Oliver all over again between them – herself included. She had saved him before, but this time? Perhaps it would be third time different.

456

How ridiculous!

Chel tossed over onto her other side and her thoughts went round and round like a caged mouse on a tread wheel, getting nowhere.

Oliver had accepted her mother's kindly plan, he had even fewer alternatives than she had, stuck in a hospital at the mercy of those who still had the full use of their legs. He had said very little, but at least he hadn't argued this time. Perhaps he felt, as she did, that they had run out of options. Or perhaps not ... perhaps he just felt that it was what she wanted to do. Only she didn't. Somewhere along the line she seemed to have severed her close emotional ties with her family. She hadn't noticed it happening, but it had.

What would be the craziest thing that they could think of?

Just wondering about it had to be the craziest thing. They couldn't do crazy things any more. If they could, she could simply kidnap Oliver from the hospital and they could run away together, as they had done once before. She couldn't do that when half an hour in the car at a time was about his limit. Half an hour would hardly get them out of Embridge, she needed more leeway than that to get him away safely – and where would they go?

It was hopeless, they must accept the inevitable and make the best of it. It would be good practice for them, making the best of it would be their lot from now on. And it could have been worse. It could have been the Dreaded Dot, not her own kind-hearted mother.

Small consolation! What a hopeless mess it had all turned out to be.

Chel slept eventually, dreamed uneasy dreams, and woke unrefreshed and weary to face another day of well-meant interference and uneasy doubt. Her mother, planning their lives as lovingly as ever, recommended that the morning be spent in packing up the bungalow.

'You can leave most of it, a house always sells better if it's furnished, and Oliver's family will keep an eye on it for you,' she said. 'If we pack up all your china and glass and personal things, then when you come to move it will be quite simple, and you probably won't even need to be there. And it will save paying storage, removers never take proper care of things in store, something always gets broken or lost.'

'All right,' said Chel, listlessly. 'I'll drop you off first thing and go and see the agent, and explain what we're doing, better than just ringing him. Susan can have the spare key.' It had to be done some time, and the bungalow couldn't hurt her with her mother there, it was when she was alone that it was to be feared. She ought to be glad of all these kindly arrangements, running on oiled wheels, sweeping them onward. It made it so easy when someone else did your thinking for you.

She ought to be thinking for herself.

She had tried, God knew. Her mind was a blank.

'Cheryl dear, are you all right?' asked her mother, concerned at her continuing silence.

'Just a bit of a headache,' admitted Chel. 'I didn't sleep too well.'

'It's been a worrying time for you.'

Chel visited the estate agent and set out to walk back to the car. The snow had nearly all melted now, the softened air held what was almost the first hint of spring, but it was wasted on the girl who walked, head down, so lost in her own thoughts that she was oblivious to anything else, even the people who shared the pavement with her.

The man heading the other way was in a hurry. He always hurried these days, keeping his life moving at such a pace that he had no time to think. He was so busy making sure he didn't think about her that he never even saw her.

They walked straight into each other, and Chel's bag, tucked carelessly unzipped under her arm, went flying and scattered its contents all over the pavement, and they were down there grovelling to pick them up and apologising before each had fully realised who the other was.

Jonathan broke off his apology in the middle, and Chel said, 'Oh!' on a faint, startled gasp.

They hadn't met since she moved out of his flat, they had nothing now to say to each other that it was possible to say. But in the present situation, it was equally impossible to get up and walk away, Jonathan had his hands full of Chel's belongings; the material goods bound them together in an awkward and stilted politeness.

'I've been wondering how you were getting on,' said Jonathan. 'How is Oliver?'

'A lot better, thank you.' The conventional phrases glossed over the awkwardness. 'He'll be out of hospital soon. We're going home – my home, that is. Just for a bit of a break.'

'Oh?' said Jonathan. 'Well, that will do you both good.' His pulses were racing, he hadn't realised that just seeing her could affect him so deeply. It was useless to remind her of what had passed between them, but the words almost spoke themselves. 'There wasn't any trouble, was there – over that night?' He didn't know what he hoped from them. For all her reaction he could have been discussing a night out at the cinema. Her thoughts were too full of Oliver to allow room for him.

'No.' She shook her head. 'Nobody knows for sure where I went. It's not their business.'

'Not even Oliver?'

Oliver had left her no choice.

'Of course Oliver. He has a right to know.'

'And didn't he mind? I mean, it isn't as if ...' His voice tailed off, and the ice crackled thinly under his feet.

'Oh, don't be silly!' said Chel. 'Of course he minded! What do you take him for?' She was angry, because the memory of just how much Oliver had minded, both at the time and later, was something that she was never going to be able to leave behind her. Because of the special bond that she had always had with her husband, it had effectively killed the last of her feelings for Jonathan. Guilt had to poison one relationship or the other, it wasn't something she could legitimately have both ways.

Jonathan understood, if not her motive, certainly the tone of her voice. He said, humbly, 'I'm really sorry.'

'Why should you be?' she snapped at him. 'It was me came to you, not the other way around.' As if he was some kind of therapist. Perhaps he had been. He smiled wryly at the bitter thought.

They were outside a small tea shop. Jonathan tipped a lipstick and a comb back into her bag and hesitated.

'How about a coffee? Just a quick one, for old time's sake. I suppose it will be the last time.'

'Why not?' agreed Chel, drifting. Her quick spurt of anger was over, she had treated Jonathan badly and perhaps she owed him ten minutes in which to say a proper goodbye.

They sat on either side of a round table covered in a demure floor-length cloth, and a languid waitress brought them two cups of insipid coffee. There was a plastic flower in a plastic vase. Jonathan pushed the sugar across, waggling the bowl to get her attention.

'No thanks.' Chel shook her head. It was the first thing she had said since they sat down, her mind was so obviously far away that Jonathan, trained to be alert for people's reactions, could hardly miss it.

'Is everything all right?' he asked, and Chel said, quite without meaning to, 'I'm so worried about Oliver.'

'Why?' asked Jonathan. 'You said he was better.'

Chel fiddled with her teaspoon, tinkling it in her saucer.

'He is, I suppose. We're leaving Embridge, did you know?'

'You told me,' he reminded her.

'Oh, not that. We're going to go and live in Cornwall.'

Jonathan looked at her carefully.

'So what's the problem? It sounds like a good idea to me. Make a new beginning.'

The necessity for answering the question concentrated Chel's mind. She found herself telling him things that she hadn't told to anyone.

'It's all wrong. Everything. Not just what's happened, but what's happening now. Everyone has made such a fuss – and then Mum coming along, and being so kind ... and it's the obvious thing to do, to take Oliver away from his interfering family and let him get well quietly in his own time. It's the right thing to do, anyone can see that – but *it's all wrong!*'

She was speaking to him about her husband as if he himself was a close and valued friend of them both. Oh God, thought Jonathan, with comfortless conviction, this has to be the end. This is the bloody last goodbye! She's only got room in her mind and in her heart for him.

'Why is it wrong?' he asked, and was surprised to hear his own voice so cool and appraising.

She thought for a moment, a frown between her eyes. The tinkling spoon fell to the cloth.

'Because ... because he's never been like that. Living with family, being fussed over by Mum, being made to be an invalid, it isn't Oliver. All this, it's like trying to cage the wind. It can't be done. Oliver always set freedom above life – above me, if you like. He must feel shackled and imprisoned and smothering to death.'

'It's hard, I know, but it happens.' Jonathan looked at her seriously. 'It's happened to Oliver. Cheryl, I'm desperately sorry for you both, for him particularly – anyone would be – but if you're not dead, you have to go on living. Him along with the rest of us. You can't dictate terms. You must see that, and so must he.'

It was the same old theme again, come to terms with it, learn to live with it, there's nothing anyone can do about it – nobody even seemed to consider quality of life! But Jonathan was somebody that she could argue with, bounce ideas off, tell he was wrong with some chance of being listened to. Chel said, 'He does see it. That's the trouble. You see, it isn't enough just to know that he must learn to accept the restrictions of being disabled. There's something in him that can't – or won't – do it. All the things that are going on now, selling the bungalow, going home like good little children to stay with Mum and Dad, planning the sort of conventional life that lots of people are quite content to lead – I think that perhaps if you're one of the kind that's born with whatever spark it is that Oliver has, you just can't do it. It's his tragedy, that his body was crippled, and his mind was left ... well, trapped. Imprisoned for life. *Caged.*'

'There's nothing that you or I or anyone else can do about it. The only person who can really help Oliver is Oliver.'

'He'll come to terms with it in the end, I suppose, but he'll never learn to take it gracefully. Why should he? It wasn't even his fault, it was a gang of mindless yobs looking for kicks –' Her voice was rising.

'Cheryl,' said Jonathan. She stared at him for a moment, rubbed a hand across her face, but to his relief, continued more calmly.

'You know what I would like to do?' she said, her thoughts and fears suddenly crystallising. 'I should like to set him free again – he gave up a lot to share with me, and now I feel as if his freedom has been trusted to me, does that sound silly? I want to go forward, not stand still. Find things – new things – that he can still do, not live among the wreckage of the things he can't. If he had been blinded, I could have been his eyes. If he was dumb, I could speak for him. Why can't I be his freedom, just the same? There has to be a way – there *has* to be!'

Jonathan thought, sick at heart, that he had never heard love so starkly defined. *Ride, ride Lancelot, only the hopeless quest for the grail is for you. Guinevere is for the King after all.* He said, 'Well, why can't you? Be his freedom, I mean.'

Chel stared at him, wild-eyed.

'Because I don't see how. I *told* you, Jonathan.'

'Drink up your coffee,' Jonathan advised her. 'That is –' he looked down at his own cup, 'if you think it's wise. Now listen, and stop flying off the handle. Tell me what you want to do, here and now. It obviously isn't to go to Whytham and be cosseted by your excellent mother. Listen to your instincts. What do *you* feel is the right thing? Never mind the rest of them, what is it you want?' *And I love you – I love you -*

Chel answered simply, straight from a conviction that came to her all of a piece, complete.

'He needs to get away from everyone, to go where he wants to go, now, immediately. If I could see how to do it, I'd take him straight down to Cornwall and the sea ... and what little freedom there still may be for us.'

'So what's stopping you?'

'What's stopping me?' Her voice rose up the scale again, indignantly. 'Isn't that obvious, what's stopping me? How would I get him there? Where would we live? Please don't say "in a boarding house," they have stairs, and they cost. Until we sell that horrible bungalow, we have to keep paying the mortgage.'

'A holiday let?'

'It'll be Easter soon. We'd never get a long let, and anyway, they cost too.'

Jonathan was silent. If he thought hard enough, maybe he wouldn't feel pain. There were things you could have, and things that you couldn't, and Chel was one of the things that he, at least, couldn't. But happiness – yes, he would like to be able to give her that. *A parfit, gentil knight* ... He said,

'If you can get him to the east coast, why not Cornwall, too? It's further, but not that much.'

'His father is going to arrange for a private ambulance.'

'I see. What it is to be rich!' He picked up his cup, but didn't drink. 'What does the hospital say about all this? He must be under a specialist, what's the general opinion?'

'Oh, that he needs an occupation, peace and quiet, light exercise to build up muscular strength, and that he must put on some weight, and most of all, he must calm down.'

'None of that sounds incompatible with the sea, and Cornwall, and being on your own.'

'I agree with you, but if I said I was going to take him there, even if I could see how, his whole family, and mine too, would shout me down. They're all so sure they know what's best for us, we'd never be allowed to get away – and they're wrong, wrong, *wrong!*'

'Then don't tell them,' said Jonathan, calmly.

'How can I not?' Chel's frustration with his lack of understanding, her desperation, shrilled in her voice. 'I've *told* you – I've tried to tell you! We've nowhere to go, and I can't just drive there in the car – he can't travel by car – or not for very long, not nearly long enough, and even that would need so much organising with rest stops on the way and never mind where we'd live when we got there. If I could see a way round all that, I could spring the trap for him, but there isn't one! I need help to do anything at all, and if I ask anyone for it, then that's the beginning of the end!'

But there was a way. Jonathan was surprised that she hadn't seen it for herself. If he didn't point it out to her, she might never think of it and her marriage might crash again, for good this time, but he couldn't let that happen to her. Not now he realised what she was prepared to give up for love. And come to that, he couldn't do it to Oliver Nankervis either, because you didn't, however you felt, grind the stuff of heroism into pulp. He had thought once that he could do it, or at least watch it happen, but he knew now that he couldn't. So that was what love did, it made a crawling, sycophantic fool out of you.

'You could ask me,' he said, steadily.

Chel stared at him, her mouth untidily open, shocked. Then she said, 'No – no, I couldn't do that to you. Anyway, there's nothing you could do. But thank you anyway ...' She let the words trail away weakly. He saw that she was near tears.

'Drink your coffee,' he said again, heavy-hearted. 'No, don't argue. Drink it, and then come with me. I want to show you something.'

He took her to College Street Motors, opposite to the Ship Inn. College Street Motors did a flourishing trade in quality used cars. He walked her past the lines of family saloons and estates and round to a yard at the back, where freedom for his rival in love and the loss of everything that he himself had wished for waited to be seen and recognised. Throwing everything away, he told himself mockingly – except that it had never really been his in the first place.

'They took it as a part exchange,' he told her. 'Bloke bought it new, top of the range, and then didn't get on with it. It's not really their sort of thing, but they were going to move it on – I expect you might get a pretty good deal on it if we try.'

Chel stood and stared. She said nothing at all for quite a long time. Jonathan waited.

It was so commonplace that it took her breath away. Trim, compact and solid, with striped tweedy curtains at the windows. After a while, she found her voice.

'A motor caravan?'

'Why not? You can travel in it, live in it, put it where you like. Oliver can lie down whenever he needs to rest, all you need is a lay-by and there are plenty of those. You can park it beside whatever bit of sea you choose. You can fatten him up on Cornish cream and pasties, or cook on the stove as you prefer. It even has a little loo and a shower room. And before you tell me that he'll never get into it, don't underestimate him. We'll get them to bolt a few grab rails on before you take it away, and he can surely manage two small steps up if there's something to hold on to. And when you need to shop, you can drive your whole home to the supermarket, and Oliver will be fine sitting in comfort with a book while you go round. What do you say?'

But Chel had nothing to say. She went on staring, her eyes like stars in a face suddenly animated. Her mind whirled.

The craziest thing they could think of?

So you took your invalid husband, crippled and in constant pain, only a short step away from a breakdown, and you lived with him like a gypsy in a little luxury holiday home on wheels, by the rugged Cornish coast, and that was crazy.

And the sheer craziness of it, the freedom and the smell of seaweed after a storm, the cry of the gulls and the feel of the wind in your faces, these gave back a little, just a very little, of what was lost. A beginning. A foothold from which to start climbing back from the abyss. The summer was ahead of them.

'It would be such fun,' said Chel, longingly.

'Of course it would,' said Jonathan. 'Do you think you could drive it?' He didn't wait for her answer, but caught the eye of a salesman who had come round to see what they were up to. 'Hi Bob, this lady would like to look inside your white elephant here, and perhaps we could have a test drive.'

'Jonathan,' said the salesman, with a nod of recognition. 'Certainly madam, I'll go and get the key.'

The inside was as neat and pristine and compact as the outside, two benches and a table that made a double bed, tiny shower, stove, cupboards, sink, a second double bed up over the cab, which would accommodate books, clothes, anything personal that they didn't want to leave behind. Even unexpected overnight guests at a push. Chel was already in love.

'It's big,' she said, peering over the front seats to the dashboard.

'It's not the biggest, it's quite small in fact for a motor home. You can handle it.' Jonathan was full of confidence.

She could, too. It felt large and unwieldy at first, after the estate car, but she liked the feel of being so high up and it ran smoothly enough. She knew that she would soon get used to the size, and more than that, Oliver would be fine.

'Listen to that engine,' said the salesman. 'Smooth as silk, runs like a bird. And we'll give it the once over, of course, before you take it away.'

'We'll need a bit more than that,' said Jonathan. He looked at Chel. 'What do you think? Go for it?'

Chel took a firm grip on commonsense.

'I'll have to discuss it with Oliver first, of course.' But she had already decided.

'Hold it for her a couple of days,' said Jonathan. 'You can do that, Bob. It isn't as if you were going to do more than send it down the line.'

'With pleasure, if your friend is really interested.'

'What would it cost?' asked Chel, belatedly.

Rather more, it turned out, than the book value of her present car, although as Oliver's father had helped her to buy it new, the gulf wouldn't be unbridgeable if they broke into their savings. The Nankervises would have a collective fit. The thought was not unpleasant.

But she had fallen among friends here – if not, she thought with amusement, among thieves.

'If you can sell privately, you would get a better price,' the salesman, Bob, told her, blithely ignoring the interests of his employers. 'Of course, I haven't seen your car, but if it's in good nick – well, don't tell the boss, but I might be able to do a deal for you. For a small commission.' He winked at her. 'Cash sale, on the QT. I know a bloke.'

He was the kind, Chel decided, who would always know a bloke. And with the money in the bank ... their sinking fund, Oliver's father called it. Well, they were sinking now and fast, if she didn't do something soon. Her heart jumped nervously in sudden excitement.

'There you are,' said Jonathan, as they walked away from College Street. 'Miracles our speciality!'

'How did you know it was there?'

'Bob's a drinking mate. He told me a few nights ago about this idiot bloke who bought the thing, and then his wife hated it, and he drove it into the gatepost – more damage to the gatepost than the van, it's rugged, that monster. As soon as you told me your troubles, I thought of it.'

'I can't imagine now why I didn't think of it for myself.' Chel was delighted, amazed.

'You're too close to the problem. Not thinking straight.' *But I am – oh, my dear love, I'm sending you away, and tearing out my heart to send it with you.* 'If you pack up the things you want to take with you and put them in marked boxes, and then give me a key, I'll get them out of the house without your mother knowing.' Calm. Matter-of-fact. Heartbroken. That's the way it goes.

'Lots of blankets and hot-water bottles,' said Chel, and laughed. 'It'll be freezing!' But spring was on the way.

Chel bought a thick, black magic marker, and drove back to the bungalow, which looked duller and more depressing than ever after her morning's activities.

'You were a long time,' said her mother.

'I had a little trouble with the car,' Chel replied.

XVIII

At one time, Susan had been in the habit of calling in at the hospital, but not since her fight with Oliver, that had broken the routine and it hadn't been re-established. Brother and sister had entered on another phase of not speaking to each other, and a very good thing too, in Chel's opinion, if that was the best that Susan could find to say. So that when she went to the hospital after lunch, she found Oliver on his own.

Her mother had tactfully offered to spend the afternoon packing up china in the bungalow, and Chel had agreed, taking this as a good omen, but the moment she walked into Oliver's room, she sensed that something was different. For good or ill, she had no idea, but she felt the change in the atmosphere as soon as she stepped through the door. Yet on the face of it, it was a tranquil scene.

Oliver lay propped up on top of the bed, not doing anything, just relaxed, watching the clouds through the window. There was a restfulness about him, a sense of release, that Chel hadn't seen for a long time, had not expected. He looked, she thought, suddenly fanciful, like a man who had laid aside a burden too heavy to bear and was now at peace. She had no idea what particular burden it could be among so many, but a small warning bell rang in the back of her mind. *Another bloody crossroads!*

Well, she could at least read one arm of the signpost.

'I've had the most amazing morning!' she cried, before he had a chance to say anything. 'I can't wait to tell you!' Oliver smiled at her.

'I've something to tell you, too, although I don't know if it's amazing.' He paused. 'Or even if you're going to like it. Hullo.'

'Hullo.' There followed a pause while they exchanged a kiss that lasted for some time. They both of them had a need for constant physical contact that was as compulsive as if they were newly in love again, reaching for each other without conscious thought, searching for what they had lost. Eventually, Chel drew back and pulled up a chair.

'All right, who goes first?' she asked. He was still smiling, she noted, lazily and with no tension anywhere to be seen. Why should that alarm her?

'Toss you for it,' he suggested.

'Why not.' She fumbled in her purse, produced a coin. 'You toss, I always fumble it. I'll call.'

Oliver took the coin, turned it over as if he expected to find two heads on it, and balanced it on his thumb. He grinned at her, whatever it was he had to say, it pleased him. She relaxed a little, but was still aware of ... *something*. Nerves, or clairvoyance?

'Here goes then,' said Oliver.

The coin flew into the air, spinning.

'Tails!' called Chel.

In the years that followed, she sometimes found herself wondering what would have happened if the coin had come down heads, and Oliver had spoken first. For if he had done so, she knew that things would have fallen out very differently. She would have spoken with reservations, with *ifs* and *buts* and *when*s, and all her fresh, driving enthusiasm would have been dissipated. They would have taken the sensible course, her own sense of responsibility would have clicked in and settled that. She would have presented her case in an entirely different way, and nothing would have happened as it did.

'Tails it is,' said Oliver, slapping the coin onto the back of his hand and looking at it. 'OK, take it away. And make it good. I feel like hearing something good.' Even his voice was different, lighter, more confident. Why did she feel his mood as a threat to her own? But he was waiting, expectant. She began her tale.

'How do you feel about running away again?'

He opened his eyes wide; that, he had not expected.

'Sounds good to me. Except that I don't see how. I wish I did.' That rang true, and she hid a smile.

'Listen.'

She had decided on her way to the hospital that it wouldn't be tactful to mention Jonathan. Once they had left for the west, she would never see him again and there was no need for Oliver to know anything about his involvement, so she described herself as having run into a friend in the town, and named no names. As she did this, she was aware that Oliver had filled in the blank in her story and become wary. But she had promised him nothing, at his own request, and the dangerous moment slipped by. The story unfolded in all its innocence, and she thought that Oliver read between the lines and appreciated that. Thought. She would never *know*. Just as he would never know. They would mend their marriage, she was sure of that now, but the damage went deep and the mend would always show. She came to the crux of the matter, to College Street Motors.

And Oliver listened, but quite obviously with none of the flaring excitement that she had felt herself, his face calm, assessing. She had thought that she would fire him with his old zest for life, fill him with new enthusiasm, and as she came to the end of the story, felt surprise and disappointment because, if anything, she felt that he was sorry – for her. Because he was about to shoot her down. She ended, lamely, 'So... that's it. What do you think?'

Oliver took time before he replied.

'If that van is in the condition you describe, it's not going for peanuts. What's the damage?'

Chel told him. 'But it doesn't matter. Bob says he can get us a good price on the car, and there's the sinking fund we can draw on. Our living expenses will be low. It doesn't matter if we've run things a bit tight, it'll build up again when next month's dividends come in. And it's our money.' She realised that she sounded defiant as she said this, but something in Oliver's stillness was getting to her. She waited for his reply, her eyes bright and fixed on his face – like a puppy asking for a pat, he thought affectionately, and loved her all over again.

'Ah ...' he said.

In the silence that followed this single syllable, Chel felt all her hopes and plans ebbing away, and could not see how or why. She said, 'It's the perfect plan, you must see that! Don't you like it?'

'Oh yes,' said Oliver. 'Yes, I like it. It sounds wonderful. Only ...'

'I think it's your turn,' said Chel.

Oliver drew a breath, but did not immediately speak. He seemed to be weighing his words, but in the end, all he said was, 'I'm sorry, Chel. I really am.'

'Why?' asked Chel, her voice suddenly unsteady.

'I've been making plans too. It's the Fund. I can't keep it.'

Bugger! thought Chel, knowing an immovable object when she saw one. The Fund, together with the insurance money, made up the sum total of all they had. The Fund had helped pay for the bungalow after Oliver's father put down the deposit for them, and the income from their investments did three things, built up capital, paid the mortgage, and fed the sinking fund. If they discarded the Fund, that effectively shifted the insurance money into the bungalow and tied it up, for the moment, tighter than the famed Gordian knot. She wasn't even certain that there would be any sinking fund left once they had paid off the mortgage, which they would then have to do because they wouldn't have enough investment income any more to cover the monthly repayments. She gave voice to her thought. 'Bugger.'

'I told you that you probably wouldn't like it. Oliver reached across to take her hand, but she snatched it away.

'That's silly, Oliver! It'll leave us with *nothing!*'

'No it won't.' Oliver had done his sums too, but he had not then known about Chel's wonderful plan. He hated to see the light die in her eyes. 'We'll still have the insurance.'

'Tied up in that awful bungalow! It might take *years* to sell!'

'No it won't, don't be silly,' said Oliver.

Chel was frightened. The bungalow would get them yet, she could see it coming – because if all their money was tied up in it, they had only two alternatives left. It was a straight choice between her parents and Oliver's. The devil and the deep blue sea. He couldn't do it to her – to them!

'But *why?*' she pleaded.

'Because ...' said Oliver.

'Because *what?*' She was angry. It wasn't just his own life he was throwing away, it was hers too. She felt she had a right to her anger. 'Just because it was *Jonathan,* I suppose!'

Oops! Bad move. She held her breath, suddenly frightened.

'No,' said Oliver. He reached out again, and this time she let him take her hand because she had scared herself, and wanted to retract. 'I'm not that smallminded, Chel – not then, or now.'

So he did guess. She felt the darkness closing in, the shadow of the tower returning.

'What, then?'

'Chel, it won't be for ever. The bungalow *will* sell, and then we can do whatever we want.'

But the golden moment would have gone. They both knew it, but still he wouldn't back down.

'Believe me, I want to do as you say, I really do. It sounds ... well, perfect. I wish we could. But we can't afford to do it, and that's ... well, it, really.'

'But we *can* afford it!' cried Chel. 'Oliver, the chance will never come again – it's now or never, you know that. You *must* know it!'

Oliver shook his head.

'The price is too high, Chel.'

'No!'

This was the second time they had fought over money, she thought suddenly, and the blood left her heart. She said, pathetically, 'If you could only tell me *why?*'

Oliver said, with a simplicity that cut straight to the heart of the problem, 'I find I can't live any more on other people's generosity. Charity. It's suffocating me.'

Chel closed her eyes.

'Oh God.'

'I'm sorry, Chel.'

'You keep saying that. It doesn't help.' *We are beyond help. I can't argue with this, it's too obviously true.* 'You can't just give it back,' she said. 'A lot of it, we don't even know where it came from. It's impossible.'

He had thought it all out. She might have known. This was the old Oliver, reappeared just when she least needed him.

'I know that. I thought we could give it all to one of those organisations that arrange sailing for the disabled.'

It had been her own suggestion, when the sore subject had first come up between them, back in that other life before the watershed. *I suppose we could easily have given the money to a suitable charity – thanked everyone and made a gesture of it.* Tears began to run down her face, after the euphoria of the morning, it was too much to bear. But the memory had brought other memories in its wake, of the dark, bitter resentment that had surged to the surface that dreadful, dreadful night, and of how long it must have been festering there inside his head, and she knew that she had lost.

'All right, then,' she said. Well, it had all been a bit too good to be true, hadn't it? Just a wonderful dream, and probably they would never have got away with it anyway. The loss of hope weighed her down. Suffolk, here we come.

Oliver had taken both her hands now, his eyes on her face. He knew, none better, what he had just done. He wished there was an alternative, but knew there wasn't. *Live now, pay later.* He hadn't realised that he had taken it for a lifeplan. He felt her hurt as if it was his own.

'Don't cry. We had a good time while it lasted,' he said gently. 'It's just, the bill's come in. It always does in the end.'

Chel's eyes flew open.

'Bill?'

'One of those things that come in brown envelopes,' Oliver began to elaborate, trying to make her smile, but Chel interrupted him.

'Shut up a moment – Bill! Not bill – Bill!'

Oliver blinked.

'I suppose you know what you're trying to say?'

'Bill,' Chel repeated. The shadows were flying, back into the dark places where they belonged. She leaned over and kissed him soundly. 'Bill!'

'Are you going to explain, or are you going to sit there for ever, saying "bill"?' asked Oliver, bewildered.

'Bill Rowlands,' said Chel.

Oliver's tone of voice was a sudden chilly warning that sent shivers down her spine.

'What about Bill?'

Eggshells crunched under her feet before she had even taken a step. He had been so like his old self, that for a few minutes there, she had forgotten that he wasn't. She sent up a brief prayer to any god who might be listening.

'A long time ago ... just after – *it* – happened, when things were at rock bottom. When I went to work as a chambermaid...' Another sore point. She winced at Oliver's expression. 'I know you hated it, Oliver, but what was I to do? I didn't want charity, either. It all happened so suddenly, and I didn't know what to do.' Silly to be sidetracked into explanations, explanations were always a bad mistake.

Oliver let it pass.

'Bill,' he said, and made it sound like a threat.

Chel said,

'He was so kind. He was the only one who seemed to understand ... well, anything at all, and I know him so little, it was strange.' She paused. 'He came one evening, he wanted to know if I was all right for money, he said ...' She paused.

'You didn't borrow money off Bill!' exclaimed Oliver. 'Chel –'

'No, I did not!' she snapped, the strain suddenly unbearable. '*Listen*, will you, Oliver? And stop being so bloody *prickly!*'

Oliver said nothing, and after a minute she dared to continue.

'He said that if we were in trouble with money because of what had happened ...' She paused there. It was hard to know how to speak of that cataclysmic event. It hadn't been an accident, it had been deliberate. It had not, in the strictest sense, been an attack, since Oliver had demonstrably started it. *It, what had happened,* sounded like spinsterish evasions of some dark and prurient truth. There had to be a way to describe it, but she had never found it.

'Go on,' said Oliver. Chel shrugged away the insoluble conundrum.

'He told me that there would be money, eventually, from the *Hesperides*. He said, if I needed it, he would advance me something against your share.'

476

'I'm not entitled to a share. I never worked on the site.'

'Oliver! Get real, do, pull yourself together! You *found* the *Hesperides!* Nobody would have a share if it wasn't for that.'

After the black tension of the past few minutes, it was like watching the sun come out.

'Shit,' said Oliver. 'I never even thought of that.'

Links that bound the chain to the heavy ball, loosening and parting. Chel began to laugh, although it wasn't funny at all.

'Oliver, you are something else! Didn't Bill say anything, ever?'

'I suppose he thought he'd already said it to you. He wouldn't see the need to say it twice, he'd know ...'

'That if we needed, we would ask? Let's ask, then. It was nearly a year ago he made the offer, things must have moved on since then. They know what some of the finds are worth now, surely? And we only need enough for the van. Let me go and see him Oliver, please.'

Oliver hadn't allowed himself to get too interested in Chel's wonderful plan, because he already knew that they couldn't afford to carry it out. Now, suddenly, it was possible. Not because of charity, or insurance policies, but because of an achievement of his own that, at the time, he hadn't given a second thought, knowing it to be happy accident as much as anything. The feeling that it gave him was as healing as a miracle.

'No,' he said, and then, seeing Chel's face, added swiftly. 'No. Let me. I'll ring him, ask him to drop by. Let's do this together, I'll be the brains, you be the brawn, and ... your friend, can help with the devious bits.'

'We can't do it without him,' said Chel, soberly.

'I understand,' said Oliver.

A silence fell between them once more, but this time it was a peaceful one. Oliver had closed his eyes as if he would sleep, but after a while, he spoke without opening them, 'Is there a game plan, or are you just planning to follow your nose?'

Chel said,

'We'll have to stop at least once, maybe twice on the way. Jo – my friend said he'd suss that out for us, find what sites were open in March.'

'Mmm. He can go round asking peculiar questions in his job, I suppose.'

'And after that,' went on Chel, deciding it safest to ignore this interruption, 'I thought we'd spend a little while in North Cornwall – not Tregothen Bay, they might look for us there.'

Oliver's eyes flew open.

'You're planning to disappear completely? Chel ...'

'My friend –'

'Call him Jonathan, please! It's me you're running off with, after all.'

'He said to smother our prejudices and get a mobile phone,' said Chel.

'Good thinking. Never a good idea to burn all your boats – all at once, that is. Then what?'

'There's no hurry, of course,' said Chel. 'I thought we'd take a bit of a holiday, let the dust settle. After all, everyone keeps saying we need one. And when we're ready, I thought then we could go on to Trelewan and find somewhere to live.' She paused. 'That's what you meant, isn't it? When you said you wanted to go home.'

'I suppose it is,' said Oliver, slowly. 'I hadn't thought about it that definitely, but you're right, of course you are. I just had this terrible longing for sea and sky and open spaces, and quiet ... and winds that smell of flowering gorse instead of petrol fumes, and the sound of surf breaking round rocks. Bloody stupid, really.' He sounded angry with himself for being so sentimental, and Chel smiled. Her pulses had stilled. It was all right. They were going to escape and it would be all right.

'Not at all. It was the first normal, recognisable instinct you had shown for nearly a year, and I was very glad of it, believe me.'

'It was a gruesome year,' said Oliver.

'It's over.'

She felt the alteration in his mood before he even spoke, the startling abrupt swing of nervous instability, and her heart leapt again, uncontrollably.

'No,' he said. He looked at her sombrely for a moment. 'It's never going to be over, Chel. Not for me. And if you stay with me, not for you, either. Have you thought about that?'

'Of course. It changes nothing. I love you.'

'As I love you. But I offered you goods that, as it turns out, I can't deliver – and not only that, I took away what you already had. Holmes must love you too – love you a lot. No – don't interrupt. It's got to be said. It isn't just what we talked about the other day, it goes much further than that. I can't take you anywhere, no dances, no parties, no fun. No adventures, no flotillas, no *Hesperides* under the sea, nothing. And because you stuck by me, in losing my own freedom, I've taken yours too. I once made a very silly remark to you, and it serves me right that it turned on me. Wherever we go now, Chel, will be your prison, and me the ball and chain. I can't do that to you, if any little bit of you longs to be free ... I know what that is like now.'

Chel sat, still as a statue, feeling as if someone had poured ice water all over her. She had thought she knew what he was going to say, that he had been going to tread the same dreary ground again, but he had somehow bypassed it, leapfrogged over it to bring them both to some strange place where sense distorted and judgement hid its face. She didn't know what she should say in reply. Oliver went on speaking, deliberately pushing out the boundaries of trust beyond their reasonable limits, testing her.

'If there's anything in you that regrets those things that we've lost – if you want the children I can't give you –' She opened her mouth to speak, but he rushed on. 'Jonathan Holmes loves you, and even I have to admit that he's been singularly faithful – and generous, if this last thing is his work. If you want to go – to him – and lead a normal life and raise a happy family, like the one you come from, then tell me now. I won't stop you, and please, you must never let pity do it. And there won't be any overdose, that's one promise that's allowable.' Once he had started to speak, although he was normally reserved he had been unable to stop. Saying it had been like wringing blood out of his own heart, but he couldn't leave it unsaid. He could never bear to feel that he had blackmailed Chel into staying when she would sooner go, he would live with despair for the rest of his life rather than do that. And Holmes, too, had to deserve better. His present generosity was humbling. And all for Chel, Oliver wouldn't deceive himself about that.

Chel's mouth had stayed open. Now, she closed it. Shock had robbed her of coherent speech, she said helplessly,

'Come on, Oliver, what brought that on? Just when things have begun to go our way for once!'

'That's why,' said Oliver. Cheryl looked momentarily bewildered.

'You mean, the idea of getting away?'

'Running away. You may as well go on calling it by its right name.'

'No.' Chel shook her head. 'What can I say to make you understand?'

'Chel –'

'You aren't the sort that runs away,' said Chel. She hesitated, seeking for the right words, and went on hurriedly before he could interrupt. 'If you were, you wouldn't be here – neither of us would, because this would never have happened. I'll tell you something, Oliver Nankervis. It's the person you are as much as anything you've ever done that makes you special. I don't know what you'll do when all this is behind us, but I do know one thing. Whatever it is, I want to be a part of it, and that should answer all your questions.'

'What can I possibly do, like this?' he asked, bitterly.

'That remains to be seen. But you've got to be famous yet, remember?'

'Aren't I that already?' asked Oliver, but what she had said must have got through to him, for to her relief he gave a reluctant laugh.

'Infamous, more like,' said Chel.

He didn't pursue the subject, she was relieved to find. It had been a bad half hour, one way and another, but they were through it now. And although she had spoken from instinct without really thinking about what she said, it surprised her now to find that she had meant every word. She didn't believe any more that Oliver's intense living of life to its last drop was over, so long as they stayed together. What was it she had said to Jonathan? *Why can't I be his freedom?* That, come to think of it, was what the love between them was all about. It always had been. Only the terms of the contract had altered.

There might still be depths to plumb, but she could breathe more easily now. They were going to be safe, she was almost sure of that.

Oliver, she thought, had really fallen asleep this time, worn out by emotion beyond his present strength. Chel moved over to the window and sat down in the chair there, and made plans in her head that felt like dreams, for all their hard reality.

Challenge, that was it. Anything that they could meet and fight together would also draw them together. Challenge was Oliver's god – and if that was something that he had also seen in her, then now was the time to prove him right. This was no small undertaking that they planned.

And they could do it. She could feel the knowledge surging through her like the flood of many waters – perhaps it was that same flood. The dark tower was falling behind. She could see sunlight glinting on water and hear the lark singing high in the sky. And there would be friends waiting for them in Cornwall, whatever Susan chose to think. There would be Jack Soames, there would be Maggie, there would be Oliver's as yet unknown relatives.

The thought of them was like a door opening. In Cornwall there were no enemies waiting, no Dot Nankervis to hate them and scheme for their downfall, no tragic Helen, whose downfall was already accomplished. No stoic, bewildered Jerry, no spiteful, jealous Susan. No loving parents of her own, either, to interfere in their affairs for their own good. No enigmatic Debbie to shout defiance, no Jonathan, they were all like water, flowing past, flowing, flowing, leaving only herself, the last handhold before the weir ... if only she could hold firm this time.

The fairy tale had been over a long time now, its magic side and its dark, the clock had struck twelve.

So, just herself. And Oliver. That was the way it had begun, that was the way it was ending – if it was the end, she thought suddenly, confused. Her heart had begun its now familiar thumping, the palms of her hands were tingling. She rubbed them together.

You have the power, use it. Go on, use it –

Just for a moment, she was afraid. It wasn't going to be easy. Oliver hadn't wanted to stay alive and perhaps he still didn't see too much point in it. He hadn't yet reached the stage where he could look ahead, he took things as they came, one at a time, carefully, well knowing that if he lost his grip on any one of them – such as his decision to give away the Fund money – he would lose his grip on everything, and this second time, the torrent would get them both and sweep them away, their love, their hopes, their fears, their future, into nothing but tatters sweeping away on the flood.

It wasn't going to happen that way.

We've been here before, only this time it's all turned around, Looking-glass Land. This time it's I who lead, I who must take the decisions, and so everything will change, quite naturally, because I'm really nothing like him at the root, nothing like Oliver. I'm firmly planted, the winds don't blow me, not to unknown adventures nor to disaster either, unless I will it. I can choose not to let them if I want.

But what will we do, what will become of us, there beside the wild, untameable sea that Oliver loves? Loves so much, indeed, that I think without it he can't be fully alive. The seabirds are still nesting on the granite cliffs, the flowers still blow in the wind, the surf still rolls in to the golden sickle beaches... but we, we are changed, and what lies ahead of us is the unknown.